MAJOR AND MINOR

MAJOR AND MINOR

MOSCO CARNER

Holmes & Meier Publishers, Inc.
New York

Published in the United States of America 1980
by Holmes & Meier Publishers, Inc.
30 Irving Place, New York, New York 10003

Printed in Great Britain

Library of Congress Cataloging in Publication Data

Carner, Mosco.
Major and minor.

Includes index.
1. Music - Addresses, essays, lectures.
I. Title.
ML60.C188 780 79-27481
ISBN 0-8419-0600-9

CONTENTS

For

FEDELE D'AMICO

'Friendships begin with
liking or gratitude.'
George Eliot

PREFACE

Of Men and Music, my first collection of musical essays and articles, came out as long ago as 1944. I have retained in this new publication those articles from that earlier collection which I think might still be of interest both to the general reader and the professional musician. The new articles cover the last twenty-five years or so, and include a paper on Goethe's ambivalent attitude to music, introductions to the orchestral music of Schubert and Schumann, an analytical guide to the Bartók string quartets and an essay on *Fidelio* which originated as my contribution to an unpublished symposium intended to commemorate the bicentenary of Beethoven's birth. In this essay I have ventured to advance a hypothesis which links the trauma of Beethoven's first knowledge that his deafness was incurable to his heroic style in the period from 1803 to 1810. The study of Simone Mayr's *L'amor coniugale* was prompted by the Beethoven bicentenary and the publication in Italy of the full score of this 'rescue' opera. All articles have been revised and, where necessary, brought up to date. The title of this new collection is, I think, self-explanatory.

My grateful acknowledgment of permission to reprint the new articles is due to the Oxford University Press, Pelican Books, Barrie & Jenkins, *Music & Letters*, *Music Review*, and the *Musical Times*.

London,
Autumn 1979

M.C.

ONE

COMPOSERS AS CRITICS

'Lisez la Correspondence de Berlioz! Peu de livres m'ont plus édifié. Il rugissait, celui-là! et haïssait le médiocre. Voilà un homme!' So wrote Flaubert to Edmond de Goncourt. The words are significant in the valuation of the literary activity of a man whose actual métier was not the writing of criticism but musical composition. They are also equally significant for a general phenomenon that made its appearance with the dawn of the last century and which persists into our own days—the creative musician as man of letters, as exemplified by Weber, Schumann, Berlioz, Wagner, Liszt, Hugo Wolf, Debussy, and Schoenberg. In these times when specialisation is often exaggerated to its extreme limits, this type of critic-composer is undoubtedly becoming less frequent. The modern conception of the 'objective' music-critic would seem to reconcile itself indifferently with such duality. The *sine ira et studio* which we demand of the critic must suffer when a composer sits in public judgment on the works of others and pronounces sentence. Oscar Wilde once said that 'an unbiased opinion is always absolutely valueless'. There may be various opinions about the application of this observation to professional criticism. But one thing may be considered to be well established: that Wilde's point of view is shared by almost all the composers who have expressed their opinion upon the musical productions of their contemporaries in critical essays and articles. That strongly-developed tendency in creative artists towards egocentricity, which in some cases rises (or descends) to actual narcissism (e.g. Wagner), often compels such natures, though frequently unconsciously, to see everything in relationship to their own creations and ideas, and to appreciate in others only what they can bring into harmony with their own personal outlook. This one-sided and irreconcilable attitude towards others frequently causes the most grotesque statements to be made, at which unbiassed readers of later times can only smilingly shake their heads; as when Hugo Wolf, for example, as critic on the *Wiener Salonblatt*, says

of Brahms: 'In a single cymbal-clash from a work by Liszt may be expressed more spirit and feeling than in all the three symphonies of Brahms, with the serenades into the bargain,' or when Weber in his fragmentary novel *Life of a Musician* passes satirical remarks on Beethoven's Fourth Symphony.

What strikes us most forcibly in the dicta of composers who have been active as critics is not so much the fact that they have delivered false judgments—for prophetic foresight in matters of art has ever been a rare gift—as that their manner of formulating their findings very often bares for our inspection all the character, the complexes and the warring emotions of the artistic soul. The writings of Berlioz, Wagner, Schumann and Wolf are examples of just that kind of involuntary psychological document. I am not speaking of letters, or opinions expressed in intimate circles, in which the artist can naturally unburden himself without restraint. It is in their critical writings and essays intended for a wide public that we discover the devil's hoof, i.e. points of view and assertions that a professional critic would not be courageous or inconsiderate enough to express.

It is probably precisely this paradox—not to speak of the witty and pointed language used—that renders the reading of such criticisms so interesting and entertaining. It is less the matter than the manner that so intrigues us and brings the personality of the writer so clearly before our eyes. It would appear that the creative artist is compelled to adopt this egocentric, often very aggressive, attitude in order to retain in undiminished force the strength necessary for his own works and the conviction that his artistic ideas are right. This is nothing other than a defence. In connection with this, the observation may be made that just those composers use the sharpest and most vehement language in their writings who have to be regarded as musical pioneers, and who have influenced musical history in a radical way, such as Berlioz (orchestration), Wagner (harmony) and Schoenberg (12-note method)—all had combative natures, the like of which were scarcely to be found in the other arts of the same period.

This unconciliatory and polemic tone is noticeable not only in the writings that are intended, in the first place, for the propagation of new ideas or reforms, but also makes itself clearly felt in the articles that deal with criticism of works, composers, musical institutions, and artistic conditions generally. The bitter sarcasm and the mordant ridicule of a Berlioz, or the clever though frequently malicious judgments of a Wagner, endow their writings with a characteristic atmosphere. Nothing is spared; the penetrating, wounding bitterness of their pens knows no consideration and gives no quarter. It is as if they scented enemies everywhere, and I believe that this is largely due to a sense of intense anxiety that the novelty and boldness of their ideas might meet with utter resistance and suffer shipwreck, an anxiety which has to be hidden behind a mask of sheer aggressiveness. This fear as to the success or failure of their creation seems to be present in all pioneering artists.

At the same time there are predispositions and tendencies in the artist himself which he feels to be inimical and disturbing to his daring ideas, and in consequence there is a constant inner struggle in progress so that he may be able to realise these novel and sometimes revolutionary ideas. The more daring the new idea, the more intense the inner struggle. Yet this struggle is exteriorised by way of a projection or transference to someone else, such as artistic coteries, the press and individuals who thus take on the status of a menacing symbol. When Berlioz takes up arms against certain musical circles in Paris which he calls *musique parisienne*, or when Wagner directs fierce attacks against Meyerbeer and Mendelssohn, there is naturally a certain amount of justification on purely objective grounds. But this criticism *ad hominem* is very largely directed against the artist himself, against those tendencies in him which he instinctively feels to be a danger to his new and bold ideas, a danger that is, as said, symbolised or personified by the *musique parisienne*, Meyerbeer and Mendelssohn.

Debussy, after having been an adherent of Wagner, became one of the bitterest enemies of his works. In spite of intrinsic recognition, he turned from Wagner in the interests of French national music. He felt that he had to free himself from all Wagnerian influence before he could become the leader of French impressionism. The epithet *musicien français* is in his eyes a rampart that will protect him from alien influences. He carries this attitude to such lengths that in his *Lettre ouverte à Monsieur le Chevalier W. Gluck* he holds the dead composer responsible—in ironical and witty language—for the fact that *'de vous avoir connu, la musique française a tiré le bénéfice assez inattendu de tomber dans les bras de Wagner'*. With Hugo Wolf all the hatred of which he is capable is concentrated against Brahms and Dvořák. The vision of Brahms haunts him like an obsession, and the way in which Wolf drags in his name, often in totally uncalled-for situations and generally *mal à propos*, can only be described as pathological. He denies Brahms practically everything that can be denied a musician. To him Brahms is 'a remnant surviving from primitive times'. Referring to the E minor Symphony he writes: 'The art of composing without ideas has most decidedly found in Brahms its worthiest representative.' In the case of Philip Heseltine (Peter Warlock), whose tragic figure seems to show a striking spiritual affinity to Hugo Wolf, we meet a similar attitude with regard to

Stravinsky. A more striking aversion to this composer than that demonstrated in Heseltine's article 'Sound for Sound's Sake' would be difficult to imagine. It culminates in the sentence in which he says that Stravinsky's works show 'in an extreme form the commonest and most unmistakable symptoms of decadence—the fear and resultant atrophy of vital instincts'.

On the other hand, enthusiasm knows no bounds when the man is found in whose art and personality the composer-critic thinks he sees a relationship with his own ideas, a confirmation of his own artistic views. The severely critical attitude is abandoned in order that words of unlimited appreciation and admiration may have unrestricted play. 'Hats off, gentlemen, a genius!' says Schumann in his article on Chopin, and 'this is one of the chosen, a genius!' are the words with which he greets the appearance of the youthful Brahms in 1853. Similar extravagance of language is exhibited in the article on W. Sterndale Bennett, which Schumann wrote when he introduced the young Englishman to Germany. But this enthusiasm is not only called forth by young aspiring talents whose way it is intended to smooth. Composers of the same age or older and dead masters find the same recognition, if they show the features with which the particular critic feels himself to be in complete sympathy. The talents that are personal and valuable for developing the writer's own tendencies in creative work are primarily the ones that are appreciated and admired in others: this is the explanation of Liszt's long essay on behalf of Wagner, Debussy's words on César Franck, and Hugo Wolf's struggle for the recognition of Berlioz and Bruckner. That this unconditional siding with others is not confined to courageous newspaper articles or enthusiastic essays but can also lead to results of permanent worth is shown by Heseltine in his book on Delius; and that intervening centuries need present no obstacles to the appreciation of the relationship between two composers Heseltine also proved, in the study which he published in collaboration with Cecil Gray on Gesualdo, Prince of Venosa.

It is a striking fact that most of these composers suffer in some way or other under this duality and would dearly like to rid themselves of it. It is as if they felt the antagonism between their creative and critical activity, and were at times conscious of the inner division this brought about. Very significantly Schumann says: 'The best way in which to speak of music is to keep silence,' and in another passage: 'What is a whole annual volume of a musical journal compared with *one* concerto of Chopin?' Berlioz refers to his criticism as 'slavery'; Debussy too does not appear to have loved this métier very deeply, and Heseltine surrendered the editorship of the *Sackbut* to another after a very short time. With Hugo Wolf the case is still more serious. It would seem that three years of activity as a critic had so heavily burdened his soul that he could compose nothing of any great importance during the whole of that time. The moment at which he resigned his post as critic (1887) was followed by the most fruitful epoch of his creative life, and as if by magic the Mörike songs, most of the Eichendorff set and the Goethe songs appeared within a short period.

This division of their own personality, leading to internal conflicts —even to a tragic sequel in the case of Heseltine—is so clearly felt by certain composers that they feel constrained to give expression to it in their writings in a peculiar literary form. This consists of the introduction of fictional characters which are only separate entities of their own divided personality, and which in the form of dialogues and conversations convert the criticism into a little dramatic scene. Schumann, in his criticisms, did this very well with the figures of Florestan, Eusebius, and Raro, and explained the meaning of these three imaginary persons in the words: 'Florestan and Eusebius form my dual nature, which I as well as Raro would like to mould into a man.' Berlioz allows various groups drawn from the public to express their opinion when he discusses Gounod's *Faust*; and Debussy invents the curious Monsieur Croche Antidilettante, a kind of double who incarnates Debussy the critic.

From all that has been said, the fact that emerges—differences in personality, time, and style notwithstanding—is the fundamental one that a creative artist employs his critical faculty almost exclusively *pro domo*; he ventilates opinions wholly favourable to his own work. For him to criticise is a safety-valve through which is let out all the toxic air engendered by his intense inner struggles. Due to his marked personality and egocentricity, without which no creation would come into being, he is unable to see both sides of the coin. His criticism does not constitute criticism in the generally accepted sense and its chief value lies in the fact that it provides material for a psychological study, enabling us to catch a glimpse of the man behind his art.

TWO

GUIDO ADLER: A PIONEER OF MUSICOLOGY

THOUGH the name of Guido Adler is little known to the great musical public, to musical scholars and research students it is a household word. It was Adler who more than a century ago stood, with a few others, at the cradle of the young science which we now have come to term 'musicology'. He has done invaluable service towards establishing this branch of learning and causing it to be recognised as an independent subject at a number of European universities.

To Guido Adler we owe that systematic and scientific criticism of musical style which, it is hoped, will finally replace the hazy method of writing about music which is still rife among musical writers. And without Adler the monumental undertaking of the *Denkmäler der Tonkunst in Oesterreich* would have scarcely been promoted. In these *Denkmäler* Adler has, with the aid of a number of younger scholars, collected and edited music written in the different parts of the old Austrian Empire, from the time of the troubadours up to the period of the early romantic composers.

Adler was only twenty-five years old when he published his first important treatise on mediæval music. At twenty-six he became lecturer in music at Vienna University, side by side with the mighty Hanslick; and a few years later he founded the *Vierteljahresschrift für Musikwissenschaft*, a quarterly publication of the highest scientific standard, which he edited in collaboration with two much older men, Spitta and Chrysander, the great German authorities on Bach and Handel respectively. Thus while still a young man Adler gave proof of his exceptional gifts of musical scholarship. Like two other famous Austrians, Gustav Mahler and Sigmund Freud, Adler comes from one of those old and highly cultured Jewish families who settled in Moravia (now Czechoslovakia) and whose love of art and science provided a fertile soil and a congenial atmosphere to budding talent.

In 1937 it was my privilege to visit the great scholar at his home in Doebling, a beautiful garden-city in the west of Vienna. Close by are

Nussdorf and Heiligenstadt, and in the distance the vineyards and woods of the Wiener Wald grace the landscape so beloved of Beethoven and Schubert. Here, at the age of eighty-two, Adler lived almost completely retired from the world. I had not seen him for many a year, and as one of his former students, counting as I do the years spent under him among my most cherished recollections, I was particularly happy to be allowed to visit him. He received me with the kindness and the keen interest that delighted us when we were students. I entered his home with feelings of awe and respect, and left it with the elation one feels after a long talk with a wise old friend. This was characteristic of Adler the teacher. He never treated us in the cold, distant manner of the 'Herr Professor', but endeared himself by regarding us as equals or, in some cases, as friends.

The department of musical history (Musikwissenschaftliches Seminar) at Vienna University was his creation, and he directed and watched it for nearly thirty years until 1927. Age would not weaken his forceful personality. Even in his outward appearance he has remained much the same as in former years. 'Herr Hofrat', as we called him—a distinguishing title received from the Emperor Francis Joseph I—was small of stature. His vigorous body, still full of vitality, might well have deceived one as to the true age of the man. A huge iron-grey beard framed his face, and his bright clear eyes gleaming through narrow and old-fashioned spectacles testified to a surprisingly alert mind. Our conversation proved that he was well versed in contemporary thought and current events. During my brief visit we touched upon the most diverse subjects. Music naturally came foremost. Adler was devoting himself almost exclusively to his work on the *Denkmäler* which had now grown to eighty-two volumes. Visits to concerts and the opera, in which he used to take a keen interest in order to keep in close contact with living music, had now to be abandoned as they proved too great a physical strain. The intimate contact with living music, the close and reciprocal relationship between artist and scholar, is a point to which Adler attached great importance, and to which he referred repeatedly in the course of our conversation. In this respect he set the best example himself. In bygone years he was on friendly and sometimes intimate terms with the leading musicians of Vienna. At his instigation, Brahms, Mahler and Richard Strauss were invited to serve on the committee responsible for the publication of the *Denkmäler*, and in 1912 he entrusted Schoenberg with the realisation of the continuo in a cello concerto in G minor by G. M. Monn published in that great collection. He also appointed Egon Wellesz and Han Gál as lecturers in his Seminary. While still a young man he fought to win recognition for Wagner, with whom he was personally acquainted, and was thus prompted to found the *Wiener Akademischer Wagnerverein*. (In this he was greatly helped by Felix von Mottl, who later became famous as conductor of Wagner's operas.) Another of Adler's achievements was the great Music and Theatre Exhibition held in Vienna in 1892; he was the principal organiser and, incidentally, took occasion to introduce Smetana's *The Bartered Bride* to Vienna. In later years Adler's energy and great organising talent were chiefly responsible for the success of the great musical festival which was held in Vienna in 1927 to celebrate the Beethoven centenary.

Journeys to various music congresses abroad have made Adler's name internationally known. He spoke to me with pleasure of his stay in London in 1911, when he attended the congress of the International Society for Music. Here he met among others Arthur Balfour and Hubert Parry (who, by a curious coincidence, published a book on style in music in the same year as Adler). He also told me of an interesting meeting with Toscanini in Milan. After conducting *Die Meistersinger*, the latter asked him how he liked the performance, whereupon Adler replied: 'It was *I Maestri Cantori* that I admired rather than *Die Meistersinger*.' These words sum up in a most concise manner what so many of us find in Toscanini's readings of certain non-Italian works.

These travels abroad ceased. For, as he jestingly said about himself, 'the old Adler ("eagle" in German) had grown tired of flying'. All the same, his many links with other countries remained in the form of a large correspondence with old pupils and foreign colleagues. Adler always aimed at imparting an international character to his school by keeping in contact with the research work carried out in foreign countries. The best proof of this is his great *Handbuch der Musikgeschichte*, in which a great number of scholars of all parts of Europe collaborated. His breadth of mind is also proved by his principle of putting talent and ability above national and racial considerations. His gift to discover and appreciate whatever is of artistic and historic value in the music of other nations is one of Adler's outstanding characteristics.

Adler died in 1941, at the age of eighty-six.

THREE

A BEETHOVEN MOVEMENT AND ITS SUCCESSORS

VOLUMES HAVE been written, and will continue to be written, on the amount and importance of the influence Beethoven exercised upon his successors in the field of the symphony. Any study of this influence will, above all, have to answer two main questions: How was Beethoven's symphonic technique taken over by later symphonists? And in what light did they regard his symphonic ideas, the spiritual world that he embodied in his great works? Though the first is a technical and the second a philosophical question, the two are closely linked, for Beethoven's symphonic work is perhaps the most striking example of the idea behind the music creating and shaping its appropriate means of expression. The present article is an attempt to study and possibly answer those two questions, not in a general way, but by choosing a special case that seems in more than one respect particularly suited to such a task.

In common with other musicians I have often felt that certain similarities and analogies exist between the *Allegretto* of Beethoven's Seventh and the second movements of Schubert's C major and Mendelssohn's A major Symphonies. However, before starting to investigate the justice of this view I came across a remark in a book by Gerald Abraham[1] which confirmed it and, at the same time, added a third case for study by drawing attention to the second movement of Berlioz's *Harold in Italy*, of which the author says that 'it was obviously suggested by the corresponding movement in Beethoven's Seventh'. A comparative analysis of the four movements in question makes the hypothesis highly probable that Schubert, Berlioz and Mendelssohn must all have, consciously or unconsciously, taken the Beethoven *Allegretto* as a model for the corresponding movements in their respective symphonies. Considering the differences of personality, artistic temperament and style it was natural that the results

[1] *A Hundred Years of Music* (London, 1938).

should be widely different; but it is these very differences that furnish the most interesting points for analysis.

As the object of this essay can be achieved only by comparison of the four movements the analysis must rest chiefly on those points which represent the *tertium comparationis*. Beethoven's *Allegretto* is in rondo-cum-sonata form:

A—	B—	A—	C—	A—	B—	Coda
(A minor)	(A major)	(shortened)	(development of A)	(only hinted at)	(shortened)	

The movement opens and concludes with three bars of a held six-four chord, a kind of 'curtain'. The exposition of theme A shows a rather uncommon structure which suggests the idea of a terrace. Beethoven repeats theme A three times, the melody rising each time an octave higher. Correspondingly the scoring becomes richer and the dynamics increase until on the last repetition, the whole orchestra is employed *fortissimo*. Beethoven enriches the texture, too, by introducing, at the first repetition, a most expressive counter-melody. Thus the tremendous build-up to the climax at bar 75 is achieved not only through a mere mechanical increase of the dynamics, but by a combination of means. The increase of the sound-volume in several stages by a gradual enriching of the orchestration produces yet another result. These stages coincide with the architectural outlines, which are thus brought into sharp relief. It is as though each step of the terrace received a new and brighter colour.[2]

Let us look for a moment at the themes themselves:

Ex. 1

[2] In his *Bolero* Ravel used this device in a highly effective manner.

Theme A is a strict period of two eight-bar sections. Beethoven seems to stress this squareness of build by regularly repeating the second section and by putting in 'full stop' rests in bars 8, 16 and 24. Another characteristic of the theme is the rhythmic pattern

♩ ♫ | ♩ ♩

suggestive of a slow march, which pervades the whole movement. The actual tune seems to have been born of this rhythm, as shown by bars 5 and 6, where the merely rhythmic figure crystallises into a melodic germ-motif of dominant importance. In contrast to A, theme B has no such deep-cutting caesurae, but flows continuously without breaks. The markedly rhythmic character of the whole movement suggests a heavily throbbing march which is dominated by a feeling of heroic pathos. The only bright colour is provided by theme B

Ex. 2

(in A major), which has a slight hymn-tune flavour and introduces a marked contrast. (The tune is supposed to derive from an old pilgrims' song once in common use in Lower Austria). Though not marked as such this *Allegretto* is really a symphonic march of a kind Beethoven had produced earlier in the funeral marches of the *Eroica* and the Piano Sonata Op. 26. It appears, therefore, that Beethoven saw in the symphonic march a special vehicle for expressing his idea of relentless and inevitable fate. He was to the best of my knowledge, the first to introduce a symphonic march with this particular significance into the symphony and sonata.[3]

The *Allegretto* in the Seventh Symphony is undoubtedly one of Beethoven's most beautiful and impressive movements. This was at once recognised by the public at the first performance of the work in Vienna in December, 1813, and a Viennese critic on that occasion hailed this particular movement as 'the crown of the more modern

[3] The marches of the divertimenti, cessations and serenades of the Viennese school belong, of course, to a different category altogether.

instrumental music'. It is thus more than probable that the outstanding qualities of the *Allegretto* induced successive composers to model one or another of their symphonic movements on its lines.

The first to do this seems to have been Schubert with the *Andante* of his C major Symphony (1828). It is very likely that he was much impressed by this *Allegretto*, the whole character of which is curiously Schubertian. There is, for instance, a striking similarity between a passage in the song 'Der Kreuzzug' and the final bars of the famous *Allegretto* tune, a similarity that is tantamount to a literal quotation. Compare the cadence in C sharp minor in the song with that in bars 6–8 of the Beethoven theme:[4]

Ex. 3

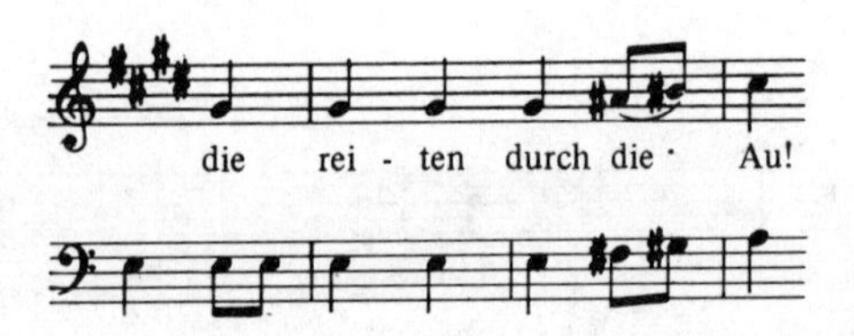

The group of Leitner songs to which 'Der Kreuzzug' belongs was written in 1827–8, that is, about the time of the C major Symphony. It is significant that Schubert uses this Beethoven motif in a song containing the idea of wandering and pilgrimage. About this important fact I shall have more to say later.

Let us now examine the *Andante* of the C major Symphony. Its position in the order of the movements, its key (A minor) and its time signature are identical with those of the Beethoven *Allegretto*. So is, essentially, the tempo. For although Beethoven's tempo is *allegretto*, the composer is credited with remarking later that he really meant an *andantino quasi allegretto* which, in practice, comes very near Schubert's *andante con moto*. Like Beethoven, Schubert cast his movement in sonata-cum-rondo form:

A———	B———	A———	C———	B———	A
(A minor)	(F major)	(shortened)	(development	(A major)	(Coda)
(A major)	(D minor)		of A)	(F sharp minor)	

[4] In his *Ludwig van Beethoven*, Thayer draws attention to this fact, but he quotes there a less characteristic passage from the song, and Richard Capell, in his *Schubert's Songs*, speaks of certain rhythmical relations between the song 'Die Sterne' (1828) and the Beethoven Allegretto.

Beethoven's three-bar 'curtain' is here replaced by a seven-bar introduction which shows theme A in its embryonic form. Here follow the two main ideas of the movement:

Ex. 4

Ex. 5

Schubert's main theme has the same strictly periodic, two-section build as Beethoven's, yet is extended by a new thought in the major key to 36 as against 24 bars of the *Allegretto* theme. To treat this gigantic theme—gigantic, of course, if we think in terms of the classical symphony—in the manner of Beethoven's 'terrace', would have resulted in a monster exposition that would have entirely upset the formal balance of the movement. (As it is, the *Andante* is not completely satisfactory in this respect.) That Schubert, however, had something like the 'terrace' in his mind is shown by his repeating theme A twice, though in a shortened form. Bars 2 and 3 of the theme clearly point to Beethoven's germ-motif (see Ex. 1) and, as in the *Allegretto*, it plays an essential part here too. Theme B shows certain similarities with its 'opposite number' in the Beethoven movement in that it avoids sharp caesurae, flows more continuously than A and possesses a hymn-like character. The march element is strongly emphasised in the marked rhythm of the dotted motives of theme A and the processional

of the accompaniment figures.[5]

[5] It is worth pointing out a characteristic and, from a psychological point of view, significant difference, within the same metre, between the quaver movement in the Schubert piece, which makes for a lighter and more even flow of music, and Beethoven's weighty ♩♩ rhythm.

I suggest that the Schubert *Andante* is essentially a symphonic march built on the lines of Beethoven's *Allegretto*, yet with the difference that the heroic expression of the latter is here superseded by a feeling of wistful melancholy. Schubert's *Andante* stands for the same idea as Beethoven's *Allegretto*, that is, the symphonic march as the musical symbol of tragic fate, but conceived by a different mind and temperament.

That this interpretation of the Schubert movement is not an arbitrary and wholly subjective supposition can be seen from the cycle *Die Winterreise*, written the year before the C major Symphony. These songs make it perfectly clear that for Schubert the idea of marching and restless wandering was symbolic of an unhappy life. It is no mere coincidence that we find a number of motifs and rhythmical patterns in these songs which also occur, either note for note or in some modification, in the A minor movement of the Symphony. It is fairly safe to say that the symphonic movement was born out of the same despondent mood as that which produced the songs of *Winterreise*. Richard Capell, discussing 'Gute Nacht' of this cycle,[6] calls attention to that kinship when he says that 'the general movement [of "Gute Nacht"] recalls the processional threnodies in some of the instrumental works, for instance . . . the A minor movement of the Symphony in C'. Compare the monotonous and continuous accompaniment of 'Gute Nacht' with that of the symphonic movement, or motifs taken at random, such as:

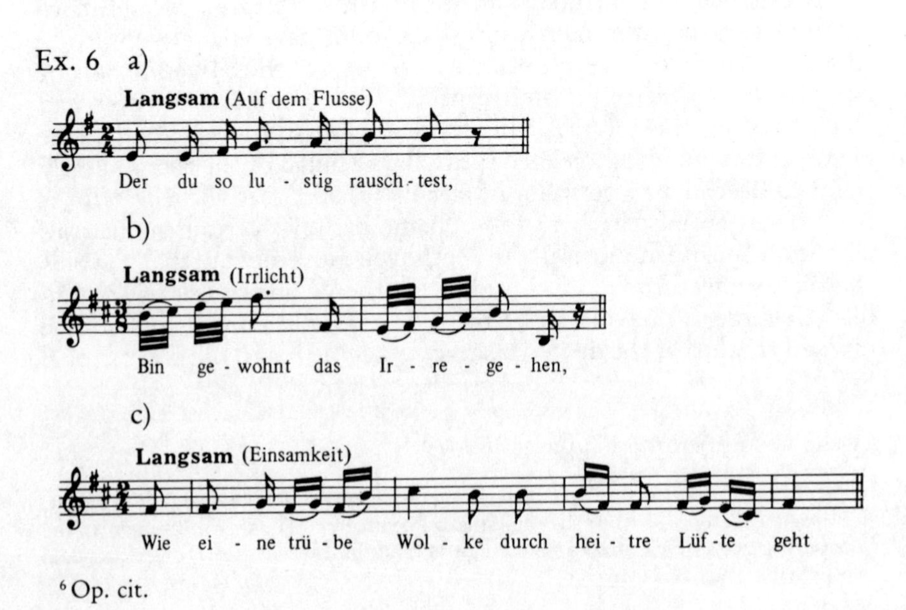

[6] Op. cit.

with some of the *Andante*. All these motifs, with their characteristic rise up to the fifth are Schubert's typical 'wander motifs', suggestive of motion. (Note also the meaning of the words.)

The most striking example, however, of this kinship is provided by 'Der Wegweiser', which perhaps best expresses Schubert's idea of an unhappy earthly pilgrimage and is, in its mood as well as thematically and rhythmically, closely related to the A minor movement. The identity of mood seems so striking, indeed, that one feels tempted to put the line of the song, 'Eine Strasse muss ich gehen, die noch keiner ging zurück', as motto over the *Andante*.

The stylistic relation is equally close. 'Der Wegweiser', like the *Andante*, is in a minor key (G minor); it has the same time-measure and the same sad, monotonous movement which, exactly as in the A minor movement, dies away in almost motionless, tired crochets. And its main motif[7] is a sort of free augmentation of the characteristic motif in bars 2–3 of the *Andante* tune, which, in its turn, goes back to the germ-motif of the Beethoven theme:

Ex. 7

Is it too bold to suggest that Schubert expressed in the symphonic movement the same idea that lies behind this simple song? If he did so—and much appears to point to it, as we have seen—then there is no doubt that the A minor movement is a symphonic march. And the notion of treating this idea symphonically and incorporating it in the Symphony must have come from Beethoven's *Allegretto*.

The next composer after Schubert to follow Beethoven's precedent by introducing a symphonic march into a symphony was Berlioz. He did this first with the 'Marche au supplice' of his *Symphonie fantastique*. Apart from the mere fact, however, that it is a march in the form of a symphonic movement, there seems to be no relation between this 'Marche' and the corresponding movements in Beethoven's *Eroica* or Seventh Symphony. Yet it may be that the generating idea of the *Eroica*, the artist as hero—in Beethoven's conception the representa-

[7] It is significant that Mahler used a very similar melodic and rhythmic pattern in the fourth song of his *Lieder eines fahrende Gesellen*, a song-cycle with the same general idea and mood as *Winterreise*.

tive of an ideal humanity—had something to do with Berlioz's grotesque 'Episode de la vie d'un artiste'. In his *Harold in Italy* (1834), however, we do find a close relation with Beethoven's Seventh. The *allegro* section of Berlioz's first movement, 'Scènes de mélancholie, de bonheur et de joie', with its vivacious 6-8 theme, corresponds very nearly to the 6-8 *vivace* of Beethoven's first movement. Similarly, the finale of the *Harold* Symphony, 'Orgie de Brigands', a furious *allegro frenetico*, seems to be modelled on the lines of Beethoven's fourth movement, the main characteristic of which is wild frenzy and excessive energy.[8]

Let us now turn to the 'Marche de Pélerins' in the *Harold Symphony*. Like Beethoven's *Allegretto*, it is a second movement and an *allegretto* march. Apart from this little else seems at a first glance to point to the Beethoven movement. Its structure is different, being in true march form with a sort of trio (the 'Canto religioso' section); it is in the major (E and C major); and as regards mood, its superficial religiosity is poles apart from Beethoven's profundity. More about this will be said later. Nevertheless, there are enough important points of resemblance which would substantiate my theory. Like Beethoven, Berlioz opens and concludes the movement with a 'curtain' of sustained chords; the first theme is in strict periodical form and square-cut, only that Beethoven's 'full-stop' rests are here filled in with the so-called murmuring of the pilgrims. The chant-like tune itself moves along in heavy, monotonous ♩ ♩ a rhythm that is kept up throughout the movement, just as in the Beethoven *Allegretto*:

Ex. 8

[8] It is interesting to note that Wagner, in describing this Beethoven finale, actually used the word 'orgies' when he said that 'here the purely rhythmical movement, so to speak, celebrates its orgies'.

Again, the codas of the movements are strikingly alike. Both die away *pianissimo* and split the rhythmic pattern of the main theme: the *Allegretto* ♩ ♫ | ♩ ♩ and the 'Marche' ♫ | ♩ ♩ It will be remembered that Beethoven's second theme had a somewhat hymn-like character. Now Berlioz's second theme—that of the trio—is a 'Canto religioso'. This, of course, was dictated by the programme. But is the analogy with Beethoven just a mere coincidence?

Further, a good deal in the formal structure of the exposition of the 'Marche' points to the 'terrace' of the Beethoven *Allegretto*. Though Berlioz does not repeat the theme, he does something very much the same in order to get the effect of Beethoven's 'terrace'. He follows the theme by a chain of melodic variants which, however, retain the original rhythmical pattern, and, like Beethoven, with his expressive counter-melody, he effectively introduces as a counterpoint from bar 64 onward the augmented *Harold* theme from the first movement, thus enriching the texture melodically too.[9]

But there is a fundamental difference between Berlioz's way of 'scoring' the *crescendo* in order to reach the climax and Beethoven's architectural scoring. Berlioz is not concerned to bring the architectural outlines into sharp relief by means of an instrumentation in which the changes are mainly conditioned by the structural plan of his music. The theme and its variants are given chiefly to the strings while the wind add ever-changing colours to the sequence of 'scenes' in the programme. The determining factor in Berlioz's scoring is its pictorial element, which contrasts sharply with Beethoven's much less imaginative, architectural handling of the orchestra.[10] Yet one advantage of Beethoven's scoring lies in that it secures, *per se* and practically without the aid of the conductor, a natural *crescendo* to the climax. Highly coloured and varied as Berlioz's is, it helps little in producing a gradual dynamic increase. Berlioz seems to have been aware of this, for he expressly demands the aid of the conductor when he advises him in the score at the beginning of the 'Marche': '*Si deve eseguire questo pezzo crescendo poco a poco fin al forte ed allora diminuendo a poco fin alla*

[9] Though the introduction of the *Harold* theme is dictated by the programme, the analogy with Beethoven's procedure shows that Berlioz is employing a purely musical device that can be understood without reference to his programme. This is one of the many examples which go to prove that Berlioz, though he got most of his inspirations from non-musical (literary) sources, followed established musical laws in the working-out of his material.

[10] The orchestral style of Liszt, Wagner, Strauss and Debussy belongs to the pictorial order, while that of Schumann, Brahms and Bruckner follows more or less Beethoven's line of scoring.

fine.' If the *crescendo* had been 'scored', this remark would have been unnecessary.

Another far-reaching difference already referred to lies in the functions of the symphonic march in Beethoven and Schubert on the one hand and in Berlioz on the other. Whereas the Viennese composers saw in it the musical symbol of a quasi-metaphysical thought—life seen as a tragic pilgrimage—the Frenchman ignores this concept and replaces it by a far more mundane idea in which the descriptive and the pictorial play the main role.

We now turn to our last example: Mendelssohn's Italian Symphony, which, like *Harold in Italy*, seems to have been modelled in three of its four movements on Beethoven's Seventh. The key is A major, the *allegro vivace* first movement in 6-8 time reminds one very much of the corresponding movement in the Beethoven Symphony, and its finale, the 'Saltarello', is a wild, exuberant dance movement exactly like Beethoven's *allegro con brio*. And there is some local colouring in both the finales—Hungarian and Russian in Beethoven's and Italian in Mendelssohn's. Yet a much closer relation exists between the second movements of the two symphonies. We know that the Italian Symphony was inspired by impressions the composer received during a visit to Italy in 1830–1, and that its second movement, like Berlioz's 'Marche' in the *Harold* Symphony, is a march of pilgrims to Rome, the march element being clearly marked in the dull steady tramp of the accompaniment figures—again a symphonic march as second movement of a symphony. Like Beethoven's, it stands in a minor key and has, to all intents and purposes, the same tempo. Its *andante con moto* is practically the *andantino quasi allegretto* of the Seventh. Though the time is 4-4, the rhythm is actually *alla breve*, for the music moves along in weighty 𝅗𝅥 𝅗𝅥 their duration corresponding very nearly to that of the ♩ ♩ in the Beethoven movement. The march is cast, however, in free sonata form with an incomplete recapitulation:

A———	B———	C———	B———	Coda
(D minor)	(A major)	(development of A)	(D major)	

A short motif from a bridge-passage between theme A and B represents the 'curtain' with which the piece opens. Theme A is, like Beethoven's first subject, a strict period, square-cut and showing the same 'full-stop' rests to underline the caesurae:

Ex. 9

The exposition of theme A follows Beethoven's 'terrace', the two eight-bar sections of the theme being both repeated separately (Beethoven repeats only the second), and the melody rises an octave higher with each repetition. At the same time a two-part counterpoint on the flutes is added. The result is much as in the Beethoven *Allegretto*—a natural increase of the sound-volume and a brightening of the orchestral colours. But Mendelssohn does not go on repeating as Beethoven does. He is content with building a two-storey terrace, as it were, instead of Beethoven's four-storey one. Nor has he in mind a *crescendo* on Beethoven's lines. On the contrary, the dynamic curve that started with the repetition, an octave higher, of the first section of A is reduced to zero again by the 'low' scoring of the second section:

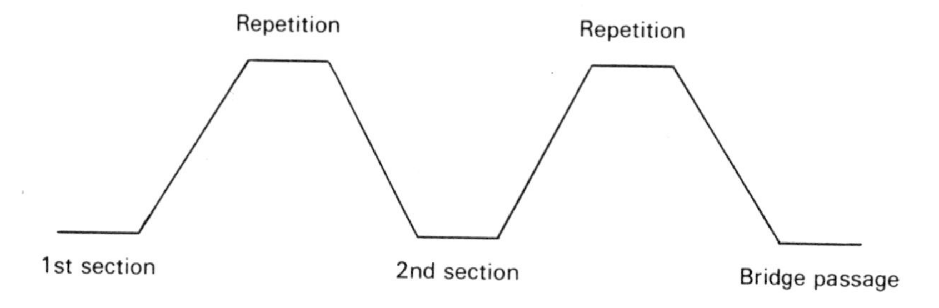

But it becomes clear that Mendelssohn's principle of scoring is here an architectural one, for his instrumentation follows in the main a structural plan and is designed with a view to stressing the architectural outlines.

Two points in this neatly-built exposition betray Mendelssohn's dominant weakness: his formalism. First, the scoring of the two sections of theme A are exactly the same, and so are those of their repetitions; secondly, the counterpoint that Mendelssohn introduces on the flutes is a mere filling in with dry, lifeless lines. (What a contrast to Beethoven's beautifully expressive counter-melody!) But this should not stand in the way of our appreciation of the purity and shapeliness of the movement as a whole.

Though Mendelssohn had apparently modelled his movement on the lines of Beethoven's *Allegretto*, we are again reminded by it of what has already been said of Berlioz's 'Marche': Mendelssohn writes a symphonic march but fails to imbue it with the profound feeling of its prototype. Beethoven's heroism is replaced by a sweet religious sentiment, much more genuine than Berlioz's, but lacking that overwhelming impact which characterises the symphonic marches of the Viennese master.

FOUR

SCHUBERT'S ORCHESTRAL MUSIC

EVEN A CURSORY glance at Schubert's orchestral music shows that the works written during the period between 1812, when the composer first launched upon orchestral composition, and 1821, the year of the sketch for the E major Symphony, are marked by a singularly close adherence to the style of the Viennese classical school. For all their distinctive signs of a great talent, they are dominated by the influence in varying degrees of Haydn, Mozart and Beethoven. To compare these early works with the songs of the same period makes one almost wonder whether they are by the same composer who wrote the Goethe songs. While Schubert here revealed himself at once as a superb master, in his orchestral music up to about 1822 we see him groping his way and only very gradually growing to full maturity. Admittedly, as an orchestral composer Schubert found himself in a difficult position. Orchestral music during the first two or three decades of the nineteenth century chiefly meant the symphonic works of Haydn, Mozart and Beethoven. They not only influenced, but even obscured, the contemporary production of orchestral music in practically the whole of Europe. Moreover, geographically Schubert was placed at the very source from which all that great music flowed. A younger contemporary of Beethoven's, he lived in the same city, where the master's titanic genius must have weighed almost crushingly upon any other native composer. In these circumstances it is not to be wondered that the young Schubert adhered so closely to the tradition of the Viennese school. Yet it was Haydn and Mozart rather than Beethoven who first served him as his chief models.[1] Whether you take his orchestral dances or his concert overtures or the bulk of his first six

[1] This tendency to gravitate to the style of the two elder Viennese composers was characteristic, not only of Schubert, but of practically all Beethoven's German contemporaries. It was not until the romantic period that Beethoven's music, chiefly the works of his middle period, began to produce progeny.

symphonies, you will find that, if not always in idiom, yet in general æsthetic attitude, they are true children of that late eighteenth-century spirit which found such perfect expression in Haydn's and Mozart's instrumental works. They are what has often been termed *Spielmusik*: music of a predominantly charming, pleasant and playful nature rarely seeking to sound a deeper and more subjective note. Chiefly written to satisfy the refined taste of a very special public, this kind of music strove first and foremost to entertain and to create an effect similar to what the older Italian composers so aptly described as *titillazione degli orecchi*. It was this ideal—which, incidentally, partly conditioned the *style galant* about the middle of the eighteenth century—that guided the young Schubert in most of his early orchestral music. Moreover his typically Viennese temperament inclined him from the very beginning to a 'hedonistic' tendency in his music.[2] It not only stamps the general character of his early instrumental works, it is also felt in his mature compositions (viz. the scherzo and finale of the great C major Symphony, the Octet, the *Trout* Quintet and the Quintet in C). Consequently we find great similarity in mood and character between the various orchestral works of his early period. Not only are there affinities between his concert overtures and the first six symphonies, but the individual works of each group resemble one another in various ways. Like Haydn and Mozart, who often expressed a complex of ideas in a whole series of works, Schubert seems unconsciously to have written his early symphonies as if, with one exception, he had intended to form a set of related works. The fact that he composed them for similar occasions, performances by amateur orchestras, also of course determined their more or less similar character.

The exception to which I have just referred is the Fourth Symphony in C minor. In mode of expression—its programmatic title *The Tragic* is, significantly enough, Schubert's own—and partly also in treatment, it differs from the rest of the early symphonies. This work shows the first signs that Beethoven's example, since the *Eroica*, of creating with each new symphony an individual musical character, was beginning to influence the young composer. For the first time in his symphonies, Schubert attempts here to introduce a more individual and serious note and it is his first symphonic work to be cast in a minor key, the poetic significance of which is obvious. Yet this attempt at emulating Beethoven was not very successful. Schubert seems not yet sufficiently

[2] It seems no mere coincidence that it was Vienna where this tendency found its happiest expression. The love of the pleasant, graceful and entertaining element in music forms a common bond between Haydn, Mozart, Schubert and Johann Strauss. Even such non-Viennese composers as Beethoven and the serious-minded Brahms were in the course of time infected by this germ in the Viennese atmosphere.

mature to grasp the full spiritual significance of his models such as the Fifth Symphony and the overtures to *Egmont* and *Coriolanus*. Or if he does grasp it, he has not yet adequate power to express it in his own way. For, save the slow introduction, the predominating formalism of the work as a whole seems to militate against a truly moving expression of tragedy and pathos. It is less Schubert than Beethoven seen through the eyes of a very gifted yet immature disciple.

With the Fifth Symphony in B flat Schubert returns to the more congenial climes of his first three symphonies. Yet with this difference: not only has he here completely mastered the classical style, but what is more important, he now fuses the traditional idiom with a remarkable individual expression, and the result is a work in which Haydn's wit and Mozart's gracefulness and light touch combine in perfect union with the composer's happy flow of melody and exuberant expression. The Fifth is thus the most successful and most representative of Schubert's early symphonies. It was, to all intents and purposes, his conscious farewell to the two masters of his youth. For in the Sixth Symphony in C, Schubert aims at something bigger and more ambitious, intending to write a 'Grand Symphony', an aim that he achieved only ten years later in the Ninth Symphony, the great C major. True, there is a certain massive broadness of feeling, a tendency to explosive climaxes and a remarkable expansion of the formal dimensions, all pointing to characteristic features of his symphonic swan-song. Yet, written at a critical stage in the composer's development—the transition from his youthful style to maturity—it shows a curious conglomeration of various heterogeneous elements which as yet he had not the power to amalgamate into an organic, coherent whole. One sees him trying to free himself from Mozart and Haydn without, however, succeeding completely; Beethoven is again much in evidence in the scherzo and the finale pays homage to a composer whom one would not expect in that company: Rossini. Thus the Sixth Symphony assumes almost the character of a pastiche all the more disappointing after the excellence of the Fifth.

Here we may pause for a moment and touch upon the vexed question of Rossini's influence on Schubert. Schubert's attitude towards the 'Italian nightingale' was admiration mingled with a good deal of ironic mockery. It is thus difficult to establish whether his occasional Rossini-isms were introduced as skits on, or homage to, the Italian's racy and brilliant yet rather facile invention. They probably served both purposes. However, I think that too great an importance has been attached to the whole question. Compared with the intrinsic and most fruitful influence of the three Viennese masters, Rossini's may be best described as but an intrusion on Schubert's music and thus it is of a minor and episodic character. While rather out of place in the finale of the Sixth Symphony,[3] in a number of other works, particularly in the second of the two overtures *In the Italian Style* in C major, the Rossinian element gives an attractive and amusing cachet.

To return to the symphonies. I said above that with the Sixth Schubert had arrived at a critical stage in his development as a symphonic writer. He was outgrowing his apprenticeship, which meant that the eighteenth-century ideal no longer satisfied him. He became increasingly aware that what he had now to say could no longer be said in terms of an idiom that was so closely modelled upon Haydn and Mozart. Nor had his attempt to follow Beethoven so far produced a satisfactory result. It would appear that the significant break in his symphonic production after the Sixth Symphony had something to do with this critical state of affairs. Moreover opera and piano music were exercising an increasing hold on his creative interest, and thus we see the composer pausing for nearly three years before returning again to the symphony.

This he did with the Seventh Symphony, of which he left a sketch complete in all essentials. Its spacious lay-out, its lyrical feeling, here incomparably more developed than in any of the previous symphonies, and the marked, in some instances striking, individuality of certain themes make this work appear as the bridge between the inconclusive Sixth Symphony and the masterpiece of the *Unfinished*. With the year of the Seventh Symphony (1821) Schubert's musical vision begins to broaden and gain in emotional power and depth. Moreover, a new introspective and at times almost self-torturing note makes itself felt, a change that was already heralded by that stirring piece of music, the Quartet Movement in C minor of 1820. More and more his music seems to become a vehicle for expressing dark and melancholy moods. What could be more symptomatic of that attitude than the pathos and pessimism that pervade the torso of the *Unfinished*, the D minor Quartet and *Die Winterreise*?[4]

Parallel with this development ran Schubert's growing understanding of the intrinsic significance of Beethoven's great instrumental

[3] Schubert's singular lack of taste in this respect is best seen in the Largo from the Piano Fantasy in F minor where the unexpected Rossini reminiscence forms a bad patch in an otherwise great movement.

[4] Cf. the entry in Schubert's diary from March 1824: 'My compositions in music are the product of my mind and spring from my sorrow; those only that were born of grief give the greatest delight to the outside world.' Illuminating, too, is his letter, of the same month, to his friend Kupelwieser, in which the composer compares his own state of mind to that of Gretchen in his famous Goethe song. That this did not, however, stifle the spontaneous and refreshing gaiety of the Viennese in him is proved by the Octet and the finales of the A minor Quartet and the Ninth Symphony.

works. What seems to have impressed him with particular force was the great human element in them; to express that in his own music became now his chief aim. It is true that Beethoven's spiritual searchings and his heroic optimism had no parallels in Schubert's genius. His was a passive nature that had none of Beethoven's power to combat the oppressive and pessimistic thoughts of his later years. He often succumbed to them in a state of hopeless despair. Yet what he unquestionably learnt from Beethoven was how to fashion instrumental music into a most powerful and at the same time most subtle medium to express his innermost feelings and thoughts. Hence, it is no coincidence that the mature Schubert concentrates more and more on large-scale instrumental works each of which represents a musical character of highly individual traits. The contrast in this respect with his early symphonies is most illuminating for the unfolding of the composer's musical personality.

This contrast is also shown in the superior technical quality of his later works, more so perhaps in his chamber music than in the symphonies. Altogether, Schubert's thematic treatment is here more ingenious and more flexible, the texture becomes infinitely richer and more varied, and even the handling of form shows on the whole a firmer grip. One feels that there is one central idea controlling and holding together the various sections of the movement. Rather than being put together in that formalistic way in which the composer treated his early symphonies, the music seems now to grow from within. This central idea is not only felt behind the individual movement but seems to determine the character of the work as a whole, and it is interesting to see how Schubert, consciously or unconsciously, uses a germ-motif to link together the main themes of the four movements.

Yet all this would not altogether account for the greatness and individuality of the composer's mature instrumental style. There is one essential factor at the bottom of it all. That is Schubert's unique lyrical genius. His early songs had already shown a rare power of lyrical invention which, though to a much lesser extent, is also felt in the slow movements of his early symphonies. Yet with that wonderful ripening and widening of Schubert's inner world, his lyricism now begins to dominate his instrumental music with ever-increasing power. It now demands a wider scope than it had in the songs. Its greater intensity requires a larger and more powerful medium, and thus the composer turns to chamber music and the symphony to fill them with a lyricism of rare poetic beauty. It is in this fusion of pure lyrical feeling with the large-scale instrumental form that lies, to my mind, the greatness and historic significance of Schubert as symphonist and instrumental composer generally. He was the first to introduce on a large scale a truly romantic feeling into the classical form of symphony and chamber music. Of his symphonies it is the *Unfinished* in which he achieved that in the most perfect manner. It is the first example of a lyrical romantic symphony. Here pure lyricism fills every bar, affecting not only the melodic invention but the harmonic and orchestral treatment. There was nothing in the whole of the classical symphony to compare with it. The only work that in a way foreshadows the world of the *Unfinished* is Mozart's G minor Symphony in which pathos and grief find a similar expression. Otherwise, Schubert's work stands entirely in a class by itself, not only in the composer's whole symphonic output but also in the whole of the nineteenth-century symphony. Its uniqueness places it alongside such great music as the above-mentioned Mozart symphony, Beethoven's Fifth, Brahms's Fourth, and, to draw a wider circle, *Tristan* and Mahler's *Lied von der Erde*—all works in which the innermost core of their creators' artistic *and* human personality reveals itself so perfectly that repetition seems impossible. It is in this light that we have to see the primary significance of the *Unfinished*. Why Schubert never completed it is a mystery which will perhaps never find a wholly satisfactory solution.

The notion cannot entirely be dismissed that Schubert, influenced as he was by Beethoven's symphonic conception, may have felt that the path on which he had started in the *Unfinished* was not the one he really intended to follow. Its passive, almost feminine feeling, its introspective attitude in which sentiment and emotion predominated over a more objective, intellectual concept—in short, its pure romanticism—was so very different from Beethoven's symphonic ideal. True, it was Schubert's first symphony in the grand style, but it was not *the* 'grand symphony' which he meant to write. Some such thoughts must have been in Schubert's mind when he wrote in 1824 that he had composed various works for chamber music and that he thus wanted to pave his way to the grand symphony. Here, I think, we have the explanation of the fact that the Ninth Symphony is not a continuation of the style of the *Unfinished* but rather a return to more classical conceptions. Its general character, a certain heroic feeling, and the noticeable restraint in lyrical expression, which is in the main confined to the slow movement, all point to Beethoven's influence.

Admittedly, the Ninth Symphony has little of that powerful intellectual appeal which emanates from the mature Beethoven symphonies. Its greatness lies elsewhere. As in the *Unfinished*, it lies in the wonderful purity of the musical content, the grandiose and spontaneous sweep of ideas, and in the broad swell with which the music surges up to overpowering climaxes almost smashing the symphonic framework to pieces. The result is formal dimensions of extraordinary proportions. Together with Beethoven's Choral Symphony it is the first example of the *kolossal* which was to characterise the symphonies of Bruckner and Mahler. Thus Schubert's deliberate attempt to return to a more classical manner succeeded only in parts. He was carried away by the romantic element of his genius, not only in those passages of elemental grandeur but also in the quiet sections where his mature lyricism manifested itself with singular beauty. Hence the Ninth Symphony stands half-way between the worlds of classicism and romanticism, and perhaps nothing is more characteristic of that dualism than the first movement, with the pure romantic feeling of the slow introduction and the classical cut of the allegro.

So much for a rough outline of Schubert's inner development as a symphonist. In turning to the more technical aspect I may briefly touch here upon such general features of melody, harmony and rhythm as are characteristic of his orchestral writing. It is significant that, broadly speaking, Schubert's melodic invention is at its best in those sections and movements which by tradition demand lyrical expression (viz. the second subjects of movements in sonata form, slow introductions, and andante movements). Not that we do not find equally inspired melodies in quick movements but, as a rule, it is those in the slow pieces that show the composer's typical fingerprints in their fully developed form.[5] Though their extended compass and their wider intervals clearly distinguish them from the composer's vocal melodies, they often contain sustained lines of a singable and markedly lyrical expression which frequently results from the Schubertian hovering and floating round a central note. And as in his vocal style, Schubert invents his instrumental melodies on a diatonic basis.[6]

The harmonic idiom of his orchestral works, notably of the last two symphonies, reveals typically romantic traits. Schubert uses dissonances much more frequently than his predecessors, especially in the form of suspensions, appoggiaturas and passing notes, and his favourite discords are the German sixth and the dominant with a minor ninth. In his modulations he generally prefers chromatic progressions as they allow him sudden and unexpected changes of key. Altogether, quick harmonic shifts are a particularly characteristic feature of his late symphonies and his chief methods in this respect are

[5] The *Allegro moderato* of the *Unfinished* is, owing to the markedly lyrical nature of its thematic material, practically a slow movement.

[6] Such melodic chromaticism as occurs in his orchestral works is in most cases the result of harmonic progressions.

the technique of the so-called interdominants,[7] the abrupt jump to the dominant of a new key, the turn to the key a major or minor third away from the tonic (*Mediantenrückung*), the alternation between major and minor, and the abrupt modulation by a one-note pivot at the entry of a new section. Of singularly beautiful effect is Schubert's device of temporarily obscuring the tonality by wavering between two keys and by introducing a succession of dominant sevenths without their 'true' resolutions. As I have said, all these devices clearly point to the composer's romantic leanings, though some of them made their first appearance in the preceding century.[8]

Rhythmically, Schubert shows considerably less imagination and variety. Many of his instrumental melodies suffer from rhythmic monotony due to his clinging to the same rhythmic pattern. This weakness is also felt in his phrasing. Schubert prefers the square build of two-bar and four-bar phrases, rarely introducing such irregularities as the clipping of phrases and the interspersing of one-bar and three-bar units as the classical masters often did in order to conceal the fundamental squareness of their melodies. In this respect Schubert was typically German and it may be that his closeness to German and Austrian folksong had something to do with it. If he does occasionally resort to some rhythmic peculiarity it becomes all the more conspicuous as, for instance, the three-bar phrasing of the introductory theme in the first movement of the Ninth Symphony, and the opening theme of the same work's second movement.[9] His rhythmic rigidity is not only confined to self-contained themes but marks less solidly built sections such as bridge passages and developments in which a freer and varied rhythmic treatment is almost *de rigueur*. Yet this does not mean that Schubert was altogether incapable of rhythmic variety and subtle articulation of phrasing. The slow introduction to the Fourth Symphony and the slow movements of his last two symphonies provide excellent instances of the fact that at times he could free himself from a stereotyped pattern. Moreover, Schubert's rhythmic style often has great power and drive, notably in his quick symphonic movements, thanks partly to his fondness for march rhythms or

[7] The English equivalent for the German *Zwischendominante* was first introduced by Gerald Abraham in his *Chopin's Musical Style* (O.U.P., 1939).

[8] The quick shift to the key a major or minor third away from the tonic had been used by Mozart and Haydn, not to mention Beethoven, and the alternation between major and minor is already found in early eighteenth-century music.

[9] An early example of a true three-bar phrase is the first subject of the opening movement of the Quartet in E flat, D. 87, No. 1. See also the opening themes of the first movements from the Piano Sonata in A minor, D. 537, and the duet Fantasy in F minor, D. 940.

rhythms that in a more general way suggest a continuous forward movement such as

(Altogether, this march-like element is very characteristic of his general style.)

Let us now turn to one of the most essential points in Schubert's symphonic style: his handling of form both as regards the four-movement cycle as a whole and the individual movements. The first question here is: how did Schubert approach the symphonic problem as raised and solved by Beethoven? This comparison is necessary in view of Schubert's various attempts to model his technique on the founder of the modern symphony. Now one of the main features of the mature Beethoven symphonies is the fact that each of them represents an organic whole in which the four movements constitute different yet complementary treatments of the same basic idea. This idea is discussed in the form of an argument and from various angles, as it were, until the finale brings a satisfactory solution. Thus Beethoven not only achieves inner coherence between the movements but, what is equally important, under his hands the finale assumes the function of a climax and general summing-up. Now nowhere in his symphonies did Schubert ever attempt to give the finale this concluding character. True, in the Fourth Symphony and, to a much higher degree, in his mature instrumental works he achieves a certain inner unity. Yet the four movements remain more or less on the same emotional plane. There is no inner development or growth that inevitably leads to a last climax in the finale. Different facets of the idea are shown, yet the idea itself is not elaborated or put through a dialectic form of argument and counter-argument. To find this in his early symphonies is perhaps not to be wondered at in view of his close adherence during that period to the eighteenth-century ideal. He builds them on the principle of mosaic-like juxtaposition of contrasting movements, relying on the simple effect of alternating moods. It would be quite possible to interchange movements from the different symphonies without fundamentally altering the character of the single works as a whole. Yet even his mature instrumental compositions do not, in spite of their inner unity, possess that cogent logic in the sequence of four movements that would impart to the finale a feeling of inevitability. Perhaps the finale of the Ninth Symphony comes nearest to that. But here, I think, it is solely the immense rhythmic impetus that creates the impression of a final climax to the preceding movements; otherwise it represents just another aspect of the 'wanderer' idea which seems to underlie the whole work. In other words, for all its romantic features the fundamental æsthetic conception behind the Ninth is still very much that of the eighteenth-century *Musiziersymphonie*, the symphony which integrates into a whole, not by gradually unfolding a psychological plan but by an alternation of contrasting and in mood complementary movements.[10] In this respect, Schubert's last symphony looks back rather than forward, which is yet another pointer to the singular position he occupies as an intermediary between the pre-Beethovenian and the later romantic symphonists.

All Schubert's completed symphonies are in four movements, in the orthodox order: allegro—slow movement—minuet (scherzo)—finale. Nowhere does he change this order or introduce as many modifications and novel features of construction and thematic treatment as he does in his piano and chamber music.[11] Altogether it would appear that in these more intimate media the composer is on the whole more enterprising than in his orchestral works.

Schubert's symphonic first movements are all in strict sonata form and, with the exception of the Fifth and Eighth Symphonies, open with slow introductions. These slow introductions contain some noteworthy features. Most of them are built in two sections of different character, the first being usually in the festive and solemn manner of the early classical operatic overture (Gluck, Mozart) and invariably scored for tutti, while the second section is of a more intimate and somewhat improvisatory nature. To this must be added the characteristic *morendo* at the conclusion of this second section where Schubert is fond of creating the effect of a lingering and haunting echo, particularly when he resorts to a suggestive interplay of melodic fragments which at times evoke the nostalgic feeling of a farewell. This is greatly enhanced by his delicate and imaginative use of

[10] Judging from the piano sketch of the third movement of the *Unfinished*, printed in the critical notes to the Breitkopf *Gesamtausgabe*, not even in the most romantic of all his symphonies did Schubert think of developing the emotional plan of the two preceding movements.

[11] In the String Quartet in E flat, D. 87, No. 1 (1813), the first movement is followed by a scherzo, with an adagio coming third. The running of one movement into the next—the apparent models were Mozart's piano fantasies and Beethoven's fantasy sonatas—is found in the *Wanderer* Fantasy and the duet Fantasy in F minor. The use of a single basic motif in the main themes of the various movements is illustrated by the *Wanderer* Fantasy and the late string quartets; though, indeed, it is also found in the last two symphonies. And, finally, the introduction of melodies from the songs occurs in the *Wanderer* Fantasy and the A minor and D minor Quartets.

the woodwind which helps to give an atmosphere of intimate chamber music. It is here that we usually get the first breath of lyricism. As in the second movements, the slow tempo seems to coax the composer into beautiful lyrical expression. The contrast between these two sections is often so marked that one has the impression that Schubert first intended to write the introduction in the traditional style yet, as he went on, turned to a more personal and individual manner. This is the reason why these slow introductions appear at times more remarkable than the main movements proper. (This applies, of course, only to the early symphonies.) Another interesting feature is that Schubert considered these introductions as more or less integral parts of the whole movement. Already in his First Symphony he re-introduces part of the slow introduction into the recapitulation of the allegro, and derives, as in the Third, Fourth and Ninth Symphonies, the first subject from material used in the introduction.[12] The most beautiful example of this close connection is to be found in the first movement of the Ninth Symphony with the magnificent apotheosis of the introductory theme at the very end of the allegro.

What strikes one in the first place in Schubert's first movements proper is their formal expansion. It is true that the process of enlarging the sonata form had started already with the late Mozart (in the three masterpieces of 1788) and was carried on by Beethoven. It was the result of the deeper emotional and spiritual content which the two composers began to express in that form. It affected every section: instead of the single-theme subjects of the early classical symphony, we now meet with subjects of more complex build, and the development, formerly not much more than a mere playground for new thematic formations and interesting modulations, changes now into a battle-ground of conflicting ideas of a programmatic and poetic nature. Similarly, from an extended repetition of cadential chords the coda grows into a second development in which, after the reconciliation of the recapitulation, the dramatic conflict flares up again. This was Schubert's model; most of his first and second subjects are of complex build, the themes invariably stated twice with the repeat in richer orchestration, and, following Beethoven's example, he handles his bridge-passages and codas in quasi-development fashion, often modulating to remote keys and thus extending the symphonic canvas. Yet here the first criticism arises. Why is it that despite their formal extension neither the late Mozart nor the Beethoven symphonies

[12] He ostensibly took the hint from the three Viennese masters who occasionally brought the two sections thus closer together. See Haydn's Symphonies Nos 98, 102 and 103, Mozart's *Haffner* Serenade (K.250), and Beethoven's *Pathétique* Sonata, Op. 13.

provoke the feeling of superfluous length while with Schubert we cannot overcome the impression that the composer often takes too long over what he has to say? This, of course, has little to do with their length as expressed in terms of bar numbers. With Schubert it is much less a question of absolute length than of proportions and, in the early symphonies, of congruity between content and form. For, in addition to their generally playful, naïve character, emotionally not very significant, they do not possess that degree of musical quality and interest which would justify their lengthy treatment. In this respect the position in the last two symphonies is different. Their incomparably greater and deeper content—in other words, the immensely broadened vision of the composer's symphonic world—required a larger framework. Yet even here his tendency to expansion at times upsets the formal balance.

It is Schubert's peculiar thematic treatment that lies at the bottom of his formal problems. With Haydn and Beethoven—and it is on their technique that Schubert tried to model his own—thematic treatment is the elaboration of a theme or themes in such a way as to yield the chief material for building and filling the complex form of a sonata movement. To put it differently, the formally more fluid sections such as bridge passages, development and coda should *grow* out of the themes. Now the principal weakness of Schubert's symphonic technique is the fact that more often than not he fails to see the possibilities of *growth* in his themes; he is often inclined to dodge genuine thematic treatment and to resort to unsymphonic devices. The reason for that lies in the specific cast of his musical personality. I have spoken before of his all-pervading lyricism. It forms the core of his genius, and no matter from which angle we approach his music we must keep this basic fact constantly before our minds. It is this strong lyricism that throws light upon his frequent failures in building up his symphonic first movements in a well-knitted, organic way. To start with, his attitude towards the symphonic theme is that of the typical song composer. He is inclined to see it as a *tune* rather than a *theme*. He looks upon most of his symphonic ideas as self-contained and self-sufficient units, and not as melodic material which will prove its *raison d'être* by its elaboration. They are not for him the means to an end but the end itself. If I use the antithesis of tune and theme, it is not to say that Schubert was altogether unable to invent themes with symphonic possibilities in them. The first subjects of the opening movements of the Fourth, Fifth and Ninth Symphonies prove that on occasion he could hit upon truly symphonic ideas. Yet what mattered with him in the first place was the indivisibility, cohesion and wholeness of a melody which, I suggest, are the typical characteristics of a tune as compared with a theme. This tendency was admirably suited to his songs and those of his instrumental movements which are based on the song form. But it was a wrong approach in a symphonic first movement where an essentially dynamic and forward tendency militates against static lyricism.[13] It is true that in his mature period he was able to achieve a greater measure of reconciliation between these two opposing tendencies, but this curious 'tug-of-war' is still felt in one way or another. It manifests itself in a mixture of true thematic treatment and more or less wholesale transposition and reiteration of self-contained melodic phrases, the latter method predominating up to his Fifth Symphony. Though the composer tries to make up for the inevitable monotony resulting from such a method by widening his harmonic range, he partly defeats this end as his static lyricism inclines him to remain too long in the same key. Add to it his often exasperating adherence to the same rhythmic patterns, and you have the factors that make for the 'divine lengths' of his large-scale instrumental works. This weakness in the structure of Schubert's first movements applies also to his symphonic finales and his concert overtures, which are without exception cast in sonata form.

I have just referred to Schubert's widening of the harmonic range, and that brings me to another important point. This is his freedom in treating the key-organisation of the classical sonata form. One of the most characteristic features here is his frequent deviation from the orthodox key sequence in both exposition and recapitulation. In the former he alters the traditional opposition of tonic and dominant (or relative major) as the respective keys of first and second subjects, by casting the second subject in other related keys such as the subdominant, the subdominant of the relative major, the relative minor of the dominant, and the mediant of the tonic.[14] These irregularities are

[13] A similar problem confronts us in the Schumann symphonies. See Chapter 10.

[14] Here are some instances: subdominant, first and last movements of Second Symphony and finale of Third Symphony; subdominant of relative major, first and last movements of Fourth Symphony and first movement of Eighth Symphony; relative minor of the dominant, first movement of Ninth Symphony; and mediant, finale of Sixth Symphony. Schubert was, however, not the first to introduce such changes. Haydn, Mozart, and especially Beethoven had occasionally chosen an unorthodox key for the second subject. But with the difference that, compared with Schubert's marked practice, theirs was much more tentative. In this connection it is interesting to recall that in the very beginnings of the sonata form (first half of the eighteenth century) the second subject was often introduced in the minor form of the dominant, and it was not until the heyday of the great Viennese period (from 1780 to about 1814) that the major form became the established rule. It is thus wrong to describe Schubert's harmonic irregularities as unconscious blunders, as some writers have done. Rather must they be interpreted as a deliberate attempt to introduce novel features into the traditional key scheme.

clearly a romantic trait and foreshadow the wide orbit of keys that became so characteristic of the later nineteenth-century symphonies. Yet Schubert, standing as he does between the classical period and the dawn of romanticism, still feels his bond with the classical tradition. This is seen in the fact that after venturing with the second subject into an unorthodox key, in the codetta of the exposition he returns to the dominant as if to make amends for breaking the classical rule. Thus we arrive at those Schubertian three-key expositions with each of the three main sections in a different key. This was another factor that made for formal expansion, for, given the pronounced static element of his style, Schubert consolidates each new key on a melodically broad and extended basis.

A similar picture is presented by his recapitulations. Here the harmonic irregularities are perhaps even more striking. It is true that most of Schubert's recapitulations are, in every respect but the harmonic, identical with his expositions. He does not seem to care for such alterations as Haydn, Mozart and Beethoven introduced in order to avoid a complete replica of the exposition: another pointer to Schubert's rather formalistic view of the sonata form. Hence his harmonic alterations are all the more conspicuous. For one thing, he often obscures the tonic key at the entry of the recapitulation by introducing the first subject in some related key, flattened mediant (finale of the Ninth Symphony), dominant (finale of the Third Symphony and first movement of the Fourth Symphony) and subdominant (first movements of the Second and Fifth Symphonies). This last choice incidentally allows him to repeat the exposition wholesale a fourth up without having to modify the modulation of the bridge passage between first and second subjects.[15] A similarly characteristic feature of his recapitulations is the choice of key for the second subject. The idea behind the classical practice of introducing, in the reprise, the second subject on the tonic was to indicate the solution of the harmonic conflict between the two poles of tonic and dominant, a conflict which imparted to the exposition some of its dynamic, forward movement. Schubert ignores that idea by frequently bringing back the second subject in a key other than the tonic and thus creates a tension of tonalities similar to that in the exposition.[16] This seems to

[15] Classical precedents for such irregularities are to be found in some of Haydn's recapitulations and in several works by Mozart and Beethoven (see the first movements of the Piano Sonata in C (K.545), the *Kreutzer* Sonata, and the *Coriolanus* Overture.

[16] In the finale of the Second Symphony, the second subject returns in G minor instead of in B flat major; in the first and last movements of the Third Symphony, in G instead of in D; in the first movement of the Fourth Symphony, in E flat instead of C; and in the first movement of the Ninth Symphony it is cast in the tonic minor.

suggest that what mattered with Schubert was not so much the functional and structural significance of the keys as their more sensuous appeal as patterns of different harmonic colour. In other words, the romantic feeling in Schubert's harmonic style began to affect even the basic tonal relations of classical sonata form.

So much for his first movements. If his lyricism here often seems at loggerheads with the dynamic element of sonata form, no such discrepancies are to be found in his second movements. The slow movement of the classical symphony was by tradition the very place where the composer could give expression to his lyrical ideas. In contrast to the first movement, it is static rather than dynamic. Hence, it is no wonder that with a composer of Schubert's type it should become the most characteristic and perhaps the most successful of the four movements. The slow tempo and the form—with the exception of the andante of the Second Symphony, Schubert's second movements are all in tripartite song form, A—B—A, or an extension of that basic scheme—allowed him to indulge his lyrical vein almost without let or hindrance. His rich melodic invention stood him in good stead when it came to writing broad, sustained melodies; and the mere juxtaposition and alternation of contrasting sections—the essence of song form—was completely in accord with his general approach to the symphony. As in his slow introductions, here too we find felicitous touches of orchestration, particularly on the woodwind, such as delicate echo effects (notably towards the end of a movement) and subtle blendings of woodwind, horns and strings. Moreover, Schubert shows here considerably greater care for details, and an altogether more elaborate treatment of the texture than we usually find in his first and last movements. In short, many of those features that Beethoven once describe as *obligates Akkompagnement*—an infinite variety in the use of technical devices, from a mere block harmonisation of a top melody to elaborate part-writing—are to be found in Schubert's slow movements, notably in those of his last two symphonies. In passing, it is worth mentioning that in none of his symphonic slow movements does he introduce a melody from his songs as he did several times in his piano and chamber music. There are, however, general affinities with his songs which in the last two symphonies assume a more tangible character in the form of melodic, harmonic and rhythmic parallels. These parallels give us some clue to the poetic and emotional significance of the individual movements.

Up to the Sixth Symphony Schubert's third movements are all entitled 'Minuet'. Actually they are no longer true minuets, standing as they do half-way between the *Ländler* of the Haydn-Mozart type and the Beethoven scherzo, though in some cases rhythmic and instrumental features of the old minuet are still noticeable. Their tempo is very fast, *allegro vivace* or *allegro molto*, thus pointing to Beethoven's influence which is also felt in the melodic shape of certain themes and the characteristic preference for strong and sudden dynamic contrasts and the frequent use of *sforzati*. This is particularly true of the third movements of the Fourth and Sixth Symphonies, which come very near to being real Beethoven scherzi. For, in addition to their considerable formal extension, they are marked by the absence of those pronounced dance rhythms which distinguish the minuet and *Ländler* from the true scherzo. Yet it would appear that to the Austrian in Schubert the *Ländler* and its younger brother, the slow waltz, were more congenial than Beethoven's wild and demoniac movements—which may be the reason why even in his very last symphony the third movement is much more like a heavy peasant dance than a real scherzo though it is thus entitled. The Austrian flavour is even more pronounced in the trios, where Schubert at times models the tunes on Viennese popular songs. A delightful pastoral note is often sounded in them and their lyrical melody and more deliberate tempo[17] strike an effective contrast to the rather turbulent and rumbustious language of the first part. This contrast is enhanced by Schubert's more intimate treatment of the orchestra in which, taking a leaf out of Haydn's trios and the classical serenades, he occasionally introduces on the woodwind short imitations, canons and concertante passages of arresting effect.

As the finales are all in sonata form there is little to add here to what has been said of the first movements. Structurally they are looser and more diffuse. Some of them give the impression that the composer, glad to have reached the last part of a large-scale work, has let himself go without much regard to formal balance and proportion. This is particularly true of the finales of the Second, Third, Fourth and Ninth Symphonies. There is a constant and relentless urge springing from a characteristic figure or a pronounced rhythm, like an ostinato, driving the music from beginning to end. Whether it is the rhythm of a galop (Second Symphony) or a Rossinian tarantella (Third Symphony) or an animated march (Ninth Symphony), the composer's adherence to the same rhythmic figure, plus the quick pace, results in the impression that some mechanical force is propelling the music on an interminable course. The general character of such movements is that of a *perpetuum mobile*. It is probable that Schubert took the idea from

[17] Schubert rarely indicates the change of tempo, yet it is a Viennese tradition to take the trios at a more deliberate pace in order to do justice to their 'leisurely' feeling.

certain Beethoven finales,[18] yet he developed it into a more characteristic feature, as may be also seen from the finales of some of his chamber music and piano sonatas.

Schubert's various dances, the Concert Piece for violin and orchestra and the eight concert overtures are all contemporary with his first six symphonies and, like them, were written for amateur orchestras—which explains their light, entertaining character. Their musical quality is more or less on the level of the early symphonies: a number of individual touches being mingled with immaturity of invention and technique and an obvious tendency to imitate Haydn and Mozart. Of these minor works the overtures are the most substantial. They are, along with Beethoven's *Zur Namensfeier*, the first examples, to my knowledge, of completely independent and self-contained orchestral overtures—a fact that must be stressed in view of the widespread notion that Mendelssohn was the first to introduce this form. Following the classical tradition (Gluck, Mozart) Schubert's overtures are all in one single movement[19] and in form are identical with symphonic first movements, (usually) a slow introduction of a solemn and festive character followed by an allegro with either a short development or a mere transition passage of a few bars leading to the recapitulation. They are less elaborate and structurally looser than Schubert's symphonic first movements, though rather similar in character. Some of them might easily take the place of first movements in the composer's early symphonies. Yet there is no mistaking the element of the traditional operatic overture which comes out in such features as frequent passages up and down the scale, tutti repetitions of cadential chords, and a generally brilliant and at times noisy orchestration. Broadly speaking, Schubert's orchestral writing strikes one here as more varied and perhaps more imaginative than in his early symphonies. (This is even more pronounced in his overtures to stage works where programmatic and poetic ideas provided an additional incentive.) And as with his symphonic slow introductions, here too the slow openings, notably of the overtures of 1816 and 1817 are often marked by intense poetic feeling and enchanting effects of woodwind colour.

Having occasionally touched upon Schubert's orchestration, it may be as well to give here a brief outline of his general methods. As long as he stood in close allegiance to Haydn and Mozart, his orchestral

[18] E.g. the Seventh and Eighth Symphonies and the Piano Sonatas Op. 10, No. 2, Op. 26, and Op. 32, Nos 2 and 3.

[19] The change from the older three-movement form seems to have originated with the overture of the eighteenth-century *opéra comique* (Monsigny, Grétry, Philidor, etc.).

writing was more or less along their lines. The size of the orchestra in his early symphonies does not extend beyond the typical combination used by the two older masters: strings, double woodwind (one flute in the First Symphony), two horns (four in No. 4), two trumpets and timpani. Significant of the general change of style in his mature period is the addition of three trombones in the last three symphonies. Yet in his concert overtures Schubert uses trombones as early as the D major overture of his schooldays.[20] In his early works it is still the strings that carry the main burden. The first statement of themes is usually entrusted to them and, especially in the openings of his slow movements, Schubert is fond of treating them in chamber-music style. It is also interesting to note that while at first the first violins have most of the melodic say, with growing maturity the rest of the strings, notably the cellos, take an increasing share. Excellent examples of this are to be found in the last two symphonies.

Yet it is Schubert's treatment of the woodwind that lends his orchestral palette its individual character. Not only does it abound in original touches—even in his early symphonies—but it is here that Schubert's orchestra shines in its warmest and most beautiful colours. The romanticist in Schubert found here a wide and more or less unexplored field for his instrumental imagination.[21] His favourite woodwind instruments were the clarinet and oboe, which are often given solo passages in which one feels that the peculiar tone-colour and technique of the instrument inspired the particular tune. This is especially true of the slow introductions, slow movements and second subjects. Moreover Schubert blends the various woodwinds in a most suggestive way both with one another and with the other departments of the orchestra, notably the horns. Another characteristic feature is the composer's *durchbrochene Arbeit* or 'broken work',[22] that is, the division of a melodic phrase between different instruments, a method that often creates the impression of a dialogue. The natural ease and variety in the handling of this device is a hallmark of Schubert's orchestral style and is seen at its best in the slow movements of the last two symphonies.

As Schubert had only 'natural' horns and trumpets at his disposal, his treatment of these instruments was necessarily much less characteristic. In his early works he uses them in the classical manner as pedals,

[20] The other overtures with trombones are those in D (D. 26) of 1812 (G. A. II, No. 2) and E minor (D. 648) of 1819. See also, his *Eine kleine Trauermusik* (D. 79) of 1813.

[21] Of the classical composers it was chiefly Mozart who in some ways anticipated him in this individual treatment of the woodwind, and there are a good number of woodwind passages in Schubert's works instinct with Mozartian feeling.

[22] An apt term coined by the Austrian musicologist Guido Adler.

for punctuation and, in conjunction with the timpani, underlining of the basic rhythm, and as dynamic reinforcement of the *tutti*. He also uses the horn as the bass or inner part of woodwind harmony, thus anticipating a characteristic of Wagner's orchestral style. Moreover, this favourite instrument of the German romantics is at times entrusted with a more prominent rôle in solo passages, rarely in the composer's early works (D major Overture of 1817, G.A. II, No. 4) but with greater frequency in the last two symphonies. One need only recall those enchanting bell-like effects in their slow movements and the magical opening of the great C major. The individual use of the trumpet is chiefly confined to calls and signals which originate in the composer's penchant for march-like elements. Perhaps the best example of this is to be found in the second movement of the Ninth Symphony. I have already spoken of Schubert's early predilection for the trombone. The massive style of some of the concert overtures and certain portions of the last two symphonies is partly due to his frequent use of this instrument, which at times, however, leads to an overloading of the texture and thus sorely upsets the orchestral balance.[23] Yet, for all that, how imposing is the introduction of the trombones in the climaxes, and how wonderful the mysterious, supernatural effect of the famous *pp* passages in the first movement of the Ninth Symphony![24]

[23] Schubert probably never heard either of his last two symphonies, which may account for his occasional misjudgment. It is said that, apparently not quite certain of the effect, he consulted his friend Lachner on the question of the trombones in the Ninth Symphony. In order to restore the balance it is the general practice today to double the horn parts—to my mind, a legitimate alteration and a noticeable improvement.

[24] Prophetic of this are certain trombone passages in the early D major Overture of 1812, and even more strikingly, in the overture to his opera *Des Teufels Lustschloss* of 1813–14.

FIVE

BRUCKNER'S ORGAN RECITALS IN FRANCE AND ENGLAND

IT IS CURIOUS that France and England—countries in which during his lifetime, and for a long time after, his music failed to gain a footing—were the only two countries outside Austria in which Bruckner appeared publicly as an organist. These two concert-giving expeditions of his—the first to Nancy and Paris in the spring of 1869, the second to London in the summer of 1871—belong to a period of Bruckner's artistic development when he was still young as a symphonist. He was over forty when he wrote his first Symphony—an extraordinary case of delayed maturity. It is true that beside this first symphony he had produced by 1869 a number of church compositions, including the magnificent Mass in E minor that looks back in spirit and technique to Palestrina. But Bruckner as a composer was still practically a blank page to most of his contemporaries, with the exception of a small circle in Upper Austria, his native country.

With Bruckner as an organist it was a different matter. From early childhood the organ had been his favourite instrument. At twenty-one his free contrapuntal treatment of a Haydn theme and his improvisation of a fugue had attracted considerable attention at his examination for a school post. But what developed Bruckner into Austria's greatest organist was the period of eleven years (1845–56) as assistant schoolmaster at the seminary of St Florian, near Linz. The baroque splendour of this Augustinian abbey was matched by its monumental organ, at that time the second largest in Austria. (The largest was that in St Stefan's, Vienna.) It was here that Bruckner got the organ and its style into his very bones. The stylistic roots of both the Chorale themes in his symphonies and the 'registration' effect of his orchestral scoring are evidently to be found in his intensive study of the organ during this period.

During these years at St Florian's he made himself a complete master of the technique of organ-playing. In 1856 his brilliant success in a competition won him the post of organist at Linz Cathedral, a post which he gave up only after twelve long years, to go to Vienna as professor of theory and organ-playing at the Conservatorium der Musikfreunde (1868). By the time he was invited to Vienna he must have enjoyed a very high reputation as an organ-player. Yet Vienna was (and is still) no easy ground for a newcomer, particularly for one from the provinces, no matter how good his reputation. It was necessary for Bruckner to establish his new position on a sound basis and he set about this in the field in which success seemed most certain, namely, as organist. A favourable opportunity soon occurred.

The organ of the newly-built church of St Epvre in Nancy, which counted among its patrons the Emperor and Empress of Austria, was to be opened with a competition. On the advice of Hanslick, pope of Viennese music, all-powerful critic of the *Neue Freie Presse*, and at that time Bruckner's friend (though in later years he became his bitterest enemy), Bruckner decided to compete. His two recitals, on 28 and 29 April, had such a resounding success that one French newspaper hailed him as '*un homme de goût le plus élevé, de la science la plus vaste et la plus féconde*'. Bruckner, highly surprised and delighted by the result, wrote in his characteristic naïve and childlike way to Herbeck, the director of the Vienna Conservatorium: 'I have only the oral judgments of the professionals in my favour[1]—a point on which modesty bids me be silent—and also the applause of the public. Charming young ladies of the highest aristocracy even came to the organ-loft and expressed their appreciation.'

This success gave the head of the Paris firm of organ-builders, Merklin-Schütze, the idea of asking Bruckner to give a recital at their Paris factory. But the timid and conscientious master hesitated, for the leave Herbeck had granted him for Nancy had expired. He characteristically wrote to Herbeck asking 'that my leave may be extended for three days. I send your Excellency, though with a very heavy heart, this request from me and all these gentlemen (he means the Paris firm) most humbly, and beg you to be so kind as to do all you can with the authorities to get them to grant what I ask. And will you be so very good as to tell my pupils?' The permission was 'most graciously' granted and Bruckner played in Paris not only at Merklin's, but at Notre Dame before a distinguished audience said to have included Franck, Saint-Saëns, Auber and Gounod. His success at Nancy was repeated and again it was his inspired improvisations that made the deepest impression. 'At the end I asked for a theme,' he writes to Linz. 'It was given me by C. A. Chauvet, one of the greatest organists in Paris, and

[1] 'Oral' in contrast to the printed notices, which (as he explains in the same letter) he was unable to read.

when I had developed it in three sections, the success was unbounded. I shall never experience such a triumph again.' It is very probable that the success of this foreign trip helped to get Bruckner the appointment of organist at the Vienna Hofmusik-Kapelle in the following September.

Two years later a second opportunity to go abroad presented itself. In the summer of 1871 an International Exhibition was held in London and the Exhibition Committee invited the Chambers of Commerce of the various countries to send their most prominent organists to London. During the Exhibition organ recitals were to be given on the giant organ just built by Henry Willis for the Albert Hall, close to which the Exhibition was held. When Bruckner heard of this, he applied to the Vienna Chamber of Commerce to be sent to London and, after a trial, he was unanimously chosen from a number of candidates. The conditions were: beginning on 2 August he was to play twice daily for a week, for a fee of £50, including travelling and hotel expenses. A detailed description of the Willis organ was sent with the contract.

A journey to London was not such a simple matter in those days and Bruckner, ever timid, implored a friend to travel with him. 'Then we can come back in fine style by way of Switzerland,' he wrote temptingly. But nothing came of this and Bruckner had to make the journey to London alone. He arrived at the end of July and stayed at Seyd's Hotel, a German hotel in Finsbury Square.[2]

A story of rather doubtful veracity is told of his first day in London. He had no sooner arrived than he went to the Albert Hall to try the organ. It was a Saturday and the manager of the Hall explained to him that it was too late. There was very little steam up—the organ was blown by steam—and Bruckner could play only as long as the steam lasted. Undisturbed the master seated himself at the organ and began to practise and improvise. Enthusiastic at what he heard, the manager had the fires stoked up and sent for various friends, so that when Bruckner finished he found to his astonishment that he had a considerable audience. *Si non è vero . . .*

Besides Bruckner, six other organists had been engaged for these several weeks of recitals: W. T. Best, the official organist of the Hall, who had opened the series on 18 July, Saint-Saëns from Paris, Mailly from Brussels, Löhr from Budapest, Heintze from Stockholm, and Lindeman from Norway. Although Bruckner had already played for the first time on 2 August, the then widely-read *Musical World*

[2] In its place (39/45 Finsbury Square) now stands the new City Gate House. In April 1976 a plaque showing Bruckner's face in profile was unveiled on the front of this building.

published on 5 August the following rather reserved announcement: 'Herr Anton Bruckner, Court Organist at Vienna, and Professor at the Conservatorium of that city, has arrived in London to play on the great organ of the Royal Albert Hall. The dates of his performance will shortly be announced. It takes some little time to become acquainted with the details of so large an instrument. Herr Bruckner's strong points are said to be classical improvisations on Handel, Bach, and Mendelssohn.'

The programme of Bruckner's London debut was:

> Toccata in F major (Bach).
> Improvisations upon the foregoing.
> Fugue in D minor (Handel).
> Improvisations (original).
> Improvisations on Bach's Fugue in E minor.

From this programme one sees how very fond Bruckner was of improvisation, in which art he was, by all contemporary accounts, a past-master. Shortly before his journey to London he said to a pupil in his Upper Austrian dialect: '*No, i werd net lang den Bach einwerggen, dös sollen die machen, die ka Phantasie haben, i spiel über a frei's Thema,*' which might be rendered: 'Noa, I doan't care for grindin' out lots o' Bach. They can do that as 'as no imagination o' their oawn. I plays away as I likes.'

In the course of a week Bruckner gave six recitals at the Albert Hall with such success that August Manns, the famous conductor of the Crystal Palace Saturday Concerts, engaged him for four more. I quote here a letter of 23 August from Bruckner to an influential Linz acquaintance—the only one so far published from which we can glean further particulars of his stay in London: 'Just finished. Played ten times; six times at the Albert Hall, four times at the Crystal Palace. Tremendous applause, endless every time. Encores demanded. In particular I often had to repeat a couple of improvisations. Both places the same. Heaps of compliments, congratulations, invitations. Kapellmeister Manns of the Crystal Palace told me he was astonished and that I was to come again soon and send him my compositions. . . . Yesterday I played before 70,000 people[3] and had to give encores as the Committee asked me to—for I didn't want to, in spite of the tremendous applause. On Monday I played with equal success at the concert . . . N.B. Unfortunately the critic of *The Times* is in Germany: so hardly anything will be written about me *now*. Please let the Linz papers know something of this.'

[3] This was at the German National Fête at the Crystal Palace on 19 August.

The postscript betrays clearly that Bruckner attached some importance to having his recitals noticed by the critics. As a matter of fact, the important dailies published nothing but the bare announcements. It was summer and these recitals, given mainly for the benefit of visitors to the Exhibition, were apparently not taken very seriously in musical circles. Still, in the already mentioned *Musical World* we find reports striking a by no means enthusiastic note. There is mention of 'second-rate foreigners' and of the 'modest mediocrity' of some of the foreign organists and 'a little discretion in the selection' of the artists is demanded (a little too late) of the management. Bruckner himself comes off comparatively well: 'He has given us a grand extempore Fantasia, which although not very original in thought or design, was clever, remarkable for its canonic counterpoint and for the surmounting of much difficulty in the pedal passages.' But now comes the blow: 'There can be nothing said extemporaneously upon the National Anthem of Austria, and still less upon the "Hallelujah" Chorus of Handel; nor do we think any improvisation with any effect can be given upon the Toccatas of Bach or the Sonatas of Mendelssohn. Great composers exhaust their themes. Nothing can be added to the "Hallelujah" Chorus, nothing to a toccata of Sebastian Bach.'

What impression was made on Bruckner by London as a town we do not know. He left at the end of August—by the way, he had begun the Finale of his second symphony here on 10 August—intending to return next year and tour the provinces. But nothing came of this. Four years later he received from the Royal Exhibition Commission a medal for his successful collaboration. Once later, in 1886, he thought of coming to London to conduct his seventh symphony in place of Hans Richter, who was ill. But this plan, too, came to nothing. A few trips to Germany to hear performances of his works were the only occasions on which Bruckner went abroad in later years. Moreover, organ-playing gradually drifted into the background as Bruckner began to concentrate more and more on symphonic composition. As he once put it: 'What my fingers play is forgotten, but what they have written will not be forgotten.'

SIX

MAHLER'S VISIT TO LONDON

MAHLER'S ONLY VISIT to London was in 1892, when he directed the German season at Covent Garden. He was then in his early thirties, but in spite of his comparative youth he had already made a remarkable reputation as a conductor, particularly as an interpreter of Wagner. At twenty-eight he had been made Director of the Royal Opera, Budapest, and during his three years' reign had raised this institution from a state of artistic decrepitude to an astonishingly high level. It was not surprising, therefore, that Bernhard Pollini, the able and far-seeing Intendant of the Hamburg Opera, selected him as principal conductor at Hamburg in 1891. Mahler's brief connection with Covent Garden also came about through Pollini.

The Hamburg Intendant had been for many years a friend of Sir Augustus Harris, then manager of Covent Garden, and Harris was contemplating as a special venture for the spring of 1892 the production of the whole 'Ring' for the first time in the Covent Garden German season. *Tristan*, *Tannhäuser* and *Fidelio* (in German) were to be given as well. London had heard the complete 'Ring' for the first time in 1882, when Angelo Neumann with his travelling Wagner company appeared at Her Majesty's; but for various reasons the complete cycle had never been performed throughout the following decade, so that Harris's project promised to be of outstanding interest.

Harris was a man with genuine theatrical instinct, full of initiative, and he knew the secret of successful opera production—to employ nothing but the best: first-rate singers, and first-rate *décor*. (It is on this principle that all the great opera-directors have worked successfully, from Angelo Neumann at the Prague Landestheater to Toscanini at La Scala.) Accordingly, Harris engaged through Pollini the finest German artists obtainable. In addition to the Bayreuth stars, Rosa Sucher and Theodor Reichmann, his singers included others then less known but who were later to become celebrities: Ernestine Schumann-Heink, Katharina Klafsky, Katarina Bettaque, Max Alvary, Julius Lieban, and others. The magnitude of his plan obliged Harris also to engage a fifth conductor for the German operas in addition to the four for the Italian and French works: Mancinelli (afterwards Puccini's friend), Bevignani, Randegger, and Jéhin. He thought first of Wagner's faithful apostle, Richter. But Richter was engaged in Vienna and could not come for the whole season. So, on Pollini's advice, Harris decided to engage Mahler instead, and, with him, a part of the Hamburg Orchestra.

Harris had now collected a choice band of German artists and was justified in announcing that his company included 'an unprecedented combination of the first musical talent of Europe'.

Directly his journey to London was decided Mahler began to learn English. For this purpose he kept a note-book in which he conscientiously entered the expressions and phrases used in the theatre. A certain Dr. Berliner, a Hamburg friend of Mahler's, to whom were addressed the letters given below,[1] has told, later, how on their daily walks he had to 'examine' Mahler and make him introduce these idioms of the theatre into conversation. At the beginning of June Mahler came to London to direct the rehearsals at Covent Garden and Drury Lane, and at once wrote to Berliner in English, so as to show his friend what progress he had made. There is no date—the majority of Mahler's letters were hardly ever dated—but the letter is post-marked 9 June, 1892:

69 Torrington Square, W.C.

DEAR BERLINER!

I shall only to give you the addresse of my residence, because I hope to hear by you upon your life and other circumstances in Hambourg.

I myself am too tired and excited and not able to write a letter.

Only, that I found the circumstances of orchestra here bader than thought and the cast better than hoped.

Next Wednesday is the performance of 'Siegfried' which God would bless.

Alvary : Siegfried, Grengg : Wotan,
Sucher : Brünnhilde, Lieban : Mime.

This is the most splendid cast I yet heard, and this is my only trust in these very careful time.

Please to narrate me about all and am

Yours, Mahler

I make greater progress in English as you can observe in this letter.

[1] From *Gustav Mahler Briefe*, edited by Alma Maria Mahler, Vienna, 1925.

After the performance of 'Siegfried' on 8 June he writes enthusiastically to Berliner, again in English:[2]

DEAR BERLINER!
Siegfried—*great* success I am *myself* satisfied of the performance. *Orchestra: beautiful* Singers: excellently—Audience: delighted and much thankfull.
Mittwoch: Tristan (Sucher)
I am quite *done up*!
Yours, Mahler.

The success of the Wagner season under Mahler must indeed have been enormous, judging from the press notices, which were unanimous in praise of the new conductor's extraordinary ability. In *The Times* the sentence 'Herr Mahler conducted excellently as usual' recurred invariably, and the *Morning Post* wrote of his *Tristan*: 'Only the word "perfect" can describe the orchestra, which achieved wonders under the direction of Herr Mahler.'

During his stay Mahler made the acquaintance of Herman Klein, then the critic of the *Sunday Times*, who has given a graphic impression of Mahler's personality and manner of conducting in his book, *The Golden Age of Opera* (1933):

Mahler was now in his thirty-second year. He was rather short, of thin, spare build, with a dark complexion and small piercing eyes that stared at you with a not unkindly expression through large gold spectacles. I found him extraordinarily modest for a musician of his rare gifts and established reputation. He would never consent to talk about himself or his compositions. Indeed the latter might have been non-existent for all that one ever heard about them[3]; but his efforts to speak English, even with those who spoke German fluently, were untiring as well as amusing, though they tended to prolong conversation.

Klein was afterwards present at a rehearsal of *Tristan* at Drury Lane, at Mahler's own invitation. He writes:

And then it was that I began to realise the remarkable magnetic power and technical mastery of Mahler's conducting. He reminded me in many ways of Richter; he used the same strong, decisive beat;

[2]The italics indicate those words which Mahler underlined.

[3]Mahler had already made a name for himself as a composer with his completion of Weber's sketches for the opera, *Die drei Pintos*, his 'Lieder eines fahrenden Gesellen' and his First Symphony. He was then working at his Second Symphony.

there was the same absence of fussiness or superfluous action, the same clear, unmistakable definition of time and rhythm. His men, whom he rehearsed first of all in sections, soon understood him without difficulty. Hence the unity of idea and expression existing between orchestra and singers that distinguished these performances of the 'Ring' under Mahler as compared with any previously seen in London. . . .

(It was this 'unity of expression existing between orchestra and singers' that later made the Vienna Opera, during the ten years of Mahler's directorate, the foremost artistic institution in the world.)

In the course of this brilliant season Mahler also conducted *Fidelio*, which was given in London for the first time in German. The London public had hitherto known Beethoven's opera only through a few performances in Italian, with recitatives by Balfe and others, and had no great opinion of it. All the more remarkable, therefore, was the popular success of the German production, a success to which the superlative performance of Katharina Klafsky (announced as 'the great German Fidelio') contributed not a little. On the other hand, Mahler received sharp criticism from one section of the press on account of his novel interpretation—particularly of the *Leonore* Overture. The critic of the *Daily Telegraph* wrote:

Mr Mahler and his orchestra showed the ill-success which generally attends new 'readings' of old works. As to this, his interpretation of the *Leonore* Overture was really and truly a 'caution'. It is common nowadays to regard unconventionality as a virtue, and he who protests against it must be prepared for hard words; nevertheless, we venture to say that the greatest of operatic preludes was very badly treated. What authority has the Hambourg conductor for the slow opening of the Allegro and the *accelerando* which immediately followed: or for similar interference with the tempo at the beginning of the Presto Coda? These are but examples of several features that went to make up the unconventionality of the whole. But why complain? The works of great masters are fair game for editors and solo executants; should not conductors also have a share in the maltreatment? They are all superior to the composers, who, unluckily, died without the advantage of their wisdom.'

However, judging from the following letter to his Hamburg friend (this time in German), Mahler does not seem to have taken this very much to heart: 'My performance of *Fidelio*—particularly the *Leonore* Overture—has been most violently attacked by half the critics here; all the same the public absolved me from my blasphemy with a regular *hurricane* of applause—in fact, they overwhelm me with endless tokens of sympathy. I've got to go before the curtain literally after *every act*—the whole house yells "Mahler" till I appear. . . .' Incidentally, in these performances Mahler still played the *Leonore* Overture before the beginning of the second Act; it was, I believe, only later, in Vienna, that he first inserted it before the Finale as 'transformation music'. This practice has been adhered to ever since by almost all conductors, with the exception of Weingartner.

Mahler was also to have conducted Nessler's sentimental opera, *Der Trompeter von Säckingen*, which was then enjoying a considerable vogue in Germany. But he managed to evade the task and the *Morning Post* noted curtly that 'Herr Mahler is evidently not in sympathy with this work, for he relinquished the baton to Herr Feld. . . .'

Why did Mahler never return to London, in spite of his great success here? Undoubtedly because his work as a composer absorbed him more and more, and the theatre holidays at Hamburg—and later in Vienna—were the only periods in which he was able to devote himself undisturbed to his creative work. The next occasions on which he conducted in a non-German country were (besides a concert in Moscow in March 1897) during the years 1908–11, when he was in America.

SEVEN

BRUCKNER VERSUS MAHLER

FOR A LONG TIME it was always 'Bruckner and Mahler' in this country. Now it is 'Bruckner versus Mahler', a confrontation forced upon us by our vastly increased familiarity with the music of both these composers. If formerly they appeared to us as a kind of Siamese twins, due to an incomplete and exaggerated view of the binding force of the Austrian symphonic tradition, this has now been succeeded by our recognition that their status is almost that of opposites. The qualifying 'almost' is necessary because there were a few things which Mahler took over from Bruckner: the tendency towards the monumental (first manifest in Beethoven's Ninth and Schubert's great C major symphony), the invasion of the expository section of a symphonic movement by developmental elements, and the use of a large brass choir to give powerful weight to climaxes. To that limited extent there was a common *stylistic* denominator between Bruckner and Mahler, but the crucial point is that, with each, those features are seen to serve entirely different *expressive* ends.

In a famous essay, Schiller divided creative artists into two diametrically opposed categories—the 'naive' and the 'sentimental' artist—and Bruckner and Mahler are textbook illustrations of these two contrasting types. Bruckner, descended from Upper Austrian peasant stock, was unspeculative, non-intellectual, and fully integrated as man and artist. Mahler, on the other hand, displayed some typical traits of the cultured Central European Jew of his time: a highly developed intellectualism which is mirrored in the extreme sophistication of his symphonic thinking, a pronounced conflict between the life of his emotions and the life of his mind resulting in a disharmonious, divided personality, and, lastly, a perennial sense of inner insecurity which his conversion in 1897 to Roman Catholicism did nothing to dispel. In short, it is difficult to imagine two more profoundly antithetical musicians working in an identical tradition.

That Mahler was emotionally the more subtly organised artist, and was musically far more wide-ranging than Bruckner, is paramount. In every one of his nine symphonies he may be said to embark on a new quest, on a fresh adventure of the mind: no two symphonies of his are alike in vision and spiritual content. Moreover, his late works show certain technical features which were to become common coin in the music after him. In marked contrast, Bruckner was no pathfinder. He contented himself with the formal-thematic devices he found in Beethoven and Schubert and with the harmonic language of Wagner. And however unique his utterance and novel his symphonic conception—the tidal waves and the use of static chorale themes in the context of a developing dynamic form are among its most notable features—Bruckner never varied in the ethos of his music. There is a grain of truth in the aphorism that he wrote, not nine symphonies, but one symphony nine times. Throughout his career he kept his mind's eye most firmly fixed on an unalterable goal: the glorification of his Creator and a mystical union through identification with elemental, primitive nature as part of God's creation. Something eternal, something beyond time and space, emanates from a Bruckner symphony: its author stood too close to Heaven to reflect and speculate on himself. In a sense Bruckner was an outsider whose spiritual habitat was not the nineteenth century but the Middle Ages. Mahler, on the other hand, was a typical product of the *fin de siècle*: he mirrored the cultural climate of Central Europe most accurately and at the same time anticipated something inherent in our own *Zeitgeist*, which may partly account for the extraordinary popularity which his music has enjoyed since the last war.

But the impression cannot be avoided that his spiritual aspirations, summed up in the comprehension of a 'whole world' in a symphony, surpassed the power and strength of his musical genius. It is, significantly, in those symphonic movements where he turns from self-identification with the lot of mankind to a reflection of his own self that he succeeds in carrying the listener with him all the way. No such disequilibrium exists in Bruckner. Every movement of his mature symphonies is a satisfying exteriorisation of the thought that moved him, of the image that stirred him. This is perhaps nowhere more immediately manifest than in his adagio movements, which for profundity, purity and breadth of invention stand completely apart in the body of the post-Beethovenian symphony. This harmony between the idea and its realisation is, most likely, a corollary of Bruckner's integrated and 'positive' personality, a personality poles away from Mahler's tormenting self-questionings, his doubts, and the pessimism characteristic of the *fin de siècle* mentality.

EIGHT

FORM AND TECHNIQUE OF MAHLER'S *LIED VON DER ERDE*

THE MAIN TENDENCY of the post-Beethovenian symphonists was to interpret the symphonic form in terms of psychological drama. This tendency, first to be noticed in Beethoven, chiefly accounts for the changes which the symphonic form underwent in its treatment by the various composers. The tone-poem on the one hand and the 'psychological' symphony on the other—the symphony with a programme—were the offsprings of this new approach. With Mahler it became the basis of his symphonic thinking. That is why in every one of his symphonic works we are faced with some interesting formal and technical problem. If for Mahler the various stages of music's course within the symphonic form became identical with the unfolding of a drama, it is equally true that by force of habit or otherwise he had to express everything in a symphonic manner. Thus it becomes clear why even in those cases where he wrote vocal music the form of which was in the first place conditioned by the words, he attempted an amalgamation of vocal and symphonic style, as witness the vocal sections in his second, third, fourth and eighth symphonies, and his many songs, most of which, significantly enough, were written to an orchestral accompaniment. This amalgamation of two intrinsically different styles is noticeable both in the form and the technique adopted in these sections. Seen in this light Mahler's *Lied von der Erde* will provide us with a good object for study.

Mahler called this work a 'Symphony for tenor, contralto (or baritone) and orchestra'. At a first glance this seems rather odd. Had he called it a cantata nothing would have puzzled us in this title. But as there was an intention behind this title, it will be interesting to see its significance and ultimate justification. Mahler chose from an anthology of Chinese verse six poems and arranged their sequence in such a way that they must be taken as representing a drama with the 'catastrophe' in the last poem. Now Mahler could have set them in the same manner as he did with his *Kindertotenlieder*, that is, as a cycle of songs in which the symphonic treatment was of secondary importance. Not so in the *Lied von der Erde*. What Mahler sought to express here was to him so fraught with meaning that to treat these poems as mere songs would have been inadequate. Short of writing a symphony with a programme, which would have been based on these Chinese poems, he chose to steer a novel course, that of combining features of the symphony, cantata and song in one, and of amalgamating them to such an extent that the result was a wholly novel work.

Generally speaking, the features of the cantata and song are more easily recognisable—as, for instance, in the six-movement form of the work, the employment of two soloists, the strong, all-pervading lyricism, and the almost constant use of the human voice. But closer examination of the contrasting character, different 'weight' and sequence of the six movements shows that Mahler had the model of a four-movement symphony at the back of his mind. No. 1 (*Allegro pesante*) takes the place of a symphonic first movement; No. 2 (*Etwas schleichend, ermüdet*) stands for the andante. And No. 3 (*Behaglich, heiter*), No. 4 (*Commodo, dolcissimo*) and No. 5 (*Allegro*), which are related in mood, combine to represent the scherzo. That these three movements belong together is also borne out by their respective keys, which are all in the major (B, G and A), whereas the 'heavier' movements, Nos 1, 2 and 6, are in the minor (A, D and C). Finally, No. 6 (*Schwer*) provides the symphonic finale. In accordance with the tendency of the symphony since Beethoven to shift its centre of gravity from the first movement to the last and thus work through the individual movements up to a climax and final solution of conflict, the finale of *Lied von der Erde* is not only the largest of the six movements, but also in its depth of feeling and emotional poignancy the greatest. So much for the general formal outline.

As regards the relation between voice and orchestra, a similar synthesis of song and symphonic elements is to be found. The vocal line expresses the general feeling and mood of the poems, whereas the orchestra deepens the expression, discusses the detailed meaning of the words, and follows the slight changes of mood more closely than the voice could ever do. This procedure is quite in Wagner's style. But Mahler, with his strong lyrical vein, follows the line of Schumann and Brahms and never lets his vocal melody become declamatory. Almost throughout the work the voice-part retains a truly singing quality; and in spite of irregularities caused by the inter-play between voice and orchestra, the periodic structure of the vocal melody is quite noticeable. The symphonic element appears in the growth of the main themes out of a germ motif which represents a segment of the 'white-key' Chinese pentatonic scale, and which appears in every possible shape and disguise throughout the work:

Ex. 1

It thus provides a close link between the six movements.

After these general remarks it might be well to examine a few points in detail. In the first movement the song-element lies primarily in its strophic form, each of the three stanzas having essentially the same music, and in the cantabile nature of the voice part. Against this must be set the symphonic relation between the voice and the instruments in the manner described above. Moreover, the three stanzas show a definite modulatory scheme which is very similar to the modulations in the development sections and, in fact, Mahler extends the last stanza by a kind of development of the main theme. The second movement also has strophic form, and a sustained vocal melody embedded in the orchestra, which is treated symphonically. There is also a kind of second subject, which appears first in the sub-mediant and later in the tonic major, the key being D minor. Remarkable in this piece is the polyphony, which already points to the linear style of modern music:

Ex. 2

In passages like this the influence of Bach's treatment of the voice with one or two obbligato instruments is easily detected. In others, again, with an orchestral accompaniment richly endowed with thematic motifs, Mahler adopts the principles of what Beethoven used to call *obligates Akkompagnement*.

It is significant that in movements 3, 4 and 5, which belong together, the symphonic treatment is much less marked. If we remember the suggestion that these three movements combined represent the scherzo of the symphony, and that even the classical minuet and scherzo show a comparatively simpler and less symphonic texture than the other movements, it will be easy to see why Mahler here preferred a more homophonic treatment. Moreover, the relation between voice and orchestra is here much less intricate and subtle than in Nos 1 and 2, and the vocal line is for the most part identical with the instrumental melody, so that No. 4, for instance, could be played as a purely orchestral piece without the voice, which would be quite impossible in the case of Nos 1, 2 or 6. That Nos 3, 4 and 5 take the place of the classical minuet or scherzo is further borne out by their dance-like character, which is particularly noticeable in Nos 3 and 4.

With No. 6 we get to the most complex movement of the work. It has the finale character of the later romantic symphony and perhaps shows best the amalgamation of elements from the symphony, cantata and song. As in the previous movements the song-character lies in the cantabile voice part and its periodic structure; the three recitatives—modern examples of eighteenth-century *recitativo accompagnato*—and the juxtaposition of three lyrical and self-contained sections with themes of their own point to the cantata. These three sections are linked together by the text, and musically by the germ motif. Yet one feels that this link would not have been sufficient to prevent the movement from falling to pieces and thus losing its unity. Mahler's great constructive skill is shown in the way in which he avoids this danger. He casts the whole movement in a free sonata form with three different subjects, with a 'development' of the first subject—a kind of funeral march—and with a regular recapitulation in which even the modulatory scheme of the classical *reprise* is observed (exposition in C minor, recapitulation in C minor–C major). Thus the movement is welded into an organic and logical form which, at the same time, follows the drama of the text. The manner in which the various sections of sonata form are here made to fit quite naturally the different stages of this drama is a masterpiece of structural ingenuity. One might be tempted, and with much justification, to see in this an anticipation of Alban Berg's use of pure instrumental forms in his opera, *Wozzeck*.

NINE

THE SECRET OF JOHANN STRAUSS

WAGNER HARDLY EVER had a good word for his contemporaries, but he made one notable exception: Johann Strauss. Strauss had, in his view, 'the most musical headpiece in Europe'. One suspects that Wagner's unstinted praise was not quite so disinterested as it looks. Had not Strauss, long before official Vienna took any notice of the composer of *Tristan*, introduced him to the most conservative of all musical cities in Europe by being the first to play excerpts from *Tannhäuser*, *Lohengrin* and *Tristan* to the open-air audiences in the Prater? However, we need no words of Wagner's to convince us of Strauss's musical genius. It is still with us. It lives in the *Blue Danube*, *Tales from the Vienna Woods*, *Voices of Spring*, *Fledermaus* and *Gypsy Baron*. A century and more have passed since these works were written and not one of them has lost its magical grip on us. How are we to account for the lasting and undiminished appeal of this music?

Strauss left more than half a thousand dances of all kinds, fifteen operettas and an opera—a truly miraculous output and comparable only with Mozart's and Schubert's fertility. But fertility and ease of production alone are no safe key to the gates of immortality, particularly not in the field in which Strauss was working: music for entertainment. Here prolificness is a *conditio sine qua non*. No other branch of music is more subject to the ever-changing fashion of the day and the fickle tast of the great masses. Successes achieved in this genre are ephemeral. We witness it every day in our popular music: the hit of today is stale by tomorrow and forgotten the day after. Strauss's music was no exception. Most of his waltzes, marches, galops, polkas and quadrilles were written for the day and for a special occasion, after which the almost inexhaustible tap of melodies had to be turned on again immediately to satisfy the never-ending demands of the Viennese public for something new. Nearly everything that Strauss wrote was *Gebrauchsmusik* in the truest sense of the word: 'utility music'. He meant it to be that, and nothing more. Yet some of it turned out to be much more, and it is here that we have to look for part of the secret of Strauss's genius. Like Mozart's and Haydn's serenades and divertimentos, like Schubert's *Deutsche Tänze* and *Ländler*, the round dozen of waltzes which Strauss wrote at the height of his career are great because they far transgress the very narrow and workaday purpose for which they were originally intended. True, they are dance music in the first place, yet they are filled with pure and beautiful music, music of a unique charm and grace. These waltzes are a musical incarnation of that kind of hedonism that has become proverbial in all lands: the Viennese spirit, that rare amalgam of lively temperament and slight sentimentality, of *joie de vivre* and nostalgia, of an inborn ease and nonchalance. But the reverse side of the picture is indifference, laziness, slovenliness, irresponsibility, and lack of seriousness. Strauss was a typical manifestation of this spirit and he was often indifferent and slovenly in his work, too, as witness his perfunctory modulations from one waltz to another or his settings of fatuous and insipid lyrics and libretti. In the case of the latter he often did not bother to know more than the words of the song numbers—one of the reasons why only two out of sixteen works for the stage have survived.

Strauss was called the Waltz King, and justly so. The supremacy of his great waltzes remains as unchallenged today as it did about a century ago. But this is not exclusively due to the spirit of the music. Vienna was rich in waltz composers such as Pamer, Gung'l, Fahrbach. Lanner, the elder Strauss and his two other sons, Joseph and Eduard. Yet what mainly distinguishes their waltzes, for all their charm and invention, from those of Strauss, is the latter's technical accomplishment; while still retaining its original dance character, Strauss transformed the waltz into a concert piece. Under his hands it became fit for both the ballroom and the concert hall. He once modestly said that his merits were weak attempts to enlarge the form that his father and Lanner had handed down to him. I would add that he made the waltz a more organic whole—as far as is possible in this dance form—than any of his predecessors and contemporaries had ever done. The exceptions are the waltzes of Weber (*Invitation to the Dance*) and Chopin which, apart from presenting an organic entity, are intended, not for dancing, but to be listened to as concert music pure and simple.

It took Strauss half a lifetime to shape that form which we now acclaim as the classical Viennese waltz. Not wholly uninfluenced by Wagner, Strauss transformed the originally rather short introduction into a kind of symphonic prelude—'symphonic' must here be taken with a pinch of salt—which is thematically linked with the suite of four to five waltzes that follows, and which paints the general mood of the suite. A further step towards a more unified form was the extension of the coda into a summing-up of the main waltz themes. But where Strauss hits the bull's-eye is as a melodist. Instead of the short eight-bar phrases of his predecessors, his melodies swing now in ever-changing curves over sixteen and, at times, even twenty-four bars. True, his technique is in the manner of a mosaic rather than a development of motifs, but what variety and contrast he achieves in a single melody! (For instance, Waltz No. 1 in 'Roses from the South' has five and the 'Brüderlein-Schwesterlein' waltz in *Fledermaus*, seven different motifs.) And if we consider that any of the great waltz-cycles contains five separate waltzes, every one with its own melody—and sometimes two—the wonder of Strauss's fertility *and* quality of invention becomes all the more impressive. Equally admirable are the subtlety and delicacy with which Strauss achieves balance of rhythm and expression within this kaleidoscope of motifs; to follow the rising and falling curves, the leaps and skips of his lines is like looking at a graph of a dancer's variegated movements.

There are rolling figures, stamping and swaying figures, there are yearning chromatic *appogiature* to suggest a sense of urgency; there are sensuous and languishing tunes, gay and capricious tunes which electrify both ear and feet. The best of the Strauss waltzes display a felicitous amalgam of *Schmiss und Schmalz* which is Viennese slang for snappy rhythm and rich tunefulness. Many of the Strauss waltzes, like those of his father and Lanner, show the influence of the violin—all three were excellent fiddlers. (Incidentally, they directed their band by alternately conducting and playing, now using the violin bow as baton, now joining in with the orchestra—a tradition which is preserved today by Willy Boskowsky and the Vienna Philharmonic Orchestra in their regular New Year's Day concert of the music of the Strauss family.) Thus, we find exploitation of the open strings—hence the choice of the keys of G, D, A and E for the large majority of the waltzes. Then there are double stops, euphonious sixths and thirds which in combination with *glissandi* lend the Strauss waltzes a slightly languid, sentimental note; there is playing on the G string and the effects achieved by different bowing (*legato, staccato, spiccato, saltando* and *sul ponticello*) and finally short, crisp up-bows at the beginning of a waltz.

Naturally, the stereotyped One-two-three cannot be avoided, but in the best of the Strauss waltzes one is hardly conscious of the mechanical thump. The rhythmic variety of his melodic patterns hides it as blossoms and leaves hide the bareness of a tree. How irritating for the dancers, but how intriguing to our rhythmic sense when Strauss upsets this tyranny of the three-fours by harnessing a two-beat rhythm on to them, as he does with such electrifying effect in No. 3 of his *Morgenblätter* and in No. 1 of his *Wiener Blut*! Besides, the typically slipshod way in which Viennese orchestras are fond of playing the accompaniment with a slight anticipation of the second beat: ♩.♪♩ ♩ instead of ♩ ♩ ♩ tends to smooth out the rigidity of the three-four time and imparts to the music at the same time a characteristically swinging lilt.

A word on Strauss's orchestration. It is rich, colourful and often sumptious. To a much larger extent than Lanner and his father, he makes pointed use of the wind instruments and percussion. Short imitative passages and counterpoints in the middle parts are often given to the brass, and the woodwind are not only employed to reinforce the strings but embellish the texture with figurations in an almost Mozartian *concertante*. Yet Strauss, for all his innovation in the scoring in which he was certainly influenced by Wagner, preserves the hegemony which the strings have in his father's and Lanner's waltzes.

At heart an instrumental composer, Strauss was no born writer for the stage. He cared as little for dramatic characterisation, for which he lacked the necessary technique, as he did for a careful setting of his words. Yet despite these serious shortcomings, *Fledermaus* and *The Gypsy Baron* are masterpieces of comic opera. To compare them is like comparing champagne with heavy Tokay. The one lives by a most happy union of Viennese humour and French lightness of touch (now and again Offenbach peeps out of its sparkling 2-4 numbers), the other by the almost Verdian vitality of its music and the colourful atmosphere of its setting. But the hallmark of both is the waltz. To cut the waltzes would be to sap the very life-blood of these operettas.

TEN

SCHUMANN AS SYMPHONIST

TO CALL Schumann one of the Cinderellas among the important nineteenth-century symphonists may seem severe. Yet what are the facts? Though much more firmly established than Bruckner's and Mahler's,[1] his symphonies—to say nothing of the rest of his orchestral music—enjoy far less popularity than those of Schubert, Mendelssohn, Brahms, and Tchaikovsky. To the public at large he is the composer of delightful piano miniatures, of the Piano Concerto, and the Piano Quintet. In the sphere of the *Lied* we greet him as one of Schubert's few great successors—an eloquent and inspired singer of the bliss and sorrows of romantic love. Yet Schumann the symphonist and orchestral writer takes a back seat in our esteem. In the programmes of orchestral concerts his symphonies and overtures make but rare appearances, for the simple truth is that their lack of brilliance and generally ineffective orchestration make it difficult for conductors to earn kudos with them. 'Schumann we cannot and will not play' was Steinbach's curt reply when invited to London in 1902 to conduct a series of concerts with the celebrated Meiningen Orchestra. And Weingartner considered the symphonies far more effective if played as piano duets.[2] It might be argued that the likes and dislikes of conductors and orchestras are often an uncertain guide to the intrinsic qualities of an orchestral work. Yet even the unbiassed cannot help boggling at the clumsiness and unevenness of Schumann's symphonic technique, his frequent lack of orchestral sense and insight into the mechanics of an orchestra.

Yet despite such weaknesses the symphonies contain some of his most inspired music, and it is no exaggeration to say that without them the literature of nineteenth-century orchestral music would be greatly

[1] This article was written in 1950 before the extraordinary upsurge of enthusiasm for Bruckner and Mahler in England, and when the Schumann symphonies figured but rarely in orchestral programmes.

[2] *Die Sinfonie nach Beethoven* (Stuttgart, 1901).

the poorer. We do not value them for their classical attributes but for the romantic spirit that keeps breaking in. Schumann's deliberate turn from the romantic miniature of his early period to the larger and stricter forms of the classical symphony and chamber music—thus forcing upon himself a change of approach, style, and technique—could not altogether stifle his romantic Muse. In fact, it is in those very movements in which the Romantic overcomes the neophyte to classicism that he made his individual contribution to the history of the nineteenth-century symphony. About the sincerity and nobility of his symphonic utterances there can be no doubt. And compared with Mendelssohn's, as for patent reasons they must be, the Schumann symphonies are far more original in thought, more adventurous in their formal novelties, at once more inward and powerful, issuing as they do from a greater depth of feeling. True, they have nothing of Mendelssohn's brilliance, polished elegance, and *savoir-faire*—much to their detriment in the concert hall. Yet Schumann was emotionally the richer personality, possessed by an elemental, and at times demoniac, urge which was lacking in the genius of his involuntary rival. It is perhaps for that very reason that Schumann, unlike Mendelssohn, was unable to find the formula by means of which to integrate the classical heritage with his own brand of romanticism. This battle between two opposing ideals was not peculiar to Schumann only; it had to be fought out by every romantic symphonist. But in his case it was less likely to resolve itself because underneath, as it were, went on another battle, the fight to reconcile the limitations of his genius with the self-imposed demand for an extension of its creative range. It is here that the chief problem of Schumann as a symphonic writer lies.

By nature a lyrical miniaturist, his self-chosen domain was first the short self-contained piano piece and song. In both these media Schumann was able to create undisputed masterpieces. There is nothing of the *petit maitre* about his diminutive works. In fact, had he died in 1841, posterity would have acclaimed him along with Chopin as a great master in the small forms. Yet, unlike Chopin, he had the ambition 'to fight his way through to the larger forms', as a much lesser figure—Grieg—said of himself. (However, Grieg was wise enough not to persist in this endeavour.) These 'larger forms' included, in Schumann's case, not only symphony and chamber music but also opera and oratorio. It is of course difficult to say whether this aspiration to conquer the whole vast field of musical composition originated in a veiled desire to emulate his foremost models, Beethoven and Schubert, or resulted from a genuine instinctive urge. The fact is that this expansion to new regions proved too great a test for a composer of Schumann's particular genius. It can be no coincidence that with a very few exceptions the music after 1841—the year when he seriously embarked on composition other than piano works and songs—shows a decline, though a very gradual one, in spontaneity, freshness, originality, and inventive distinction. It would appear that the necessity to face and solve formal problems of a new order tended to sap his power of inspiration.

The special problem that confronted Schumann in his symphonies was two-fold. First, how to deal with the sonata-form in the single movement, and secondly, how to create an inner unity between the four movements? Not that he had not come across this problem before 1841, as witness the abortive G minor Symphony of 1832, and the Piano Sonatas in F sharp minor and G minor. And we know how inadequate they are from the point of view of formal treatment. I shall not expatiate on the general technical handicap of a composer who up to his eighteenth year was much more interested in literature and writing, and for years was only an amateur musician, albeit a highly gifted one, who, to all intents and purposes, acquired the knowledge of his craft by self-tuition. The technique that served him well in the congenial media of short piano pieces and songs was certainly not sufficient to make symphonic writing an easy task. And what he himself first thought of the sonata-form may be gathered from his dictum in 1839 that 'isolated beautiful examples of it will certainly still be written now and then—and have been written already—but it seems that this form has run its life-course'. Yet two years later he made a complete volte-face and concentrated for a time almost exclusively upon works in sonata-form.

How did he handle it in his symphonies? His first handicap here was his inability to invent true symphonic themes, themes capable of development and further growth. One of the virtues of his small-scale works was the short epigrammatic theme. With a few exceptions, he applied the same method to his symphonic first and last movements, the testing-places of the true symphonist. Even so, superior technique, as Brahms has shown, could have made something of such unsymphonic static ideas. Yet development from within is very rare with Schumann. Like Schubert's, his normal way of filling the large canvas is by repetition and sequence of square-cut patterns, and, in the development sections, by transposition of large blocks wholesale. This is not to say there are no attempts at real working-out, as in the Second and Third Symphonies, but Schumann's instinctive tendency was towards mere juxtaposition of mosaics: the formal style of his piano pieces. When he suddenly reverts to true development, one gets the impression that he resorted to it chiefly because 'thematic work' was the way of the classics. One feels much the same kind of formalism in his cumulative use of canon and imitation—a favourite device long before his more intense Bach studies of 1845 (e.g. in the first movement of the early G minor Symphony).[3] In short, there is much to show that in his symphonic writing Schumann often paid mere lip-service to the masters of the past. Another weakness (which he also shares with Schubert) is his clinging too long to the same rhythm, thus adding to his melodic unwieldiness. This seems all the more surprising in a composer who was so much given to rhythmic experiment as Schumann. Yet once he has hit upon a fresh rhythmic pattern, he is inclined to do it to death.

This brings us to another, related, feature. It is Schumann's tendency to build up a whole movement from a single-pattern theme, to swamp it with a melodic-rhythmic ostinato, the most characteristic example of which is the first movement of the D minor Symphony. It is psychologically interesting to note that it is usually in movements or single pieces of a curiously restless, one might almost say, demoniac, character that Schumann resorts to this toccata-like treatment.[4] It has much in common with his device of retaining the same accompaniment figure throughout a whole song. True, such technique makes for thematic unity, yet in a symphonic movement, with its greater length and more complex texture, the advantage is bought at the price of melodic and rhythmic monotony. Schumann was no Beethoven to bring off such a monothematic *tour de force* as the Viennese master did in the first movement of the Fifth and the outer movements of the Seventh Symphonies. Moreover, thematic unity by itself does not create that higher form of coherence which results from the ability to think in a sustained and consistent manner. With the exception of the first movement of the *Rhenish*, there is nowhere in the Schumann symphonies a wide sweep of ideas, a continuous growth from within. Even the extraordinary thematic economy of the first movement of the D minor Symphony does not succeed in creating an organic whole, nor do the various thematic cross-references between its four movements make for an inner unity. One cannot dismiss the impression that in his, at times obsessional, preoccupation with the monothematic device, Schumann consciously attempted by a purely technical means

[3] Cf. his remark in one of his early letters that 'it is most extraordinary how I write almost everything in canon, and then only afterwards detect the imitations and often find inversions, rhythms in contrary motion', &c.

[4] Piano Trio in G minor, Op. 110, first movement; Violin Sonata in A minor, Op. 105, first and third movements; Violin Sonata in D minor, Op. 121, first and fourth movements; *Concert sans Orchestre*, Op. 14, finale; *Fantasiestücke*, Op. 12, *In der Nacht* and *Traumeswirren*; and *Kreisleriana*, Op. 16, Nos 1 and 7.

to achieve the inner coherence which was not inherent in the fabric of his symphonic thought.

Now on turning from the single sonata-movement to the symphonic form as a whole we shall not be surprised to find other symptoms of Schumann's structural weakness. The supreme criterion of a symphony since Beethoven is whether it presents a whole in the sense that a central idea informs *all* the movements and makes them appear as inseparable parts of the musical organism. Herein lies the crux of the symphonic form, classic, romantic or modern. Barring the Second Symphony, Schumann never fully obtained an organic unity between movements, a unity by which a movement is felt to be the corollary of the preceding one. To repeat: a born miniaturist, his primary, instinctive way of musical thinking was in terms of small, static, self-contained, and independent mood-pictures.

And here we come to another important factor. Schumann appears to have needed the stimulus of poetic ideas and literary images to bring his imagination to the boil, and this was bound to have a decisive bearing on the way he conceived of formal coherence. Take his cycles of piano works and songs. What holds them together is less inner, musical, unity than the intellectual link provided by a literary programme. In other words, his cycles represent a succession of musical tableaux whose progress and purpose are chiefly determined by extra-musical thoughts and such general aesthetic considerations as contrast and formal balance. In his symphonies Schumann still clings to the tableaux manner. Here too we find a more or less loose succession of romantic mood-pictures and character pieces, only with the difference that the adoption of the symphonic form forced upon him greater formal discipline and a more sustained manner of thinking. Up to a point Schumann gradually acquired both; yet something of the loose, casual character of a suite remains. Hence the difficulty of forming a unified picture of a Schumann symphony. Like Mendelssohn's symphonies Schumann's are at bottom romantic *Spielmusik*—music in which the capricious play of romantic fancies and moods dominates over a more abstract, more intrinsically musical, central thought. The whole is less than its parts.

Only once, when under the impact of a terrifying personal experience, the spectre of madness was before him—and a very real spectre, as it later turned out—did Schumann abandon his *Spielmusik* conception and, stepping out of his romantic dream-world, make a real-life experience his symphonic 'theme'. This was in the Second Symphony, his only symphony with something of Beethoven's 'moral character'. Hence its greater *inner* unity and the feeling that the four movements flow from one central idea and in their sequence illustrate the peripeteia of a psychological drama. Yet Schumann achieved this higher symphonic aim at a considerable cost, for, with the exception of its adagio, musically the C major Symphony does not rise above mediocrity. The thought suggests itself that once Schumann tried to detach himself from literary programmes and poetic fancies and looked into his inner self for inspiration, his creative powers sagged, producing but laboured, aesthetically disappointing music.

That literary subjects, poetic images, and nature impressions played upon his fancy, Schumann admitted both explicitly and by implication in his various writings, notably his long essay (1835) on the *Symphonie fantastique*.[5] Yet while most of his piano pieces have titles, in his symphonic music he was much more reticent, fearing no doubt that an open admission of the presence of a programmatic background would be likely to detract from the absolute, purely musical significance. As he said in the essay on the Berlioz work, 'If the eye is once directed to a certain point, the ear can no longer judge independently'. Hence the subsequent suppression of the titles which he originally intended for each of the four movements of the B flat Symphony and two movements of the Third. Yet for all his circumspection there is sufficient internal evidence to suggest a programmatic origin for his symphonies. It is this very intrusion of poetic ideas that gives Schumann's symphonic work its special place in the history of the post-Beethovenian symphony. He opened to the symphony a world of Romantic imagery and lyricism which was at once new and personal. It was a world both truly German and truly Schumannesque, created from the fantasies of Jean Paul and E. T. A. Hoffmann, the magic of the German fairy-tales, the old-world atmosphere of ancient Rhenish cities, and from the intimacy and hidden poetry of Schumann's domestic hearth.[6] Who but the romantic Schumann could have written a *Spring* Symphony or thought of such things as the romanza and the slow introduction to the finale of the D minor Symphony, and the 'Cathedral' movement of the Third? Yet there was little in Schumann of Schubert's romanticism which was naïve, mystical, cosmic. Schu-

[5] Cf. his *Gesammelte Schriften über Musik and Musiker*; also his letter to Clara, of 13 April 1838: 'I am affected by everything that goes on in the world and think it all over in my own way, politics, literature and people, and then I long to express my feelings and find an outlet for them in music. That is why my compositions are sometimes difficult to understand, because they are connected with distant interests; and sometimes striking, because everything extraordinary that happens impresses me and impels me to express it in music.'

[6] I find it difficult to square this with the fact that Schumann's music enjoys such marked popularity in, of all countries, France. It is, by the way, the same world in which the Mahler of the first four symphonies and of the early songs felt very much at home.

mann fed his mind on the *rational* element of German literature. His was the romanticism of the rising German middle-class, the German burgher with his solid education and his genuine love of *Kultur*. Consciously or unconsciously, Schumann departed from that universality of audience at which the Viennese classics aimed. In his symphonies he no longer addressed himself to a European élite, the public of Haydn, Mozart, and Beethoven, but to a public with the same national and social background as his own. This has often been described in a derogatory sense as the bourgeois element in Schumann's artistic make-up. Yet while it is true that it sometimes produced music of an innocuous, homely Philistine nature, it was on the other hand responsible for the wonderful inwardness and *Versponnenheit* of many of his mood-pictures. In fact such introspective, non-classical movements as his andantes and scherzi were Schumann's most personal contribution to the post-Beethovenian symphony; they are symphonically extended character-pieces.

Yet while for obvious reasons more felicitous in the simple form of such movements, the inspired Romantic in Schumann is by no means absent from the formally stricter, more complex and more 'classical' outer movements of his symphonies. In particular, the slow introductions turn into inspired mood-pictures: idyllic in the First Symphony, sombre, dream-like and solemn in the Fourth, tormenting and restless in the Second. (It is significant that the first movement of the Third, Schumann's most 'classical' movement, dispenses with a romantic preamble.) In form these introductions all present the same picture: two parts, the first more static, lyrical, the second, more dynamic and mostly containing a tempo acceleration to the ensuing allegro. Another characteristic is that without exception these introductions contain some of the chief material of the allegro. (Schumann thus made a principle of what Haydn and Schubert did only occasionally.) This thematic integration is carried a long step further when other movements as well derive some of their ideas from the opening introduction, as in the Second Symphony and, most strikingly, the Fourth. It seems more than probable that Schumann's love of thematic germcells, mottos, and the monothematic device in general was nurtured by such precedents as Beethoven's C minor Symphony, Schubert's *Wandererphantasie* and Berlioz's *Symphonie fantastique*. In fact, there is an unmistakable echo of Berlioz's *idée fixe* in the Schumann symphonies which so far seems to have escaped notice. In three out of the four, Schumann introduces the same characteristic figure of three notes rising step-wise to the major third.[7] The manner

[7] Cf. motto-theme of the First, chorale-theme of the slow introduction to the finale of the Fourth, and scherzo and adagio of the Second.

of its use suggests a special programmatic significance for the composer. With one exception, it is always scored for the brass and the three notes are to be played with an accent. I venture to suggest that Schumann associated with it a signal or call, perhaps a kind of 'sursum corda', for that is the effect it creates. And its reiterated appearance in works so different in character points to its being a 'fixed idea' in the literal sense of the term.[8]

So much for Schumann's borrowings from immediate forerunners. More important, however, is the fact that in his D minor and C major Symphonies he foreshadows diverse techniques in the more advanced use of mottos and theme-relations: Liszt's theme-transformation, Wagner's leitmotive, Tchaikovsky's motto, and Franck's *idée cyclique*. And strange as it may seem, there is an intrinsic affinity between Schumann's 'thematic reservoir' (e.g. the introductions to the Second and Fourth Symphonies) and the basic tone-row of twelve-note music. *Mutatis mutandis*, he might have said with Schönberg, 'I was always occupied with the aim to base the structure of my music consciously on a unifying idea which produced . . . all the other ideas'.[10] For all his structural weaknesses, Schumann was a pathfinder in the means of achieving formal-thematic compression and thus forms an important link between Beethoven and the 'intensive' instrumental writers of a much later period.

If this is perhaps the most striking positive feature of Schumann's symphonic technique, there are others equally characteristic. I would mention in the first place his predilection for melodic surprises which he springs on us in the form of fresh tunes—introducing them, as often as not, into the development section and, notably, the coda. His inclusion in his scherzo movements of two contrasting trios is of this order.[11] Schumann was a born melodist; a glance through his piano and song cycles proves it beyond doubt. Yet while such loose succession of melodies was for obvious reasons banished from the sonata-form, Schumann would not altogether restrict himself here to two main themes, and used the formally more fluid sections for smuggling in fresh ideas. Some may have originated in poetic intentions such as the Beethoven quotation in the finale of the C major Symphony, and the unexpected lyrical parenthesis in the coda of the first movement of the

[8] Careful analysis might discover it in other works.

[9] It is as well to recall the fact that the root of all these nineteenth-century devices is the 'reminiscence' of the eighteenth-century opéra comique, also found occasionally in the music of an earlier period.

[10] See Schönberg's letter to Nicolas Slonimsky, published in the latter's *Music since 1900*.

[11] Cf. his First and Second Symphonies, and the coda of the scherzo of the *Rhenish*.

B flat. Others again serve the purpose of providing new material for a second development, or lyrical contrast, or to crown a movement with a final apotheosis, as in the *Overture, Scherzo und Finale*. Here again Schumann foreshadows what was to become a characteristic feature of the late nineteenth-century symphony.

To complete this list of novelties, mention must be made of a characteristic device by which Schumann achieves harmonic surprise. This is the statement of a theme, usually the second subject, in what I would call harmonic inversion. Instead of introducing it at once in the expected key, he starts his theme in a related one[12] to lead it subsequently to its 'right' key. This inversion has a two-fold effect: it momentarily obscures the tonality, and if such harmonic duality is maintained for a longer stretch, the impression is created that Schumann's exposition and recapitulation are laid out on three different harmonic planes. Beethoven has it sometimes but only on a small scale,[13] with Schubert we find it more frequently and extensively, yet Schumann's reiterated use of it makes it a fingerprint of his harmonic style.

A few general words about his scoring have already been said at the outset. It forms a sorry chapter in the critical evaluation of his orchestral works. Brilliant, colourful, varied—in short, imaginative—scoring has a way of covering up, or at any rate detracting from, structural weaknesses. Striking cases in point are the Tchaikovsky symphonies; Tchaikovsky's formal defects are much the same as Schumann's, yet as *orchestral* music the Russian's symphonies are singularly effective. Had Schumann been endowed with a better grasp of the orchestral mechanics and with a more sensitive ear for the blending and balancing of instrumental colours, his Cinderella rôle as an orchestral composer might have been less marked. For his symphonies are tuneful and generally lively in rhythm. It might be argued that the specific character of his orchestral music is such as *not* to demand a dazzling garb.[14] And this could be supported by a reference to Brahms's orchestra. Whatever one may think of Brahms as an orchestrator, it is indisputable that his orchestral style is part of his musical thought and thus serves the purpose of his symphonic utterances admirably. To a certain extent this is also true of Schumann. On the other hand there is ample evidence that his

[12] Usually the supertonic or upper mediant, occasionally the relative major or minor.

[13] See the recapitulation of the first movement of the *Waldstein* Sonata, Op. 53, second subject first in A, then in C.

[14] Even his writing for the piano, the medium from which he started and which remained most congenial to him, is not brilliant; consider his limited use of the high and low registers and the crowding of the texture by inner parts.

orchestral technique *was* deficient, leading him into such well-nigh incredible blunders as the revision of the D minor Symphony. Not that Schumann was congenitally unable to think in orchestral terms, as is frequently stated. But, with a few startling exceptions, he failed to make the orchestra an eloquent, flexible instrument of his thought. As early as 1832, while working on his youthful G minor Symphony, he confessed to putting in 'often yellow instead of blue' and considered orchestration an art 'so difficult that it'll take long years' study to give one certainty and self-control'. The bane of Schumann's orchestra is its thickness and heaviness, caused by superfluous doublings, notably of the inner parts, and the preponderant, injudicious use of the brass for inner pedals and mere rhythmic accentuation. In addition, the woodwind are often employed in registers where they do not 'speak' readily. Though the handling of the strings shows greater experience, Schumann often scores a melody for the first violins only, so that they have to contend single-handed against a heavy accompaniment. Nor does he allow his orchestra to 'breathe' sufficiently, using the various instrumental groups uninterruptedly for too long a stretch. The frequent result is unrelieved thickness of texture and murky opaque colour.[15] The puzzling thing is that at times Schumann would score with a delicacy, economy, and sensitiveness to colour and balance that make one almost wonder if such passages are by the same pen which put in 'yellow instead of blue'. And it is interesting to find that it is largely in the slow movements that Schumann shows himself inspired and imaginative in handling the orchestral palette.

A propos of Schumann's revisions in the Fourth Symphony, Tovey makes the interesting suggestion that it was the composer's inadequacy as a conductor that induced him to make 'all entries fool-proof by doubling them and filling up the rests', a possible but not plausible explanation resting on the assumption that if one group of instruments missed Schumann's cue, the other would not. Yet it must be presumed that even in Schumann's times professional orchestral players could be relied upon to count their bars and come in on their entries. Nor does Tovey's suggestion explain why Schumann's scoring was at times as good as it was. The striking discrepancy in one and the same work between good and bad scoring seems to argue a more fundamental reason than incompetence and lack of practical experience. It is true that Schumann had no particular knack for the orchestra and often appears to have conceived his orchestral music in terms of the piano, which would partly explain the doublings and the massiveness of texture. Yet I venture to suggest that the marked

[15] It is for this reason that Weingartner and Mahler revised the orchestration of the four symphonies. For a detailed account of Mahler's rescoring, see Chapter 11.

unevenness of his orchestral writing may have had something to do with his mental illness, the first outward symptoms of which date back to 1834, if not before. We know that intermittently it affected his auricular sense, and it may be that during these periods it also affected the clarity of the inner sound-picture of the music Schumann happened to be writing at the time. It is conceivable that its projection into concrete orchestral terms carried with it the mark of such disturbances—a hypothesis which of course would need substantiation on the part of a psychiatrist conversant with Schumann's pathological history, but for all we know it may account for the disconcerting inequality of his orchestral style.

ELEVEN

MAHLER'S RE-SCORING OF THE SCHUMANN SYMPHONIES

IT WILL ALWAYS remain a moot point whether the revision of a work by any other hand but the composer's can at all be justified. The purist will always be opposed to it and he will find strong support for his uncompromising attitude in the over-riding importance we nowadays attach to *Werktreue*, i.e. strict faithfulness to the original in every respect, notably the manner and form in which its author presented it. Yet the eighteenth and nineteenth centuries thought quite differently, as witness Mozart's additions to the score of *Messiah*, Wagner's revision of Gluck's *Iphigenia in Aulis* and his orchestral retouches of Beethoven's Ninth Symphony, Strauss's edition of *Idomeneo*, Rimsky-Korsakov's so-called 'improvements' to the score of *Boris Godunov* and the Bruckner symphonies in the revisions of Ferdinand Löwe and the brothers Josef and Franz Schalk. The time has long passed when the revised versions of those works were far more frequently heard than the originals, and this applies in particular to Handel's oratorio and the Bruckner symphonies, which nowadays are always performed in the version in which the composer intended them to be heard. The exception is the Schumann symphonies, which have always been given in the composer's own orchestration, in spite of the fact that they show serious defects in scoring and in instrumental balance, defects which indeed prompted Mahler to subject their instrumentation to a thorough revision. It is odd, however, that we never hear his versions, the performance of which would certainly be an interesting (and perhaps rewarding) experience. Mahler, himself a master of orchestration, inevitably stumbled over Schumann's lack of insight into orchestral mechanics and his difficulty in thinking in pure orchestral terms, though the surprising thing is that at times his scoring shows a large measure of imagination, delicacy and skill, as we find for instance in his Piano Concerto, the *Romanze* of his Fourth Symphony and parts of the *Manfred* Overture. But taken by and large Schumann handled the orchestra in an awkward, clumsy manner and it will be interesting to see in what ways Mahler tried to improve it.

Mahler was an experienced hand at the business of revisions, alterations, and orchestral retouches, witness his completion with the help of sketches of Weber's *Die drei Pintos*,[1] his revision of *Oberon*, and his retouches in the scoring of Beethoven's Ninth Symphony. Moreover, Mahler was a typical romantic whose affinity with Schumann is very marked and expresses itself in certain stylistic resemblances. Mahler thus possessed every qualification necessary for his intricate and complex task.[2] How did he set about it?

His alterations may be classified under seven heads:

(1) Lightening of thick instrumental textures.
(2) Throwing into relief of thematic lines and rhythmic patterns.
(3) Changes in dynamics and re-scoring of certain dynamic effects.
(4) Improvement of phrasing.
(5) Changes in the manner of playing.
(6) Thematic alterations.
(7) Suggestions for cuts.[3]

The result of these changes is greater orchestral transparency, greater prominence of thematic lines and essential rhythms, and subtler gradation and greater variety of tone-colour and dynamics. Not a single movement in the four symphonies remained untouched, and in some of them Mahler's alterations and corrections cover many pages of the score. It is, of course, impossible to give here a detailed account of all these, but a number of examples will suffice to illustrate Mahler's methods.

Schumann's heaviness of texture is usually the result of unnecessary and often clumsy doubling of melodic lines and unessential middle-parts. Take, for instance, the passage in III. 2, bars 25–9. It is a quick and short *piano stretto* with a subject in *staccato* semiquavers. Schumann scores this passage for strings with all the woodwind—except oboes—doubling them, and adds insignificant rhythmic note-repetitions on horns and trumpets. The polyphonic nature of the

[1] Mahler's version was first performed under his direction at the Neue Stadt-Theater, Leipzig, on 20 January, 1880.

[2] There is no printed edition of Mahler's version. But his alterations have been entered on a number of copies of the original scores which are on hire from Messrs. Boosey & Hawkes (Universal Edition), London, who have kindly given me permission to use them for the purpose of this article.

[3] The last four groups have, strictly speaking, little to do with the actual business of re-scoring. But Mahler's work was a thorough revision rather than merely a re-orchestration.

passage demands, however, a lighter and more transparent scoring, so Mahler eliminates the woodwind and brass, and by this simple alteration arrives at a lighter texture, a softer *piano*, a better *staccato*, a crisper string tone, and a welcome contrast of colour when the woodwind enter after this string passage.

Such lightening is frequently associated with colour contrasts and freshness of tone, as in Mahler's alteration at the opening of IV. 3, Trio. Schumann here doubles the flutes (which have the theme) with the clarinets in the lower octave for sixteen bars; Mahler allows the clarinets to rest during the first eight bars and only then continues with the original scoring. He thus gets both increased sonority and a new blend of colour in the second phrase.

There are, on the other hand, instances when Schumann, for the sake of colour contrast, introduces fresh instruments which only thicken the texture by unnecessary doublings, and also tend to disturb the basic colour scheme, as at the opening of III. 3, with its addition, after two bars, of oboes and horns which are given merely harmonic filling, and upset the balance of colour which Mahler restores by the simple elimination of the added instruments.

Another frequent device of Mahler's for loosening the texture is to alter *a due* passages, or passages scored for different instruments in unison or octaves, into *soli*, as in the cadenza-like figure of I. 1, bars 19–20, with Mahler's solo flute in place of Schumann's flute *and* oboe.

Unnecessary doublings of inessential middle-parts are for obvious reasons more keenly felt in the brass than in any other group. This accounts for the great number of alterations to be found in Schumann's brass parts. His treatment is generally rather clumsy here—partly because he frequently uses the brass in the manner of the classics, chiefly for sustained harmonies and rhythmic accentuations. This is no defect in itself, but is hardly adequate in view of the greater complexity of Schumann's style.

One of Schumann's most common faults is his doubling of the string basses with bassoons *and* trombones, resulting in a thick and heavy bass line, examples of which can be found in practically every movement. In such cases Mahler eliminates the trombones altogether, and the same thing happens to Schumann's many superfluous horn and trumpet doublings of unimportant middle-parts. Schumann also indulges in heavy orchestral pedals which he usually overscores by combining horns with trumpets. These Mahler corrects as a rule by eliminating the trumpets. An instructive example of how Mahler, by reducing the number of doublings, lightens heavy brass combinations is his alteration at the very opening of II. 1. Schumann scores this *pianissimo* (!) passage for two horns, two trumpets, and alto trombone. In Mahler's version this call is announced by trumpets only—an alteration which has the additional advantage of allowing the soft background of string crochets to be better heard.

Another factor that largely contributes to the heaviness of Schumann's brass scoring is his tendency to over-stress the rhythm by mere repetitions which represent the rhythmic skeleton of a particular melodic pattern. Take the D major section from IV. 2, with its monotonous bare horn rhythm ♪♪♪ | ♩. ♪♪♪ | ♩ or IV. 1, 7 bars of *lebhaft*, with its 'bark' of | 𝄾 ♪♪♪ | and | ♪ ♪. ♬ ♪ ♪. ♬ | by the combined forces of horns, trumpets, and timpani. In these and similar other cases Mahler uses his blue pencil ruthlessly, or else he resorts to the ingenious device of distributing these skeletons between two groups of instruments, adding at the same time contrasting dynamics as in I. 1, bars 209–13:

Ex. 1

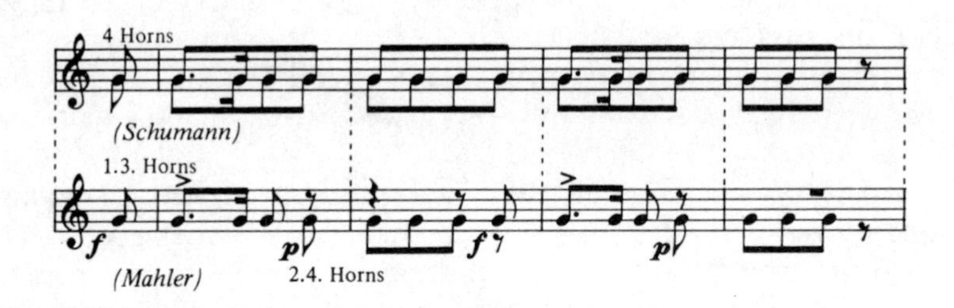

an altogether subtler and more effective way than Schumann's scoring for four horns, *fortissimo* in unison.

The timpani being rhythmic instruments *par excellence* it is not surprising to find here similar overstatements of the rhythm. Schumann's usually reinforces the timpani with purely rhythmic trumpets —a characteristic device of the classical method of scoring which Schumann applies, however, too mechanically and perfunctorily. Mahler's version uses the reinforcement only occasionally.

If Schumann's treatment of the strings cannot be regarded as model scoring he had at any rate a greater experience and knowledge of their special technique than of any other instrument except, of course, the piano. Yet even with them he makes the same mistake of superfluous doublings as in II. 1, four bars after B:

Ex. 2

By allowing the upper strings to rest for nearly three bars Mahler not only rids the melodic line of its thickness and thus, incidentally, gives it more edge, but also keeps the violins fresh for their entry on the *legato* phrase. Instead of wholesale elimination as in the above example, Mahler sometimes distributes the melodic line more subtly between the two originally doubling instruments, as in I. 4, bars 10–13:

Ex.3

Somewhat similar is the alteration in the D major section of IV. 2. Mahler here changes the original violin solo into an alternation between solo and tutti and thus creates both a contrast of colour and an instrumental dialogue of good effect.

Mahler's throwing into relief of thematic lines and rhythmic patterns is generally based on the technique of what I called elsewhere 'architectural scoring'.[4] This technique is guided by considerations of structural clarity as opposed to more pictorial and colouristic methods. In practice these two opposite ways of scoring—comparable to the antithesis of line and colour in painting—are rarely separated—if we disregard such exceptional cases as the music of the true impressionists or the *Farbenmelodie* of Schönberg's middle period.

[4] See Chapter 3: 'A Beethoven Movement and its Successors'.

Composers have by instinct always tried to strike a fair balance between these two principles. It is, however, natural that in the symphony where the architectural and thematic elements are of particular importance, architectural scoring should often predominate. On the whole this applies to the Schumann Symphonies. But Schumann's lack of a keen sense of the orchestral *palette* often jeopardises his intention of scoring architecturally. His thematic lines are often blurred and drowned by over-scored middle-parts, his melodies often lie in a register—usually a low one—in which the particular instrument does not 'speak' or carry well, or else are scored too thinly or given to the wrong instrument altogether. He also pays insufficient attention to the marking off of larger and smaller architectural units, such as periods, middle sections in tripartite forms, first and second subjects, etc., by contrasted scoring. To correct such organic defects was a much more difficult task than the lightening of thick textures. But Mahler's skill in getting under Schumann's skin helped him to make good quite a number of such deficiencies.

One simple device he uses is to transpose melodic woodwind passages an octave higher, particularly the oboes and clarinets which Schumann frequently uses in their lower middle register. Sometimes Mahler scores melodic lines for woodwind *a due* where Schumann employs only a single instrument, or he doubles the original scoring by the addition of instruments which in the original have only harmonic fillings to play. This latter procedure has the advantage of combining the re-drawing of the melodic line with the loosening of the texture, as it reduces the number of 'thick' background instruments.

Schumann also seems to have had an aversion to using flutes and clarinets in their highest registers. He sometimes breaks the logic of his part-writing either by transposing the flutes and clarinets into the lower octave, after a few initial bars, or by taking parts to a lower note of the harmony, thus distorting the melodic line. Mahler corrects this by simply continuing the part in its initial register.

A singularly effective device of Mahler's is to free the brass, particularly horns and trumpets, from their task of stodgy harmonic padding and use them more for melodic purposes—chiefly to underline themes and important motifs as far as this was consistent with the general balance of sound. The markedly melodic treatment of horns and trumpets is, however, characteristic of late romantic and modern music and the result partly of the greater complexity of symphonic writing, partly of the technical improvements in the instruments, during the last hundred years. To introduce this method of brass scoring into Schumann's symphonies was stylistically questionable. Yet the gain to the orchestral texture in flexibility and clarity is so great that even the purist may well close his eyes for once. In order to appreciate the full import of the following alteration (I. 1, bars 281–9):

Ex. 4

the passage should be compared with its original. It is a *stretto* with the main thematic motif as subject, and one can see at a glance how much more distinct its various entries become in Mahler's re-scoring. Schumann here uses horns and trumpets in the most insignificant way, whereas Mahler makes them play an important part in clarifying the structural build of the passage. It is usually in *stretti* that Mahler resorts to such melodically treated brass.

Somewhat similar to this treatment are certain alterations of Schumann's timpani parts. They originated in the composer's peculiar tendency to keep on the whole to the tuning indicated at the beginning of each movement. The result is that his timpani part often does not coincide with the true bass, but consists of any middle note of the harmony which happens to be identical with one or the other note of the initial tuning, as in the following example (I. 4, bars 66–71):[5]

[5] Schumann's slipshod treatment of his timpani basses reminds one of the curious practice in the eighteenth and early nineteenth centuries when, since notes on the timpani are not very distinct in pitch, composers did not bother about the necessary *mutano* after they had modulated to other keys and thus actually wrote wrong notes—mostly, however, in *forte* tutti passages where such clashes could hardly be heard. Thus Verdi, in the first finale of *Un Ballo in Maschera*, continued to write notes on the timpani which do not fit into the harmony at all. This was as late as 1859.

Ex. 5

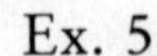

Mahler's version of such timpani parts has the true bass, which makes the line altogether clearer. Similar in effect is Mahler's addition of fresh notes, which also adds more bite to the rhythm in the bass. These corrections demand frequent and often very quick changes of the tuning which, if they have to be made in fast tempo, require either pedal timpani or the use of three kettle-drums, as in the first and last movements of the Fourth Symphony.

A singularly curious alteration which occurs in the slow movement preceding the finale of the Third Symphony deserves special mention. In bars 50–2 and 65–7, Mahler transposes the original timpani E flat an octave lower to a note which to my knowledge is never used on this instrument, though it is possible to tune it down to such low pitch. By this most unusual alteration Mahler apparently aimed at a very hollow and muffled sound in order to enhance the religious and mysterious character of these passages.[6]

The string department shows fewer alterations made for the sake of clearer thematic outline. Yet such alterations as do occur are of importance. Schumann is often inclined to score quick melodic runs rather thinly, usually for the first violins only, so that this group has to contend against a heavy accompaniment single-handed. Mahler's common procedure in such cases is to reinforce these runs by doubling the first with the second violins and violas, in unison or octaves. As in Schumann's scoring, the latter are usually given the accompaniment. Mahler's corrections not only throw the thematic line into better relief, but loosen the string texture by reducing the number of accompanying parts. A excellent large-scale illustration of this procedure is to be found in Mahler's version of the string parts of the first movement of the Fourth Symphony, particularly in the development section with its characteristic alternation between first violins and 'cellos and, later, between strings and combined woodwind. Another device of Mahler's to improve such thinly scored passages is to transfer the accompaniment from the second violins to the violas *divisi* and to use the former for the support of the first-violin melody, as at the

[6] It will be remembered that this beautiful movement was inspired by the solemn ceremony of the Cologne Archbishop's elevation to the cardinalate.

opening of the *Larghetto* from the First Symphony, where the rich sound of the combined violins add greatly to the beauty of the passage.

Mahler's skill becomes particularly evident when we come to passages in which he combines various devices. One of the best examples is to be found in III. 1, eight bars before N:

Ex. 6

This passage—significantly enough, again a *stretto*—marks the end of the development section and leads at N—the climax of the movement—to the recapitulation. Mahler's alterations in these eight bars are a model of architectural scoring, and a comparison with Schumann's original yield the following points: (1) greater prominence of the thematic line on double basses, 'cellos, violas and first violins, by (*a*) augmentation of note-values; (*b*)reinforcement by the second violins; (2) loosening of the texture by (*a*) elimination of trumpets and timpani with their bare rhythmic skeleton, thus keeping them fresh for their entry on the climax; (*b*) introduction into the horn parts of occasional breathing spaces; (*c*) reduction of doublings in the middle-parts; (3) greater differentiation and grading of dynamics. The result is a considerable increase in clarity and plasticity of texture, rhythm and dynamics.

As for alterations of, and additions to, Schumann's dynamic markings, Mahler simply records what every experienced conductor does by word of mouth in rehearsal in order to achieve a good balance of sound and a contrast of light and shade. For it is a common experience with most orchestral music before Wagner and Liszt that its dynamic markings do not seem to take into full account the peculiarities of orchestrated dynamics as revealed in practice. For instance, the woodwind can never be toned down to the same level of *p* or *pp* as the strings. Accompaniment on the brass will always—to the annoyance of every conductor—stand out conspicuously if marked with the same dynamics as the rest of the orchestra. There are long-drawn *crescendi* and *diminuendi* which orchestral players will for certain psychological reasons always start too soon, thus jeopardising an evenly distributed increase or decrease in the volume of sound; and other such pitfalls of orchestral playing. Paradoxical as it may seem, the conductor who in classical and romantic works keeps faithfully to the original dynamics will never quite achieve the dynamic balance intended by the composer, as the conductor does who introduces intelligent modifications. This applies particularly to symphonic works of the romantic period in which emotional and pictorial elements play a preponderant part and which, consequently, require a greater measure of dynamic contrast and shading. Naturally, such alterations are partly subject to individual taste. Yet provided the conductor is a sound musician—not merely a deft gesticulator—and endowed with a natural feeling for style, his dynamic alterations will unquestionably improve the quality of the performance.

Now Mahler's qualifications in this respect are beyond dispute. All the same, in his dynamic alterations of the Schumann symphonies, he tends to over-mark the scores, to introduce too many dynamic gradations, and thus to impart to the symphonies a degree of restlessness that seems too high for Schumann's style, although one has to admit that an element of nervous agitation does underlie much of Schumann's music. But taking a broader view, it is arguable whether Mahler's dynamic alterations do not come nearer to Schumann's intentions, despite his occasional lapses, than the drily objective readings of certain modern conductors.

On practically every page of Mahler's version there are new < > or <*f* or >*p* marks, which, in most cases, correspond to what every orchestral player with a natural musical feeling does by instinct. Moreover, Mahler makes more frequent use of both extremes of the dynamic scale (*pp* and *ppp*, *ff* and *fff*) and the intermediate (*mp* and *mf*) than Schumann does. This at times leads to exaggerated dynamic contrasts as Mahler is inclined to change over, within a very short space, from *pp* to *ff* and vice-versa. Such sudden contrasts are clearly not in keeping with Schumann's general orchestral style and are not free from superficial effects as in the coda of the third movement of the First Symphony, where at the transition from the *come sopra ma un poco più lento* section to the *quasi presto* conclusion, Mahler alters the original *pp-mf* into *ppp-ff*, or—even more strikingly—at the opening of the finale of the Third Symphony, where he changes the original *f* of the first eight bars to *pp* and follows this in the next eight bars by a *ff* instead of the original *f*.[7]

But there is a group of dynamic alterations which is more than justified. Bearing in mind the dynamic peculiarities of the various orchestral departments and their individual instruments, Mahler introduces changes that aim at a more varied gradation and a better balance of sound. Take the passage in IV. 1, at letter G, where Mahler replaces Schumann's uniform *ff* by the following gradation:

Woodwind *fff*
Horns *ff*
Trumpets *p*
Trombones *mf*
Timpani *ff*
Strings *ff*

By toning down the trumpets and trombones, which have only harmonic fillings to play, and bringing up the woodwind, Mahler throws the thematic motif into greater relief. In I. 1, bars 126–8, Mahler alters the original *ff* of the woodwind and brass to *ffp* while the

[7] Mahler's own works are full of such sudden contrasts, and suffer from dynamic over-markings which only hamper the flexibility and natural flow of orchestral playing.

strings continue *ff* so that the sustained chords of the first two groups are prevented from drowning the strings, as they are bound to do in Schumann's scoring.

In a second category of alterations, Mahler tries to achieve certain dynamic effects, particularly long-drawn *crescendi* and *diminuendi*, by appropriate re-scoring. This 'scoring of dynamics' is a more organic and at the same time subtler way of getting the intended dynamic results than merely putting in the usual markings. Mahler's alterations of this kind are legion, and he uses here all the various devices discussed previously. An excellent large-scale illustration of this method is his scoring of a long *crescendo* in the *coda* of II. 2. Schumann scores the whole of this coda *tutti* and *forte*, inevitably resulting in dynamic monotony. Mahler builds up a gradual *crescendo* with the dynamic climax about the middle of the coda, as seen from the following:

(*Schumann*)

Horns Trumpets Timpani Strings	Flutes Oboes Clarinets Bassoons Horns Trumpets Timpani Strings
2 bars	*36 bars*

(*Mahler*)

Horns Trumpets Timpani Strings	Oboes Clarinets Bassoons Strings	Strings	Clarinets Bassoons Horns Strings	Flutes Oboes Clarinets Bassoons Horns Strings	Flutes Oboes Clarinets Bassoons Horns Trumpets Timpani Strings
2 bars	*4 bars*	*7 bars*	*4 bars*	*5 bars*	*16 bars*

Mahler was, in his own works, very explicit and generous with his phrase markings, and a prominent feature of his conducting was his insistence upon intelligent and intelligible phrasing. Therefore it is not surprising that he also tackled this aspect of the Schumann symphonies. A device most frequently applied is his introduction of short rests which contribute largely to a clear articulation. Schumann's uneconomical way of keeping the strings busy most of the time explains why this kind of alteration is to be found chiefly in this department. In some cases short rests are also introduced to heighten the original *staccato* effect, as in the first Trio of the First Symphony.

Other of Mahler's changes in the manner of playing include additions of fresh *pizziccati, sul tasto*, the demand for 'Schalltrichter aufheben' (the raising of the bell) of trumpets, thus increasing the carrying power of the tone,[8] and the use of muted trombones.

Mahler wisely refrained from any major thematic alterations. There are only a few minor changes, the most important of which is to be found at the very beginning of the first movement of the B flat Symphony where Mahler restores Schumann's original version of the opening call on the horns and trumpets. This motif originally read B flat—G—A—B flat, that is, a major third lower than the present version, and thus it corresponded with the very opening of the *Allegro* section (1st and 2nd violins). Due to the fact, however, that Schumann had only 'natural' brass instruments at his disposal, the notes G and A had to be stopped while B flat as the eighth harmonic on an instrument in B flat was an open note. Thus the phrase must have sounded very uneven and almost comic in its sharp dynamic and colour contrast. Hence Schumann's subsequent transposition, which presented no such problems to the players as the notes C and D constitute the respective ninth and tenth harmonics of the fundamental B flat. It was one of those cases where the limitations of valveless instruments interfered with the composer's full realisation of his intention as is, for instance, so well illustrated by Beethoven's treatment of the horns and trumpets in his Seventh and Ninth Symphonies. Mahler, thinking of the modern instruments with valves for which Schumann's original phrase has nowadays no difficulties, quite logically went back to it.

Another perfectly reasonable alteration occurs in II. 2, at four bars after the letter M, where Mahler transforms the insignificant rhythmic figure on horns and trumpets into the trumpet call, with which the first movement opens, combining it with the chief motif of Trio No. 2.

Ex. 7

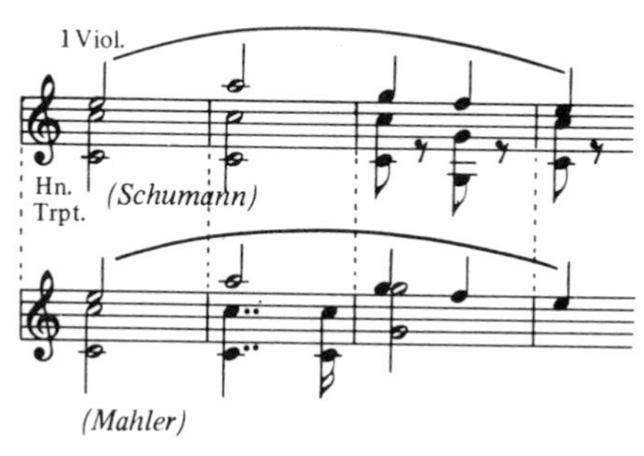

[8] In his own works Mahler makes frequent use of this device.

Mahler suggests a few justifiable cuts in the lengthy and repetitive finale of the Second Symphony. They are:

(*a*)	From bars 398	inclusive to	422	inclusive.
(*b*)	,, 438	,,	441	,,
(*c*)	,, 492	,,	507	,,
(*d*)	,, 528	,,	560	,,

In conclusion, I should like to make it clear that in writing this article I am not advocating the replacement in the concert repertory of the Schumann originals by Mahler's versions. What I suggest is a few occasional performances of the latter so as to enable critics and public to judge for themselves. I appeal to enterprising conductors.

TWELVE

GOETHE AND MUSIC

IN HIS CONVERSATIONS with Eckermann, which took place during the poet's late life, Goethe often discusses his attitude to the various arts. One aspect that seems to have occupied his mind in particular was what we today would call the 'subconscious' or 'instinctive' of artistic creation. Goethe calls it *Das Dämonische*, the demonic—something that to him appeared as irrational and hence incapable of analysis by the critical and logical mind. It has, he says, an effect that casts its spell over everything and no one is able to account for it. Of all the arts it is music in which he feels this demonic element at its strongest and that, he says, would explain the magic power which music has exercised over mankind since its earliest days. But he makes the following reservation: '*Das Dämonische liegt nicht in meiner Natur, aber ich bin ihm unterworfen*' ('The demonic is not in my nature but I am subject to it').

Although Goethe's attitude to music was positive and appreciative, in this predominance in it of the demonic, the irrational, he felt something unsettling, disturbing and perhaps even dangerous. It is interesting to recall that Thomas Mann held similar views on the nature and effect of music, going, however, further than Goethe, for Mann ascribes to music a disruptive pathological power, as he made clear in *Doktor Faustus*, in which the hero, a German composer, eventually ends in madness. Not that Goethe ever drew such conclusions, although his description of Beethoven as a composer 'possessed by demons' may have implied something of the kind. Goethe's difficulty was that his clear, logical and rationalistic mind was unable to come to fully satisfactory terms with an art in which so much rests on the instinctive and purely emotional. He describes it as an intermediary between us and the unspeakable, by the unspeakable implying emotions, feelings and subconscious desires. He thus finds it beyond interpretation on the part of the intellect. It also seems that its abstract nature, its intellectual elusiveness, baffled him and while he admits that it has form and content, he declares its content as immaterial, defying clear and intelligible definitions.

Yet throughout his life Goethe attempted to discover an intellectual approach to music. One often has the suspicion that in this approach he was inclined to regard music less as an art and rather as a fascinating activity of the human intellect, an activity in which he tried to fathom the general laws of nature governing it. Thus music became for him almost a subject of natural science. As in his theory of the colours, he attempted to analyse music in terms of a natural phenomenon, and in his abortive *Tonlehre*, a theory of musical sound, he probes into the laws by which intervals and chords are built and related. And there was a considerable correspondence going on between him and the composer Zelter, his musical mentor and adviser, on the important function of the interval of the third on which the enigmatic difference between the major and minor modes depends. These enquiries and speculations were the manifestation of an urge to penetrate intellectually into the secret of this 'demonic' art. As Goethe said to Eckermann: 'It is more through *reflection* and therefore in a more general way than through *enjoyment* that I approach music.' The crux of the matter is that Goethe failed to understand music *in* and *on* its own terms. To put it more bluntly, Goethe was not musical in the intrinsic sense of the word. The specific nature of what we call a 'musical experience', an enrichment of our artistic consciousness, which only music and no other art can provide and which no amount of verbal metaphors can define, for this Goethe seems to have had no ear and no response. How odd in a poet whose verses are imbued with inner music and whose lyrical genius was so largely responsible for the flowering of the German *Lied* from Schubert to Hugo Wolf!

It was partly this inability to appreciate music *qua* music that inclined Goethe to deny it a purpose in itself. The modern principle of *l'art pour l'art* he would have found both incomprehensible and wrong in music. Only inasmuch as music served a purpose beyond itself, would he admit its *raison d'être*. He would thus demand of a composer to write with an extra-musical purpose in mind, to relate his composition to something that the intellect could grasp. By implication he would postulate that music should be the product of pure reason.

In all this Goethe reflected the rationalism of the eighteenth century which regarded music, as Leibniz once said, as 'an unconscious mathematical problem of the soul'. Despite Rousseau, and despite Beethoven who proved that utmost intellectual clarity and deep powerful emotions could be fused into a most satisfying musical whole, Goethe was never able to change his rationalistic one-sided view. Yet it is reported that on occasions a piece of music, notably a song, could stir him most profoundly and even move him to tears. How are we to square this with his cold rationalistic views? This contradiction between his own reaction and his general attitude to music is only an apparent one. For here, too, Goethe was a child of his time, adhering as he did to a theory that played an important part in the musical aesthetics of the eighteenth century. This was the so-called *Affektenlehre*, a theory according to which every piece of music had to express a certain clearly defined emotion—joy, sorrow, gladness, melancholy and so on. The aesthetic value of a composition depended on the extent to which it succeeded in arousing in the listener the emotion which the composer set out to express. It was an accepted thing, in fact it was expected, for the listener to show his emotional reaction quite openly and visibly—break out in tears, rise from his seat according to what the music expressed. And Goethe as a listener was no exception in this respect. In his *Sorrows of the Young Werther* there is a scene in which he illustrates the pronounced emotive function which according to the *Affektenlehre* music was endowed with. Lotte is playing something on the spinet and this is how Werther reacts to it:

> It is all over, my dear friend; I can support this state no longer. Today I was sitting by Charlotte; she was playing on her spinet with an expression it is impossible for me to describe to you. Her little sister was dressing her doll upon my lap; the tears came into my eyes; I leaned down and looked intently at her wedding-ring; my tears fell—immediately she began to play the favourite, the divine air which has so often enchanted me—I felt comforted by it; but soon it recalled to my mind the times that are past—grief, disappointed hopes.—I began to walk with hasty strides about the room.—I was choked.—At length I went up to her, and with eagerness said, 'For heaven's sake play that no longer'. She stopped, looked steadfastly at me, and said with a smile that sunk deep into my heart, 'Werther, you are indeed very ill; your most favourite food disgusts you. Pray go, and try to compose yourself'.—I tore myself from her.—Great God! thou seest my torments, and thou wilt put an end to them!

Goethe here uses music purely as a means to arouse in Werther emotions and evoke in him extra-musical associations. Equally rationalistic was his view that music should serve the purpose of education and be used for our moral and religious edification. He would thus place church music on the highest pinnacle. But if divorced from such lofty aims music should at least provide a highly refined entertainment for the mind. It should delight us by well-proportioned forms, by polished craftsmanship, by a clear and neat expression of emotions as demanded by the *Affektenlehre*. He would not allow for music of high emotional tension, of strong dramatic and tragic accents. The 'demonic' must not enter this sphere, because it would upset the Olympian calm and serenity which the mature Goethe regarded as the ultimate aim of classical art. This explains why Goethe's favourite instrumental composers were Haydn and Mozart. But it also explains his marked coolness toward Beethoven and Schubert. Their individualism, their subjective expression, their clear break with the eighteenth-century ideal of music as a means of refined entertainment—in short, their romantic tendencies—Goethe would not and could not accept.

Altogether, the music that in Goethe's later years would have been called 'modern'—Weber, Spohr, Beethoven and Schubert—Goethe politely but firmly rejected. 'Music in the best sense,' he said to Eckermann, 'needs little novelty, in fact the older it is, the more familiar, the greater is its effect.' It is an attitude falling not very short of the Philistine. This is what he says to Eckermann after a musical party at his house at Weimar at which some modern quartet was played. The date is January 1827:

> 'It is odd,' said Goethe, 'to see where our modern composers are leading us with their most highly developed technique and clever tricks; their compositions are no longer music, they go beyond the limits of the human emotions and it is impossible to read into them any meaning. How is it with you? With me all goes as far as the ear and not further.' I replied that I felt about the same in this case. 'Yet,' Goethe continues, 'the Allegro had character. This endless whirling and swirling suggested to me the Witches' Dance on the Blocksberg and so I was able to supply to this curious music a mental picture.'

The last sentence is most revealing. For it shows Goethe's characteristic approach to music. Only if he could associate some image, some programme with the music he heard, was he able to make anything of it. Unless it suggested to him something that could be grasped in terms of a situation, an event, a mood picture, and could thus be defined in words, Goethe failed to appreciate it. That is why pure instrumental music found little favour with him, and it is significant that he preferred to listen to such instrumental music that was outspokenly programmatic. One of his favourite pieces of that kind was the Capriccio by Bach in which Bach describes his feelings at the departure of his beloved brother.

Goethe's programmatic approach to music was also responsible for his marked preference for vocal music. For here the words gave the intellect a clear direction to what the music meant to express and illustrate. Here Goethe found a rational equation between music and meaning. Vocal music, he felt, was free from the tantalising elusiveness that disconcerted him in pure instrumental music. There is a scene in his novel *Wilhelm Meisters Lehr und Wanderjahre*, in which Goethe makes this very point. Wilhelm and his friends have been listening to the playing of an old harper. The piece was a purely instrumental one and Wilhelm now asks him to sing something:

> He began the prelude on the harp, which he had placed before him. The sweet tones which he drew from his instrument very soon inspired the company. 'You can sing too, my good old man,' said Philina. 'Give us something that shall entertain the spirit and the heart as well as the senses,' said Wilhelm. 'The instrument should but accompany the voice; for tunes and melodies without words and meaning seem to me like butterflies or finely-variegated birds, which hover round us in the air, which we could wish to catch and make our own; whereas song is like a blessed genius that exalts us towards heaven, and inspires the better self in us to attend him.'

'The instrument should only accompany the voice,' says Wilhelm. In this sentence Goethe sums up his view about the relation between voice and instrument in a song, an eternal bone of contention between poet and musician. In this emphasis on the purely accompanying character of the music in a song Goethe, however, was not alone. He shared it with most eighteenth-century writers and musicians, who held that the task of a song composer was chiefly to throw the words of the poet into sharper relief, to intensify the effect of the words as such. The measure of the perfect song composer lay in the degree of his subservience to the poet. To re-create the mood of a poem in such terms that the music becomes an equal of the poem, a full counterpart to the mood and imagery of the verses—in which Schubert and the later *Lieder* composers saw their great task—this Goethe and his time would have regarded as an arrogant encroachment on the territory of the poet. It would have endangered the effect of the words and obscured their meaning. It was from this angle that Goethe judged the musical settings of his own verses. Do we now wonder why he preferred the respectable mediocrity of such song composers as Reichardt and Zelter to the soaring genius of a Schubert? Yet one has to be fair to both Goethe and his favourite musicians. Reichardt and Zelter had the merit of being among the very first to see how supremely suitable Goethe's lyrical verses were for a musical setting. Yet bound by the rationalistic aesthetics of their time they contented themselves with underlining the verses with more or less adequate melodies, mostly melodies of a simple, straightforward character, almost in the nature of a folksong, so that the words always remain in the foreground and intelligible. And they provided an instrumental accompaniment perfectly in keeping with the neutral character of the vocal melody. It had no particular musical significance or, if at all, it attempted to characterise the mood and physical situation of the poem only in a timid and tame fashion. Even Mozart, with his incomparable genius for dramatic characterisation, dared not to go far beyond the limits set by the song conventions of his time when he came to write his only Goethe setting, 'Das Veilchen'.

Goethe was deeply impressed by Zelter's setting of his poem 'Um Mitternacht' (At Midnight), saying to Eckermann 'It remains beautiful no matter how often one hears it. There is something perennial, imperishable in the melody.' True enough, it is certainly one of Zelter's best songs, comparatively free of the self-conscious primness and stilted expression that characterises many of his other songs, but Goethe's praise seems to us nowadays rather exaggerated.

The great difference of approach that existed between Goethe's favourite song composer and Schubert, can be appreciated best when one hears three different settings of the same poem, the 'Erlking', by Corona Schröter, Reichardt and Zelter, and tries to hear them, as it were, against the background of Schubert's masterpiece. Different as these three settings are from one another, they yet have common characteristics: the words are the chief thing, the song melody is simple and allows of clear enunciation of the words while the accompaniment is rather self-conscious in its suggestion of the nocturnal ride. Particularly with the first two settings, one feels that the music is almost incidental, not much more than a help to a more heightened recitation of the words. And it is significant that all the three settings are strophic, the music of the first stanza having to do duty by the other stanzas, and, with the exception of Zelter's song, completely ignoring the dramatic development of Goethe's ballad. One is by Corona Schröter, an eminent opera singer, who wrote her 'Erlking' in 1782. It is a strophic setting of eight bars with no attempt at the merest musical characterisation. Reichardt's setting was written in 1793 and shows some attempt at musical characterisation. It is in a minor key and the piano accompaniment with its marked rhythm speaks for itself. But the vocal line is purely declamatory without any lyrical relief, and stanza upon stanza follows to the same music. A third, the 'Erlking' by Zelter, was finished in 1807. Again a strophic setting, yet, significantly enough, there are already variations, though minor ones, in both melody and harmony. And at the climax where the child breaks out in the terrified cry *'Mein Vater, mein Vater, jetzt fasst er mich an! Erlkönig hat mir ein*

Leids getan!' Zelter introduces a most dramatic passage, almost prophetic of Schubert's setting.

Zelter's song is clearly the most advanced of the three 'Erlking' settings. But except for the dramatic climax, it can hardly compare with Schubert's setting. While Zelter still confirms the hegemony of the poet over the musician, the young Schubert swept it away with one stroke and, free from fetters of antiquated rationalistic aesthetics, raised the music of his 'Erlking' to the plane of Goethe's verses. To Goethe this must have seemed an unpardonable arrogance which he returned by completely ignoring the composer who had sent him a copy of the song. We wonder what Goethe would have thought of Hugo Wolf's settings of his various poems. He might have perhaps approved of the declamatory treatment of the voice, but he would have been dismayed at Wolf's 'symphonic' accompaniment.

THIRTEEN

THE STRING QUARTETS OF BARTÓK

BARTÓK'S FIRST ESSAY in string quartet writing (later suppressed) is said to date from 1899, when he was a youth of eighteen; his last, from December 1944 (nine months before his death), when he sketched out a few brief ideas for a planned seventh quartet. Between lie the six published quartets, whose dates are as follows (the figures in brackets indicate the composer's age at the time of composition):

No. 1, Op. 7	1908	(27)
No. 2, Op. 17	1915–17	(34–6)
No. 3	1927	(46)
No. 4	1928	(47)
No. 5	1934	(53)
No. 6	1939	(58)

A glance at this table and consultation of the complete list of Bartók's works elicit the significant fact that, along with the piano, the string quartet was the sole medium that held the composer's undiminished interest, from his student days up to almost the very end of his life. The six quartets occupy a central position in Bartók's creative career, they form its very backbone. Or to change the metaphor, they may be likened to the pages of a diary to which a great artist confided the most private experiences and adventures of his heart and mind. In point of style they contain the quintessence of Bartók's musical personality and as a series they afford a fascinating study in creative development. Each may be said to stand at the culmination of the respective phases of his artistic growth and each, with the possible exception of No. 1, is a masterpiece in its own right. Certainly, we may declare our preference for this or that quartet, we may find the one more immediately accessible than the other, yet this is irrelevant to the objective recognition that within its terms of reference, each of the quartets from Nos 2–6 is a rounded whole and sums up the essential problems, tendencies, and aspirations peculiar to the successive stages of Bartók's maturity.

Beethoven comes to mind, with whom the string quartet possessed the same significance in his creative career; and it can be said without fear of contradiction that not since the Viennese master has an outstanding composer made this medium so intimately his own as Bartók has. The parallel can be extended. Just as the series of seventeen Beethoven quartets constitute the apogee of the classical form, so do the series of six Bartók quartets mark the consummation of the modern genre. For profundity of thought, imaginative power, logic of structure, diversity of formal details, and enlargement of the technical scope, they stand unrivalled in the field of modern chamber music.

The quality of uniqueness that attaches to these quartets is enhanced by the following fact. One of the mainsprings of Bartók's creative life was to achieve a synthesis of East and West. In the quartets this synthesis may be said to reach its most sublimated form, and we realise the full measure of Bartók's achievement when we bear in mind that this consummate fusion of two such very different musical cultures is effected in a medium which we regard as at once the purest and most subtle manifestation of Western musical thinking. To have harnessed so fruitfully the instinctual forces residing in Eastern (Magyar) music to the most intellectual of our musical forms—therein lies, to my mind, the historic significance of the Bartók of the quartets.

This synthesis, however, was achieved at a price. A criticism that must be levelled against Bartók's quartet style (as, indeed, it must be brought against Beethoven's too, from the Rasumovsky Quartets onward) is, that sometimes it bursts the framework of the medium with explosive vehemence. Responsible for it in Bartók's case was not (as it was in Beethoven's) a powerful symphonic urge, but the percussiveness of his harmony, rhythm, and dynamics. Bartók does not aim at orchestral effects, though occasionally he writes passages of a quasi-orchestral texture and sonority (second movement of No. 2, first part and coda of No. 3, finale of No. 4): it is the complex of features we connote with the 'barbaric' quality of his general style that militates against the intimacy and inwardness of the string quartet medium. However, if seen in the whole context of Bartók's achievement, this aspect moves into proper perspective and must be accepted as an integral part of his conception of string-quartet writing. Without it, the quartets would not be what they are.

Before dealing with the six works individually, let us first attempt a general outline of their style and see in which way they reflect Bartók's development over the years. Broadly speaking, five stages may be discerned:

1. The early period when Bartók was under the influence of the late German romantics: First Quartet.

2. The period during which a purer, more individual kind of romanticism fuses with elements of Magyar folk music: Second Quartet.

3. A phase of technical experimentation and intellectual abstraction, the period of the 'difficult', expressionist Bartók: Third Quartet.

4. A gradual relaxation of the expressionist tension and a return to a more lyrical expression: Fourth and Fifth Quartets.

5. The 'classical' phase, characterised by a comparative simplicity in form, texture, and tonal relations and by a newly gained equilibrium between the intellectual and emotional aspects of Bartók's personality: Sixth Quartet.

The series thus shows, in respect of aesthetic and technical difficulties, a crescendo and diminuendo—a kind of arch, if you like, in which the 'keystone' is represented by the Third Quartet. (Yet supposing one wished to study the quartets in their order of progressive difficulty, the best method, I suggest, would be to begin with the first two, then tackle No. 6, and work one's way back through Nos 5 and 4 to the Third Quartet.)

One of the most striking aspects of the quartets lies in Bartók's varied and highly individual treatment of the classical form. He never abandons it but he introduces a number of significant modifications and novel features, most of which serve the purpose of achieving a greater organic coherence, both in the single movement and the quartet as a whole. His chief device for obtaining unity between movements is the romantic one of the cyclic idea which in the mature quartets he develops and applies in an original manner. In No. 1 the young Bartók is still content with deriving the first subject of the Finale from an *ostinato* figure in the preceding *Scherzo*, while in No. 2 first and last movements are thematically linked. But in Nos 4 and 5 the cyclic idea is extended to four of the five movements and applied in a manner at once more intellectual and intrinsic, by means of the so-called arch-forms A–B–C–B–A. This enables the composer to establish between the movements not only thematic but also formal and emotional correspondences. Bartók may have derived the five-movement form from Beethoven's Opp. 130 and 131 or from Hindemith's String Quartet No. 2, Op. 10 or Berg's Lyric Suite which he heard at Baden-Baden in the summer of 1927. In No. 6 we find him resorting to the cyclic idea in the form of a motto-theme, but here too its application shows individual modifications. No. 3 stands apart, in that overall unity is achieved by its one-movement form, in which the four sections relate to one another in the pattern A–B–A–B (coda), the last two sections constituting greatly modified recapitulations of the first two.

In the form of the individual movements, however, Bartók closely adheres to classical models: sonata, *rondo*, and a simple A–B–A in the fast movements, while the slow ones are always three-sectional. The one exception is provided by the *Lento* of No. 2, in which Bartók appears to be reproducing the serial, chain-like arrangement characteristic of a certain kind of Magyar music: four thematically unrelated sections, but held together by the typically Western devices of a recurrent cadential motif and a coda of reminiscences.

This is the appropriate place to say something about Ernö Lendvai's thesis[1] that the law of the Golden Section governs the structure of a good many Bartók movements. In support of this thesis I cite Guido Adler who states[2] that the proportions of the Golden Section, in which, in terms of length, the smaller part relates to the large part as the latter relates to the whole, apply virtually to all sonata movements of classical music.

I have been in correspondence with Mr. Lendvai who writes that the 'Golden Section or GS appears *not* as a mathematical rule, i.e. it would be useless to seek for a mathematical logic in it, for it is an organic element of *musical dramaturgy*. It can be observed that themes of a *dynamic* nature follow the rules of GS . . . while themes of a static character have a well-balanced symmetrical structure.'

I asked Mr Lendvai to provide me with a table of his calculations of GS for the Fourth Quartet, my reason for choosing this particular quartet being that it is the only one whose score (Philharmonia) is prefaced by an outline of its formal structure (possibly by Bartók himself) which I could compare with Mr Lendvai's computations. (The two do not quite tally.) On p. 112 I reproduce in parts Mr Lendvai's figures but I should say here that he mostly considers only sections and not the whole movement.

With so searching a mind as Bartók's it is not surprising that the detailed structure of the traditional forms should undergo significant alterations. This is particularly true of the recapitulation of a sonata movement and, more generally, of any repeat of previous material. Bartók carries the conception of the classical reprise to the point where it sometimes takes on the character of a complete reorganisation and radical 'rethinking' of the exposition, with the result that in certain movements the correspondence between exposition and recapitulation becomes so vague and tenuous that one is tempted to speak of an

[1] *Béla Bartók. An Analysis of his Music* (London, 1971), pp. 17–26.
[2] *Handbuch der Musikgeschichte* (Berlin, 1930), p. 783.

ideal reprise rather than a real one, a return in the spirit rather than in the letter. The most remarkable instance of this will be found in the *Ricapitulazione della prima parte* of the Third Quartet and in the slow movements of the Fourth and Fifth Quartets. Again, in the opening *Allegro* of No. 5, the recapitulation partly reverses the order in which the themes follow each other in the exposition; in addition, the themes themselves reappear in their inverted form. Occasionally, however, the recapitulation will represent a simplified, more straightforward version of the expositions as in the first movement of No. 2 and the *Prima parte* of No. 3 (p. 7, [11]).[3] In short, Bartók knows no mere formal repeat but revitalises it by an organic regeneration of the expository material.

Organic regeneration is also the secret of Bartók's motif development (as it is of Beethoven's). It accounts for that compelling logic and cohesion which are felt even in his most complex and difficult works; and the immense subtlety and pliability of this process is perhaps nowhere shown to more remarkable effect than in the mature quartets. Like the Beethoven of the late quartets and piano sonatas, Bartók concentrates on a few and often insignificant motifs, and by a variety of devices he evolves from these germ-cells the ever-changing tissues of his fabric: stretching and contracting of intervals, diatonic and chromatic versions of the same figure, fragmentation, inverted and retrograde forms, and rhythmic variation. In certain movements the music seems to stem from a single protoplasmic cell which proliferates into the most unexpected and multifarious shapes. It would take a large number of pages to show how in, say, the first *Allegro* of No. 4 the texture of the whole movement has grown out of a simple six-note chromatic motif. Such movements are not merely monothematic but, to coin an appropriate word, *monocystic* (one-cellular), the theme, or themes, being offshoots of the cell, and the whole movement showing *continuous* growth.

In an interview given in 1939 Bartók named Bach, Beethoven, and Debussy as the three masters from whom he had learned most.[4] Beethoven's influence we have noted in Bartók's motif development and the close attention he paid to matters of form. As for Debussy, it is true he had shown Bartók one of the ways by which to emancipate himself from the classical concept of major-minor tonality, and he also coloured (to some extent) the Hungarian master's harmonic style, yet there is little direct influence of the French composer to be felt in the

[3] All page numbers refer to the miniature scores. No. 1 is published by Ròzsavölgyi, Budapest, No. 4 by the Wiener Philharmonischer Verlag, Vienna, and the rest by Boosey & Hawkes, London.

[4] See *Béla Bartók*, by Serge Moreux (London, 1953).

quartets—one or two Debussyian fingerprints occur in the first two quartets. And although Bartók's impressionism, as exemplified in the 'night music' of the slow movements of Nos 4 and 5, can be traced back to Debussy, it is so personal as to *appear* to have grown on his own soil. Bach, however, who revealed to Bartók 'the transcendant significance' of counterpoint is, like Beethoven, more in evidence, and for the patent reason that the four individual parts of the string quartet medium offer an especially wide scope for polyphonic writing. In his later quartets Bartók cultivates a predominantly linear (non-harmonic) counterpoint in which harmonies are mostly the accidental result of the part-writing. This largely accounts for the marked harshness of the harmonic idiom of Nos 3–5. In addition, the scholastic 'automatic' devices of inversion, retrograde motion, canon, imitation, and *stretto* are used in profusion, and on several occasions subjects are stated in canon, as in the opening movements of Nos 1, 3 and 5. At times, however, the impression cannot be resisted of a *de trop*, a feeling that Bartók is straining these devices and making too self-conscious a use of them, as witness the contrapuntal *tour de force* of the Finale of No. 5. On the other hand, he handles them with remarkable freedom and rarely sacrifices the shapeliness and equipoise of his melodic lines to the demands of strict logic. Another characteristic is his habit of making a fugue the centre of a development section, and it is worth noting that all these fugues share a common feature, in that they are fast scurrying pieces in subdued dynamics and in *leggiero* style. Unlike the fugues of the late Beethoven, Bartók's are not dramatic but (like some of Bach's) of a 'motoric' kind and greatly intensify the rhythmic drive of the movement in which they occur.

If we once again cast a comprehensive glance at the melodic and harmonic style of the quartets, we observe a characteristic change as the series progresses. In the melody a gradual process of fragmentation takes place. Themes are replaced by motif-generated configurations, which change their shapes in kaleidoscopic fashion; and there is a preponderance of small (mostly) chromatic intervals over wider diatonic ones. It is largely in what has aptly been called 'imaginary folk tunes' (Moreux), melodies invented in the style of Magyar music, that Bartók's melodic writing gains in consistency and sweep: as witness the *Seconda parte* of No. 3, the fourth movement of No. 4, and the slow movements of Nos 4 and 5. From the Fifth Quartet onward, however, Bartók's melodic writing gains in consistency and sweep:as witness the singularly beautiful motto-theme of No. 6.

To turn to the harmonic aspect. The quartets clearly reflect Bartók's emancipation from romantic (Wagnerian) chromaticism and the traditional major-minor tonality of his early period to the individual style of his maturity. Under the influence partly of his native folk music, partly of Debussy and Stravinsky, Bartók turns to a 'diatonicised' chromatic writing in which the five chromatic notes stand in their own right, equal in status to the seven diatonic notes (their former 'parents') and often replace them. Lendvai has shown[5] that in Bartók's harmonic thinking there operated an axis system based on the circle of fifths which enabled him to replace tonic, dominant and subdominant by the opposite poles or counterpoles of the axis, *without change of function*, e.g. C=F sharp; G=C sharp; F=B. These replacements are not to be confused with Bartók's tendency to deliberate mistuning of perfect intervals by supplanting them with their augmented or diminished forms. One senses here Stravinsky's influence, notably from his *The History of the Soldier*, as for instance in the Third Quartet, but traces of this influence are still felt in as late a quartet as the Sixth. Bartók's axis system with its replacement technique leads to a marked extension of the tonal orbit and at the same time to a receding perspective of the tonic, to the point where it is scarcely perceptible and where frequently a single note or single chord serves as the point of departure and return at the end. Providing that we discard the restricted classical notion of tonality, we may say that No. 3 is 'on' C sharp, No. 4 'on' C, and No. 5 'on' B flat. Here again the Sixth Quartet marks a return to a more clearly defined key, the first and last movements being in what is a much expanded D major-minor. Hand in hand with the composer's free handling of chromaticism and tonality goes an increase in the dissonant character of his harmonic texture. To the classical principle of chord-building by superimposed thirds, is now added that of superimposed seconds, tritones (augmented fourths), and perfect fourths, the latter (in descending form) being a characteristic feature of the melodic style of Magyar folk music. And to heighten their pungency, Bartók will often present the discords in an exposed, naked form. It is significant of his harmonic development that while in the Second Quartet he would still mollify the harshness of certain harmonies by a special layout and scoring (see, for example, the bitonal passage on p. 17, Tempo I), in the Third Quartet he intensifies it by percussive triple and quadruple stops, played 'at the heel' and *martellato* (pp. 6–7).

Lastly, a word or two on Bartók's special sound effects. Up to the Third Quartet he confined them to the traditional *arco-pizzicato*, *con sordino*, and an occasional *sul ponticello*. In the subsequent works other devices are introduced, some for the purpose of increasing harmonic and rhythmic percussiveness. We already mentioned *martellato*, 'at the

[5] Op. cit., pp. 2–3.

heel', and difficult triple and quadruple stops (sometimes with the use of open strings). To these must now be added *col legno*; extended and simultaneous *glissandi* on all four instruments, sometimes in double-stops; 'brush' *pizzicati* in which plucked chords are linked by *glissandi*; up-and-down arpeggio of a guitar-like effect; a new kind of percussive *pizzicato* in which the string is plucked with such force that it rebounds off the fingerboard producing a snapping sound; and lastly, quarter-tones in the *Burletta* of No. 6, employed with the (apparently) satirical intention of suggesting 'out of tune' playing.[6] But we must add that Bartók shows himself fully aware of the fact that the effect of such special contrivances is in inverse ratio to the frequency of their use, and, on the whole, he resorts to them with circumspection and a fine ear for their fitness in the context.

In the following pages no elaborate analysis is attempted (which would be impossible in the space at my disposal) but merely a more detailed description of salient points of the form and other aspects of each quartet. If my personal experience be any guide to the student who is making his first acquaintance with these quartets, he should pause to reflect that even the most detailed analysis will fulfil its purpose only if that which is first grasped by the intellect, eventually becomes an imaginative experience. To reach this point, close study must go hand in hand with a realisation of the actual sound: and the inner ear ought to be assisted by frequent hearings of this great yet certainly difficult and in some respects esoteric music, in live and recorded performance. Only then will it gradually yield its full meaning, scope, and wonderful inner coherence.

First Quartet, Op. 7
Lento–Allegretto–Allegro vivace

The First Quartet bears eloquent witness to a young mind at once powerful and ardent in expression and resourceful in form and technique. Yet in the light of the composer's later development it is only natural that we should find it uncharacteristic and immature in several respects. The texture is thick, often overcrowded with thematic tissues, there is insufficient 'air' in it; and in the second and third movements one cannot help the impression that Bartók's youthful impulses ran away with his formal discipline. (In later years he criticised this quartet for its lack of economy). It is a romantic work—intensely so. Curiously enough, while in the immediately

[6] Characteristic passages in which these devices occur will be cited in the more detailed discussion of the quartets.

preceding Fourteen Bagatelles, Op. 6, and the Ten Easy Piano Pieces the composer had cast off the spell of the German romantics, in the First Quartet the influence of Wagner and Brahms is still potent. Both melody and harmony are saturated in Wagnerian chromaticism (which must be distinguished from Bartók's later 'diatonicised' chromaticism), as may be seen from the opening theme of the *Lento*. It bears an almost twelve-note appearance, and its un-Bartókian, expansive tortuous line recalls Brahms:

Ex. 1

This is stated in the form of a fugato, and it may well be that the opening *Adagio* fugue of Beethoven's Quartet in C Sharp Minor, Op. 131, was at the back of Bartók's mind when he conceived this beginning. Here and there also Debussy's influence makes itself felt, viz. the whole-tone passages in the *Allegretto*, p. 11, after [9], and at the end of the Finale; and the *Lento* contains a passage (p. 6, at [9]) which bears a strong textural resemblance to a passage occurring in the first movement of Debussy's Quartet (p. 2, bar 17 *et seq.*), in that an expressive cello theme is being set against fast-moving chords in parallel progression.

In point of style No. 1 cannot be said to be fully integrated. There is, indeed, a marked cleavage to be noted between the first two movements on the one hand, and the last on the other. The Finale is undoubtedly the most Bartókian of the three, for here we hear the first unmistakable echoes from his growing absorption in Magyar folk music. (His researches in this field began in 1905, three years before the composition of the First Quartet.) Already the Introduction shows characteristic features: a division into *tempo giusto* (upper strings) and *rubato-parlando* (cello recitative), a stamping percussive rhythm, and, in the melody, an emphasis on the Magyar fourth. The *Allegro* proper opens with those obstinate note-repetitions in grating seconds which Bartók later often uses as a kind of ritornel to set off the various sections of his dance-like movements. Similarly, the chief thematic material of the movement proclaims a native flavour: the first theme, in its marked rhythm and syncopations (2*a*); the lyrical second, in its pentatonic steps (2*b*)[7], and the fugue subject (derived from (*a*), in the ornamental triplet 'kink' (2*c*):

Ex. 2

a)

b)

c)

Although we are still far from the 'barbaric' quality of Bartók's later style, the rhythmic drive of this movement is considerable and here and there we already find those percussive triple and quadruple stops which will increasingly occur, as we progress in the quartet series (pp. 32, 33 and at the very end).

The form of the First Quartet is uncommon. Instead of the traditional *Allegro* in sonata form, the opening movement is a rhapsodic *Lento* in a simple A–B–A. With the two succeeding movements, which are both sonata movements, the tempo quickens progressively from *Allegretto* to *Allegro vivace* and thus the whole quartet is given a firm sense of direction toward an agogic (tempo) climax. Overall unity is achieved by the ubiquitous presence of a semitonal *appoggiatura* motif while the main subject of the Finale (2*a*) stems from an accompanying *ostinato* in the preceding *Scherzo*:

[7] It has a family likeness to the beautiful cantabile theme in the first movement of No. 6, composed thirty-one years later (see Ex. 20).

Ex. 3

The first and second movements are also linked by a short transitional figure in thirds, which leads, without a break, from the end of the *Lento* (viola and cello) into the somewhat Brahmsian *Scherzo* introduction. The recapitulation of both these movements already shows the young Bartók's concern with a greatly varied repeat, notably in the remarkable compression and modification of the *Scherzo* reprise. The key of the First Quartet is A minor, though it opens in something like F minor.

Second Quartet, Op. 17
Moderato–Allegro molto capriccioso–Lento

During the period of nine years, which lie between the completion of the First and the Second Quartets, Bartók reached his first maturity. He became increasingly engrossed in the collection and study of folk music, the direct fruit of which were various settings of Magyar and Rumanian songs and dances; he had composed such large-scale works as the opera *Duke Bluebeard's Castle* and the ballet *The Wooden Prince*, and written the famous *Allegro Barbaro* which marked, so far as his piano music was concerned, his first wholly individual and characteristic work. The Second Quartet occupies the same position in his chamber music. It may be said to contain the essential features of his subsequent quartet style—partly fully developed, partly in embryonic form. If it looks backwards at all, it is in the romantic feeling of the first and last movements, but Bartók's romanticism has now shed the strong emotional colour of the First Quartet. It is restrained, subdued, more inward, though moments of impassioned outbursts are not absent.

In point of style the Second Quartet is a fully integrated work. True, in the first movement we still hear a Debussyian echo in the organum-like progressions of perfect fifth (p. 8 at [9]), and occasionally Bartók's harmonic experiments are too obviously contrived, as witness, in the Finale, the too-frequent use of 'false relations' and fourth-chords. But these, if anything, are very minor blemishes in a work otherwise so homogeneous, rounded, and poetic in utterance. Moreover, the assimilation of features of Magyar folk music is here complete. And although Bartók's harmonic idiom has considerably gained in pungency since the First Quartet—the opening of the Finale, for example, constitutes a little study in clashing major and minor seconds—on the whole the composer appears anxious to tone down such harshnesses by a careful choice of layout, dynamics, and scoring. Thus, in the bitonal passage of the first movement (p. 17, Tempo I) the clash between C in the treble and C sharp in the bass is hardly perceptible, owing to the *pp pizzicato* of the cello; and in the Finale the *con sordino* serves to mollify the grating effect of the opening seconds, apart from lending the whole movement a veiled, mysterious colour. Altogether, the relative euphony and marked melodiousness of No. 2 makes it, perhaps, the most immediately attractive of the series.

Again, the form shows a departure from the norm: three movements, of which the last is a *Lento*, the order of the First Quartet being here almost reversed. And again thematic cross-references are established, the first and last movement being linked by the figure *x*, which opens the first subject of the *Moderato* and in rhythmic augmentation pervades the *Lento*:

Ex. 4

a) 

b) 

The *Moderato* is a movement of great lyrical beauty proclaiming its marked *cantabile* character in such themes as the expansive second subject. Beginning with an expressive violin theme (p. 5, [5]) it proliferates into passionate, truly Bartókian phrases which are marked by Magyar triplets. (This ornamental figure is anticipated in the first subject.) And the nostalgic coda (p. 17, Tempo I), which establishes a clear A major-minor, is sheer poetry.

The ensuing movement fully bears out its title *Allegro molto capriccioso*. It may best be described as a series of capricious Magyar-inspired dances, written in a vein of which the *Allegro Barbaro* is so characteristic an example. In all such movements an almost savage rhythmic drive sweeps everything before it. The music derives a further impetus from the conflict between a major and minor third, D–F sharp–F natural, a conflict which ends with the assertion of the minor interval. The seed of this struggle lies in one of Bartók's *Ur*-motifs or basic motifs (figure *x*) which generates the movement's main theme, a rocking dance-like phrase, with augmented seconds and Magyar ornamentation in its tail; it is also possible to see in this theme an influence from Arabic music, viz. the repeated small intervals on the 1st violin and the percussive octaves on the viola. (In 1913 Bartók visited the Bay of Biskra to study Arabic folk music):

Ex. 5

Technically speaking, the whole movement may be said to be 'about' the critical interval which for our Western ears decides the fundamental difference between major and minor. It is worth noting that in one of the pieces of his later *Microcosmos* (Vol. IV, No. 108) Bartók dealt with the same problem, giving this study the significant title *Wrestling*.

The form of this movement is highly interesting: a *rondo* in which most of the episodes are variations of Ex. 5; moreover, the seven-bar introduction not only serves to set off a number of episodes but turns itself into an episode (p. 24, [11], and p. 30, [22]). The thematic economy of this movement is indeed most remarkable, and as an illustration of the immense plasticity of Bartók's variation technique the passage on p. 25, [13], may be cited in which the introduction is so transformed as to be almost unrecognisable.

The muted coda is a brilliant piece of string writing, tearing along in *Prestissimo* and producing a strange effect in its heterophonic character.

If the *Allegro* is a dynamic extrovert piece, the following *Lento* is static and highly introspective in the bleakness of its opening, which almost conjures up the desolation of a lunar landscape. In mood it seems to be prophetic of the melancholy Finale of the Sixth Quartet of twenty-two years later. Except for brief impassioned moments, the music is subdued to the point of almost motionless tranquillity. Impressionist and Magyar elements commingle in a highly original manner. Note, for example, the alternative 'high' and 'low' in the scoring of the opening, and the etiolated colour produced by the muted strings. At first there is no theme but merely wisps of a melody, and not until p. 48, [4], does the music really crystallise into a sustained coherent phrase, a broad folksong-like theme moving in (chiefly) pentatonic steps and harmonised in fourth-chords. Mention has already been made of the fact that this movement seems to reproduce the chain-like sequence of unrelated sections peculiar to Magyar peasant music: there are four parts with their own material: *Lento—Un poco più andante—Lento assai—Tempo I*. The coda p. 50, *Lento assai*, briefly reviews the whole movement at the same time reorganising the thematic material.

Third Quartet
Prima parte—Seconda parte—Ricapitulazione della prima parte—Coda

During the ten years which separate the Second from the Third Quartet, Bartók's development moved toward a *ne plus ultra* of concentration and subtilisation. It is Bartók's expressionist period represented by such works as the two Violin Sonatas, the Piano Sonata, and the First Piano Concerto—works that show him at the height of his intellectual modernism. This is the 'difficult' Bartók of whom all his commentators speak—elliptic, elusive, enigmatic, uncompromising, and harsh to the point of aggressiveness. Like the expressionist Schönberg, the Bartók of the years between 1922–7 appears almost exclusively concerned with the projection of an inner world in which the frontier dividing the conscious and rational from the unconscious and irrational is practically non-existent. The music of this period takes on a significance at once private, symbolic, and arcane. Not unlike the Beethoven of the late quartets and piano sonatas, Bartók here seems to be communing with himself rather than attempting communication with the outside world. It is for this reason that the Third Quartet is the least accessible of the six, making extraordinary demands on our perceptive and imaginative powers. Yet it is no less a masterpiece than the others and differs from them only in that its aesthetic and intellectual premises are more difficult to apprehend.

With a composer of Bartók's type concentration of form goes hand in hand with an intensification of expression. The Third Quartet is, thus, the most concentrated and intense of the series. It is in one movement yet divided into four sections which follow each other in the simple pattern Slow—Fast—Slow—Fast. Thematically they are related in a manner which may be illustrated by two interlocking spans:

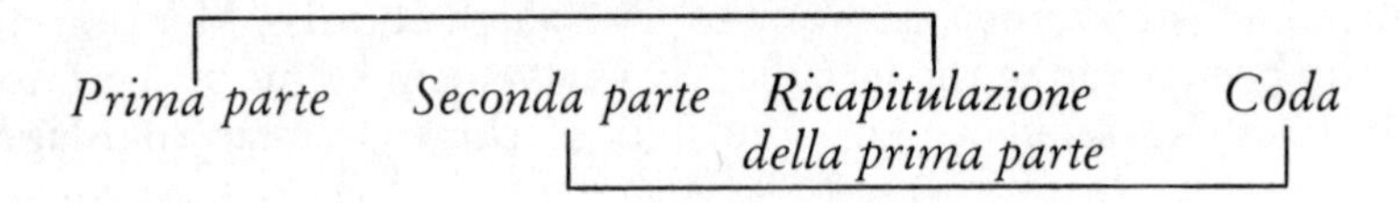

In the following analysis the sections will be taken according to their thematic correspondences and not their actual order of sequence. The First Part constitutes a supreme example of Bartók's technique of developing virtually the whole of a movement from a single germ-cell. Here the *Ur*-motif is a simple pentatonic figure consisting of a rising fourth and a falling minor third. We first hear it at the beginning of the opening theme (after five curtain-like introductory bars):

Ex. 6

(This theme, incidentally, is stated in the form of a free canon.) The immense power of regeneration which lies in figure *x* can be seen from these three examples:

Ex. 7

The First Part is in three sections, the middle one of which recalls, in its fragmentary texture and subdued dynamics, Bartók's 'night music' style. Although it introduces new material, not derived from the basic motif, the bitonal bass reiterates figure *x* in *ostinato* fashion. The development (starting p. 6, [7]) is punctuated by savagely percussive double and triple stops for all four strings which by their simple homophony achieve a dramatic contrast with the surrounding contrapuntal texture. In the repeat of the first section (p. 7, [11]) Bartók introduces the 'real' theme of the movement, a broad swaying tune of Magyar flavour which grows out of the first three notes:

Ex. 8

The suggestion may be ventured that the theme, or at any rate its first three bars, was perhaps Bartók's initial idea, and that instead of stating it at the very beginning (as most composers might have done) he seized upon its most characteristic motif and evolved from it the best part of the movement before showing us in Ex. 8 the purest and at once most beautiful manifestation of the *Ur*-motif's generative power.[8]

The recapitulation of the First Part compresses the material to such an extent that sometimes a few bars have to do duty for perhaps a dozen bars of the exposition. This last section has seventy bars, as against 122 of the first section. Moreover, by means of most subtle transformations, Bartók achieves the effect of psychological rather than physical return to the First Part. He has perhaps never written music more fascinating in its elliptic and recondite allusions than this *Ricapitulazione*.

The Second Part yields to our understanding more readily. With its relentless forward-driving rhythm, its percussive chords, syncopations, and *glissandi*, it clearly springs from the soil of native dances. The form is that of Variation-cum-Sonata-form. Here is the variation theme, a folk-dance-like tune harmonised in 'primitive' parallel triads:

[8] There is a certain parallel here with Sibelius's method of gradually assembling a symphonic theme from previous particles.

Ex. 9

No sooner has it been stated than it throws off a brief semi-quaver motif, Ex. 9*b*, which is already a kind of variation retracing the theme's characteristic dome-shaped outline in rhythmic diminution. It is actually this motif which provides the basis for the ensuing variations, to which Ex. 9*a*, also varied, furnishes the bass. While the melodic pattern undergoes relatively minor changes, there are frequent alterations of the rhythmic units (2/4, 3/4, 6/8, 5/8, and 3/8). On p. 13, a bar before [10], cello and viola introduce the 'second subject' in the form of another variation, characterised by syncopations, whole-tone progressions, and descending fourths:

Ex. 10

The treatment of this theme is largely in imitation and *stretto*. The development (beginning p. 17, Tempo I) deals with both 'subjects', contains such special sound effects as *col legno* and *sulla tastiera*, and finally culminates in a light-fingered fugue whose subject derives from Ex. 9*b* (p.20, [31]). Imperceptibly, the fugue leads into the recapitulation, when the variation theme is at once stated in canon while the second subject appears both in diatonic and chromatic versions (p. 24, at [38] and [40]). There is a short reference to the *martellato* passage of the First Part which presently returns in the much altered version of which we have already spoken.

The Coda is nothing else but the transformed reprise of the Second Part. The pace is increased from *Allegro* to *Allegro molto*, the basic metre changed from 2/4 to 3/8, the contrapuntal texture becomes denser, canon and inversions in *stretto* predominate, and towards the end the aggressive character of the music is greatly heightened by obstinate note-reiterations, incessant motif repetitions, double-stop *glissandi* and up-and-down arpeggios. The movement concludes on a chord of three superimposed fifths based on C sharp, which represents the 'key' of the Third Quartet. Bartók's free conception of tonality during his expressionist period may be seen from the fact that, apart from the very opening and a brief passage in the First Part, C sharp is not in evidence again until the last few bars.

Fourth Quartet

Allegro—Prestissimo con sordino—Non troppo lento—Allegretto pizzicato—Allegro molto

In the Third Quartet Bartók advanced furthest in the direction of intellectual severity, uncompromising harshness of emotional expression, and formal experimentation. The Fourth, written a year later, marks a certain retreat from the 'exposed position' taken up in the preceding work though the first movement still has some hard things to say. Not that his style shows an intrinsic change. We still find a (predominantly) linear counterpoint, a predilection for scholastic devices, pungent discords, ferocious rhythmic drive (Finale), and special sound effects. Yet the new gains acquired in the Third Quartet are now seen to be in the process of consolidation on a broader formal basis, and such movements as the wonderful elegy of the third and the delightful serenade of the fourth suggest a mind of more mellow humanity and more accessible to gentler, more relaxed moods.

Nevertheless, the quest for creating overall unity and correspondences between movements by novel means continues. Thus the five movements, of which the Fourth Quartet consists, are conceived in the so-called arch form A–B–C–B–A, in which the two outward and the two inner movements, respectively, mirror each other, while the central piece C stands by itself. In a sense, the music progresses from A to C and then retraces its step.[9] Correspondences between the four movements are not merely thematic but are also felt in the form and character of the music:

Allegro—Prestissimo—Non troppo lento—Allegretto—Allegro molto

[9] Gerald Abraham has made the interesting suggestion that the arch form may have been suggested to Bartók by Alfred Lorenz's book, *Geheimnis der Form bei Richard Wagner*, which appeared in 1924. (See 'The Bartók of the Quartets', *Music and Letters*, October 1945). Yet it is also possible that Bartók derived it from Alban Berg who employed the arch form on a smaller scale in the second movement of his *Chamber Concerto* (1925) and in the third movement of the *Lyric Suite* (1926).

As in the Third Quartet, it will be more expedient for our purpose not to follow the actual order of the movements, but to take the corresponding pairs together. The first and last movements—in sonata and ternary form, respectively—derive their complete material from a single germ-cell of six notes which is concealed in the seventh bar of the *Allegro's* opening subject (Ex. 11*a*):

Ex. 11

What an unpromising idea it looks! It is the measure of Bartók's structural thinking that from it he evolves a well-nigh inexhaustible fund of seemingly new motifs of which I quote some important ones from both movements (see above). Yet it would, I believe, be extremely hard to detect the relation between Ex. 11*a* and *f*, without hearing the intervening stages of this metamorphosis. As one of Bartók's American biographers aptly remarked, it is because the composer allows us to share his thought-processes rather than leaping from the basic motif to its furthest transformation, that his music carries such logic with it.[10]

The first movement is an abstract piece of music wholly concerned with problems of form, design, and texture. It provides a most rewarding study of Bartók's monocystic motif-development. Not a single phrase is to be found which has not grown, in one way or another, from the simple six-note motif. And as though the composer wanted to press home its fundamental importance, he closes the movement with Ex. 11*a*, *pesante* and doubled in three octaves. Although this *Allegro* represents one long and continuous development, the traditional four 'sonata form' sections can be clearly

[10] *The Life and Music of Béla Bartók*, by Halsey Stevens, rev. ed. (New York, 1964).

discerned: exposition, up to bar 49, development proper to bar 92, recapitulation to bar 126 (but slightly reversed, with the basic motif now preceding the opening theme), and coda.

The corresponding fifth movement evokes the atmosphere of a ferocious Magyar dance. The introduction with its stamping triple and quadruple stops, widely spaced and using open strings, completely breaks the framework of the string quartet medium and produces a most resonant orchestral sonority. Again, the main theme (Ex. 11*d*) is set against a throbbing percussive accompaniment punctuated by *sf* chords which create an exciting cross-rhythm (3/8 and 2/8 versus the basic 2/4 (or 4/8)). By contrast, the middle section (beginning p. 52, bar 152) is deliciously airy and graceful, with crisp mordents and guitar-like arpeggios on all four open strings (second violin and cello). As in the first movement, the recapitulation (beginning p. 57, bar 238) opens with a slight reversion of the material, the main theme now preceding the introduction. In order to fashion the link between first and last movements still firmer, Bartók reintroduces, in the coda of the Finale, the few final bars of the *Allegro*, and again closes with the *pesante* version of the germ cell. Both movements are 'on' C, though tonality here is more clearly defined in the Third Quartet.

The correspondence between the second and fourth movements is on several levels. Both are light-weight *scherzi*, both are played throughout in a special manner, *con sordino* the *Prestissimo*, *pizzicato* the *Allegretto*, and both share the same thematic material:

Ex. 12

a)

b)

c)

d)

(*c*) represents the diatonic extension of the involuted chromatic (*a*), while the identical changing-note motifs (*b*) and (*d*) are free inversions of a figure in the tail of (*a*). Yet this is not all. One is tempted to assume that (*a*) is itself a variant of the chromatic *Ur*-motif Ex. 11*a*, so that in the last analysis not only the two outward movements but also the two inner ones appear to have sprung from the same germinal idea.

Though the *Prestissimo* and the *Allegretto* are, as has been said, *scherzo* movements, there is a marked contrast of mood between them. The one may be described as a *perpetuo mobile* to which the muted strings lend a strange shimmer, not unlike that of the *Allegro misterioso* of Berg's *Lyric Suite*; while the delicate guitar-like accompaniment of the other conjures up the intimate atmosphere of a serenade. It is here that Bartók first uses the 'snap' *pizzicato*.

In this dynamic quartet the only point of repose is provided by the expressive lyricism of the slow central movement. Its form is a simple A–B–A plus coda. Section A is introduced by a sustained chord, *pp*, first *non vibrato*, then *vibrato*. This forms a most delicate harmonic background for a wistful cello recitative of Magyar character: melismatic embellishments, syncopations, and drooping fourths and fifths. There are three 'verses' of it, each beginning in a new key.[11] This kind of grave melody is said to be peculiar to the music of the *tárogató*, a woodwind instrument of ancient (Eastern) origin, whose dark colour is somewhat akin to that of our clarinet.[12]

The middle section (beginning p. 33, bar 34) is an exquisite atmospheric study evoking the mysterious sound of nocturnal nature. The extent to which Bartók developed a personal impressionist style, may be seen from an instructive comparison of this and other examples of his 'night music', with Debussy's *Les sons et les parfums tournant dans l'air du soir*, the fourth piece in Book I of the Piano Preludes.

Lendvai's calculation of the Golden Section for the first three movements is as follows:

1st Mvt. The exposition clearly shows the proportions of GS. Its total length is 48 bars; the second subject enters in bar 30 which figure represents the geometrical mean between the whole and the smaller part. Accordingly the proportions are 48:30:18.

2nd Mvt. The ratio between scherzo and trio is the precise GS the proportions of which are 188:116:72.

3rd Mvt. The structure of this slow movement reflects the pro-

[11] The opening theme of the *Allegretto* is stated in a similar manner: four entries in successively rising fifths (A flat–E flat–B flat–F).

[12] Originally it possessed a double reed, but Bartók must have heard its more modern, single-reed version.

portions of GS as expressed in the so-called Fibonacci series, a number sequence in which every number is equal to the sum of the two preceding numbers:

2-3-5-8-13-21-34-55 etc.

Three consecutive numbers contain the proportion of GS, with the geometrical mean in the second number:

5-bar introduction
1st entry of *8*-bar theme up to bar *13*
2nd entry up to bar *21*
3rd entry up to bar *34*
4th entry up to bar *55*

According to Lendvai, the recapitulation is static—hence the symmetrical 8 + 8 structure. It is true that this last section has the marking 'Tranquillo', but the interplay of the original theme (cello) with its inversion (1st violin) seems to me to introduce a far from static element into the music.

Fifth Quartet

Allegro—Adagio molto—Scherzo—Andante—Finale: Allegro vivace

The Fifth Quartet followed the Fourth after an interval of six years, yet in general style and form it stands far closer to its immediate predecessor than the latter stands to the Third Quartet, from which, we recall, it is separated by one year only. Intrinsically, the Fourth and Fifth Quartets are sister works, they form a pair, the chief difference between them lying in the fact that the later work carries the process of intellectual relaxation and lyrical expansion another stage further. Significantly enough, we now have two slow movements (while No. 4 had only one), the melodic lines have become ampler and the harmonies on the whole less astringent.

But the formal organisation is the same as in No. 4: again the arch form A–B–C–B–A, yet C is now a *Scherzo* flanked by two slow movements, in which Bartók reaches a new height of evocative lyrical poetry.

Let us again consider the related movements in conjunction. The opening *Allegro* and the Finale are both in sonata form, both are 'on' B flat, and both share some of the material. Their thematic correspondence may be seen from a comparison of their first subjects. That of the *Allegro* consists of three distinct ideas, while that of the Finale is essentially a simple scale figure within the range of a tritone:

Ex. 13

The connection between the two subjects is a remarkably subtle one: the repeated B flat of (*a*) corresponds to the repeated E of (*d*) (with Bartók tritone relations often assume the function of the classical tonic-dominant); similarly, the ascent in (*b*), from B flat to E, is mirrored in (*d*) in the descent from E to B flat, and the chromatic 'kink' *x* of (*b*) appears inverted in (*d*). In other words, the main subject of the Finale represents a free inversion of part of the first movement's opening theme.

As for the second subjects of the two movements, they too derive from the *Allegro*'s main theme:

Ex 14

(*a*) is a free version of Ex. 13*c*, while (*b*) suggests a variant of the chromatic 'kink' *x*.

In the first movement such subtle relations extend also to seemingly unconnected ideas as at [A] and [B], which contain tissues stemming from the opening theme, in particular figure *x*. Essentially, it is the same monocystic development as we noted in the first movement of No. 4; but as a sign of Bartók's advance towards a more clear-cut melodic articulation, we find here the thematic material so moulded as to produce more differentiated, readily recognisable shapes. Thus we can speak again of themes in the more established sense of the term, themes whose contrasting character clearly sets them off from each other: there is the percussive first subject (stated in canon); there is the dance-like transitional theme at [B], with its wide leaping intervals, and changing cross-rhythms which produce a rhythmic 'canon' between treble and bass; and there is the gently undulating lyrical line of the second subject, at [C]. Moreover, a clear sense of tonality is felt in the individual themes as well as in the movement as a whole, and the beginnings of the three sonata sections show a simple quasi-classical pattern: tonic: B flat—'dominant': E (tritone again!)—tonic: B flat. The recapitulation (beginning at [F]) represents a clearly recognisable return of the exposition yet with a characteristic modification. The order in which the themes appear in the exposition is now largely reversed and, in addition, all are reintroduced in their inverted versions. In other words the recapitulation represents the 'mirror' of the exposition.

The Finale is, broadly speaking, similarly organised. In character it belongs to Bartók's 'motoric' or *perpetuo mobile* movements. Of a predominantly polyphonic texture, it abounds in inversions, canons, *stretti*, and passages in reversible counterpoint. The development centres on a fugue (beginning p. 75, bar 369) whose subject derives from the first movement's opening theme:

Ex. 15

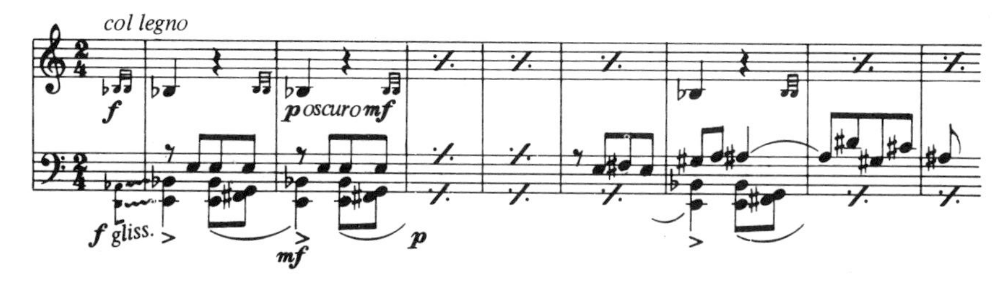

It is a most uncommon fugue. The subject has the marking *oscuro* and is at once stated against a purely harmonic (colouristic) background: percussive note-reiteration on the two violins, *col legno*, and a drone-like ostinato on the cello. The whole fugue constitutes an illuminating examle of the meeting of East and West in Bartók's music.

Uncommon in a different sense is a brief episode, marked *Allegretto con indifferenza*, in the coda, p. 88: a trivial tune in a clear A major and harmonised in *cliché* fashion with alternating tonic and dominant, to be played *meccanico.* The whole passage produces the effect of barrel-organ music. One is here strongly reminded of Mahler's deliberate use, in his symphonies, of trite tunes to suggest mundane, commonplace aspects of life. Bartók's strange episode is like a sudden grimace, an ironic sneer—an impression heightened by the strident dissonances produced by the bitonal passage (A major against B flat major, bars 711–720).[13]

Like the first and last movements, the *Adagio* and the *Andante* share the same ground plan, A–B–A plus coda, and some of the material. Both open in an atmospheric manner, the fragmentary motifs and trills of the one corresponding to the repeated *pizzicato* notes, slurs and *gruppetti* of the other. Then the music gains substance leading to a middle section based on a Magyar-inspired theme of serene lyrical expression (Ex. 16*a*), which the *Andante* presents in a beautifully expanded version (Ex. 16*b*). Note the perfect balance between the two halves of this theme, the second half representing a free and embellished inversion of the first:

Ex. 16

Both movements contain a chorale, the *Adagio* at [A] and the *Andante* at [D]—a feature almost invariably associated with Bartók's 'night music' (see, for example, the respective slow movements of the Second and Third Piano Concertos).

The *Andante*, which is the more extended piece, develops Ex. 16*b* in an impassioned ecstatic section (p. 53, *Più mosso, agitato*) to which the 'cry' of a leaping minor third adds a poignant accent.[14] This remarkable

[13] The Finale of the Viola Concerto contains a passage of similar triviality, also in A major and extended over more than fifty bars.

[14] The same motif occurs in the slow movement of the Viola Concerto where it is marked *piangendo*.

movement ends mysteriously on a cello passage of plucked triple-stops linked by *glissandi*.

The central movement is a most engaging *Scherzo* in *alla Bulgarese* rhythm, for which Bartók evinced a predilection in his later period (see the last six pieces of his *Microcosmos* and the Trio of the third movement of his *Contrasts*). The asymmetrical pattern of the *Scherzo* proper is $\frac{4+2+3}{8}$. There are three sections, the first of which is marked by fleeting figures (mostly in up-and-down arpeggio). In the second section they form the delicate background for a sprightly theme of folk dance character (Ex. 17*a*, below).

The Trio is cast in a more complex 'Bulgarian' rhythm, the initial pattern $\frac{3+2+2+3}{8}$ alternating with $\frac{2+3+2+3}{8}$ and $\frac{2+3+3+2}{8}$. The string writing here represents a real *trouvaille*. The first violin, *pp* and muted, traces out a delicate arabesque consisting of a ten-note ostinato which is repeated (in several transpositions) no less than sixty times. This lends the movement a sense of feverish excitement which reaches its highest pitch on p. 38, *accelerando*, when the second violin adds the 'mirror' version of the *ostinato*, and the viola, a few bars later, doubles the treble and ninth an octave lower, *ff*. Before and after this climax the string texture is of a shimmering diaphanous quality and into it Bartók weaves an enchanting melody which seems in the vein of a (Magyar?) children's song (Ex. 17*b*):

Ex. 17

Sixth Quartet

Vivace—Marcia—Burletta—Mesto

With the Sixth Quartet, written five years after the Fifth, we reach the 'classical' Bartók, the Bartók of such works as the Music for Strings, Piano and Percussion, the Violin Concerto, and the Divertimento for

Strings. The chief characteristics of this period are: a relatively greater simplicity of form and technical devices, themes of a more sustained, broader nature, harmonies of lesser harshness, a sharper tonal perspective, and greater transparency of texture. So far as the quartets are concerned, these changes, which first began to show in No. 4, reached their culmination point in No. 6. It is significant that in No. 6 Bartók reverts to the classical scheme of four contrasting movements and uses a simpler, less intellectual device than the arch form, in order to achieve an overall formal unity—a *ritornello* or motto-theme. This theme is a sad, mournful viola melody with a marked drooping tendency, most beautifully shaped and balanced and, like the variation theme of the Violin Concerto, an exquisite example of the perfect fusion of the melodic and rhythmic inflexions of Magyar music with Bartók's personal manner:

Ex. 18

As already intimated, the motto as such was a favourite device of the romantics but Bartók applies it in a novel manner. Ex. 18 prefaces each of the first three movements but on each occasion in a different setting and scoring (viola; violincello; 1st violin) and with increasing length (13 bars; 17 bars; 20 bars). In the finale the *ritornello* extends to 45 bars and determines the character of the whole movement. Instead of serving as a device for 'rubber-stamping' the different movements (as we find in Liszt and Tchaikovsky) Bartók achieves an organic integration with the main body of the music. Moreover, the codetta of the first movement (p. 4, *Vivacissimo, agitato*) appears to derive from the opening motif of Ex. 18, while the theme of the *Marcia* seems to stem from bars 5/6 of the motto.

The opening of the first movement proper echoes the beginning of Beethoven's *Grosse Fuge*, Op. 133, in that the first subject is anticipated in the last eight bars of the *pesante* introduction, in rhythmic augmentation, before appearing in its 'true' form:

Ex. 19

The remarkable transformations which this theme undergoes in the course of the movement is yet another illustration of Bartók's art of continuous progressive development. And for a most instructive example of his variation technique, I refer the student to the passage (p. 4, bars 81–99) where Bartók follows up the statement of the lovely Magyar-inspired second subject (Ex. 20) with two successive variations (second violin—viola).

Ex. 20

Two other features worth noting are the almost classical manner with which the three main sections of this sonata movement are set off from each other, and the clear sense of tonality which is a Bartókian D major-minor. If the general mood of the music is exuberant, even gay, this suffers a complete reversal in the following three movements.

The ensuing *Marcia* is harsh, aggressive music through which a fanfare (p. 21, beginning at bar 59) cuts like a sharp knife. (The march theme shows a family likeness to the *Verbunkos* of *Contrasts*, written a year before the Sixth Quartet.)

The Trio is in *rubato* style, with agitated *tremoli* on the violins and strummed, guitar-like chords on the viola. Against this nervously excited accompaniment is set a high-lying passionate cello recitative, marked by a restless succession of minor thirds later, and *glissandi*. (This recitative represents an excellent example in stylised form of the so-called *doină* or *horă lungă*, which is an important branch of Rumanian folksong in the regions of Maramures and Ugocsa. Its characteristic features—*parlando-rubato* passages, chant-like, incantatory repetitions of the same note, and frequent use of downward thirds—are all to be found in the Bartók melody.) A polytonal *cadenza* for all four instruments leads to the recapitulation of the March which is now greatly changed, some of its material being inverted.

Somewhat related to the mood of the *Marcia* is the grim, sardonic humour of the *Burletta*. Its harmonic, rhythmic, and dynamic ferocity recalls the Bartók of the expressionist period. Grating discords, fiercely percussive chords 'at the heel', much down-bow playing, *glissandi*, and slurs lend this movement its 'barbaric' quality. Moreover, the quarter-notes of the first violin played against the 'true' notes of the second violin (bars 26 *et seq.*) create a deliberate 'out of tune' effect.

Relief is introduced by the wistful lyrical middle section, an *Andantino*, whose two ideas are freely derived from the first movement's two subjects: both are free inversions of Exx. 19 and 20, respectively, and are themselves linked by almost identical cadential figures (*x*) in the tail end:

Ex. 21

The repeat of the first section shows interesting modifications: the opening in *pizzicato* (some of it of Bartók's 'snap' variety), the addition of a new triplet motif with a skipping fourth in its tail, and a singularly dramatic effect in the coda (p. 40, bar 135 *et seq.*) where Ex. 21*b* makes three vain attempts to break the mood of this savage burlesque.

So far, the motto has played an all but preludial part in the work. In the Finale it becomes the generating theme of the whole movement revealing its full emotional significance in the poignant sadness of this *Mesto*. And when on p. 44, bar 46 *et seq.*, the two subjects from the gay first movement are recalled *p, molto tranquillo*, the second of which is to be played *più dolce, lontano,* it inevitably calls to mind Dante's *Nessun maggior dolore che ricordarsi del tempo felice nella miseria* ('There is no greater sorrow than to recall the time of happiness in misery'). There is a sinister shudder in the *tremolo* chords, *sul ponticello*, on the last page, and after a last heartrending cry, the movement closes in darkness, on the dying motto.

Considering the extraordinary nature of what was to be Bartók's swan-song as a quartet writer, one cannot resist the feeling that the work possesses a poetic, extra-musical significance—perhaps even a 'programme'. There is the peculiar use of the motto—an *idée fixe*, three times rejected until at last it is accepted, there is the melancholy character of the motto itself, there is the brief dramatic interlude in the *Burletta*, there are those wistful reminiscences from 'the time of happiness' in the finale, and there is the bitter irony of the two middle movements and the sombre introspection of the *Mesto*. A sense of profound personal tragedy seems to emanate from it all. Perhaps a clue to it is to be sought in the fact that Bartók completed the quartet when the conflagration in Europe had already broken out. He was then in Budapest and may well have experienced a feeling of despair and spiritual isolation, if not frustration. We do not know. Yet the work suggests with an almost aching poignancy some such state of mind which the composer may well have consciously depicted in the music. At any rate, No. 6 is the only one among his mature quartets in which we have the clear impression that strong subjective emotions press to the surface with uncommon insistence.

FOURTEEN

THE MASS FROM ROSSINI TO DVOŘÁK

THEORISTS HAVE OFTEN discussed whether there exists in reality such a thing as a musical style which is definitely ecclesiastical, or whether it is not a mere question of convention and the association of ideas. The problem is not an easy one to decide. During the nineteenth century most composers of the front rank devoted themselves—with the exception of Bruckner, and he only during his earlier period—to secular music and only occasionally wrote a work for the church. Symphony and opera, concerto and chamber music—these were the principal fields in which such musicians worked; if they turned their attention to a Mass or a Requiem, it was wholly natural that they should treat these works in a style closely related to, if not indeed identical with, their customary manner, except that counterpoint played a more conspicuous part.

Of course the nature of the text asked for emotional restraint, for the replacement of subjective romantic feelings by a more impersonal objective attitude; but in France and Italy this was the case more in theory than in actual practice. Berlioz's Requiem can certainly not be held up as a paragon of how to write in an ecclesiastical style. Rossini's Mass (*Petite Messe Solennelle*) and Verdi's Requiem admittedly contain sections where a comparative restraint has been practised, but it is evident that the two masters approached the text from a quasi-operatic angle, treating it with a dramatic conception that goes beyond what listeners in northern Europe and America may find appropriate to the setting of a religious work. But it is just as well to remind ourselves of the fact that it has always been the custom of southern peoples to dramatise their religion, and the Roman Catholic Church in these countries is giving true expression to national tendencies in surrounding its services with the splendour of a stage spectacle. In other words, it is the prerogative of the composer of opera in those lands to make his offering to God in dramatic terms.

In dealing with Gioacchino Rossini (1792–1868) some words will not be found amiss on his *Stabat Mater* of 1842, one of the many settings by composers of the Latin poem about the vigil of Mary by the Cross. This work had a curious history. It was begun in Spain at the request of the Spanish prelate Varela, but on his return to Paris Rossini was seized with a severe attack of lumbago after the composition of the first six numbers. Being continually pestered to deliver the work, he entrusted the remainder to Tadolini, the conductor of the Théâtre Italien in Paris. In 1837 Varela died and his heirs decided to sell the publication rights to a French publisher, Aulagnier. Rossini, however, informed the latter with the utmost firmness that he would do everything in his power to prevent this, since he alone possessed these rights, and sold them to his own publisher, Troupenas. He also revised and completed the work himself. The final fugue was written some time in the summer or autumn of 1841. By then eleven years had passed since Rossini had composed his last opera, *William Tell* (1829).

Rossini modelled his *Stabat Mater* on Pergolesi's. If we approach it as a religious work we shall be disappointed, for it is more secular in spirit than Verdi's Requiem, and in parts unashamedly theatrical. But if it is taken as music pure and simple, then not much fault can be found with it. Admittedly the last four numbers are superior, but there are also delightful things to be found in the first six. The introductory 'Stabat Mater' is perhaps the best of these—an expressive quartet for soli and chorus in G minor which Rossini repeated in the final number. Except for an unfortunate passage in 6-8, the succeeding 'Eia Mater' has an eloquent chorus, and there is much harmonic variety in the ensuing 'Sancta Mater'. But the next number, 'Cuius animam', is a facile operatic aria for the tenor, and the following duet, 'Quis est homo', abounds in sentimental florid writing. Of the last four numbers every one commends itself. There is much tender grace in the *cavatina* 'Fac ut portem', and the 'Inflammatus' impresses by the dramatic cut of the soprano solo which is set against a vivid chorus and reaches up to top C. As for 'Quando corpus morietur', recognised by Rossini himself as one of his most felicitous inspirations and much admired by Wagner, it is a splendid example of unaccompanied four-part writing. Perhaps the most successful number is the final double fugue, with two subjects in complementary rhythm; the first, 'In sempiterna saecula, Amen', has a boldly rising line which is freely imitated in the second fugue, on the word 'Amen'. There are several expositions and *stretto* sections, separated by episodes. Then, after the interpolated repetition of the first number, a mainly chordal coda brings the fugue to its impressive end. The first public performance of the *Stabat Mater* took place at the Salle Ventadour in Paris in January 1842, when it was an unqualified success.

More than twenty years later Rossini wrote the most successful of his sacred works—the *Petite Messe Solennelle*, which in an inscription to God he described as 'the last mortal sin of my old age'. He added: 'Have I written music that is blessed, or just some blessed music? I was born for *opera buffa*, well Thou knowest! Little knowledge and a little heart is all here. Be blest and grant me Paradise.' The idea of writing the work was not, as usually stated, due to a performance of Liszt's Mass in the Church of St Eustache, in Paris. The work had been contemplated by Rossini for some time before, and work on it made him, apparently, moody and irritable. Far from being '*petite*', it is longer than most Masses. The word must either have been a jest or must have referred to its original form, in which the four solo voices and small mixed chorus were given an accompaniment of two pianos and an harmonium only. Rossini later scored it for full orchestra, so as to prevent someone else doing it after his death, but he himself preferred it in the original version.

The Mass is far less operatic in style than the *Stabat Mater* and, although Rossini professed indifference to scholastic ingenuity, it contains contrapuntal sections of masterly skill which can easily stand comparison with Cherubini's Masses. Rossini told his friend, Michotte, that his main ambition in it was to leave a final legacy which might serve as an example of how to write for the voice. Beauty and originality of melody, and audacity of harmony are other characteristics, though the latter is, in Rossini's own words, 'often coated with sugar'.

The Kyrie, in A, contains some of the best ecclesiastical counterpoint—notably in the 'Christe eleison', in C minor, where, at one bar's distance, the choral voices are linked in pairs, bass with alto and tenor with soprano. The Gloria, in F, opens in a jubilant manner, but from 'Et in terra pax', which is chiefly for the four soloists, the mood is subdued. The ensuing 'Gratias agimus tibi' is a tenderly moving trio; the tenor aria in D, 'Domine Deus', smacks perhaps too much of opera but is remarkable for its modulations to distant keys. In the following 'Qui tollis peccata mundi' the two women soloists are given music of tragic nobility to sing; the piece begins in F minor and ends in F major. 'Quoniam tu solus sanctus' is an extended aria in A for the bass soloist, rich in melodic and harmonic beauties. One of the finest things in this Mass is the double fugue 'Cum sancto spiritu' (see example).

Not only is the subject full of character and variety, but the treatment, if somewhat lengthy, is most varied, containing a *smorzando* section, in which counterpoint yields to effective homophonic contrast, and a most imaginative coda.

Ex. 1

The Credo derives its great impact from the combination of the voices with an *ostinato* figure for the piano which is first one bar and then half a bar long. The piece modulates from E through various keys to A flat in which key the soprano solo intones the 'Crucifixus'. Then, after the repeat of the Credo music, there follows the powerful double fugue, 'Et vitam venturi'. With the ensuing 'Religious Prelude' Rossini gave proof that his subscription to the complete works of Bach had not been without its practical use; the piece, which is for organ or piano, is an admirable essay in intricate four-part writing. The Sanctus and Benedictus, which follow each other without interruption, are set for unaccompanied chorus. Rossini then breaks with the authorised text of the Mass by inserting the Latin hymn 'O salutaris hostia' ('O saving victim') which he sets as a contralto aria, notable both for the beauty and length of its phrases and for its modulations. Equally noteworthy is the final chorus with contralto solo in which, combined with an *ostinato*, the Agnus Dei is thrice uttered to the identical melody but different harmony. This is followed by a new and more contrapuntal section, which in the last bars turns to the key of E major.

The Mass was first performed in 1864 at the house of the Countess Pillet-Will in Paris. Leading artists of the Théâtre Italien sang the solo parts, and the chorus was selected by Auber from the best students of the Paris Conservatory.

It was the death of Rossini in 1868 that gave Giuseppe Verdi (1813-1901) the idea of proposing that a Requiem Mass should be written by leading Italian composers in collaboration to be performed on the next anniversary of Rossini's death in the church of San Petronio at Bologna (the town where Rossini had spent his boyhood). The scheme came to nothing—in Verdi's view, because of lack of collaboration on the part of his friend Angelo Mariani, the famous conductor, whom he suspected of resentment because he had not been included among the composers, and, more certainly, because of hostility on the part of Scalaberni, the impresario of the Teatro Comunale at Bologna, who refused to permit his singers and orchestra to take part. The net result was that Verdi was left with his own contribution to the collective Requiem, the 'Libera me' for solo soprano and chorus. Then, in 1873, occurred the death of Alessandro Manzoni, author of the classic Italian novel *I Promessi Sposi* (*The Betrothed*) and one of the very few human beings before whom Verdi bowed his head. Verdi proposed to the mayor of Milan that he should write a Requiem to be performed in the following year, and incorporated in it his contribution to the abortive work in memory of Rossini.

To the smart judgement that the Requiem is 'Verdi's finest opera', the best answer is to be found in what the composer's widow said when commenting on certain adverse criticisms that had been made of the work. Guiseppina Verdi wrote:

> They talk a lot about the more or less religious spirit of Mozart, Cherubini, and others. I say that a man like Verdi must write like Verdi, that is, according to his own feeling and interpreting of the text. The religious spirit and the way in which it is given expression must bear the stamp of its period and its author's personality. I would deny the authorship of a Mass by Verdi that was modelled on the manner of A, B, or C.

We cannot indeed expect Verdi to have shed his personality in writing the Requiem. If here and there we are reminded that opera was after all his *métier*, we note on the other hand that while most of his operatic ensembles portray a conflict of emotion in the personalities on the stage, in the Requiem such conflict within ensembles is nonexistent. Superficially, the fiercest contrasts reign between its seven sections, but they are merely different manifestations of a unity that lies in the prayer for the soul's peace.

Melody and harmony in the opening 'Requiem aeternam' are given to the muted strings, the four-part chorus only whispering the prayer in more or less broken declamation until the beautiful fugal section, 'Te decet hymnus', brings the first agitation for the unaccompanied voices. With 'Kyrie eleison' begins a new section in which the four solos and, presently, the chorus share the melody with the orchestra. The longest section is a setting of the 'Dies irae', a text depicting the Last Judgment. Its great orchestral chords, with the bass drum marking the unaccented beats, its rushing of strings, and its partly chromatic choral shouts, suggest a mood of darkness and despair. This is unquestionably the most dramatic part of the Requiem.

Then trumpets, both in the orchestra and placed at a distance, suitably reproduce the sound of the 'last trumpet' in the choral 'Tuba mirum'. The bass solo, as if terrified, declaims the 'Mors stupebit' ('Death will be aghast'). This is followed by an extended dramatic section for the mezzo-soprano, while the chorus mutter from time to time their 'Dies irae'. The wide compass of this solo—from B below the stave up to high A flat—is noteworthy. After the repeat of the choral 'Dies irae', clarinets and bassoons introduce the moving trio in 6-8, 'Quid sum miser', which is sung by the two women and the tenor soloists. In 'Rex tremendae majestatis' the choral basses are entrusted with a majestic motif while the remaining parts of the chorus and the soli execute counterpoints on 'Salva me, fons pietatis'.

A lyrical duet for soprano and mezzo-soprano, 'Recordare, Jesu pie', leads to an extended tenor solo accompanied by expressive orchestral triplets; and finally a bass solo declaims, in virile tones, the 'Confutatis maledictis'. These last three sections, all for the soloists, are rounded off by the choral 'Dies irae'. Now begins once more, with great expression', the 'Lacrymosa', whose simple, almost childlike melody might have come from one of Verdi's early operatic ensembles. The mezzo-soprano opens with it, and then combines with oboe and clarinet into a lamenting counterpoint while simultaneously the bass solo repeats the melody. Out of this a choral movement of solemn beauty and musical complexity is engendered:

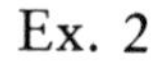
Ex. 2

Ex. 2 (cont.)

The soloists now intone, unaccompanied and in a style of great ecclesiastical purity, the final prayer to Jesus; the chorus takes the text up to the original melody ('Lacrymosa'); and the whole movement would seem about to expire—when, on the word 'Amen', there occurs an unexpected and, in the harmonic context, magical modulation from B flat major to G major which is supported by a *crescendo* to *forte* and a *diminuendo* again to *pianissimo*. The close of the movement, for the orchestra alone, is in B flat, the relative major of G minor, in which key the movement had begun. Into a mere six bars Verdi concentrated the expression of a poetic idea and the musical rounding-off of a vast movement.

The Offertorium does not invite such dramatic treatment. It is only at the words 'sed signifer sanctus Michael' ('But the holy standard-bearer Michael') that the soprano solo indulges in something like operatic behaviour. 'Quam olim Abrahae' makes a feint at a fugue but soon settles down to secure homophony, and this is followed by the peaceful strain 'Hostias et preces' for the four soloists. The Sanctus, after being ushered in by trumpet fanfares and three choral shouts, takes the form of a double fugue for two choruses. Pedants may frown upon it, but for other listeners its two themes and their treatment are most felicitous. The fugue is brought to a glorious close in augmentations to the words 'Pleni sunt coeli' and 'Hosanna'. The Agnus Dei, the shortest piece, opens with the two women soloists singing, in octaves and unaccompanied, a broad peaceful melody which shows a perfect compromise between Verdi's individual melodic style and liturgical tradition. There follows the 'Lux aeterna', which takes the form of a trio for mezzo-soprano, tenor, and bass, and begins in uncertain tonality. It is a solemn and, in parts, sombre movement.

And so we arrive at 'Libera me', surviving from the original Requiem intended for Rossini. Here at last it is the soprano solo who is given the lead. In a recitative (marked *senza misura*, that is, 'in free rhythm' in the first bar) she prays for deliverance from the pains of hell, and her prayer is repeated by the chorus. Then the 'Dies irae' returns from the earlier movement; then the soprano and unaccompanied chorus recall the opening 'Requiem aeternam', after which the introductory recitative is repeated. The ensuing fugue cannot be faulted from the technical point of view, but it is its character—cheerful to the point of jauntiness—that unfits it to be the coping-stone of this great edifice. Not until the soprano solo joins in with an augmentation of the theme does the piece approach the grandeur and tragic nobility of the rest of the Requiem. The first performance of the work took place at St Mark's Church, Milan, in 1874, under Verdi's direction.

Verdi also composed four *Sacred Pieces* (*Pezzi sacri*). The *Ave Maria* for unaccompanied chorus and the *Stabat Mater* for chorus and orchestra were written shortly before his last opera, *Falstaff* (1893); the *Te deum* for chorus and orchestra, and the *Laudi* (Praises in honour of the Virgin Mary, to a text of Dante) for unaccompanied chorus were his last works. In the *Stabat Mater*, Verdi repeats not a single word in his setting of the text, and the sombre opening given out by the chorus in unison sets the appropriate atmosphere at once. This miniature, which shows a most individual harmonic style and is admirably scored, deserves to be mentioned in almost the same breath as the Requiem.

The most considerable of the four *Sacred Pieces* is the *Te Deum*, which uses a large orchestra including an English horn. Verdi did not use the text ('We praise thee, O God') as the majority of composers do—to celebrate occasions of public rejoicing—but concentrated on the basic thought of this canticle, which is a prayer for deliverance from the wrath to come and the avowal of trust in God's mercy. The setting is very dramatic and is based upon two themes of liturgical character and provenance. The first theme opens the work, providing the subject for the subsequent chorus, and the second occurs on the trumpets before the words 'Tu rex gloriae' and is then treated in complex eight-part writing. The orchestral handling is as vivid as it is elaborate. The four *Sacred Pieces* were performed for the first time in Paris in Holy Week, 1898, and then in Italy at the Turin Exhibition that year under the young Arturo Toscanini.

Verdi did not associate himself with the Church as such. But Bruckner's almost fanatical attachment to the Roman Catholic faith not only determined his entire outlook on life but was also the chief inspiration of his art. Of the Austrian composers of the nineteenth century, Anton Bruckner (1824–96) was the most religious. Though in determining his general position in the history of music his symphonies are more important, the best of his church music raises him to the front rank of nineteenth-and twentieth-century composers for the Catholic Church. There is no fundamental difference between the style of his symphonies and that of his religious works; the former are to a large extent the continuation in instrumental terms of the latter. In the Masses in D minor and F minor, the orchestra takes a considerable share in the general texture of the music, and is given themes of its own independently from the choral material. These themes are subjected to elaboration in a truly symphonic manner. Moreover, there are many thematic similarities to be found between the Masses and the symphonies, similarities which spring from characteristic fingerprints of Bruckner's general style, as the two examples show:

Ex. 3 a) Mass in F Minor

It was while he was a cathedral organist at Linz, up till 1868, that Bruckner wrote his Masses. Thereafter, living in Vienna (where he composed eight of his nine numbered symphonies), he wrote only two major works of a devotional character, the *Te Deum* and his setting of Psalm 150, neither of which was intended for religious service. But no less than seven Masses are extant from his early period; and of these the Masses in D minor, E minor, and F minor, are masterpieces, each representing a different solution of the composer's problem of setting the text of the Mass. The first and the third are orchestral or festival Masses; characteristic of them is their symphonic form and texture. Haydn, Mozart, Beethoven (Mass in D), and Schubert are here the chief models, but Bruckner goes also further back to Gregorian plainsong and the polyphony of the Palestrina period; at the same time, the melodic and harmonic novelties of his own romantic age, especially those originating in Wagner, are not ignored. It was the symphonic grandeur of the Masses in D minor and F minor which aroused the hostility of the purists in the Roman Catholic church—the Cecilians—a hostility which, ultimately, drove the composer into the camp of their opponents.

Yet, aware of the antagonism that divided the Church in the matter of musical settings of the Mass, he had attempted a pacification in writing, in 1866, the Mass in E minor, which is an eight-part vocal work with wind accompaniment. The work was intended to conform more closely to the pattern of what was regarded as 'official' church music. Apart from being much simpler than the other two Masses, it shows a certain bridge between the old modes and modern tonality. This Mass

b) Symphony No. 5, First Movement

was repeatedly revised (mainly as to the instrumental parts) and not published till 1890.

The Mass in F minor, which is Bruckner's largest choral work, was written in 1867–8 at the end of his Linz period, and its composition was partly overshadowed by his serious breakdown of 1867. Its first performance took place in 1872 at St Augustine's Church in Vienna under the composer's direction. Brahms, who attended, was deeply moved by it, as were Hellmesberger, Herbeck, Hanslick, Dessoff, and many others of Vienna's musical notabilities. Bruckner subjected the work to repeated revisions in 1872, 1876, 1881, and 1883. In a final version undertaken shortly before publication in 1894, the number of horns was increased from two to four.

The Kyrie is dominated by a step-wise descending motif of four notes which gives expression to a feeling of contrition. (It shows a curious resemblance to the opening figure in Verdi's Requiem.) The 'Christe eleison', beginning in A flat and modulating to D and G flat, operates through a new figure of wide steps (fifth and octave), and the addition of solo passages to the chorus introduces a more subjective feeling. The third part returns to the opening but interpolates an unaccompanied 'Kyrie eleison' of great intensity before closing in an abject mood. The Gloria in C opens with a theme of jubilation. Twice in its later course it is given to the solo, and finally comes to rest in the key of D minor. 'Qui tollis peccata mundi' is set in a contrapuntal manner, with a marked symphonic treatment of the orchestra. After the next section has repeated the 'Gloria' theme in the fashion of a sonata recapitulation, a double fugue of majestic proportions follows whose festive march character is emphasised by the instrumental accompaniment.

The Credo is the most extensive movement and the centre of the Mass, having connexions with both the preceeding and succeeding movements. The first part in C is largely a unison, with a Gregorian theme for its main idea. In the 'Incarnatus' and 'Crucifixus', the tenor and bass soloists combine with the chorus against a throbbing orchestra, the pace being slow. The 'Et resurrexit' is dealt with in a mainly chordal *allegro*, with a slightly broader coda on the words 'cuius regnum'. After a reprise of the opening of the movement, to which the words 'Et in spiritum sanctum' are now set, a new section in G ensues, with a *fugato* for the four soloists. The climax of the movement is reached in the breathtaking double fugue 'Et vitam venturi' where of particular interest is the shape of the subject, based on the Credo theme: its harmonised version is tacked on as counter-subject, and this provides regular chordal interruptions in the majestic flow of choral polyphony:

Ex. 4

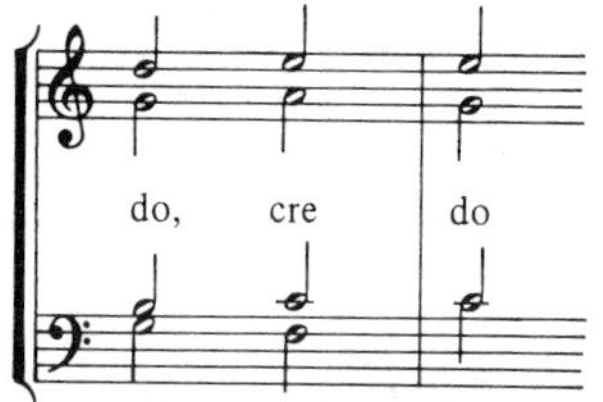

The Sanctus is the shortest of the movements. In its first part (*moderato*) it reverts to the 'Christe eleison' theme of the Kyrie; the second part (*allegro*) begins in Gregorian style but then continues in a manner more typically Bruckner's own.

The Benedictus opens (*andante*) with a tender eight-bar orchestral prelude which anticipates the first of the two choral themes. This is a melody which moves by steps and is announced by the alto solo, and repeated, at a bar's distance, by the soprano and then the tenor solo. The second melody, a wide-ranging theme (which Bruckner employed again in the *Adagio* of his Symphony No.2) is given to the bass solo and freely repeated by the women's chorus. These two melodies are twice reiterated, but each time with extensions and other modifications. An instrumental epilogue leads to an Allegro which repeats the corresponding section of the Sanctus.

In the Agnus Dei, which returns to F minor, a short orchestral prelude announces a tragic theme that forms a counterpoint to the ensuing ideas put forward by chorus and soloists. At 'Dona nobis pacem', minor changes to major, the step-wise descending fourth and the choral octave of the opening Kyrie makes a brief appearance, and shortly before the end Bruckner recalls the fugal subject from the Gloria and the first of the themes of the Credo.

For Bruckner's Czech contemporary, Antonin Dvořák (1841–1904), religious music represented not much more than a side-line in his prolific output. But for sheer beauty of invention and sincerity of expression, some of his religious works can bear comparison with the finest of his instrumental music. The place of such works as the *Stabat Mater* (Prague, 1880) and the Requiem (Birmingham, 1891), both for four soloists, chorus, and orchestra, is not on the shelves of a music library but in the live atmosphere of the concert-hall. So also with the *Te Deum* (New York, 1892), for soprano and bass solos, chorus, and orchestra. From 1877, when he worked on the *Stabat Mater*, to 1894, the date of the *Biblical Songs* for voice and piano, we count altogether eight compositions of a religious nature—a proof that, even if some were written as pieces demanded by a particular occasion, the setting of the religious music signified for Dvořák more than a mere convention to which almost every nineteenth-century composer was expected to pay his tribute. It is true that he was at heart an instrumental composer, and felt generally hampered rather than inspired by words. All the same, he succeeded in expressing the meaning and feeling of the liturgical text in an effective manner.

Broadly speaking, Dvořák may be said to be at his most inspired when setting those sections that give expression to grief, pathos, suffering, drama, and exaltation—in the movingly expressive lyricism of the *Stabat Mater*, for instance, or the dramatic climaxes of the Requiem, the Mass (1881), and the *Te Deum*. On the other hand, those sections in which the text is in a meditative vein, inviting contemplation, show in the setting a falling-off of the melodic invention and do not escape the charge of conventionality.

In his formal division of the text Dvořák follows the tradition as he found it in classical church music, though in details he goes his own way. In the musical treatment he successfully observes balance, contrast, and emotional weight. But where the 'absolute' musician in Dvořák tends to go astray is in the thematic handling of the individual numbers. He frequently resorts to the device of splitting up a vocal melody into its constituent motifs, with which he operates in the manner of an instrumental development. That the musical texture gains thereby cannot be denied, but the defects of this method in a predominantly vocal composition are only too evident. This quasi-instrumental handling leads to unnecessary length, and entails consequently the stretching of the text to fit the music. The result is tedious word-repetition. In constructing 'symphonic' texture Dvořák also fails to pay much attention to a detailed musical characterisation of word-pictures. Yet this does not mean that these works lack the sense of characterisation altogether. A splendid example is found, for instance, in the leading-motif of the Requiem, which symbolises the idea of death and mourning and which pervades the entire work, thus giving it spiritual and thematic unity.

A few words may not be amiss on the various influences to which

Dvořák was subjected. Reared as he was in the classical tradition, he saw his chief models in the church music of Beethoven, Schubert, and—this was due to his frequent visits to England—Handel. It was above all Handel's vigorous, majestic choral style that left its mark on Dvořák's choruses. It is Bach, however, with whom Dvořák shows affinity in his *Te Deum*, particularly in the vital rhythm of the first movement. Cast in the form of a miniature choral symphony, it is also full of imaginative touches in the orchestra. The *Te Deum* is a strikingly original work—perhaps the most felicitous contribution Dvořák made to religious music. Also not without influence on Dvořák were such composers of the romantic period as Berlioz, Mendelssohn, and Liszt. The principal motif in the 'Quis est homo' of Dvořák's *Stabat Mater* is almost identical with a figure in the 'Lacrymosa' of Berlioz's Requiem. Wagner's influence, which was strongest in Dvořák's early and very late periods, manifests itself chiefly in certain harmonic predilections, notably in progressions of secondary sevenths. The Verdi of the Requiem also left his mark, as may be seen in the typically Italianate character of certain melodies in the Czech composer's own Requiem—for instance, the 'Rex tremendae majestatis' and the 'Confutatis maledictis'.

A different kind of influence went very deep with Dvořák: the national element of Czech folk music. Generally speaking, the broadness and straightforwardness of his melodic style and the melancholy that informs many lyrical passages of the *Stabat Mater*, the Requiem, and the Mass are of a general Slavonic heritage. But there are numerous other passages in these works of a more tangible form of musical nationalism, such as the influence of mediaeval Czech hymns (witness the chorale, *Hospodine pomilujny*, in the finale of the sacred oratorio *St. Ludmilla*), pentatonic turns in the melody and certain rhythmic patterns which derive from Slavonic dances.

FIFTEEN

THE TWO 'MANONS'

BAUDELAIRE, SPEAKING OF *Les liaisons dangereuses*, described it as *un livre essentiellement français*. He might have said the same of the Abbé Prévost's *Manon Lescaut* (1731) which in subject, treatment, and style of language is as typical a product of the Gallic spirit as Laclos's book. Prévost's is largely an autobiographical novel in which that twice-renegade priest recounted, in imaginative form, amorous experiences of his turbulent youth, and, for once setting aside his routine as a hack-writer of popular adventure stories, succeeded in producing a genuine work of art. Intended as a cautionary tale, his book has often been compared to a Racinian drama in that it deals with the classical conflict between reason and passion illustrated in the fatal fascination of a young nobleman with a seductive but wholly unworthy amoral woman. Prévost treats this theme with the dignity and serious purpose of French classical tragedy and, to the extent to which the downfall of Manon and the Chevalier Des Grieux is the natural consequence of their moral character, the novel is a tragedy. It reads like a play: the action is swift and stripped of all superfluities, the language simple and direct. Add to this a series of uncommonly striking incidents and the allure of a corrupt Parisian society under the Regency, and it is clear why this novel has continued in its universal appeal for more than two centuries and provided the material for several operas—from Auber's *Manon Lescaut* of 1856 to Henze's *Boulevard Solitude* of 1952, with the two best-known examples between them, Massenet's *Manon* (1884) and Puccini's *Manon Lescaut* (1893).

To put the fundamental difference between these two operas into a nutshell, Massenet's is all *sentiment*, tender, refined, full of charm and prettiness; Puccini's is all *passione disperata*, full-blooded, filled with animal vitality, and coarse-fibred. Of its kind *Manon* is a masterpiece, wholly conforming to French nineteenth-century taste and written with the lightest and most elegant of touches. *Manon Lescaut* is merely prophetic of the future master and has a specific gravity incomparably heavier than that possessed by its French counterpart.

Massenet had two great advantages over Puccini. By the time he came to write his opera he was a fully mature composer and at the height of his career, while the Italian, his junior by sixteen years, was a virtually unknown musician and as yet insufficiently experienced in the dramatic craft when he tackled *Manon Lescaut*. Yet more important still was the fact that the Frenchman was *naturally* attuned to the all-pervasive erotic atmosphere of Prévost's novel and able to feel himself completely into the psychology of his main characters, bringing them to life in music inimitably delicate and most captivating in its tender melancholy charm. True, Puccini possessed a marked affinity with French sensibility, as he was to show in *Bohème* and *Butterfly,* but in *Manon Lescaut* it had not yet come to the fore. (It is conceivable that had he written this opera a few years later he would have produced a work refined, elegant, and piquant.) He simply saw the subject with Italian eyes, turning the light-hearted, frivolous, and pleasure-seeking heroine of Prévost into a woman of strong, all-consuming passion, who already in the opening act is burdened with a heavy load of Puccinian melancholy; while the refined aristocratic Des Grieux of the original becomes under his hands a callow, impetuous, and reckless youth hailing from Tuscany rather than a province of France. There is scarcely any French 'feel' in Puccini's opera.

Another important difference between the two works concerns the dramatic treatment of the subject. Massenet's two poets, anxious to follow the novel as faithfully as possible, allow us to see the heroine's moral decline in successive cumulative stages: Manon, a mixture of girlish shyness and coquetry (Act I); the sweetheart of Des Grieux (Act II); the mistress of the wealthy De Brétigny (Act III, Scene 1); the seductress of her erstwhile lover, with the *scène à faire* in the Church of St Sulpice in Paris (Act III, Scene 2); the criminal accomplice of Des Grieux and her arrest (Act IV); and finally Manon, to be deported to North America, dying in the arms of Des Grieux, on the road to Le Havre (Act V).

Puccini, in his understandable wish to avoid as far as possible a duplication of the situations presented in Massenet, foreshortened Manon's psychological development to such an extent that from the latter half of the second act when disaster befalls her, he portrays her in an increasingly dark, despairing way. Altogether, in his opera misfortune overtakes the two lovers far too soon, with the result that, in marked contrast to Massenet's balanced treatment, the emotional equilibrium of the Italian work is seriously disturbed. To sum up, the French opera is a perfect translation into musico-dramatic terms of the essence of Prévost's novel with a libretto that is extremely well tailored—qualities which are absent from Puccini's libretto.[1]

Yet, when all is said and done, Puccini scores over Massenet on three counts: in the almost inexhaustible stream of his melodic inspiration, the sensuous warmth and passionate eloquence of his lyrical invention, and the comparative modernity of his harmonic language. *Manon Lescaut* is the opera in which the composer speaks for the first time clearly and unmistakably in his own individual voice, and it is, moreover, the purest of his representative stage works free of those deliberate assaults on our sensibility to which we are exposed from *Tosca* onwards. It is conceived in a vein of romantic poetry which betrays no sign—admittedly, to its dramatic disadvantage—of the calculating man of the theatre. It has the high seriousness of youth, and a despairing passion smoulders in the music, blazing out into a fierce, scorching flame with the love scene of the second act, after which it scarcely ever abates. Indeed, in the final act the dramatist in Puccini wholly abdicates in favour of the musician, and with his predilection for scenes of mental and/or physical suffering makes the most of Manon dying in a North American desert. This act is essentially a long lament with a surfeit of minor tonalities verging on monotony and dramatically an anticlimax after the preceding act at Le Havre—the most original and most gripping of the whole opera. In the roll-call of the twelve prostitutes about to be deported to New Orleans, Puccini's gradual build-up of the tension, from disjointed fragments to a fully sustained chorus, and with Manon's and Des Grieux's broad cantilena crowning the climax, is nothing if not masterly. Not until the first-act finale of *Turandot*, which shares with the embarkation of *Manon Lescaut* the sombre key of E flat minor, do we encounter a situation as memorable for its music, as dramatic in its impact, and as impressive as a stage picture. It may well have been largely this act which prompted Shaw, after seeing the first English production of the opera in 1894, to the prophetic words: 'Puccini looks to me more like the heir of Verdi than any of his rivals.'

[1] His libretto had a multiple paternity: Leoncavallo, Praga, Oliva, Illica and Giacosa, with the composer, assisted by Ricordi, directing the operation. This is why the opera is published without the mention of the librettists—a curiosity in the annals of opera.

SIXTEEN

DEBUSSY AND PUCCINI

Debussy had the soul of an artist, capable of the rarest and most subtle perceptivities, and to express these he employed a harmonic scheme that at first seemed to reveal new and spacious and prescient ideas for the musical art. When nowadays I hear discussions on Debussyism as a system to follow or not to follow, I feel that I would like to tell young musicians of what I personally know concerning the perplexities that assailed this great artist in his last years. Those harmonic processes which were so dazzling in the moment of their revelation, and which seemed to have in reserve immense and ever-new treasures of beauty, after the first bewitching surprise always surprised less and less, till at last they surprised no more; and not this only, but also to their creator the field appeared closed, and I repeat I know how restlessly he sought and desired a way of exit. As a fervid admirer of Debussy, I anxiously waited to see how he himself would assail Debussyism; and now his death has rendered impossible that we shall ever know what would have been the outcome that indeed might have been precious.

Puccini in the *Musical Times*, July 1918

BEFORE I DEAL with the extent to which the musical and aesthetic problems raised by Debussy's innovations affected Puccini, it will be well first to consider what attitudes the two composers maintained towards each other. Edward Lockspeiser in his penetrating and absorbing study of Debussy[1] writes of the strangely contradictory views expressed by the French composer on some of his contemporaries, views which did not imply an uncertainty of critical judgment or duplicity but were, as Mr Lockspeiser suggests, the manifestation of a deep-seated ambivalence of feeling. This ambivalence seemed to spring from the complexity of Debussy's psychological make-up, more particularly from the infinite sensitivity with

[1] *Debussy, His Life and Mind* (London, 1965).

which he reacted to the flux of external impressions whose conflicting nature his mind registered in a way very bewildering to his contemporaries. He seemed both drawn to and disenchanted by the same artistic personality. Musicians on whom he expressed himself in such contradictory fashion included Fauré, Ravel, Stravinsky and apparently Puccini. Why I say 'apparently' will become clear. According to Stravinsky,[2] who met Puccini in Paris in 1913, Debussy confessed to having respect for the Italian's music, and there is furthermore Debussy's alleged remark to Falla that he knew of no one who had described the Paris of the 1830s as well as Puccini had in *La Bohème*.[3] But the point about these remarks is that they are reported to us second-hand, and are contradicted by Debussy's opinions expressed in his published writings, opinions in which he gave vent to his strong antagonism to the whole of the so-called Young Italian School. This antagonism was dictated partly by his fear of a possible influence that the School might have on French music,[4] and partly by a great aversion from all realism. For this reason he criticised the operas of Alfred Bruneau, a composer whom he otherwise much admired. In an article of 1913 he expressed himself most bitingly on Italian opera of his time:

> Inspired by scenes in the realistic cinema the characters throw themselves at one another and appear to wrench melodies from one another's mouths. A whole life is packed into a single act: birth, marriage, and an assassination thrown in. In these one-act operas very little music need be written, for the reason that there is hardly time to hear much.

He regarded it as the worst crime which Puccini and Leoncavallo had committed that they took a French novel (Murger's *Scènes de la vie de Bohème*) and made it the theme of operas wholly Italian in spirit; and that, in spite of their pretence at character study, they achieved nothing more than simple anecdote.[5] This last remark throws considerable doubt on the authenticity of what Debussy is supposed to have said to Falla about Puccini's *Bohème*. To sum up, it would appear that like the majority of French composers of that time he evinced little sympathy for Puccini, whose realism and full-blooded emotional

[2] See *Expositions and Developments* by Igor Stravinsky and Robert Craft (London, 1962).

[3] Quoted in *Manuel de Falla* by Jaime Pahissa (London, 1954).

[4] Debussy tended to judge foreign music from an exclusively nationalist, French point of view.

[5] Debussy here overlooked the fact that already the novel was hardly more than a string of very loosely connected anecdotes or episodes in which those dealing with Rodolphe, Marcel, Mimi and Musette happened to be the most important.

mode of expression were poles apart from the ethos of his own music.

Puccini on the other hand was in his own words a 'fervent admirer' of Debussy[6] in whom he saw 'The soul of an artist capable of the rarest and most subtle perceptivities', whose harmonic innovations 'at first seemed to reveal new and prescient ideas for the musical art'.[7] As far as we know, Puccini's interest in the French composer began in all seriousness after he had heard a performance of *Pelléas* in Oct 1903 when he had come to Paris to supervise the first French production of *Tosca*. But it is very probable that he had earlier heard *L'après-midi* and the *Nocturnes*, and that he knew the opera from the vocal score which was published in 1902. According to the diary of the conductor Henri Büsser, Puccini on that first Paris occasion was much impressed by the novel harmonic and orchestral colours of the work, but expressed surprise that it did not contain a single piece of vocal effect. Hearing *Pelléas* must have been an extraordinary experience for him, yet it is odd that there is no mention of this in any of his published letters of the years 1903 or 1904.

When Puccini attended, in December 1906, the first French production of *Butterfly*, he saw *Pelléas* again, and this time recorded his impressions in an interesting letter to Ricordi. As before, he found the opera extraordinary in its harmonic colours and diaphanous orchestral textures, yet added that it 'never moves you, never lifts you up. Its colour is unrelieved and sombre as that of a Franciscan habit. It is the subject that interests and that acts as a tug-boat for the music'.[8] This last remark demonstrates that Puccini had not forgotten the strong attraction which Maeterlinck's play had exerted on him in the mid-1890s, when he seriously considered it as the subject for an opera but had to abandon the idea on learning that the playwright had already given it to Debussy. Whether Maeterlinck's symbolist drama, with its dream-like, veiled atmosphere and its remote unreal-seeming characters, would have made suitable material for a composer of Puccini's type is more than doubtful. And, considering his whole mode of thinking as a musical dramatist, it was inevitable that he should have failed to appreciate in Debussy's stage work the subordination of music to poetry, and its marked tendency towards mere hints and

[6] This was much in contrast to Mascagni's attitude, who wrote in 1908 about *Pelléas* that 'the music makes one think of those cinema musicians who play, modestly and timidly, their little airs while the most extraordinary episodes unfold on the screen'.

[7] See Puccini's tribute at the head of this article. Another version, translated from a French translation, appears in Lockspeiser, op. cit. I, p. 270; the original Italian has not been traced.

[8] Quoted from Letter No. 495 in *Carteggi pucciniani*, ed. Eugenio Gara (Milan, 1958).

allusions so diametrically opposed to his own explicit, direct and earthy manner of expression.

There was an unbridgeable gulf separating the two composers in their dramatic aesthetics, yet as musicians they shared something in common and this was, as Mr Lockspeiser acutely observes, their constantly exploratory view of compositional technique. Both were of an inquiring mind and empirical in their application of technical devices, but with this fundamental difference: Debussy was the originator of a new world of harmonic and instrumental procedures which left an indelible mark on the face of twentieth-century music, whereas Puccini, for all his venturesomeness, was an adaptor, albeit an adaptor of genius, of what was novel in the music of his time—Debussy, Strauss and Stravinsky.[9] The odds are that had he lived longer he would have availed himself of dodecaphony. In marked contrast to the hermetic personality of the French composer who in his mature years shut himself off completely from all outside influences, the Italian was a born eclectic forever remaining open and receptive to stimulations coming from other composers. From almost the beginning of his career he tried, not unlike Verdi, to keep abreast of the technical innovations of his time—what he called 'tenersi al corrente' ('to be in the swim')—and in this way invest his personal style with the quality of up-to-dateness. This is well illustrated by the following anecdote: embittered by the poor reception of the *Trittico* at its first European performance at Rome in Jan 1919, and suspecting that the chief cause was the fact that the operas had not been considered modern enough, he is reported to have said to an Italian critic (Gaianus): 'If you come to Torre del Lago I will show you the scores of Debussy, Dukas, Strauss and others. You will then see how worn they are because I have read, reread and analysed them and made notes all over them.'[10] How very different from Debussy, who is said to have kept not a single score by another composer at his home!

Of all the important non-French composers who came under the spell of Debussy's music Puccini was the one who submitted to it longest. Yet seen in retrospect this influence appears far less direct than had been widely assumed during his lifetime, and manifested itself largely in the liberating and enriching effect it had on his general harmonic language; there are but few instances in which he borrowed from or directly imitated Debussy. That the latter's influence should have lasted for some twenty years—from the time of *Butterfly* to that

[9] Also Casella, as shown by John C. G. Waterhouse in 'Puccini's debt to Casella', *Music and Musicians*, Feb. 1965.

[10] Quoted in *The Magic Baton, Toscanini's Life for Music*, by Filippo Sacchi (London, 1957).

of *Turandot*—finds its explanation in Puccini's marked 'French' sensibility which made him particularly responsive to Debussy's innovations. This sensibility showed already at the start of his operatic career and set him sharply apart from the other members of the *giovane scuola*. Thus his first opera, *Le villi*, displays already his characteristic blend of Italian *passione* with French *sentiment*, the latter expressing itself in tender, intimate emotions and a delicate charm. Moreover, up to and including *Butterfly* there are clear echoes in his melodic style of Massenet's famous *phrase décadente*, and it can indeed be argued that his *morbidezza* is partly Gallic in provenance, which is the more remarkable as Puccini was so typically Italian in his *dramatic* approach to opera.

What are the Debussyisms in Puccini? They are, as I intimated, chiefly confined to the harmonic field, yet some of the devices commonly associated with the French composer were anticipated by Puccini and others, and are now seen to have been common coin in the last two decades of the nineteenth century. For instance, in so early a Puccini work as the Mass (1880) there occur already *faux-bourdon*-like progressions probably picked up from *Aida*.[11] Again, *Edgar* and *Manon Lescaut* contain a great many passages of chromatic side-slipping of diminished, secondary and dominant sevenths:

Ex. 1 a) *Edgar*

b) *Manon Lescaut*

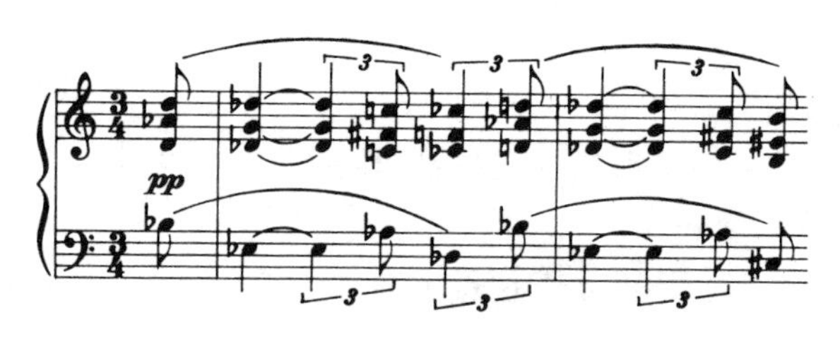

[11] See the succession of 6/3 chords in *Aida*'s 'Là tra foreste vergini'.

which Puccini may well have derived from *Otello.*[12] True, Debussy employed such and similar progressions in his Wagnerian *Cinq poèmes de Charles Baudelaire*, but it is most improbable that Puccini knew these songs, which were in any case not completed until 1889, the year of the first production of *Edgar*. Another device much used by Debussy, though its discovery cannot be attributed to him, was that of parallel fourths and fifths, which was in the air towards the end of the last century[13] and was for a time a favoured procedure with Puccini; witness, in *Bohème*, the archaic harmonisation of the Christmas Song, Act 1, and the succession of parallel fifths in the atmospheric orchestral introduction to Act 3; and, in *Tosca*, the *organum*-like passages in Cavaradossi's first aria and the parallel triads in the orchestral prelude to Act 3. Similarly the whole-tone scale, which is so prominent in *Pelléas,* occurs already in Puccini's 'Roman' opera—both composers probably deriving its use from the Russians. It was not until *Butterfly* that Debussy's impact on Puccini bore real, tangible fruits. Not for nothing did the Italian describe this opera as his most advanced work to date, and this because of the greater freedom he had learned from the Frenchman in the handling of the dissonance and because of the impressionist character of much of his 'exotic' scoring. Moreover, with the example of *Pelléas* before him, Puccini now makes a far more articulate use of the whole-tone scale than he had in *Tosca*, where this scale appears merely as the basis of chords, as in the 'Scarpia' motif and its extensions. In *Butterfly* on the other hand the whole-tone scale serves to generate clear-cut, sharply defined melodic figures:

[12] See the chromatically moving parallel fourths (augmented and perfect) at the beginning of Verdi's opera.

[13] There is a passage of parallel fifths in the bass in Iago's 'Vien dopo tanta irrision la morte', *Otello*, Act 2.

Butterfly is Puccini's only opera which, beyond showing the general influence of Debussy's harmonic and orchestral innovations, is directly indebted to *Pelléas* for two ideas—the 'Sword' motif and the off-stage chorus of the sailors. In addition to the striking similarity in the melodic shape of the Debussy and Puccini examples, there is the tritone as their most critical interval:[14]

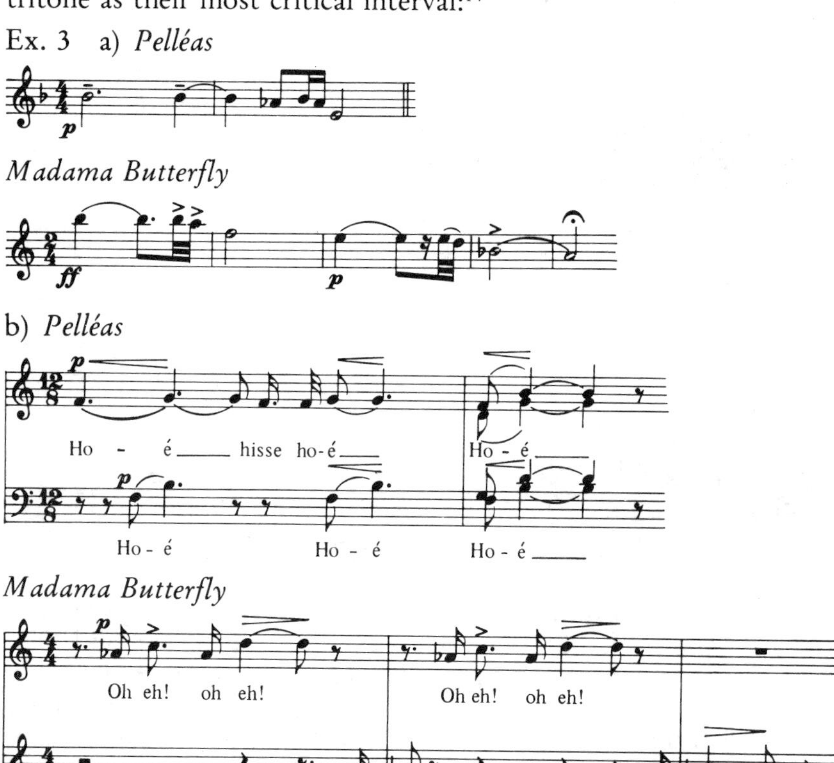

That after the first production of *Butterfly* in Febuary 1904 no Italian critic alluded to these Debussyan features is to be accounted for by the fact that *Pelléas* was as yet unknown in Italy (where it was not heard until 1907). Yet by the time that *La Fanciulla del West* was first produced at New York in December 1910 Debussy's music had conquered the world, and it was therefore not surprising that some American critics strictured what they considered to be strong

[14] In this context I must draw attention to the succession of glittering off-key chords in the scene of the presentation of the silver rose in *Der Rosenkavalier*, a passage which seems to me to have been directly inspired by *Pelléas* (Act 1, six bars before 13).

Debussyan echoes in Puccini's score. But actually there is hardly more of Debussy in *La Fanciulla* than there is in *Butterfly*—we find again the melodic use of the whole-tone scale, the great harmonic freedom resulting, as in the 'Japanese' opera, in a blurred sense of tonality, and the insistent recourse to secondary sevenths and ninths (instead of simple triads) either in parallel motion or in the harmonisation of a melody:

Ex. 4 *La Fanciulla del West*

By the time of the *Trittico* Debussy's influence on other composers had greatly diminished, but we still discern it in *Il tabarro* and *Suor Angelica*—in the predilection for sparse, attenuated orchestral textures, notably in the latter, and the exploitation of individual instruments for mere sound's sake. Moreover, the exquisite atmospheric opening of *Il tabarro* has the unmistakable 'feel' of the beginning of *La Cathédrale engloutie* about it, but is made more pungent by Puccini's bitonality:

Ex.5 a) *La Cathédrale engloutie*

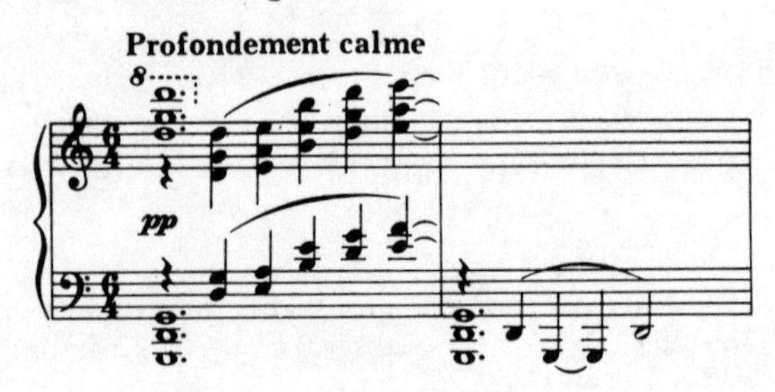

b) *Il Tabarro*

while the side-slipping of perfect fourths and fifths in the duet between Michele and Giorgetta, beginning with the latter's 'No, calmati, Michele!', somehow recalls similar progressions in the scene in the subterranean vaults of *Pelléas*. Equally Debussyan are the triads with added seconds in the archaic opening of *Suor Angelica*:

Ex. 6 *Suor Angelica*

Even in *Turandot*, composed at a time when generally a strong reaction had set in against Debussy, we are still able to hear echoes of him. There is the melodic use to which Puccini puts the whole-tone scale, as for instance in the opening 'Turandot' theme, and there are the delicate impressionist whiffs of sound on harp, flute, clarinet and celesta in the 'Moon' chorus of Act 1 which demonstrate that the French composer had not entirely ceased to exert his hold on the Italian.

SEVENTEEN

SIMONE MAYR AND HIS *L'AMOR CONIUGALE*

BEETHOVEN'S *Fidelio* was the fourth and last setting of Bouilly's drama *Léonore ou l'amour conjugal*. This drama, based on a real incident during the Reign of Terror of the French Revolution, enjoyed such an extraordinary vogue in post-revolutionary Europe that it was set, before Beethoven, by one French and two Italian composers. Gaveaux's *Léonore* (Paris, 1798), Paer's *Leonora* (Dresden, 1804) and Mayr's *L'amor coniugale* (Padua, July 1805) compare with Beethoven's opera as the planets with the sun. All three operas, it is true, achieved, unlike *Fidelio*, a notable success at their first production and even later, and there are, moreover, striking parallels between the works of Gaveaux and Paer and Beethoven which strongly suggest that he knew the vocal scores.[1] Yet in the event they were completely eclipsed by *Fidelio* and today they have only historical importance, though it will be one of the purposes of this article to show that Mayr's work contains a good deal that would make a revival a desirable and worthwhile undertaking. What prompted this study is the fact that in 1967 the town of Bergamo, where Mayr lived and died, brought out a full score of his *L'amor coniugale*[2] which makes it possible to analyse the work, notably in its orchestral aspect, in greater detail and in a more comprehensive manner than was the case with previous writers.[3] But first we must consider the composer in more general terms. Giovanni Simone Mayr (1763–1845) was a Bavarian who, after receiving his musical training in Germany, followed the custom of

[1] A score of Paer's opera was found among Beethoven's effects after his death.

[2] Vol. 22 in *Edizioni Monumenta Bergomensia*, reconstructed and edited by Arrigo Gazzaniga. I am greatly indebted to the civic authorities of Bergamo for providing me with a copy.

[3] Ludwig Schiedermair, *Beiträge zur Geschichte der Oper um die Wende des 18. und 19. Jahrhunderts*, 2 vols (Leipzig, 1907–10), Hermann Kretzschmar, *Geschichte der Oper* (Berlin, 1919). Friedrich Lippmann, *Vincenzo Bellini und die italienische opera seria seiner Zeit* (Cologne, 1969).

eighteenth-century German musicians and went to Italy to complete his studies; he finally settled in Bergamo as a composer and teacher, with Donizetti as his most famous pupil. During his life-time his was a name to conjure with, with a reputation extending far outside the confines of Italy. Zelter mentions him in his correspondence with Goethe. Stendhal refers to him in his *Vie de Rossini*[4] where he says that the reason for Mayr's success was 'parce qu'il présentait au publique une petite nouveauté qui surprenait et attachait l'oreille . . . mettre dans l'orchestre et dans les ritournelles et les accompagnements des airs, les richesses d'harmonie qu'à la même époque Haydn et Mozart créaient en Allemagne', though elsewhere in the book he denigrates Mayr in order to let his hero shine the better. Rossini himself, who was much influenced by Mayr, had this to say about him: 'Se i compositori de' giorni nostri studiassero le opera di Mayr ch'è sempre drammatico e che canta e che è melodico sempre, essi troverebbero tutto che cercano . . . e che loro sarebbe utilissimo.'[5] Mayr received at various times offers to take up appointments in places such as Vienna,[6] Paris, Lisbon, London, St Petersburg and Dresden, all of which he declined, having taken, like Hasse and J. C. Bach before him, deep roots in Italy.

Mayr is one of Tovey's Important Historical Figures now inhabiting our musical histories and dictionaries, but while he was alive he was very much to the fore on the Italian operatic scene and of far-reaching influence on the younger school of native composers. Rossini, Bellini, Donizetti and the early Verdi, not to mention such minor lights as Mercadante and Pacini, owed much to his reforms though his influence exceeded his actual gifts. He was an eclectic endowed with a strongly developed sense of the theatre. In his serious and comic operas he followed the late Neapolitans (Piccinni, Cimarosa, Paisiello), but developed further the melting cantilena of, notably, Paisiello's *Nina*, and thus formed the bridge to the *melodia di sentimento* of Bellini and Donizetti. At the same time he studied Gluck, Mozart and his contemporary Cherubini. From Gluck he learned the technique of massive choral scenes and the art of correct as well as expressive

[4] Paris, 1824, i, p. 19.

[5] Quoted by G. B. Biaggi, 'S. Mayr', *Gazzetta musicale di Milano* (1875), p. 295.

[6] Mayr was in Vienna in 1802 for the production of two of his operas (*L'equivoco* and *Ercole in Lidia*) and in 1803 was invited by Schikaneder to compose an opera for the Theater an der Wien, which did not materialise. (Schikaneder was just then engaged on a libretto for *Vestas Feuer*, for which Beethoven wrote a trio, later used in the duet 'O namenlose Freude' in *Fidelio*.) There is also a letter by Constanze Mozart to Mayr, probably written between 1806 and 1808, in which she recommends to his attention her elder son Karl, who was studying music in Milan and who had heard 'so much of your fame and great talent' (reproduced in Schiedermair, op. cit.).

declamation in the *recitativo accompagnato*, which is one of the outstanding fingerprints of his style. Moreover, in his accompanied recitative he achieves a persuasive portraiture of a character in a given dramatic situation by means of what was called *canto caratteristico*, supporting it with a highly suggestive treatment of the orchestra. The opera which shows his *accompagnato* at its most dramatic, and from which, significantly, all *secco* is banished, is *Medea in Corinto* (1813):

Ex. 1

As for his dramatic structure, Mayr found his chief models for breaking up the stereotyped succession of recitative and aria in Metastasian *opera seria*, by inserting concerted numbers in which the action continues apace, in *opera buffa* and in Cherubini. For instance, in *L'amor coniugale* there are six more or less static solo arias as against eight vividly dramatic ensembles (duets, trios, quartets and so on). In addition, Mayr broadened the finale in the Mozartian manner, drawing several scenes together into an uninterrupted musical chain which mirrors the crescendo of the action towards the dénouement. And as a composer of German origin, he attached—indeed, could not help attaching—a far greater importance to the orchestra than did his Italian-born contemporaries, taking his main cue from Mozart, notably his *concertante* writing for woodwind and horns of which *L'amor coniugale* provides a number of excellent examples. In short, what Jommelli and Traetta, under the influence of Gluck, failed to achieve for Italian opera, namely a true *dramma per musica*, was almost achieved by a lesser man who happened to come at a time when native production was ripe for reforms.

Mayr's operatic output reached sixty-odd works—*opere serie* and *buffe*[7] and the so-called *farse.* The pure *farsa* was a descendant of the old intermezzo and, as the name indicates, was always comic, and in a

[7]The most important among his serious operas were *Adelaide di Guesclino* (1799), *Ginevra di Scozia* (1801), *Il ritorno d'Ulisse* (1808), *Il sacrificio d'Ifigenia* (1811), *La rosa rossa e la rosa bianca* (1813) and the aforementioned *Medea in Corinto*. His most successful comic operas include *Che originali* (1798), *Il caretto del venditore d'aceto* (1800), and *Un vero originale* (1808).

single act.[8] Yet, influenced by French *opéra-comique*, there developed a special kind of (mostly) one-act opera which was the *farsa sentimentale* or *eroicomica* cultivated by a number of composers in the last quarter of the eighteenth century and the beginning of the nineteenth, among them Gazzaniga,[9] Paer and Mayr, whose *L'amor coniugale* is called *farsa sentimentale*. It presented a mixture of the serious and the comic, and many of the later libretti closely followed those of *opéra-comique*, notably of the 'terror' or 'rescue' type during and after the French Revolution. Mayr, in particular, apart from the musical lessons he had learnt from Cherubini, favoured also his subjects and it was he who prompted his chief poet, Gaetano Rossi, to adapt several of Cherubini's libretti to his own purposes, as in his *Lodoiska* (1796), *Le due giornate* (1801) and *Elisa* (1804), which are all 'rescue' operas like *L'amor coniugale*.[10] In contrast to the other Italian composers of *opera semiseria*, in which the serious and the comic elements were merely juxtaposed, Mayr often succeeded in blending them, the one interpenetrating the other and so achieving a greater verisimilitude in the character of the drama. Consider, for instance, this passage from *L'amor coniugale* where after the Governor's tremendous outburst the goaler Peters taunts him with stinging irony in pure *opera buffa* style:

Ex. 2

[8] Puccini's *Gianni Schicchi* is a modern *farsa*.

[9] His *Don Giovanni* (Venice, 1786), which was carefully studied by Da Ponte and Mozart for their opera, is a *farsa sentimentale*.

[10] Mayr's *Medea in Corinto*, to a text by the Bellini poet, Felice Romani, is also modelled on Cherubini's *Médée*.

Rossi, who adapted Bouilly's *Léonore* for Mayr, followed the essential outline of the French original but compressed its two acts into one, with a single change of scene from the prison courtyard to the dungeon, and eliminated the chorus. Moreover, he transposed certain scenes and made four alterations in the drama. The first was to transfer the action from Spain to seventeenth-century Poland, which necessitated altering the names of Bouilly's *dramatis personae* though not in consistent fashion. Léonore is called Zeliska/Malvino; Florestan becomes Amorveno and Pizarro, Moroski; the gaoler Roc has a German name, Peters; Marcelline is turned into Floreska and the Minister into Ardelao, the hero's brother. Why did Rossi choose a Polish setting? The most likely explanation would seem that, beginning with the first Partition in 1772 and the wars leading to second and third Partition (1793 and 1795), Poland had become a political cauldron in Europe and thus a topical subject for opera, e.g. Cherubini's 'Polish' operas *Lodoïska* (1791) (reset by Mayr five years later) and *Faniska* (1805). But it should be added that Mayr's *L'amor coniugale* is Italian in style where it is not German, and there is nowhere an attempt to introduce a Polish colour into the music. Rossi's second alteration and certainly a major one concerned the motivation for the Governor's persecution of the hero. In Bouilly, who was followed by

Paer's poet, Giacomo Cinti, and Beethoven's Sonnleithner, Pizarro's motive was political revenge—he had been denounced by Florestan; in Rossi it is Moroski's love for Zeliska which drives him to do away with her husband Amorveno. We are probably not wide of the mark to see in this change an Italian predilection for amorous intrigues. Rossi's third alteration was to eliminate Bouilly's Jacquino and so both simplify the drama and reduce its comic element. His last modification, already mentioned, was to substitute for Bouilly's Minister Amorveno's brother Ardelao who, as *deus ex machina*, arrives at the prison at the crucial moment of the drama.

Rossi's characterisation differs most from Bouilly's in the figure of Moroski, who, unlike Pizarro, is introduced not as a cruel murderous tyrant but a sly cunning coward who on receipt of the letter of warning does not break into a furious rage, as he does in *Fidelio*, but is profoundly shaken and can think only of how best to save his skin. It is not until the dungeon scene that he is shown in his true villainy, where he is filled with a lust for revenge on Amorveno. But, we must ask, revenge for what? Amorveno's 'crime' is to be the husband of the woman whom the Governor loves: hatred, and not revenge, should be Moroski's driving emotion. Yet in the dungeon scene Rossi makes him say 'Nell' orror di questo abisso piomba omai vendetta . . . Ah! vendetta m'arde il core', which is simply a paraphrase of Bouilly's text, if not an adaptation of Pizarro's words in Paer's *Leonora*. In altering the motivation for Moroski's intended murder of Amorveno, Rossi omitted to alter the words in the quartet of the dungeon scene. But psychological truth was not a *forte* of the Italian librettists until Boito. Or was this merely negligence on the part of the poet, in which Mayr blithely acquiesced? Also Zeliska is somewhat different from the Leonore we know from Beethoven's opera. She is a typically Italian heroine—ardently passionate and fired more by simple instinctive love than duty as Amorveno's wife. Indeed, she strikes us very much as a young girl who can also be tenderly pleading, but she is far away from the mature woman of *Fidelio*. In Paer she is portrayed in a way similar to Mayr's Zeliska, which suggests that Rossi must have taken Cinti's libretto as part model for his own libretto. Floreska, too, deviates from the original Marcelline and, notably, from the girl in Paer, who is a saucy, impertinent wench of typical *commedia dell'arte* lineage. In Rossi she is a noble, wholly idealistic and rather serious girl, though Mayr's music depicts her in terms of *opera buffa*. Strangely enough, when at the end of the drama her Malvino turns out to be Amorveno's wife, she gives not the slightest hint of her total dis-enchantment.[11] As

[11] In Gaveaux/Bouilly the girl exclaims: 'Mais où trouver un *vrai* Fidelio?' and in Beethoven she is made to say 'O weh mir! Was vernimmt mein Ohr!'

for Peters, her father, he is portrayed in stronger comic colours than he is in Bouilly or Sonnleithner. Rossi makes him into a true figure of fun whose exterior is already characteristic. He has a big paunch on account of his fondness for the bottle, and it is largely his circumference which renders his work for the prisoners in their cells rather burdensome: 'non so più buono a far tante fatiche e sento che mi pesa questa mia non volgar circumferenza,' as he candidly admits to Zeliska. Like the gaoler in Beethoven, yet more so, Peters is greedy for gold, which is for him the prime necessity for a happy life—in which view Floreska staunchly contradicts him. He has a father's commonsense,[12] and he can be drily cynical, as when in referring to the prisoner, he says to Zeliska: 'Moroski mi fe'economo di quel povero diavolo, non vuole ch'egli si ingrassi troppo.' And his playful irony is seen in the last scene with Moroski and Ardelao where, alluding to the Governor's first appearance in the dungeon in a mask, he taunts him with 'Vieni, maschera . . . stai fresca, è finito carnevale' (see Ex. 2). Yet this gruff, knotty and impatient man has a heart of gold; he sees his chief task in old age as 'sollevar qualche volta gl'infelici' and he shows profound compassion when he describes to Zeliska Amorveno's suffering.[13]

The dichotomy of Bouilly's libretto, which was written for a French *opéra-comique* and which is particularly striking, in the mixture of homely *Singspiel* and heroic music-drama, in *Fidelio*, is characteristic also of *L'amor coniugale*. Thus, Peters and Floreska are the 'lower' characters who provide the comic foil to the serious protagonists and are treated in *opera buffa* style. Floreska, who is to be sung by a light soprano or soubrette, is portrayed in two arias, the first of which clearly belongs to the sphere of German *Singspiel* which Mayr tried to assimilate to Italian opera. She makes her introduction in a strophic spinning song[14] in 2/4 time and suitably *volkstümlich* in its circular diatonic melody which describes the spinning-wheel and is preceded by a suggestion of the motion of the treadle:

[12] 'Ella ha troppo bisogno di marito. E onesta, è virtuosa ma l'amore è troppo traditore, e un padre che ha un buon naso, sa quelche deve far in simil' caso.'

[13] (*Con mistero e compassione*) 'sopra la nuda terra . . . all' oscuro . . . i suoi vestiti fradici stracciati . . . smunto . . . oppresso . . . languente.'

[14] In Beethoven, Marzelline irons.

Ex. 3

Her second aria, explicitly so called (her first song forms the opening part of the Introduction), is ternary and a little more elaborate. With its short, 'sharp' figures it might have come from Cimarosa or Mozart—Zerlina's music in *Don Giovanni* springs to mind:

Ex. 4

In the sentiment expressed—longing for marriage with Malvino—this aria corresponds to Marzelline's 'O wär' ich schon mit dir vereint' in *Fidelio*, though it comes later in the dramatic scheme than in Beethoven's opera.

Peters's characterisation is on a par with his daughter's, yet with this difference that, whereas Floreska sings in more sustained lyrical phrases, her father favours, as was customary with the old men in Italian comic opera, a quick-moving voluble *parlando* style of (mainly) triadic nature, e.g. his 'Gold' aria:

Ex. 5

The position of this aria is interesting. In Gaveaux it is No.3 and in Beethoven No.4, while Mayr has it as No.7, between the monologues of Zeliska and Amorveno. Since the opera was in one act, with a short break to allow for the change of scene to the dungeon, the transposition of Peters's song was evidently done to provide dramatic and musical contrast with its two flanking numbers and reassert for the last time in the opera the comic element. Beethoven did a similar thing in the first version of *Fidelio*, in which a *Singspiel* duet between Leonore and Marzelline stands between the duet of Pizarro and Rocco and the heroine's great aria. Peters's first introduction in Mayr is in the opening scene of the opera, in the shape of a duet with Floreska, though this is largely a solo for the gaoler, with the same characteristics as his later 'Gold' aria. The least important figure is Ardelao, portrayed in *opera seria* style but vocal (in both senses of the word) only in the final two ensembles.

Of the three protagonists the Governor is the motive force of the drama. He represents its dynamic element and in Mayr's opera (as also in the settings of Paer and Beethoven)[15] he is painted in music of a restless, agitated and forceful character. Since Italian opera knows no spoken dialogue, all that is dealt with in Bouilly in speech—in the Governor's case, his receiving of the letter, his reading of it and his order to the officer to man the watch-tower of the prison—is treated in *L'amor coniugale* in *recitativo secco* and *accompagnato*.[16] Moroski first introduces himself in what is nominally a duet with Peters, though for its longest part it is a solo aria, the whole number contracting the situations of Pizarro's aria No. 7 and his subsequent duet with Rocco

[15] In Gaveaux, Pizarro is largely a speaking role.

[16] The only time that Mayr resorts to the spoken word in the form of a melodrama is when Moroski reads the contents of the letter, which is done to allow the spectator to hear the words in all clarity. This device seems to go back to Alessandro Scarlatti's *La Statira* (Rome, 1690) where the heroine reads aloud Alexander the Great's decree in which he abdicates in her favour.

No. 8 in *Fidelio*.[17] Mayr's characteristic method of combining a solo and a concerted piece in a single number springs from his concern to keep the dramatic action moving, without the intervention of a *secco*. Moroski's solo is to all intents *durchkomponiert* and is in the style of the Italian 'rage' or 'revenge' arias, with wide leaps in the broken-up voice part, and short tearing figures and staccato basses in the orchestra:

Ex. 6

[17] Peters's aside sung *sotto voce*: 'C'è del torbido per aria' corresponds to the chorus of the guard: 'Er spricht von Tod und Wunden' in *Fidelio*.

This solo begins in C major but presently there comes a surprise in the form of an orchestral march in E flat major which completely unmans Moroski, who in his fear imagines that Ardelao and his troops are already arriving at the prison gate.[18]

Moroski's second solo does not occur until the last scene, where he is led into the dungeon by Ardelao's men, disarmed and in a wild despair. This is a powerful *accompagnato*, also in 'vendetta' style, with a trembling violin ostinato played alternatively *f* and *p*:

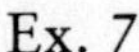

Ex. 7

[18] There is another version of the opera which at this point has the direction 'Musica che accompagna i suoi che vengono a lui'. See Lippmann, op. cit., p. 65.

It remains to be added that Moroski, like Beethoven's Pizarro, owes something to the villain Durlinsky in Cherubini's *Lodoïska*.

It was given only to Beethoven to identify his own heroic urges and aspirations with the heroine in *Fidelio* and make her into a more than life-size character. Mayr's Zeliska is much nearer to earth, she has not Leonore's 'fourth dimension': in turn impassioned and tender, she never rises to the high moral plane of her German counterpart nor has she, not unexpectedly, that *Innigkeit* which Leonore shows in Nos 12 and 13 of *Fidelio*. Dramatic thrust as well as lyrical intimacy in the Italian manner are the features of her music. She is fully portrayed in her great monologue (sc. 10), which is of considerable length—almost as long as Leonore's recitative and aria in the 1805 version of the Beethoven opera and by forty-odd bars longer than the 1814 version. The monologue follows her changing emotions faithfully and is one of the most inspired pieces in the opera. The opening section is a long *accompagnato* in which she gives expression to love as the driving force of her action, defying the 'empio Moroski' and 'la tua barbarie infame' (Allegro), to turn to a simple prayer to God to protect her in her dangerous undertaking (Adagio). It is interesting to note that the Adagio theme of the *accompagnato* returns again as the opening of the aria:

Ex. 8

The irregular build of the phrase (3 + 4 bars) is as noteworthy as the inward tenderness, which is German or Mozartian rather than Italian. That Mozart must have been very much in Mayr's mind when writing this slow section of the aria is proved by his unashamedly literal quotation of two bars from the slow movement of Mozart's clarinet concerto. In this section of the aria Zeliska expresses her intense longing for Amorveno, with whom, if she cannot save him from Moroski's clutches, she will share death. The vocal line, though beautifully drawn, is perhaps too florid to be accepted by the modern listener as a convincing reflection of her sentiment, yet this intrusion into the serious style of a 'playful' element was characteristic not only of Mayr and the Neapolitan school but is seen in even more developed form in the *dramma di sentimento* of Bellini and Donizetti. With the following Allegro, in which Zeliska oscillates between horror of Moroski and passionate love for her husband,[19] we move into high drama, with tremendous leaps in the voice part and a dramatic coloratura as the climax, of the kind which Paer and Beethoven (in the first version of his opera) wrote for their heroines:

Ex. 9 a)

b)

The traditional chromatic 'screw' of the line in (b), bars 5–7, is to be noted. Though Zeliska is for the most part characterised in terms of *opera seria*, it speaks for Mayr's dramatic conception of her that he clearly distinguishes between Amorveno's wife and Malvino, Floreska's *fidanzato*. In the trio with Peters and Floreska (sc. 2) she is almost a figure from Italian comic opera. The opening is pure Rossini, who in fact plagiarised it for Rosina's aria in *Il barbiere di Siviglia*:

[19] Most of this Allegro she sings in a state of 'esaltato terrore' and 'delirando'.

Ex. 10

while the last part of the trio might have been written by Cimarosa or Paisiello. But, significantly, when Zeliska is for a short moment left alone on the stage, she launches into a cavatina in which for the first time in this opera Mayr introduces a new note of melting tenderness, of the kind that we know best from Bellini and Donizetti:

Ex. 11

More conventional in cut is Zeliska's Romanza, which she sings at Peters's invitation ('canta che cantando si scorda la fatica') in the grave-digging scene in the dungeon (sc. 14)—willingly enough, as she hopes that Amorveno will recognize her voice. The insertion of such narrative pieces,[20] which are mostly in *siciliano* rhythm in the minor and of melancholy character,[21] was a convention in Neapolitan opera and most probably originated in French *opéra-comique*. Zeliska's strophic song is in A minor and is most appealing in its wistful melody:[22]

Ex. 12

[20] The text of this Romanza tells of a wife who has precisely the same task to achieve as the heroine in the opera.

[21] Pedrillo's 'Im Mohrenland gefangen war' in *Die Entführung* and Barbarina's 'L 'ho perduta, me meschina!' in *Figaro* are excellent examples.

[22] Rossini well remembered it in his *siciliano* in D minor in the first act of his *La Cenerentola*, in which also Mayr's modulation to the relative major via the interdominant is copied.

The Romanza is not to be taken as part of the portrayal of Zeliska's character but is a concession to a prevailing tradition. The whole scene, which opens and closes with *secco* recitative, corresponds to the melodrama in *Fidelio*.

The counterpart to Zeliska's monologue is Amorveno's long recitative and aria. It is preceded by a remarkable orchestral introduction which, as in Beethoven, is in the nature of a symphonic poem, though far looser and less closely knit. (It is noteworthy that all four settings of Bouilly's subject have this introduction in a minor key—C minor in Gaveaux, Paer and Mayr, and F minor in Beethoven.) There is about Mayr's introduction a sombre, dark-keyed feeling recalling Gluck in the unison opening and expressing both the oppressive atmosphere of the dungeon and Amorveno's despairing state of mind. It is *durchkomponiert* and contains three principal ideas all equal in suggestive power. Since it was the tradition of Neapolitan opera to repeat the instrumental prelude in the following *accompagnato*[23] the emotional significance of Mayr's themes is plain, e.g. 'Solo nell' universo':

Ex. 13

[23] Beethoven still adheres to this procedure in the opening part of Florestan's recitative.

This recitative provides an instructive example of Mayr's *canto caratteristico*, the line of the vocal phrases following the inflections of the words and expressing their mood; Amorveno sings the opening 'dolentissimo, con un filo di voce'. About half-way through this *accompagnato* the composer adds a pair of cors anglais, instruments not frequently used in those days,[24] to heighten the mournful character of this scene.

The aria consists of a Largo and an Allegretto, both of which display imaginative and pointed *concertante* passages for woodwind, while a solo violin seems to stand for Amorveno's tender love for Zeliska. As in Bouilly and the first two versions of *Fidelio*, Mayr's hero draws, at the beginning of his aria, a medallion of his spouse from his breast, at which point the composer, never greatly troubled about his plagiarisms, quotes from Tamino's 'Bildnis' aria in *Die Zauberflöte*, embellishing the phrase, however, with the elegant flourishes of the Neapolitan school:

Ex. 14

In the Allegretto, Amorveno imagines holding his wife close to his heart—a sentiment which compares with Florestan's 'Und spür' ich nicht linde, sanft säuselnde Luft' in *Fidelio*. Yet this whole section does not rise above the conventional; occasionally it is even trivial and represents a noticeable tailing-off after the magnificent *accompagnato* and the Largo of the aria.

As already mentioned, eight of the fourteen musical numbers in *L'amor coniugale* are concerted pieces, the majority of them 'action' ensembles, in which Mayr embeds lyrical solos which arise logically from the situation and thus are firmly anchored in the dramatic action. It is significant that he does not divide the opera into numbers but into scenes. There are altogether eighteen scenes, the last

[24] Cors anglais occur already in Mayr's *Le due giornate*, and in the comic opera *Che originali* he introduces a *chitarra francese*, probably taking his cue from the mandoline in Don Giovanni's serenade in Mozart's opera.

four of which are drawn together into a long continuous finale. In other words, from the quartet in the dungeon onwards the tension mounts constantly until the dénouement, which is mirrored in *accompagnati* and continuous set-pieces for a gradually increasing number of singers. Mayr's treatment of these last four scenes is a good instance of his aim at creating a *dramma per musica*.

As a more detailed discussion of all the ensembles in *L'amor coniguale* would lead too far, I shall confine myself to a consideration of the salient points of some of them. The trio of sc. 14, which corresponds to the No. 13 in *Fidelio*, starts with Amorveno, Zeliska and Peters but finishes as a duet for husband and wife, in which Amorveno interprets the gaoler's departure, who leaves to give the agreed whistling signal to the Governor, as the announcement that his last hour has come. Zeliska/Malvino is deeply affected by his state of mind and they embark on a duet in G minor which transports us to the world of a Mozart opera, particularly *Don Giovanni*:

Ex. 15

The most dynamic of the concerted numbers is the dungeon quartet (sc. 15). Like Pizarro in *Fidelio*, Moroski makes three attempts to kill his victim, all of which are frustrated by Zeliska's intervention. At the first attempt she throws herself between the Governor and her husband; the second attempt she foils by exclaiming she is 'una donna, la sua moglie!', and, at the third attempt, which occurs considerably later, she points a pistol at Moroski. From a purely musical point of view her first intervention is far more dramatic and better spaced than her second, which cannot compare with Leonore's unaccompanied

'Töt' erst sein Weib!', to say nothing of the fact that her crucial words, 'la sua moglie', are almost completely drowned by the violence of the orchestra:

Ex. 16 a)

b)

The surprise of the quartet is a Cantabile in which Zeliska appeals to Peters for help—an excellent example of how Mayr allows a lyrical solo to spring directly from the action. The purity of the vocal line and its noble flow point forward to early Verdi.

Mayr compensates for the retardation of the action by following the Cantabile with a tremendous Allegro assai, which is motivated by Moroski now unmasking himself.[25] The music presents a maelstrom of emotions, with broken-up ejaculatory phrases for the voices in the high register and the orchestra wildly working up to the climax when Zeliska draws the pistol. The trumpet signal, which is sounded only once,[26] brings the turbulence to a momentary halt. It is only Moroski who knows its meaning—the other three characters are gripped by an 'angoscioso palpito', and an intense desire that 'un fulmine quell' empio opprimerà'. Towards the end of the quartet Zeliska launches into a magnificent coloratura passage clinched by a top C:

Ex. 17

In its dramatic thrust and powerful language Mayr's quartet has little to fear from a comparison with the corresponding piece in *Fidelio*.

As in Bouilly and the first two versions of Beethoven's opera, the ensuing duet between hero and heroine (sc. 16) is dominated by two emotions: despair at their salvation and joy at being at last reunited. Introduced by an *accompagnato* for Zeliska ('Ecco tutto perduto'), the duet starts with an important *ritornello* and later shows a beautiful dovetailing of the two clarinets with the voice:

Ex. 18 a)

[25] In the *Fidelio* quartet Pizarro takes his mask off soon after the opening.

[26] Mayr had already used this dramatic device in the finale of his serious opera *Adelaide di Guesclino* (1789), where the trumpet call fills the hero (Carlo) with mortal fear only to prove, as in *L'amor coniugale*, the signal of his liberation. Trumpet and horn signals became very popular in French opera of the Revolution.

b)

Another accompanied recitative (Largo) conveys, most eloquently, in the funereal dotted rhythm of the horns and the shuddering string figures in B flat minor, the pair's resignation to death. This is comparable to the beautiful recitative which in the 1805 version of *Fidelio* preceded the duet between Florestan and Leonore. But Mayr's following set-number, an Allegretto in B flat major ('In questo tenero estremo amplesso') is a disappointment. With its two bar phrases in the voices and trills and *Schleifer* on the first violins it belongs, incongruously, to *opera buffa*, suggesting that, when it came to express joy in love, Mayr found it difficult to continue in the serious style which he had so successfully applied to the two protagonists in their previous music. Beethoven's 'O namenlose Freude' duet remains most firmly fixed in heroic music-drama.

The ensuing quintet (sc. 17) announces with trumpet flourishes the arrival of Ardelao and his men, accompanied by Peters and Floreska, who are heard off-stage shouting 'Vendetta'. This confirms the apprehension of Zeliska and Amorveno, who interpret these shouts as being intended for them. In Bouilly-Gaveaux and Paer (also in the first two versions of Beethoven's opera) the scene is for chorus. It is therefore puzzling why Mayr did not introduce at this point—the cast here includes soldiers and villagers—a chorus, and all the more so as his big choral scenes were a feature of most of his operas and were much praised in his time.[27] He does, however, both in the quintet and the following sextet, treat the solo voices in the choral style of his period, i.e. a syllabic note-against-note, homophonic setting.

With the entry of Moroski, 'disarmato e fremente', the last scene (sc. 18) begins, opening with the governor's powerful *accompagnato* discussed on p. 158. The sextet, called 'Finale' in the score, is verbally a paean on the power of conjugal love, yet, like the finale in Cherubini's *Les Deux Journées*, it expresses the general exultation in terms of comic opera.

A word or two should be said on Mayr's treatment of the recitatives. In both *secco* and *accompagnato* he is seen to be far more careful than his Italian contemporaries in correctly declaiming the text and in mirroring the verbal inflections even in quickly delivered phrases, at times heightening the emotional content of the words by an arioso turn. Nor must we overlook the pointed use of sudden harmonic shifts in the *secco* recitative, chiefly by means of interrupted cadences, in order to suggest a new line of thought in the character. Since characterisation is well-nigh impossible in *secco*, Mayr employs the *accompagnato* for this purpose, where he invariably draws on the resources of the orchestra[28] to intensify the expression of the vocal lines. Striking examples of this are to be found in the *accompagnati* of Moroski, Zeliska and Amorveno, all of which show a singularly dramatic use of the unison—one of the features of Mayr's operatic style. Similar in effect is Mayr's resort to *ostinato* technique, which he took over from the Neapolitans but employs far more frequently to establish and fix an emotional mood. Equally noteworthy is his *concertante* writing, especially for woodwind and horn, which he evidently learned from Mozart, and which not only throws a vocal phrase into greater relief but adds to the liveliness of the orchestral texture (see Ex. 19).

The overture,[29] which Mayr still calls *sinfonia*, wholly conforms to

[27] For another production Mayr wrote a 'Coro di prigionieri' which, curiously, is quite different in its text from the chorus in Bouilly. In fact, the words read like a paraphrase of the *Gefangenenchor* in *Fidelio*. 'Ah quest'aure più serene quant'è dolce respirar.' It is probable that both Rossi and Sonnleithner here based themselves on the text in Paer's opera. It is regrettable that Signor Gazzaniga did not see fit to include this *coro* in an appendix to the full score.

[28] The opera is scored for a classical (Haydn) orchestra including double woodwind, but one flute, and a pair each of horns and trumpets.

[29] Mayr wrote a second overture for a later production of the opera at Bergamo in 1813, which exists only in a piano arrangement to be found in a vocal score made by Giuseppe Manghenoni, one of his pupils.

Ex. 19

the Neapolitan tradition in having no connection with the music of the opera and standing completely outside the drama. Indeed, this overture might do service for an *opera buffa*. It consists of an introductory Andantino whose charming woodwind theme is treated in part-canon and accompanied by typically Italian string pizzicatos. It is pure Rossini:

Ex. 20

The Allegro is in simple sonata form with two contrasting themes, the second of which, following Neapolitan practice, first appears in the major and then the minor. Also traditional is the introduction of a completely new idea in the development section—a beautifully shaped melody for solo horn, repeated by solo clarinet:[30]

Ex. 21

What is generally regarded as a typically Rossinian device—the orchestral *crescendo*—occurs already in the coda of Mayr's overture, and in fact, goes back to Jommelli who may have taken it over from the Mannheim school.[31]

L'amor coniugale is admittedly uneven in the quality of its invention and does not avoid the trite and conventional. On the other hand, it stands out for its firm grasp of dramatic situations and gives a convincing portrayal of the characters and their governing emotions—rage and fury (Moroski), grief and pain, longing and resignation (Zeliska and Amorveno) and good-natured humour and affection (Peters and Floreska). This is under-pinned by a suggestive eloquence of the orchestral language which greatly contributes to making the opera approach a true *dramma per musica*. Last but not least, it shows everywhere a sovereign command of technical resources. These are qualities which, in addition to its interest as part of the historical background to Beethoven's *Fidelio*, should render a modern production of this *farsa sentimentale* a rewarding experience.

[30] Cf. the slow introduction in the overture to Rossini's *Il barbiere di Siviglia* or, more accurately, to his *Aureliano in Palmira* (1813), which echoes Mayr's theme.
[31] Cf. *W. A. Mozart* by Hermann Abert (Leipzig, 1923), vol. I, p. 335.

EIGHTEEN

MÁTYÁS SEIBER AND HIS *ULYSSES*

ULYSSES, A CANTATA for tenor solo, chorus and orchestra, is based on a text taken from James Joyce's remarkable novel of that title.[1] It was written in 1946–7 and received its first performance at a Morley College concert on 27th May, 1949, since when it has been broadcast several times and was performed at the I.S.C.M. Festival at Frankfurt in June 1951. The work created a profound and, in certain respects, unique impression and there is no doubt that in it Seiber had written the most outstanding work of his career so far. *Ulysses* not only shows the consummation of his mature technical style, but advances to a sphere of thought and sentiment of which he had given us but few glimpses in his immediately preceding compositions.[2] In casting a retrospective glance at the totality of his work before *Ulysses*, the picture that presented itself was that of an eminent, resourceful craftsman—the term is used here in its pre-nineteenth-century connotation—whose strong points were structure, design and cogent musical thinking. One admired in his music an intellectual clarity and strength, an unerring sense of direction and an absolute certainty as to the form and means employed. Though a direct pupil of Kodály, Seiber's essential style proclaimed him a disciple of Bartók. There was, however, an element that appeared insufficiently developed: a sense of poetry and of subjective expression which would lend the music a more emotional and personal significance, and thus gain for it a wider appeal. Seiber seemed to address himself chiefly to our intellect and less to our imagination. A change was noticeable for the first time in his *Notturno* of 1944. Here the accent was no longer so

[1] The vocal score is published by Schott & Co., Ltd. (London), to whom I am indebted for permission to quote the music examples. I also wish to acknowledge my thanks to John Lane, The Bodley Head, Ltd., for their kind permission to reprint Joyce's text.

[2] *Fantasia Concertante* for violin and string orchestra (1943–44); *Notturno* for horn and string orchestra (1944); *Fantasy* for string quartet, flute and horn (1945).

exclusively laid on the formal-technical aspect—an atmospheric, or better, evocative element entered the music, loosening Seiber's intellectual severity in favour of a relatively more sensuous lyrical note. The *Notturno* was a mood-picture, not emotional but emotive, that is to say, it suggested a conception in which the primary incentive still seemed intellectual but in its artistic projection produced emotional overtones. If *Ulysses* shows fundamentally the same approach, there is, however, this difference that in it the composer has allowed a wider scope for the evocative and emotive, to the extent of making these elements the exclusive stimulus in one or two numbers. To put it in another way, if the very choice of the text argues an unaltered preference for the intellectual incentive over the emotional, the music, however, proves that the composer was able to distil from his words a poetic substance which I believe to be the chief reason for the lasting impression the work has made.

In deciding to set a cantata to an excerpt from Joyce's book Seiber accepted a formidable challenge. That he has met it so successfully may be taken as the measure of his mature creative imagination. In order to bring home the difficulty of his musical proposition and also to facilitate reference in the later analysis, I quote below the full text of the Cantata. It is taken from Joyce's penultimate chapter, in which Ulysses-Bloom returns home with his young friend Stephen Dedalus and embarks on meditations ranging over an immense sphere of human experience. It is the middle of the night, with Stephen about to leave. Bloom sees him out of his house, and it is here that the Cantata begins:

I. What spectacle confronted them when they, first the host, then the guest, emerged silently, doubly dark, from obscurity by a passage from the rear of the house into the penumbra of the garden?

The heaventree of stars hung with humid nightblue fruit.

II. With what meditations did he accompany his demonstration to his companion of various constellations?

Meditations of evolution increasingly vaster: of the moon invisible in incipient lunation, approaching perigree: of the infinite lattiginous scintillating uncondensed milky way: of Sirius, 10 light years (57,000,000,000,000 miles) distant and in volume 900 times the dimension of our planet: of Arcturus: of the precession of equinoxes: of Orion with belt and sextuple sun theta and nebula in which 100 of our solar systems could be contained: of moribund and nascent new stars such as Nova in 1901: of our system plunging towards the constellation of Hercules . . . ever-moving from immeasurably remote eons to infinitely remote futures in comparison with which the years, three-score and ten, of allotted human life formed a parenthesis of infinitesimal brevity.

III. Were there obverse meditations of involution increasingly less vast?

Of the eons of geological periods recorded in the stratifications of the earth: of the myriad minute entomological organic existences concealed in cavities of the earth, beneath removable stones, in hives and mounds, of microbes, germs, bacteria, bacilli, spermatozoa: of the incalculable trillions of billions of millions of imperceptible molecules contained by cohesion of molecular affinity in a single pinhead: of the universe of human serum constellated with red and white bodies, themselves universes of void space constellated with other bodies, each, in continuity, its universe of divisible component bodies of which each was again divisible in divisions of redivisible component bodies, dividends and divisors ever diminishing without actual division till, if the progress were carried far enough, nought nowhere was never reached.

IV. Which various features of the constellations were in turn considered?

The attendant phenomena of eclipses, solar and lunar, from immersion to emersion, abatement of wind, transit of shadow, taciturnity of winged creatures: emergence of nocturnal or crepuscular animals, persistence of infernal light, obscurity of terrestrial waters, pallor of human beings.

V. His logical conclusion, having weighed the matter and allowing for possible error?

That it was not a heaventree, not a heavengrot, not a heavenbeast, nor a heavenman. That it was a Utopia, . . . a past which possibly had ceased to exist as a present before its future spectators had entered actual present existence.

Taken by itself the text, in which, incidentally, the composer has for an obvious reason made several cuts, might almost have stepped out of a text-book on natural science. It is little short of being a scientific enumeration of phenomena appurtaining to astronomy, physics and biology. What was here, one first wonders, that could have fired a composer's fancy? But Seiber's setting of seemingly so unpromising a text[3] has its precedents. Modern opera and oratorio have provided us with instances in which music is successfully harnessed to an abstract or merely factual text though, it must be added, such passages are usually woven into a tissue of dramatic and lyrical writing.[4] The intellectual *tour-de-force* of basing a whole work on such a text is rare. True, this proposition has intrigued several composers before Seiber. Rameau declared himself ready to set the *Journal d'Hollande*, and Tchaikovsky saw musical possibilities in an advertisement for corn-plasters! Richard Strauss maintained that a professional composer should be able to set acceptable music to a list of laundry articles and an income-tax demand—thinking, no doubt, of the domestic idyll suggested by the first and the stern drama implied in the second. And there are Milhaud and Eisler to prove the inspirational power of such somewhat unpoetic texts as a catalogue of agricultural implements and newspaper clippings. Seiber is thus in good company. The great difference, however, is that with him the attempt was made not in a spirit of frivolous *bravado* but to produce a serious and well thought-out work of art.

What inspired him in Joyce's text was, as the music clearly proves, far less Bloom's arid meditations than the nocturnal setting of the scene and the sentiments underlying it: the feeling of utter loneliness and insignificance which human beings experience when confronted with the vastness of the cosmos and its inscrutable mysteries; the sense of frustration and futility when Bloom recognises that his meditations lead to one conclusion only: '*that it was a Utopia . . . a past which possibly ceased to exist as a present before its future spectators had entered actual present existence.*'

If that represented to Seiber the emotional substratum of the scene, there was also its atmospheric aspect to be made use of: the pallid darkness of the summer night and the cold oscillating light of the stars. (To judge from the *Notturno* and the string quartet *Fantasy*, nocturnal moods appear to have a special appeal for the composer.) And last, there is the verbal music of certain sentences which beyond their intellectual meaning must inevitably impress themselves on a musician's ear, such as '*The heaventree of stars hung with humid nightblue fruit*', the alliterative '*nought nowhere was never reached*' and so on—lines that, as so often with Joyce, must be read aloud in order to disclose their sensuous beauty. Yet even allowing for such musical

[3] I should make it clear, however, that the composer wholly disagreed with my view as to the uninspiring quality of the better part of his text.

[4] Cf. *Intermezzo* by R. Strauss; Britten's *The Rape of Lucretia*, and Hindemith's oratorio, *Das Unaufhörliche*, to mention works that come immediately to mind.

stimuli as sentiment, atmosphere and verbal sound, it is no exaggeration to describe as a feat of the imagination a setting which not only makes perfect sense *qua* music but interprets Joyce's words in terms of a truly poetic quality.

Corresponding to the five paragraphs of the text, the Cantata is divided into five movements:

I. *The Heaventree*
II. *Meditations of Evolution increasingly vaster*
III. *Obverse Meditations of Involution*
IV. *Nocturne—Intermezzo*
V. *Epilogue.*

Since the prevailing mood underlying Joyce's scene is static and atmospheric, three movements (I, IV, V) are slow, lyrical and evocative and may be described as *Nocturnes*, though only No. IV is explicitly thus entitled. Nos II and III present, in contrast, a dramatic interpretation of the text. The choice of a solo voice alternating with the chorus was evidently suggested by Joyce's division of his paragraphs into a short opening question and a long answer—a formal-dramatic element of which Seiber makes use in the following manner: in the first three numbers, the solo tenor has, in addition to other passages of the text, the question: the chorus the reply; in No. IV this order is reversed, while in the *Epilogue* both question and answer are given to the chorus, the soloist singing only the very last sentence. The contrast is not only of individual voice against a choral mass, i.e. of different timbre and volume, but also of texture: the soloist mostly sings in an *arioso*-cum-recitative style with florid writing in the more lyrical passages while the choral parts either flow in long, undulating lines or move *en bloc* with harmonies often chosen for their suggestive effect. In the last movement there is also a *Sprechchor*.

For the purpose of achieving musical unity the composer allows the five movements to be dominated by a central motive whose characteristic feature is the alternation between a major and minor third:

Ex. 1

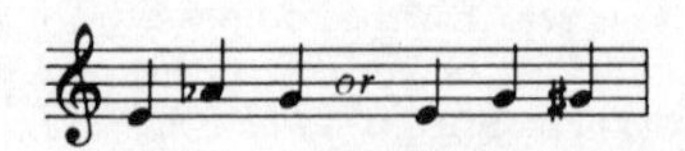

This 'circling' motif is used both to 'rubber-stamp' the movements and, more organically, as a generating thematic cell. In this latter respect the composer has resorted to an unusual procedure in that in the third and last movements he derives from it a twelve-note series which, contrary to one's first assumption, came to him as an afterthought. Thus, in No. III the *allegro* section is based on:

Ex. 2

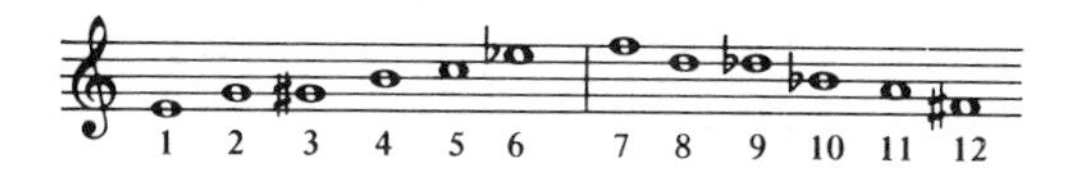

A closer glance at this series shows it to be what Křenek once described as *hochqualifiziert*[5]—not just a seemingly improvisatory succession of the twelve chromatic notes, following no deliberate pattern, but characterised by a special order of sequence. The feature of Seiber's row is its symmetry. The twelve notes are divided into two groups of six each, the first ascending and the second descending; at the same time the second group represents the mirror of the first transposed a semitone up. In addition, the only intervals used are minor thirds and semitones in regular alternation, with a single whole-tone at the apex. The shape of this series may be described as 'question and answer' of which feature the composer has made ingenious use in the melodic structure of the *allegro*.

In the *Epilogue*, Ex. I generates a twelve-note series of a less distinguished character which serves as the subject for an introductory orchestral fugue in eight parts:

Ex. 3

Yet this does not complete the composer's recourse to twelve-note devices. In No. IV, the *Nocturne*, he introduces yet another tone-row which, unlike the two previous ones, is wholly independent of the germ

[5] See *Über Neue Musik* (Vienna, 1937).

motif, Ex. I, and which partly originated from a work of Schönberg's. More will be said about this later but here we may make the general observations that in none of these three movements does Seiber apply the Schönbergian technique with a strict observance of its rules.[6] Except for the *Nocturne*, his handling of it is considerably freer than in, say, Berg's *Lyric Suite* and Violin Concerto. There are tonal chords and a tonal pull is felt, notably in the scherzo of No. III and the fugue of No. V. Broadly speaking, the five movements of the Cantata present an intentionally symmetrical, classical key-scheme: E–A–E–B–E. In other words, *Ulysses* is 'on' the tonality of E which is defined by its dominant and subdominant keys, yet greatly expanded and complicated by chromaticism and harmonic shifts reminiscent of Bartók's method of expanding tonality.

So much for general features. Turning to the individual movements, our chief interest concentrates on the way in which the composer has responded to his text. To start with, what in No. I seems to have caught his imagination in the first place, were the image and the rich verbal sound of *'The Heaventree of stars hung with humid nightblue fruit'*. After 'setting the atmosphere' in the tenor's introduction, a prologue darkly-coloured, slow and brooding, the chorus opens in close thirds and branches out into swaying, long-drawn arabesques calling up the image of Joyce's 'Heaventree':

Ex. 4

[6] This is also true of his *Fantasia Concertante* which is written wholly in the twelve-note style.

Though no mortal has yet heard the 'music of the spheres' the continuous weaving and revolving of lines of Seiber's chorus suggests something of that mysterious effect.

Joyce's second paragraph presented a considerably more difficult proposition. This long meditation on '*Evolutions increasingly vaster*' consists of the enumeration of a multitude of astronomical phenomena. It was apparently the underlying idea of a constant yet varied motion of different stellar bodies that suggested a musical treatment in the form of a *passacaglia*—a masterly solution of the problem of finding a musical form which would both symbolise the intellectual contents of the text and hold the structure of the whole movement together. The ground-bass of the *passacaglia* may thus be taken to stand for the idea of the Universe while the variations upon it illustrate the diverse evolutions occurring within the infinite space. The theme with its triple-time and chromatic descent is clearly modelled on the old *passacaglia* type:

Ex. 5

As with the tone-rows in the third and last movements, Seiber handles it in a completely free manner, now extending it, now shortening it and, in addition, using figure *x* (a variant derived from the central motive, Ex.1) for development. Moreover, the theme also moves to the upper part so that 'chaconne' would perhaps be a more accurate description. While Ex. 5 is used in some variations more than once, each variation has a melodic and rhythmic pattern of its own, yet the basic 3/4 metre is retained throughout, thus imparting to the *passacaglia* an overriding rhythmic unity. One of the most impressive variations is set to the words, *'of our system plunging towards the constellation of Hercules'* whose dramatic image the composer has transmuted into a vigorous fast-moving *fugato* on three subjects divided between chorus and orchestra:

Ex. 6

and culminating in a powerful unison of the choral subject which is crowned in the following variation by a close four-part canon on the whole orchestra, representing the climax of the movement.

In the third paragraph, *'Obverse Meditations of Involutions increasingly less vast'*, Bloom turns from the Universe to our planet, from the macrocosm to the microcosm, from the inorganic to *'organic existences'*. To suggest Joyce's obverse picture, Seiber opens the movement with a mirror-like inversion of the orchestral introduction of the preceding movement reminiscent of similar 'tricks' in the word settings of the mediæval polyphonists. The main section of the movement is a fast scherzo-like *allegro* which, as already mentioned, is based on the tone-row, Ex. 2. As in the *passacaglia*, each sentence of the text is set to a variation of the basic row (also used in its *cancrizans* version in the recapitulation of the scherzo) and the whole is held together rhythmically by the pervading 6/8 metre. The several divisions of the chorus and the almost continuous splitting of the lines into small fragments inevitably conjure up the image of the microscopic multitude of organisms of which Bloom speaks. A subtle touch here is the change, at the words, *'of the universe of human serum'* from the impersonal chorus to the solo voice. This section is to be taken as the contrasting trio of the scherzo. Equally suggestive is the setting of the last sentence, the alliterative '*nought nowhere was never reached*', which is spoken by the chorus *senza voce* while the orchestra dies away on increasingly shorter fragments of the tone-row.

In the fourth paragraph Joyce describes the nocturnal aspect of our planet which is mirrored in music of a strangely pale, wraith-like character. There is a cold, impersonal and at times eerie air about it—it is all atmosphere rather than *Stimmung*. The movement is by way of a homage to Schönberg. It is based on a tone-row whose first six notes have been taken from the sixth of Schönberg's Piano Pieces, Op. 19. As in Schönberg, Seiber introduces them in their chordal version to which he adds two more chords of his own to complete the series:

Ex. 7

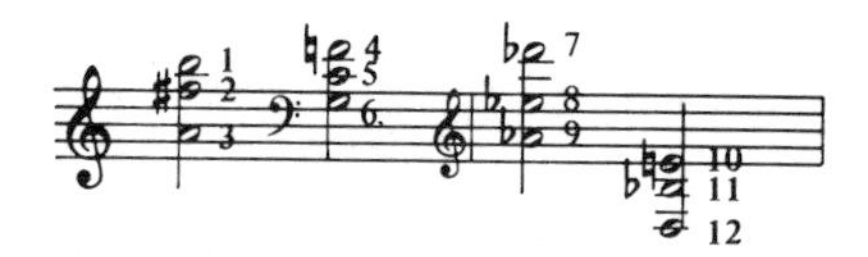

There are repetitions of individual notes, changes of their original sequence in the series and chordal versions of them with tonal implications. But unlike the other two movements employing the twelve-note technique, the *Nocturne* derives the *whole* material from Ex. 7 and consists of continuous variations of it.

The reason for Seiber's borrowing from Schönberg was the fact that the two chords struck him as a perfect embodiment of the idea of nocturnal stillness and pallor. It is precisely this impression which the piece creates from its very beginning: low-lying choral parts in block-harmonies with 'hollow' fourths and fifths and broken and shadowy figures in the orchestra which are scored in such a way as to produce the effect of pale, etiolated colours. The *Nocturne*, which owes something to the style of Bartók's 'night music', is a masterly study in evanescent sounds and perhaps the most immediately impressive of the five movements.

The *Epilogue* refers back again to the opening movement and for a subtle reason. It will be seen that while in the opening paragraph Bloom and his young friend are subject to an illusion, 'the heaventree', in the last paragraph they realise that '*it was a Utopia*', a negation, as it were, of all they had imagined they might see in the cosmos. Therefore, the *Epilogue* takes up where the *Prologue* ended: the concluding violin solo of No. I is, in No. V, spun out into the twelve-note fugal subject of Ex. 3. This eight-part fugue is the most extensive orchestral piece of the Cantata and seems to suggest the mental process of Bloom's '*having weighed the matter*' (does it also stand for Bloom's '*allowing a possible error*' ?!). The rest of the movement is mainly choral, recapitulating some of the material of the first movement such as 'the heaventree' music. But there is now a significant change. While in the first movement the music gradually rose from dark to bright colours, in the *Epilogue* this process is reversed; moreover, the texture becomes increasingly thinner, disintegrates into mere particles and sinks back to the low solitary E on which the Cantata began—an ending strangely moving in its transcendental suggestion of human frustration.

NINETEEN

ELGAR AND THE SYMPHONY

WHEN A COMPOSER settles down to writing a symphony he means business of the first musical importance. Beethoven has taught us this, and ever since we have, rightly or wrongly, come to regard the symphony as the most highly organised of our instrumental forms—a form that puts the whole of the composer's creative faculties to the severest test, that challenges all the resources of his intellectual and emotional powers. In short, to write a symphony is to give the totality of both one's musical experience and one's artistic personality. This has been essentially the view of most symphonic writers since Beethoven. It was also Elgar's view.

His two symphonies are conceived on a grand scale, and one feels a strong and rich musical personality behind the music, speaking a markedly personal language. There is an abundance of beautifully poetic and truly inspired moments, and the treatment of the orchestra shows the hand of a composer used to thinking in orchestral terms. Yet on examining the two works more closely, one begins to wonder whether Elgar's method, or rather the particular cast of his musical mind, was altogether that of a born symphonist. The symphonies suffer from one basic weakness: the essentially rhapsodic nature of Elgar's conception. In other words, instead of letting the music grow—one of the fundamental characteristics of the symphonic form—the composer is inclined to string together the various structural sections in a more or less kaleidoscopic way. They do not seem to flow naturally into each other and the cogent logic of an organic sequence is at times completely lacking. This is not a failing that owes its origin to any purely technical deficiency. That Elgar knew how to handle the symphonic technique, particularly as regards thematic treatment, is amply shown in the orchestral parts of his oratorios, the First Symphony (his use of the motto-theme is most varied and ingenious), and in his *Falstaff*. His formal failing is due fundamentally to the particular case of his musical mind. Elgar was a lyricist with marked programmatic tendencies. He was thus a romantic composer of the Schumann type. (It is significant that he confessed to a special liking for that composer's music, particularly his symphonies.)

If we want to find the essential Elgar we shall do so in the *Enigma Variations*, which show Elgar at his orchestral best, and represent the quintessence of his instrumental style: a series of self-contained contrasting mood-pictures permeated with strong lyrical feeling and illustrating a certain inner programme: the different personalities of his various friends. Does this not remind us of Schumann's *Carnaval*, the *Davidsbündler* and the *Etudes Symphoniques*? Is not Elgar's approach essentially the same? I suggest that, broadly speaking, the character and the formal type of the *Enigma Variations* return in the symphonies in more or less ingenious disguise.

For 'mood-pictures' read 'structural sections', which are, however, strung together by symphonic methods, and you arrive at the type of Elgar's symphonic movement. This chiefly accounts for its rhapsodic character. It also accounts for another typical feature: the continuous rise and fall of Elgar's emotional curve. His symphonic movements are given a special stamp by these unsteady and often very sudden and dramatic changes of mood, which are particularly disturbing in those movements which are the chief carriers of the symphonic thought, the first and last. With Elgar the essentially epic character of the symphony changes to a lyrico-dramatic one. And to assume an underlying programme which to a certain extent conditions and directs the character, treatment and formal course of the music, is not only justified in view of the programmatic nature of most of Elgar's compositions, but is also the corollary of internal evidence. Despite the fact that Elgar upheld Brahms's Third Symphony as the perfect model of symphonic writing because of the absence from it of any clue to what was meant, he gave us in his own E flat Symphony a clear indication of its spiritual meaning by prefacing it with a quotation from Shelley, while the character of General Gordon was, on his own admission, the inspiration of the central mood of his planned first symphony, though whether this was the later Symphony in A flat is uncertain.

Once we have recognised these tendencies and the failings to which they lead, we shall have cleared the chief obstacle to a more positive appreciation of Elgar's symphonic style. His symphonies are certainly no model symphonies. Yet what lends them an indisputable distinction is their very personal language, particularly as regards their melodic style. There is no mistaking those typical Elgarian curves of rising and falling intervals with their preference for wide upward leaps, the rising sixth forming here a special feature. Elgar's melodic gift seems to unfold its greatest richness in two special types of phrase: the melody which, by its fiery *élan* and its overflowing exuberance, takes you, as it were, by the scruff of the neck (see the very beginning of the E flat Symphony), and the quietly lyrical line imbued with yearning, wistful expression. It is particularly with this second type that Elgar the melodist scores over Elgar the symphonist. There is no more beautiful example of this than the slow movement of the A flat Symphony, with its characteristic string writing. (It is, incidentally, the strings—the most flexible and most expressive group of orchestral instruments—that give Elgar's orchestra its cachet.)

It is in such passages that what has been termed the Englishness of Elgar's musical genius seems to manifest itself with singular intensity. These passages are the first to arrest the attention of the non-British musician, and it is interesting to see how some of the younger school of British composers have been influenced by this Elgarian trait, witness the slow movement of Ireland's Piano Concerto (particularly the string passages), Bliss's Clarinet Quintet and Music for Strings and the slow movement of Vaughan Williams' F minor Symphony. This English element in Elgar is a striking proof that national characteristics in music need not necessarily originate in folk-song. There is nothing folk-songish about Elgar's lyrical phrase, yet it will always be felt as something intrinsically English. Nationalism in music is not always a matter of literal quotation of folk-song motifs, or the absorption, however complete and organic, of folk-song elements into one's personal style. It often expresses itself in a certain characteristic attitude of the musical mind, in a certain way of musical thinking and of tackling technical problems. This higher and more subtle kind of musical nationalism is the kind we meet in the Elgar Symphonies. It does not lie only in the shape and the expression of Elgar's lyrical phrases. It is also felt in those quiet moments which Elgar is fond of introducing after his great emotional outbursts, moments in which the music reaches a maximum of beautifully poetic expression tinged with wistfulness. The foreign musician is perhaps better able than the Englishman to detect these national elements; they strike him at once as something new and different from the symphonic style of German music. True, the symphonies betray certain influences, notably Wagner's in the orchestration and Brahms' in the symphonic texture. Yet for all that, they represent for me the first great examples of English symphonic thinking.

TWENTY

FIDELIO

1. Genesis of the Opera

BEETHOVEN'S FIRST ACQUAINTANCE with opera dates from his early years at Bonn where between 1789 and 1792 he sat as a viola player in the Elector's theatre orchestra. In this capacity he heard the best operas of his time—operas by Gluck, Mozart, Cimarosa, Paisiello and others—and he may have formed then some ideas about the dramatic stage. Up to 1803, however, there was only little sign that he was interested in operatic compositions, his main domain being instrumental music and oratorio.[1] But then an event occurred which in retrospect seems to have been providential for *Fidelio.* In April 1803 his oratorio, *Christus am Ölberg*, had its first performance in Vienna; it proved that Beethoven possessed a marked gift for a stirringly vivid and imaginative representation of Christ's agony in Gethsemane, though in later years he dismissed part of the oratorio as being written 'in modern operatic style'. It was most probably this dramatic quality which induced Schikaneder, then director of the recently built Theater an der Wien, to commission from Beethoven in the spring of 1803 an opera on a classical subject to his own libretto, *Vestas Feuer*, of which the composer, however, completed only the first scene, a trio, since financial difficulties had arisen with the running of the theatre forcing its owner, the Viennese merchant, Bartholomäus Zitterbarth, to sell it in February 1804 to Baron Peter von Braun,[2] the manager of the Hoftheater am Kärnthnerthor. Von Braun dismissed Schikaneder (though he had to take him back by the September of that year), and it is possible that this change

[1] In about 1796 Beethoven wrote two tenor arias to be interpolated in Ignaz Umlauf's singspiele, *Die schöne Schusterin* (1779), and from the same year dates his dramatic scena, *Ah perfido!*, not to mention dramatic settings of three more Italian texts between 1801 and 1802.

[2] Beethoven was on friendly terms with the Brauns, dedicating to the Baroness the two Piano Sonatas. Op. 14 and the Horn Sonata, Op. 17.

of management was the likely cause for Beethoven abandoning *Vestas Feuer*.[3]

His erstwhile contract with Schikaneder was dissolved and it was not until the latter's reinstatement in the theatre in the autumn of 1804 that von Braun drew up a new contract with Beethoven for an opera to a libretto, adapted by Joseph Ferdinand von Sonnleithner,[4] from a French original, *Léonore, ou l'amour conjugal. Fait historique espagnol en deux actes*, by Jean Nicolas Bouilly. Bouilly's subject was then very much in the air of post-revolutionary France and Central Europe, proof of which is the fact that it was set no fewer than four times in close succession by composers of three different nationalities—the Frenchman Pierre Gaveaux (Paris, 19 February, 1798), the Italian Ferdinando Paer, in an adaptation by Giacomo Cinti (Dresden, 30 October, 1804), the German-born Simone Mayr in a version by Gaetano Rossi (Padua, 1805) and Beethoven.[5]

Beethoven started the composition of *Fidelio* in late 1803 and probably completed it in sketch-form by August or early September 1804. He insisted, however, on calling the opera *Leonore*, but von Braun, in order to avoid confusion with the works by Gaveaux and Paer, named it *Fidelio*. Incidentally, Bouilly seems to have derived his heroine's incognito from 'Fedele', the name adopted by Imogen, another faithful wife, who appears disguised in boy's clothes in Act III sc. vi of Shakespeare's *Cymbeline.* The first production was fixed to take place at the Theater an der Wien on 15 October, 1805, but difficulties were raised by the Imperial censor in a ban, dated 30 September, on the grounds that the libretto was subversive of political authority. In a letter to the censor of 2 October Sonnleithner appealed against the prohibition pointing out his chief reasons for adapting the French libretto. These were: firstly, that the Empress herself (the wife of Francis II) had found '*the original very beautiful*'—in fact she had

[3] This libretto was subsequently set by Joseph Weigl (1766–1846) and his opera first produced in Vienna on 10 August, 1805.

[4] Sonnleithner (1766–1835) was Secretary to the Court Theatre from 1804 to 1814, and was one of the founders of the famous Gesellschaft der Musikfreunde in 1812.

[5] Pierre Gaveaux (1761–1825) was a fertile composer with forty-odd operas to his name, as well as a singer who sang the tenor part of Florestan when his *Léonore* was first given in Paris. Gaveaux's first venture into 'rescue opera' was *L'Amour filial* (Paris, 7 March, 1792).

Ferdinando Paer (1771–1839) was a composer of an equally prolific output, whose stage works have historic significance for showing the trends of Italian opera around the turn of the eighteenth century. He was particularly experienced in the management of stage-craft and his *Leonora, o l'amor coniugale* was one of the several models for Beethoven's *Fidelio*.

For details of Mayr, see Chapter 17.

told Sonnleithner that no other libretto had pleased her as much as that of *Fidelio*; secondly, that Paer had already brought out an opera on the same subject at Dresden and Prague; thirdly, that Beethoven had worked on the opera for more than a year and a half, and since no one had expected difficulties with the censor, rehearsals had begun in time to produce the opera on the name-day of the Empress (15 October); fourthly, that the action had been transferred to sixteenth-century Spain, and, lastly, that there was a great dearth of good libretto and that that of *Fidelio* was indeed a very fine specimen presenting a moving picture of female virtues. In a second letter of 3 October Sonnleithner reinforced his plea by saying that the only stumbling-block was the fact that a minister (Pizarro) had abused his power but, Sonnleithner stresses, he had abused it in a private matter for which he was punished—and punished by his King.[6] The censor relented on 5 October and the first performance of *Fidelio* was given at the Theater an der Wien on 20 November, 1805, preceded by the *Leonore* No. 2 Overture, and conducted by Ignaz von Seyfried in the most unfavourable circumstances. Napoleon's troops had occupied Vienna on 13 November, while the Court and the nobility—the very people with a true appreciation of Beethoven's music—had fled to the country. Thus the audience at the first-night consisted largely of French officers, very few among them with a knowledge of German. Moreover, the opera was said to have been put on very hurriedly, the singer of Florestan (Demmer) was unsatisfactory, and Anna Milder, later an outstanding Leonore, had great difficulties with her aria;[7] besides, her acting was not up to the demands of her great rôle. All the press notices were without exception severely critical of the opera pointing, among other things, to its excessive length—the first version was in three acts—the incessant repetition of words and whole sentences and the lack of invention and true characterisation in the music. There were two more performances on 21 and 22 November, both badly attended, after which Beethoven withdrew the work. Since excessive length was one of the points in which all critics had concurred, some of Beethoven's aristocratic friends, convinced of the excellence of most of the opera, undertook a rescue action and attempted to persuade the

[6] Sonnleithner's two letters to the censors are reproduced in A. Sandberger, '*Léonore* von Bouilly und ihre Bearbeitung für Beethoven durch Josef Sonnleithner', *Beethoven-Jahrbuch* (Munich, 1924), p. 141.

[7] Milder, who was later to take part in the first performance of the Ninth Symphony, told Anton Schindler, Beethoven's one-time amanuensis, in 1836, of the 'hard struggle' she had had with the composer over some passages in the 1805–6 version of the *Adagio* section in Leonore's great monologue, passages which she described as 'ugly, unvocal and inimicable' to her voice. See Thayer-Forbes, vol. I, pp. 383–99.

composer, much against his own stubborn conviction, to make radical cuts.[8] (The parallel with Bruckner and his well-meaning friends is noteworthy.)

Stephan von Breuning, who knew Beethoven from his early days in Bonn, undertook the revision of Sonnleithner's libretto, contracting its three acts into two acts (as in Bouilly's original), transposing certain scenes and altering some of the text. In this shortened version, for which Beethoven wrote his *Leonore* No. 3 Overture, the opera was produced at the Theater an der Wien on 24 March, 1806 and repeated on 10 April. On this occasion the press reports were far more favourable. While they still inveighed against Sonnleithner's libretto (Breuning's name did not appear on the play bills), they found much to praise in the music, and the odds are that this second version would have had more than just two performances but for the fact of Beethoven's congenital mistrust and suspicion in money matters. He accused von Braun of misrepresenting the box-office receipts—in lieu of a fee Beethoven received a percentage of these takings—and a quarrel ensued in consequence of which he angrily demanded the score back.

This is the last we hear of *Fidelio* until eight years later. Early in 1814 three members of the Hoftheater—Saal, Vogl and Weinmüller—who were entitled to a benefit performance decided, no doubt prompted by the fact that Beethoven's fame was now at its height, to approach him for permission to produce his opera. He readily acceded to their request, but in marked contrast to his earlier attitude towards revision in 1806, it was he himself who insisted on making considerable improvements in the opera.[9] At his invitation Georg Friedrich Treitschke, the poet and stage-manager of the Hoftheater, took (with Sonnleithner's consent) the libretto in hand, tautening the action even more than Breuning had done, chiefly by reducing the spoken dialogue, providing a

[8] There is a long description of the crucial meeting at Prince Lichnowsky's in December 1805, which J. A. Röckel, the singer of Florestan in the second (1806) version of *Fidelio*, gave to Thayer in 1861. See Thayer-Forbes, vol. I, pp. 388–9.

[9] That financial considerations also entered into his decision to revise the work is attested by a list found together with his sketches for alterations in the 1814 version. In this list Beethoven noted down the sums he hoped to obtain from productions elsewhere:

Hamburg	15 Thaler in gold
Frankfurt	15 Thaler in gold
Carlsruhe	12 Thaler in gold
Graz	120 Florins (one thaler = 12 florins(?))
Darmstadt	12 Thaler in gold
Stuttgard (*sic*)	12 Thaler in gold

(See Nottebohm, *Zweite Beethoveniana*, p. 299). Beethoven's expectations however remained unfulfilled. *Fidelio* was produced in none of the above cities before 1831—four years after his death.

new text for several musical numbers and dividing the second and final act into two scenes. While in both the Sonnleithner and Breuning versions—which faithfully followed the French original—the whole of this act played in Florestan's dungeon, Treitschke transferred the great finale to the bastion of the prison—an effective symbolic change from darkness to light.

In this version the opera was produced at the Kärnthnerthor Theater on 23 May 1814 when the part of Leonore was again sung by Anna Milder;[10] Florestan was the Italian tenor Radichi, Pizarro, Vogl, Weinmüller sang Rocco, and Saal, the Minister. Beethoven, now completely deaf, nominally conducted but behind him stood Michael Umlauf[11] to prevent any mishaps. For this third version Beethoven composed the so-called *Fidelio* Overture in E major, but it was not played on the first-night because it was not yet finished. According to Treitschke, the *Prometheus* Overture was performed while Seyfried states that the overture to *Die Ruinen von Athen* took its place, which is corroborated by a notice in the *Sammler*.[12] It also appears that for the first few performances Milder sang the original version of her aria and the revised version[13] not until 18 July when also Rocco's fine couplet, which had, strangely, been omitted from the 1806 version,[14] was included. The success was tremendous and the opera soon made its way abroad, with Weber being the first to produce it outside Vienna (Prague, 21 November, 1814). The first full score of *Fidelio* was published in France in 1826 by the Paris firm of A. Farrenc with a French and German text, yet still in the original three acts and with the action transferred from Spain to Germany![15]

II. The Opera of 1814

Fidelio has often been called the 'first political' opera. How much truth is in this description? Let us for a moment grant the 'political', yet what of the ordinal 'first'? As a matter of historical fact, *Fidelio* came, as we have seen, chronologically last in the series of four operas based on Bouilly's subject. And as for terming it 'political', this would seem

[10] Originally a Madame Hönig was to sing but a day before the performance she was replaced by Milder.

[11] Michael Umlauf assisted the composer in this way in performances of other works of his. Michael was the son of Ignaz Umlauf (1746–76) with whom he is often confused.

[12] See Thayer-Forbes, vol. I, p. 582.

[13] My table on pp. 258–9 shows the respective lengths of the different versions of this aria.

[14] However, a revised version of this couplet is found in a draft score of the 1806 version, with music different from the original.

[15] Publication order of *Fidelio* is as follows:

to ignore the transcendental aspirations and the great message of Beethoven's work which rises far above the political implications of the libretto—the conflict between the *ancien* and *nouveau régime* played out in the cruel persecution of an innocent, courageous and truth-loving man by an evil tyrant (a theme which has gained considerable actuality in the Europe of the last fifty years or so). But Beethoven was not a political animal and when setting the opera never thought of proclaiming through it a political message. His sentiment *in tyrannos* has a much wider application. *Fidelio* is a paean to the great humanitarian ideas of the French Revolution, ideas which subsequently became deeply rooted in the civilised Western world—liberty and justice for every individual and the brotherhood of men. 'Es sucht der Bruder seine Brüder und kann er helfen, hilft er gern' sings the Minister in the second-act finale. At the same time the opera is a glorification of a wife's unbounded loyalty to her husband and her readiness for heroic self-sacrifice on his behalf. 'Töt erst sein Weib!' exclaims Leonore in the great quartet (No. 14) of Act II. These two sets of ideas—humanity and utter conjugal devotion, ideas not necessarily related—are brought into the closest interplay and form

---

1805 version, HV 109 [Op. 72a]
- 1905, vocal socre, edited E. Prieger; Breitkopf & Härtel privately (Brandstetter, Leipzig)
- 1908–10, full score, edited E. Prieger; Breitkopf & Härtel privately (Brandstetter, Leipzig)
- 1956, early version of Marzelline's aria (C minor) in score, HV 122 *Rivista Santa Cecilia*, Vol. 5, No. 4
- 1960, early version of Marzelline's aria (C major) in score, HV 121; Breitkopf, Supplement Vol. II to *GA Ed.*
- 1967, full score, edited W. Hess; Breitkopf, Supplement Vol. II to *GA*

1806 version, HV 110 [Op. 72a]
- 1807, Trio, 'Ein Mann ist bald genommen'; canon-Quartet; Duet, 'Um in der Ehe froh zu leben' (vocal score); Cappi, Vienna
- 1810, vocal score (by Czerny), incomplete; Breitkopf & Härtel
- 1815, new edition of above, with additions; Breitkopf & Härtel
- 1843, Pizarro's aria, 'Auf euch nur will ich bauen', Act I finale (Hess gives 1841 as publication date, but *see* O. E. Deutsch, *Musikverlags-Nummern* [Berlin, 1961], p. 10, '6821–7003'; number of present extract is 6893); Breitkopf & Härtel
- *1851/53*, vocal score, edited O. Jahn, with two early versions of Marzelline's aria as supplement; Breitkopf & Härtel

1814 version (principal publications, excluding miscellaneous arrangements [Kinsky-Halm, pp. 185ff]), Op. 72b
- 1814, vocal score (by Moscheles); Artaria
- 1815, vocal score; Simrock
- 1826, vocal score and full score (French translation); A. Farrenc, Paris
- 1828, vocal score and piano (4 hands) arr. Breitkopf & Härtel
- 1847, first full score in German original (*see* 1826 above) Simrock

This list was compiled by Ates Orga, the editor of the Beethoven Symposium for which my article was originally intended. I reproduce it with Mr Orga's kind permission.

the spiritual core of *Fidelio*. No other musical stage-work can claim the same measure of lofty idealism, moral uplift and ethical force. Its only forerunners are Gluck's *Orfeo ed Euridice* and Mozart's *Die Zauberflöte*; and if it has found a modern successor at all, it is Berg's *Wozzeck*, which proclaims the message of humanity and dignity of man by representing on the stage, in poetic irony, the very opposite.

We mentioned the French Revolution in which the subject of *Fidelio* had its origin. Beethoven was a spiritual child of this tremendous upheaval in the history of humanitarian ideas—he was but a boy of eighteen when it first broke out in 1789. He came to believe most profoundly in its tenets—liberty, equality and fraternity of men—to which he set a crowning monument in the finale of his Ninth Symphony. For the development of Beethoven's *Weltbild*, his spiritual outlook on life and the world, the ideas of the French Revolution were of crucially formative importance. They inspired some of the greatest works of which *Fidelio* is the most explicit in its message wholly conforming to Schiller's concept that the theatre is a moral institution. Its subject, born during the most turbulent stage of the Revolution, struck, apart from its great musico-dramatic potential, a basic and fundamental chord in his ethical personality. Yet it would be beyond all psychology to explain why it was just Beethoven—in his private life the most despotic of men—who responded so directly and intensely to its humanitarian message. All we can say is that his nature happened to be morally so constituted as to be most readily receptive to ideas coming from across the Rhine.

Fidelio is an opera whose essence is heroism symbolised by Leonore's resolve to liberate Florestan against tremendous odds or die in the attempt. The subject accorded with Beethoven's own heroic concept of life, a concept so much to the fore during his middle period. But his view that existence was suffering and endurance, and that this could only be mastered by an heroic act of will, seems to have had little connection with the French Revolution. It was formed, I suggest, in the agony of a personal tragedy—his deafness. When in 1796 he first became aware of it[16] he took it as a passing affliction, but his realisation in 1802 that it was incurable and that he was doomed to total deafness appears to have come to him with the force of a traumatic shock; at first it had the impact of a catastrophe on him which he thought he would not survive. Proof of this is the tragic document he addressed to his two brothers (Caspar Carl and Nikolaus Johann) which is known as

[16] The general medical view today is that Beethoven was afflicted by otosclerosis which is due to a constitutional tendency of a hereditary nature. See E. Larkin, 'Beethoven's Medical History', in Martin Cooper, *Beethoven: The Last Decade, 1817–1827* (London, 1970), pp. 440–1.

the Heiligenstadt Testament of 6 October, 1802. This was a true *De profundis clamavi* from which I quote the sentences revelant to my hypothesis. Beethoven introduces them by saying that he was completely unable to hear the sound of a flute or the song of a shepherd, and then continues:

> Such experiences brought me to the verge of despair, a little more and I would have put an end to my life—it was only *art* which held me back. O! it seemed to me impossible to leave the world until I had produced all that I felt in me to produce . . .

And a little later:

> Virtue, it alone can give happiness, not money; I speak from experience. . . It is due to it and to art that I did not end my life by suicide . . .

What do these sentences imply? Clearly, that Beethoven conquered his suicidal thoughts by an act of iron will-power, by a heroic resolve to stay alive and go on composing. This presumes an intense inner struggle, and it is my conviction that this struggle was the matrix out of which his heroic works were born. Is it not significant that in the eight years following the Heiligenstadt Testament Beethoven wrote the *Eroica* and the Fifth Symphony, *Fidelio*, the Fifth Piano Concerto and the overtures to *Coriolanus* and *Egmont*? They are the works of which the heroic element, a sense of intense conflict fought out in the most dramatic of terms, forms their most salient feature. (Also the considerable formal expansion to be noted in such compositions as the 'symphonic' *Rasumovsky* quartets, the *Waldstein, Appassionata* and *Kreutzer* sonatas can be interpreted as a corollary of Beethoven's heroic concept since 1802). Take the *Eroica*. Certainly, it was partly inspired by Napoleon, the Consul of the French Republic and in Beethoven's eyes, as indeed in the eyes of so many others, the fighter for liberty, equality and justice. The original title of the symphony was *Bonaparte*. But, as J. W. N. Sullivan, the author of a most perceptive book on Beethoven (London, 1927) and on the ethos of his music, writes:

> No amount of brooding over Napoleon's career could have given Beethoven his realisation of what we call the life-story of heroic achievement, as exemplified in the *Eroica*. This is obviously a transcription of personal experience. He may have thought Bonaparte a hero, but his conception of the heroic he had earned for himself.

'A transcription of personal experience', says Sullivan. This personal experience, I suggest, was the composer's shattering realisation reverberating so poignantly through the Heiligenstadt Testament, that he was now incurably deaf and that only through the mobilisation of his total will-power would he be able to survive and continue creating. True, heroism seems to have formed part and parcel of Beethoven's moral constitution, but it was brought out into the open and put to its most challenging test by his determination to fight down his suicidal thoughts and restore the sanity of his mind by a renewed devotion to his art. 'I will seize fate by its throat' Beethoven is reported to have said about the significance of his Fifth Symphony. This 'fate' I see in his affliction with incurable deafness and the self-destructive thoughts it at first induced in him while the 'seizing by its throat' stands symbolically for his desperate struggle to fight against them.

I wish to go further and suggest that there is a most intimate connection between Beethoven's personal tragedy and the drama of *Fidelio*. In what we may assume to have been unconscious fantasies he saw in Florestan's undeserved suffering his own suffering as an incurably deaf composer: just as Florestan is the innocent victim of a political intrigue, so Beethoven may have felt to have been the innocent victim of an intrigue of nature.[17] Pizarro, the cause of Florestan's suffering, may well have represented to him the dramatic symbol for the cause of his own suffering. And what of Leonore? I am convinced that in his unconscious mind Beethoven equated her seemingly impossible and heroic task of freeing her husband from the Governor's clutches, with his own resolve in 1802 to rise above his own tragic fate and try to save his mental sanity by a complete devotion to composition. Seen in this light the happy outcome of the opera would correspond to his triumphant victory in his personal tragedy.

If my theory is accepted that Beethoven perceived in Pizarro, Florestan and Leonore aspects of his own tragedy, then it will help us to explain why the subject of *Fidelio* attracted him with magnetic force and engaged his *entire* personality as man and artist. The fact that he made three versions of the opera—and that for the last version it was he himself who of his own accord suggested to revise it—is, I think, sufficient evidence of the hold this subject had on him. That the commission to compose *Fidelio* came a year or so after the Heiligen-

[17] Alan Tyson, in his probing article, 'Beethoven's Heroic Phase', *Musical Times* 110/ii (February 1969), p. 139, confirms this when he writes that if one reads in the opening of Florestan's recitative, 'deafness' for 'darkness', it is a sentiment that might have come from the Heiligenstadt Testament.

stadt Testament, which incidentally must have provided immense realease of the pent-up tension accumulated in the preceding years, was of course a mere coincidence, but it came at the psychologically right moment. True, for Beethoven his deafness was a profoundly tragic experience, but for the history of nineteenth-century music it was an immense blessing in disguise. For without this tragedy it is debatable whether his great heroic works from 1803 to 1810 would have come into being at all, just as it is debatable whether Beethoven's spiritual development would have taken the direction it did after the Heiligenstadt Testament.

My theory also helps to account for the singular fact that in spite of many subsequent operatic subjects *Fidelio* remained his only stage-work. He continued to search for subjects virtually till the end of his life, approaching a great many writers for suitable libretti. This search became an *idée fixe*, yet none of the subjects contemplated fired his imagination sufficiently strongly because, apart from other reasons, they failed to combine idealism and humanity with a story which was a reflection of his own tragedy, as was *Fidelio*. He considered most of these various projects very seriously and in great detail but his reaction was always the same—a lightning realisation of situations and incidents best suited for an effective dramatic treatment followed by doubts, irresolution and, ultimately, complete rejection.[18] It was in the last analysis this fixation to a subject of a special kind which made Beethoven so rigid, so unmalleable when it came to make up his mind

[18] After the second version of *Fidelio* in 1806, Beethoven's first substantial project was for Shakespeare's *Macbeth* in an adaptation by Heinrich Collin (1808), who also offered him a *Bradamante* (eventually set by Reichardt), which Beethoven eventually refused, having already remarked in a letter from the autumn of 1808 that 'I cannot deny that on the whole I am prejudiced against this sort of thing [magic], because it has a soporific effect on feeling and reason'; compare this with a similar reaction against a libretto offered in 1803 by Rochlitz (letter of Beethoven's, dated 4 January, 1804). In 1811 Treitschke was approached to prepare a libretto for a romantic melodrama, *Die Ruinen von Babylon*, of which Beethoven spoke with enthusiasm saying that it was difficult to find a good libretto. In a letter to Ferdinand Pálffy (11 June, 1811), Beethoven remarks 'it is very difficult to find a good libretto for an opera. Since last year I have turned down no less than twelve or more of them.' On 28 January, 1812 he wrote to August von Kotzebue: 'When I was setting your prologue and epilogue to music for the Hungarians [Opp. 117/113], I could not restrain an ardent wish to have an opera that would be the product of your unique dramatic genius. . . . I must admit that I should like best of all some grand subject taken from the history and especially from the dark ages, for instance, from the time of Attila or the like.' During the same year he discussed operatic plans with the young poet, Karl Theodor Körner (1791–1813), and the latter (10 February 1813) wrote that 'Beethoven has asked me for *Die Rückkehr des Odysseus*. If Gluck were alive, that would be a subject fo his Muse'. Beethoven's connections with Treitschke extended beyond *Die Ruinen von Babylon*

about a subject of a different character. Moreover, his ethos would not allow him to set such subjects as those of Mozart's *Figaro*, *Don Giovanni* or *Così fan tutte*—'degraded plots' which, he said to Rellstab in 1825, could never appeal to him. In his symphonies, sonatas and quartets he was, as it were, his own 'librettist', unfettered by conceptual thoughts or, to use the modern jargon, linguistic semantics, and was therefore completely free to sublimate in them precisely those emotional complexes and images which stirred him most deeply. Beethoven was not a born *operatic* composer though he was a highly *dramatic* one, and because of his fixation was, unlike Mozart, only able to identify completely with such characters as were the projection of his floating but restricted unconscious fantasies. The portrayal of an immense variety of characters in all their subtle psychological traits such as we find in Mozart was not given to Beethoven. Leonore, Florestan, Pizarro and the Minister are types rather than individual characters, more abstractions than human beings of flesh and blood, and ultimately the mouthpiece for ideas of good and evil, loyalty and villainy, suffering and heroic will. Beethoven paints his principal characters in black-and-white without the many intervening shades that we find in Mozart. In Leonore's music, for instance, there is no suggestion of any eroticism such as we find in Mozart's Countess, though she is occasionally shown in softer, more feminine colours. (Leonore is perhaps the idealisation of the kind of woman Beethoven desired all his life but could never encounter in reality). Yet it is precisely this black-and-white in which resides part of the great dramatic, as well as moral, force of *Fidelio*. It is noteworthy that Beethoven should also have succeeded as well as he did with the portrayal of Rocco and his small world.

Fidelio is the greatest example of the type known as 'Terror' or 'Rescue' opera which was the product of the French Revolution and had a short-lived vogue in France and central Europe up to about the

---

and *Fidelio*, and the *Sammler* for 13 December 1814 revealed that the subject was to be Treitschke's *Romulus und Remus*. Another theme was von Berge's *Bacchus* (1815), and in 1823 Beethoven considered two further librettos by Grillparzer for *Melusine* and *Drahomira*, the latter based on a Bohemian legend.

There was also Beethoven's petition at the end of 1807 to the newly founded Opera Board, in which he sought a permanent appointment pledging himself to produce in addition to other works 'an opera annually'. In view of the failure of *Fidelio* this petition was, not unexpectedly, rejected, but the noblemen, of whom the Board was composed, clubbed together to ensure the composer a regular income through performances of his works (at the home of Prince Lobkowitz) and the commission of the Mass in C.

first decade of the nineteenth century.[19] The taste for such stage-work, which for us would seem to contain an element of verismo—in *Fidelio*, the scene of Pizarro's attempted murder of Florestan in the dark dungeon and Leonore drawing a pistol—sprang from incidents in the Revolution, notably during the Reign of Terror when hairbreadth escapes from Jacobin persecution of persons and whole families of noble birth through the intervention of devoted spouses, friends or servants were a frequent occurrence. Jean Nicolas Bouilly (1763–1847), the author of the two most famous libretti treating of such incidents—*Léonore ou l' amour conjugal* (Gaveaux, 1798) and *Les deux journées* (Cherubini, 1800)— has told us in his *Memoirs*[20] that his stories were based on real events in which he was personally involved as administrator of the ancient Departement Touraine. Thus the subject of *Léonore* originated in the heroic self-sacrifice of a noble lady of Tour (Madame de La Valette) whose efforts to save her husband from the guillotine Bouilly himself had aided and abetted.[21] Again, in *Les deux journées* he recorded the courage of a simple water-carrier who by a cunning trick deceives the authorities and thus rescues a magistrate who was a friend of the author's parents. In both these libretti Bouilly set out to glorify a wife's unbounded loyalty to her husband and added at the end the moral lesson to be drawn from this story. To both libretti he attached the subtitle *Fait historique* to vouchsafe for the authenticity of his tale. Yet, in order not to arouse the suspicion of the political authority that he was defending the aristocracy against the revolutionary régime which might have led to his imprisonment—if

[19] The ancestor of this genre of operas seems to have been Grétry's *Richard Cœur de Lion* (Paris, 21 October, 1784), but the first genuine 'Terror' or 'Rescue' drama was Berton's *Les rigueurs du cloître* (Paris, 23 August, 1790), and Cherubini's first *opéra comique*, produced in Paris on 18 July 1791—*Lodoïska*. These works were followed in close succession by other examples from Lesueur, Dalayrac, Méhul, Gaveaux, Boïeldieu, Paer, Mayr, and, lastly, Beethoven. The subjects were not always related to incidents in France during the Revolution but sometimes dealt with events in other and remoter countries—Poland in *Lodoïska* and Mayr's *L'Amor coniugale* (Padua, 1805), and Siberia in Boïeldieu's *Béniowski* (Paris, 8 June, 1800; after a play by Kotzebue). But in all these cases, terror followed by rescue was the main feature of the plot—in Boïeldieu, the terror, however, is not a human character, it is rather the rigorous Russian climate from which the whole cast is saved in the end!

[20] J. N. Bouilly, *Mes récapitulations* (Paris, 1836–7), vol. II, 'Le Règne de la Terreur', p. 59. Bouilly, a friend of the liberal Comte de Mirabeau, was originally a lawyer and judge employed in the service of the First Republic. After the tremendous success of his *Léonore* in Gaveaux's setting, he devoted himself entirely to the writing of libretti, dramas and comedies which were greatly in demand at the time.

[21] In his recollections, Bouilly relates, with evident pride, that at a reading session of his *Léonore* in a private circle a young girl, Eugénie Revel, was moved to such an extent that she later became his wife!

not indeed, his death—he prudently transferred the action, as had done previously Beaumarchais with his subversive *Le mariage de Figaro* (1784), to another time and place: in *Léonore* to Spain in the sixteenth century and in *Les deux journées* to the seventeenth-century period of the despotic Cardinal Mazarin. Both libretti show an identical dramatic pattern: a leisurely setting of the atmosphere and a slow development of the action with the lighter characters in the foreground. This was followed by a turn to a more grim realism as the tension mounts when the serious characters enter the drama. Beethoven's *Fidelio* shows this pattern very clearly.

As already remarked, Bouilly's *Léonore* provided the subject for four operas. In the case of Mayr's one-act setting (called a *farsa sentimentale*) it is noteworthy that the action takes place in remote Poland and eliminates Bouilly's political motivation. The drama here deals with the eternal triangle springing from the unrequited love of Moroski (Pizarro) for the faithful Zeliska (Leonore), the wife of Amorveno (Florestan), and the rôle of Bouilly's Minister is played by Amorveno's brother who unexpectedly arrives at the prison. Mayr also composed a *Les deux journées* but its most famous setting, by Cherubini, was first produced in Vienna in 1803 when Beethoven heard it and was deeply impressed, so much so indeed that he not only modelled his *Fidelio* on it but actually borrowed from it.[22]

Beethoven's marked dependency in *Fidelio* on other composers—in some instances amounting almost to plagiarism—is a strange fact. A possible explanation is that, while in his instrumental music he was in his own element and showed little direct influences, at the time of the composition of the first *Fidelio* he was inexperienced as an operatic writer. It would appear that he did not feel quite sure of himself, did not always know how best to proceed with the setting of the text and therefore consulted works by such experienced stage composers as Cherubini, Méhul, Gaveaux and Paer who had a large number of operas to their name. Needless to say, these borrowings do not in the least affect the stature of *Fidelio* and, moreover, they are always worked to a far more imaginative purpose than their originals. But they prove the well-known fact that even the greatest of artists is in some ways indebted to the work of minor men. There are features in Cherubini, Méhul and Paer which, if we could hear their music today, would seem to us as though copied from Beethoven. (In fact Cherubini's *Les deux journées* and especially *Lodoïska* [1791] actually sound

[22] Owing to the rivalry in the pre-von Braun era, the Theater an die Wien produced it in a German version on 13 August, 1803 with the title *Graf Armand*, and on the next evening the Viennese could see it at the Kärthnerthor Theater as *Die Tage der Gefahr*, in an adaptation by Treitschke.

like second-rate Beethoven.) Yet the opposite is the case. These forgotten musicians contributed to the *lingua franca* of their period which Beethoven adopted but in the process assimilated to his own individual style, and in *Fidelio* this process can be clearly seen at work.

Let us first take Cherubini's *Les deux journées*, a 'terror' or 'rescue' drama like *Fidelio* which deals with a very similar story and, like *Fidelio*, ends with a call for humanity: 'Le premier charme de la vie, c'est de servir l'humanité.' It was one of the very few *opéras comiques* which Cherubini wrote and which, with the exception of the classical tragedy, *Médée* (1797), was his most successful opera and performed with particular frequency in nineteenth-century Germany. It starts with a weighty overture in sonata form preceded by a slow introduction, exactly as Beethoven's three *Leonore* overtures, and like them an unsuitable prelude for the homely opening scenes of the opera in the first of which a character sings a Savoyard song. Cherubini has three melodramas from which Beethoven learned how to make pointed and even better use in his own melodrama in the grave-digging scene (Act II, No. 12) which is, incidentally, asked for in Bouilly's *Léonore*.

But we now come to more tangible facts. One of the most popular numbers in Cherubini's *Les deux journées* was an orchestral *entr'acte* before Act II and the following chorus for officers and soldiers in the vein of a nocturne. The *entr'acte* contained a creeping figure (Ex. 1*a*) which clearly echoed in the mysterious bassoon motif (Ex. 1*b*) of the orchestral opening of the first-act finale in *Fidelio*:

Ex. 1

a)

b)

Similarly, the choral nocturne has a theme in ascending minims and I was astounded to find that one of Beethoven's earliest sketches for the beginning of his first-act finale (Ex. 2*b*) was all but identical with this Cherubini theme (Ex. 2*a*); Ex. 2*c* gives the final draft of Beethoven's opening to this finale (tempo indications as in the original 1805 version of the opera):

Ex. 2 a) *Les deux journées*

Again, in Cherubini's *Médée* (Paris, 13 March, 1797) the heroine rushes on the scene, at the opening of Act II, in a state of high agitation and sings a recitative ('Soffrir non posso'), accompanied by an orchestral figure which Beethoven must have remembered when in 1814 he wrote the new recitative for the Act I aria of Leonore ('Komm, Hoffnung, lass den lezten Stern') who comes on the stage in a similar frame of mind to Medea's:

Ex. 3 a) *Medée*

b) *Fidelio*

Yet, while Cherubini's figure remains dry and stilted, Beethoven's is put to most dramatic use.

As for Gaveaux's *Léonore* and Paer's *Leonora*, they were both highly successful in their time and, although there is no record of a Vienna production of the French opera, Beethoven must have known it from a vocal score which was published in Paris in 1798; while a vocal score of Paer's work was found among Beethoven's effects after his death. The French opera opens with an F minor overture in a quasi-Spanish character and ends with greatly agitated scale runs on the strings. These must have struck Beethoven as a particular apt expression of jubilant joy, for he imitated them in his own manner in his *Leonore* Overtures Nos 2 and 3:

Ex. 4 a) *Leonore*

b) *Leonore Overture No. 2*

c) *Leonore Overture No. 3*

There are a number of other parallels with Gaveaux. His opening number is an aria for Marcelline in G minor, with a middle section in the major. The 1805 first version of *Fidelio* begins with Marzelline's aria (No. 1) in C minor, with, also, a central portion in the tonic major. Similarly, the following duet for Marcelline and Jacquino in Gaveaux is marked by florid passages for the soprano and has a *stretto* at the end—exactly as Beethoven's duet (Act I, No. 10); to say nothing of the fact that, like Gaveaux and Paer, he illustrates the knocking at the gate which so annoys Jacquino while pressing his suit on the girl. Moreover, Gaveaux's couplet for Roc (this is the jailer's name in Bouilly's libretto) is in B flat and begins with a theme whose general shape is very similar to Beethoven's opening:

Ex. 5 a) *Léonore*

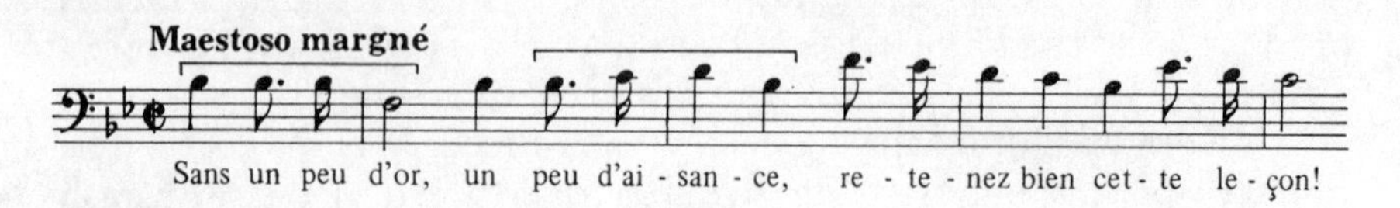

b) *Fidelio*

In the French opera, Léonore's *romance* is introduced by a long horn solo, an idea taken over by both Paer and Beethoven, the latter turning it, however, into an obbligato for three horns and bassoon. The Prisoner's Chorus in Gaveaux introduces a bass solo—Beethoven does the same with a solo for tenor and bass. Again, the *allegro* section of Gaveaux's first-act finale (his opera is in two acts) is based on a rythmic figure in 4/4 which in Beethoven's E flat *allegro molto* of his second-act finale is changed to 3/4:

Ex. 6 a)

b)

The dungeon scene in the French opera begins with a sombre orchestral introduction in C minor marked by 'sigh' figures which is followed by an accompanied recitative and a Romance for Florestan in the same key. Paer's introduction is also in C minor, and Beethoven follows suit yet in a far more stirring manner, with his orchestral prelude in F minor and a *recitativo accompagnato*. Both Gaveaux and Paer anticipate Beethoven in the realism of the grave-digging scene by illustrating the shovelling and the rolling of the heavy stone. And, lastly, the 'Joy' Duet in the French work is an *allegro agitato* in *alla breve*, with a high tessitura in Leonore's part which goes up to *a''* and *b* flat'' and, at the end, to top c'''. The duet in Beethoven is an *Allegro vivace* in 4/4, but beaten in *alla breve*, which in the original 1805 version boasted a most exacting soprano part, with seven *b''*s and, in two places, a sustained high *c'''*. Also Beethoven's rapid alternations between Florestan and Leonore: 'Du bist's!—Ich bin's!—O himmliches Entzücken! . . .' first occurs in Gaveaux's 'C'est Florestan! C'est ton époux!—Quoi Florestan? Quoi mon époux?'.

It remains to point to a most striking parallel between Paer's overture and the *Leonore* Overture No. 3. Paer's opens with a slow introduction in *adagio* tempo in which he quotes a theme from Leonora's cavatina, an idea which Beethoven must have found so suggestive that he adopted it for himself but, instead, cited a theme from Florestan's aria. The incorporation in an overture of themes from the body of the opera goes of course back to the eighteenth century, but that *both* Paer and Beethoven should have quoted a protagonist's theme suggests that the Vienna composer consciously followed the Italian's device. As for the trumpet calls in the *Leonore* Overtures they occur already in the overture to Méhul's *Héléna* (Paris, 1 March, 1803) which were taken from the finale of Act I of his opera. Gaveaux uses these signals only in the dungeon scene. It should be added that trumpet and horn calls were a much-used device in French opera during and after the Revolution.

In order to maintain a coherent discussion of *Fidelio* and not to confuse the reader I shall in the following pages ignore as far as possible the first and second versions and concentrate on the version of 1814. This is the version we see on the stage and which represents Beethoven's ultimate thoughts on a work which, he said to Anton Schindler shortly before his death, cost him greater labour pains than any other composition and was therefore very close to his heart.

In genre *Fidelio* belongs to the *singspiel*, with spoken dialogue in which the physical action advances and which links the various musical numbers; this corresponds to the *opéra comique* for which of course Bouilly's libretto was tailored. In style, however, Beethoven's work is a hybrid of the small and homely petit-bourgeois world of the *singspiel* and the world of an exalted, heroic music-drama. This was already true of Cherubini's *Les deux journées* but with the difference that the serious part of the French opera misses the tremendous power and imaginative depth of the Beethoven work. The hybrid nature of *Fidelio* is already apparent in the *dramatis personae*. Rocco, Marzelline and Jacquino reveal themselves as descendants of types from *opera buffa* (on which Bouilly seems to have modelled these characters) and, ultimately, from the *commedia dell'arte*. The young pair recalls the servant lovers and the jailer the 'heavy' father of eighteenth-century Italian comic opera. On the other hand, Pizarro and Don Fernando have their prototypes in *opera seria*, the Governor deriving from the evil magician or sorcerer and the Minister from the benevolent king in a Metastasian libretto. A parallel can also be drawn with some characters in *Die Zauberflöte*: Jacquino and Marzelline are reminiscent of Papageno and Papagena,[23] while Pizarro stands for the Queen of the Night and the Minister for Sarastro. It is Florestan and notably Leonore, who, though remotely related to the protagonists in *opera seria*, strike us in their musico-dramatic treatment as entirely novel creations. With the heroine, who is much larger than life-size, Beethoven put an operatic character on the stage who became the progenitor of such great figures as Rezia in Weber's *Oberon*,[24] Wagner's Brünhilde, Isolde, Kundry and even Strauss's Salome and Elektra.

As for the libretto, excellent though Treitschke's revision of Sonnleithner's original was, on paper there is a marked disproportion between the musical numbers of the two acts, the first containing ten as against six numbers in the second act. Yet in performance this is scarcely felt, due to the different dramatic and musical weight of the two acts. The first serves the exposition of the drama introducing the characters one by one and acquainting the spectator with the motivation for the Governor's and Leonore's actions. This opening act, apart from setting the atmosphere of the prison, is all preparation —the real happenings are all packed into the second act, viz. the grave-digging scene (No. 12) and the tremendous *scène à faire* of the quartet (No. 14) which brings the unexpected *dénouement*. All the music of Act I up to the Trio (No. 5) is in typical *singspiel* tone—immediate and popular in appeal, of an easy tunefulness and light in texture, yet it is not quite *la petite musique agréable* of French *opéra comique* at the turn of the eighteenth century. Even the wonderful canon-Quartet (No. 3) seems to me, on account of its simple, straightforward melody in almost the vein of a German folksong, to belong to the sphere of *singspiel.* The Trio (No. 5), however, stands already on the threshold of the serious part of the opera which actually begins with the March (No. 6) announcing the entry of Pizarro. It is with Pizarro that Beethoven changes from the previous *singspiel* style to music of a highly dramatic and symphonic character which he maintains uninterruptedly to the end of the work. Some writers have criticised this discrepancy of style

[23] In Bouilly there is a duet between Léonore and Marcelline in which the girl sings 'j' te ferai bientôt père con un p'tit Fidelio', after which she continues almost in the vein of the duet between Papageno and Papagena.

[24] *See* for instance, Rezia's dramatic monologue, 'Ozean! Du Ungeheuer!'; Weber himself had conducted *Fidelio* as early as November 1814.

and manner in *Fidelio*, but we find the same in *Die Zauberflöte* and *Der Freischütz* and also in the *opéra comique* of Cherubini and Méhul which became the model for romantic opera.[25] In performance when we are gripped by Beethoven's drama we are scarcely aware of this stylistic mixture which in any case does nothing to diminish our aesthetic enjoyment.

There is an apocryphal story according to which Cherubini, when he first heard *Fidelio* in 1805, considered Beethoven's treatment of the voices as inexperienced and awkward and sent him a manual on vocal writing as taught at the Paris Conservatoire. Whether Beethoven made any use of it is unknown—probably not. Yet ever since writers have seized on Cherubini's judgment, citing vocal passages in *Fidelio*, the Ninth Symphony and the *Missa solemnis* as proof of the composer's lack of insight into, and sympathy for, the human voice. Yet a mere glance at his songs and the concert arias, *Ah perfido*! and *In questa tomba oscura* WoO 133, would have been sufficient to show that the opposite is the case. It was neither inexperience nor lack of sympathy that was responsible for the fact that Beethoven sometimes piled up enormous difficulties for his singers, but the sheer power of a particular musical thought which he wished to express in such exacting terms. Just as in his instrumental music, it was the *idea* dictating the *style* which compelled him to write vocal passages of a strenuous character.[26] They are, significantly, found only in those of his works into which he projected great humanitarian and timeless concepts going for this very reason to the utmost limit of what could be expressed by the human voice. In *Fidelio* it is Leonore, the mouthpiece of his heroic vision, who in her aria (No. 9) has the most exacting passages to sing, but also the arias of Florestan (No. 11) and Pizarro (No.7) contain difficult phrases and, no less, the Act II Quartet (No. 14) and the 'Joy' Duet (No. 15) which are, significantly, numbers in which the characters are shown in a white-heat of passion and where the dramatic temperature rises to fever-pitch. The very difficulties in the vocal writing of those numbers are not imposed on the music from outside but spring directly from the given situation in which the characters are involved, and are at the same time one of Beethoven's foremost means of achieving a dramatically and psychologically true portrayal.

[25] *See* W. Dean, 'Opera under the French Revolution', *Proceedings of the Royal Musical Association*, 94 (1967/8), pp. 77ff.

[26] When Schuppanzigh once complained of a very difficult passage in one of the quartets, Beethoven's uncompromising reply was: 'Does he imagine I think of his wretched fiddle when the spirit is upon me?' *See Beethoven* by Paul Bekker (Berlin, 1912) p. 357–8, without indication of source.

Admittedly, his approach to vocal writing was that of a predominantly instrumental composer for whom structure and design, balance and periodicity of phrases counted most; hence his many seemingly superfluous repetitions of sentences which were strictured by the critics of the first *Fidelio*. The basic units of Beethoven's phraseology are four and/or eight bars but, in order to avoid a mere mechanical symmetry, he often disturbs this pattern by phrases of an irregular length as, for instance, in the opening of Trio (No. 5; 2+3 bars); Pizarro's and Rocco's Duet (No. 8) where the particular dramatic treatment of the text results in a phrase of 7+2 bars (Ex. 25a); the opening of Florestan's aria (No. 11) in which a five-bar long *ritornello* is followed by its vocal repeat in four bars; or the opening of the Act II Duet (No. 15) with its overlapping of two three-bar phrases (bars 5–9):

Ex. 7

Beethoven's word setting is mostly syllabic and it is only in phrases of a highly charged emotional content where he expands a syllable over several bars in a coloratura, notably in Leonore's aria (No. 9) but also in concerted numbers as, for example, in the first act Trio (No. 5):

Ex. 8

In marked distinction to his songs he pays as a general rule much attention to the correct accentuation of his text and lays particular stress on crucial words:

Ex. 9 a)

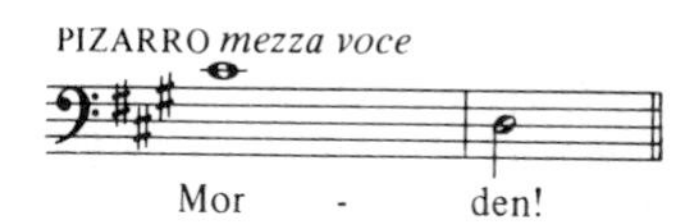

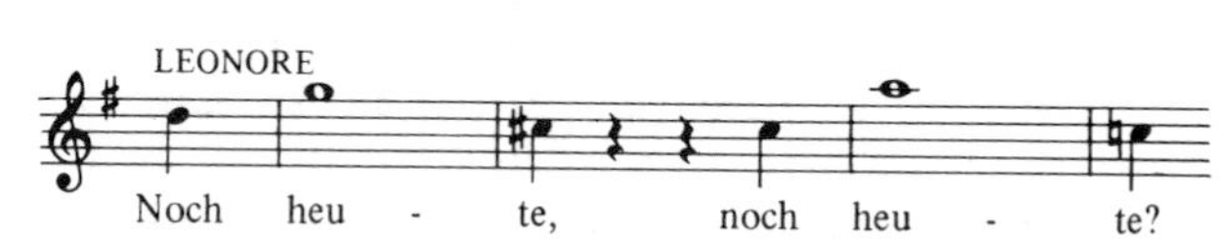

As for Beethoven's formal treatment in *Fidelio*, the sixteen numbers of which it consists show an astounding diversity and wealth of design. The way in which he modifies, for instance, a basic binary or ternary pattern in accordance with the dramatic or emotional requirements of a particular situation is a study in itself. Sometimes we find him making use of sonata and rondo forms because these formal procedures happen to correspond with the unfolding of a given situation. Take the opening Duet (No.1), which is a repeated A–B, but the to-and-fro of the amorous squabble between Marzelline and Jacquino, beginning with the latter's 'Ich habe zum Weib dich gewählet', is treated as a development of the opening orchestral *ritornello*:

Ex. 10

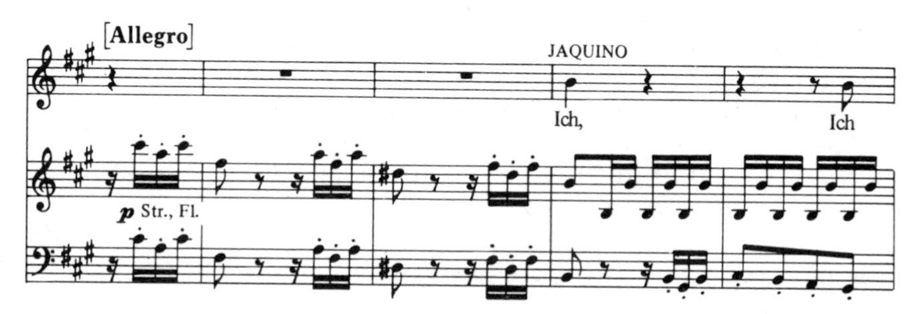

Similarly, Leonore's and Rocco's Act II Duet (No. 12) is a Rondo (A–B–A–C–A–coda) in which Rocco's opening phrase, 'Nur hurtig fort, nur frisch gegraben' recurs several times, because the jailer is so obsessed with the thought of accomplishing his task of digging Florestan's grave before Pizarro's arrival that he persists in urging Fidelio (Leonore) to hurry up. From a formal point of view the outstanding numbers are the Act I second duet (No. 8), the Act II Quartet (No. 14) and the two finales all of which are *durchkomponiert*, Beethoven inventing for each new phase of the evolving action fresh material. Yet a measure of unity is preserved in that there are thematic links and correspondences between the individual sections in the form of recurring motives. Beethoven's organic thinking could not be supressed even in these 'free' numbers.

We now come to the rôle played by the orchestra in *Fidelio*. Beethoven was a composer for whom symphonic thinking was second nature—it was, as it were, congenital in him and it is, hence, not surprising that even in his opera he approached its instrumental side from a predominantly symphonic angle. In other words, the orchestra here is as important as the voices, and though the relationship between the two may vary, the general rule is that the instruments have the main say with the voice-parts more or less superimposed and unfolding the orchestral harmony in an horizontal direction. A good example of this is the *poco allegro* section of Florestan's aria where the solo oboe has the theme while the voice fills in the harmony in linear variations, and also the E flat Duet between Rocco and Leonore in the first-act finale in which the voices now sound the notes of the orchestral harmony and now double the instrumental melody. In fact, doubling between voice and instruments occurs frequently, notably in lyrical portions such as the *adagio* of Leonore's aria (No. 9), the Act II Trio (No. 13) and the second Duet of Act I (No. 8) (Ex. 25a). Moreover, Beethoven dovetails voice-part and orchestra most intimately as when he begins a theme vocally and then continues it in the instruments or vice versa:

Ex. 11

The chief dramatic function of the *Fidelio* orchestra is to set the predominant mood of a scene in the *ritornello*, to comment like the chorus in ancient Greek tragedy on the characters' thoughts and feelings, and illustrate striking details in the physical or emotional situation. Beethoven here applies *mutatis mutandis* the same technique as in his instrumental music—statement of a theme either by the orchestra alone or shared with the voices, and splitting it up into its constituent motifs which are then used to provide a continuous symphonic texture. Variation is an important aspect of this technique as may be seen, for instance, in the above mentioned E flat major Duet of the first-act finale where a one-bar figure is constantly varied melodically, harmonically and, sometimes, rythmically to cover a long stretch of the music:

Ex. 12

The *locus classicus* of Beethoven's use in *Fidelio* of the symphonic orchestra for dramatic and expressive purposes is the introduction to Act II, really a miniature tone poem conveying in the most striking manner the sombre, desolate atmosphere of Florestan's dungeon and preparing us for the mood in which the character is first presented. Even the Act I March (No. 6) displays in the variation of its opening motif in dotted rhythm a symphonic element. In this context attention must also be drawn to Beethoven's art of *recitativo accompagnato* in the arias of Leonore and Florestan in which the orchestra, in constant interplay with the voice, follows the changing emotions of the characters with remarkable pointedness and thus achieves complete dramatic truth.

What greatly adds to the richness of Beethoven's orchestral texture is a device known as *accompanimento obbligato* with which he said he had come into the world. This device, occasionally encountered in rudimentary form in the 'galant style', was perfected by the Viennese school, notably Beethoven, into one of the most characteristic features of their music. Its aim and purpose was to free the accompaniment from its servile bondage as a mere harmonic support and transform it into an independent, wide-ranging element, thus enriching the texture with a wealth of vital tissues. While the homophonic principle of a leading voice was preserved, the accompaniment was raised to a significant rôle in that it was now given a measure of liberty and plasticity unknown before the Viennese classics, extending from a simple chord progression to melodic-rhythmic figures to quasi-polyphonic writing. The sole restriction on complete autonomy was that for all its multifarious possibilities of rivalling the principal theme it had to remain geared to the latter, like satellites revolving around a planet. Take the leading voice away and the texture, despite its melodic-rhythmic richness, becomes meaningless and collapses. There is not a single number in *Fidelio* which does not show the application in one form or another of this vital device, and we find it even in such typical *singspiel* numbers as Marzelline's aria (No. 2), her duet with Jacquino (No. 1), and Rocco's couplet (No. 4):

Ex. 13

Beethoven's occasional resort to short imitative passages between voice and orchestra is part of his *accompanimento obbligato*, but its most consummate employment in a quasi-contrapuntal manner is to be encountered in the *adagio* of Leonore's aria (No. 9) in which the voice is set against counter-motifs on the three horns and the bassoon:

Ex. 14

Leonore's solo number represents a most highly developed example of the old *aria concertata*, but the important point to be noted about it is the fact that in contrast to the strict polyphony such as we find, for instance, in a Bach aria, the instrumental parts of the Beethoven aria are invented according to the homophonic principle: the three horns and bassoon remain for all their free movement harmonically related to the vocal melody.

Before we leave the *Fidelio* orchestra something must be said about its use for illustrative purposes. Like the bird-calls in the *Pastoral* Symphony, Beethoven's musical imitation of the knocks at the gate in the opening duet (No. 1, in which he followed Gaveaux and Paer) may strike us as literal and naïve. But no such criticism could be advanced against his illustration of the grave-digging in the first duet of Act II (No. 12), with its most suggestive circular figure (Ex. 26d) on the double-bass and contra-bassoon which is subsequently subjected to symphonic treatment. Other similarly imaginative instrumental effects are the fluttering of the violins in Marzelline's aria (No. 2) expressing her joyful longing for Fidelio (Leonore), the light, airy woodwind arpeggios in the canon-Quartet (No. 3), the etiolated string passages in Pizarro's aria (No. 7; at the words, 'Schon war ich nah im Staube'), the pale, shadowy string figures in the Governor's duet with Rocco (No. 8) when he alludes to *the* prisoner in the dungeon, and so on.

In conclusion of these general observations some consideration must be given to the tonality of *Fidelio* and the order of key sequence between the individual numbers. In marked contrast to Beethoven's cyclical instrumental works and the *Missa solemnis*, the third version of *Fidelio* does not have an unequivocal tonal centre to which the seven keys used in the sixteen numbers could be closely related. It begins with an overture in E major and ends with a finale in C major whereas the original 1805 version opened with an overture in C major followed by Marzelline's aria in C minor/major, and finished in C major. In other words, C was the unifying tonality. This was destroyed in the 1814 version by the fact that the opera was now made to begin with a duet in A major (see Appendix, pp. 258–9) which compelled Beethoven to cast the *Fidelio* Overture in the dominant key. If there is a tonal pull at all in the last version it is not to C but to A, the tonality which appears in four numbers.[27] On the other hand, the key sequence between the individual numbers is governed by the classical principle of dominant, subdominant and mediant relationships, yet with one most striking exception in which Beethoven jettisons this principle. This is the

[27] In the following table, the tonalities (major/minor mode) of the 16 numbers of *Fidelio*, as well as the *Fidelio* Overture, are listed according to the frequency of their occurrence:

A	Nos 1, 8, 12 and 13
B flat	Nos 4, 6 and 10
E	Overture and No. 9
D	Nos 7 and 14
G	Nos 3 and 15
F	Nos 5 and 11
C	Nos 2 and 16

sequence E major—B flat major which are the respective keys of Leonore's aria (No. 9) and the ensuing first-act finale. These two tonalities are a tritone apart and are thus completely unrelated. My own explanation for this extraordinary and quite modern-looking sequence lies in the assumption that Beethoven may have considered the intervening spoken dialogue as a buffer for mitigating what in classical music must be regarded as a most violent tonal wrench.[28] To my knowledge Beethoven dared the same sequence only once in his instrumental works, namely the String Quartet, Op. 130, in which the second movement in D flat major is succeeded by the *Alla danza tedesca* in G major.

As to his choice of keys for the individual numbers, it would appear that it was dictated by the dramatic or emotional nature of a given piece rather than by a consideration for the cohesiveness achieved by the classical relationship. We know that Beethoven associated certain tonalities with certain emotional complexes (hence his general aversion from transpositions) and in *Fidelio* we may see this for instance in the E major of Leonore's aria, a key which seemed to him particularly suitable for the expression of noble and exalted sentiments. Significantly, E major is the key of Sarastro's lofty aria, of the supremely beautiful and inward variation movement in Beethoven's Op. 109, the tenderly expressive second movement of his Op. 90, and the hymn-like second subject in the exposition of the opening movement of the *Waldstein* Sonata. Pizarro's 'Vengeance' aria (No. 7) is in the 'turbulent' D minor, the same key as in the Queen of the Night's second aria, while the orchestral introduction to Act II of *Fidelio* shares with the *Egmont* Overture the 'desolate' F minor.

Fidelio consists of fifteen vocal numbers—five arias, eight concerted pieces and two big finales (as well as the overture and a first-act orchestral march, No. 6), which can, broadly, be divided into two groups. Although most of the drama is carried forward in the spoken dialogue, as was typical of *singspiel* and *opéra comique*, there is the small group of 'action' numbers of a dynamic, forward-driving character, while to the second group belong the static pieces which serve to project the characters' states of mind and feelings. The *données* of the libretto are such that in the first act the static numbers predominate—there are no less than six there as against three in the second act. But this must be qualified by the fact that the recitatives and arias of both

[28] The same tritonal sequence occurs in Mozart's *Die Entführung aus dem Serail* in which Blondchen's aria in A major is followed by her duet with Osmin in E flat major; but, as in Beethoven, the two numbers are separated by spoken dialogue. In Mozart's operas with *secco* recitative, the latter provides the modulating link between numbers in distantly related keys.

Leonore and Florestan, while static from the point of the outer, physical action, present an inner, psychological development such as we find in *Figaro*, in the Count's 'Vedrò, mentr'io sospiro' and the Countess's 'E Susanna non vien?'.

In the centre of the drama stand Leonore and Pizarro—they are at once its driving force and its two protagonists around whom the rest of the characters are grouped in something like an hierarchical order. Leonore is the most important and richest musical figure who has the lion's share of the music: she sings in nine numbers while Florestan and Pizarro only in five (the latter's part in the second-act finale is negligible). Leonore's essence is heroism and this is limned in her Recitative and Aria (No. 9) in a manner which shows Beethoven at the height of his powers of dramatic characterisation—not surprising if my theory about the reason for his extremely close identification with the heroine has any validity. The music conveys with utmost faithfulness and psychological truth each and every one of her quickly changing emotions—the recitative, her fury and revulsion from Pizarro whose murder plan she has overheard ('Abscheulicher, wo eilst du hin?') and then her awakening hope for a better future ('So leuchtet mir ein Farbenbogen'); the aria, her unbounded trust in the power of love to achieve her great task (*adagio*) and her heroic resolve to follow the call of duty as a devoted spouse (*allegro con brio*). Each of the recitative's various motifs is fraught with suggestiveness—from the violent scurrying rush of the strings at the opening (see Ex. 3*b*) to the gently floating and almost disembodied woodwind phrase evoking the image of a rainbow[29] as the symbol of eternal hope. Leonore's inner development is also mirrored in Beethoven's sequence of keys—from the dark G minor at the start of the recitative to the consolatory C major later and the hopeful E major of the aria.

The *adagio* section of the aria (in varied strophic form) is pure song imbued with a feeling of utter peace and calm, one of the composer's finest inventions in lyrical vein. Of its elaborate texture, with three *obbligato* horns and bassoon (see Ex. 14) we have already spoken. The horns also play an important part in the dynamic *allegro con brio* (tripartite); indeed, the heroic character of this section is, orchestrally, created by the three horns which open with a *ritornello* in widely flung triad arpeggios and close the aria with a rousing scale run extending over three octaves! It is in this *allegro* that Leonore rises to her full stature as a woman of heroic willpower; the music not merely stands *for* her—it *is* Leonore. Significantly, her voice-part contains far-spanning arpeggios upwards and tremendous skips which contrast so

[29] A very similar woodwind passage occurs at the *pianissimo* choral section, 'Ihr stürzt nieder, Millionen?', in the finale of the Ninth Symphony.

strongly with the predominantly step-wise progression in the lyrical *adagio* section (Ex. 14). Even for a dramatic soprano inured to Wagner, Strauss and Berg this last section is a tough nut to crack, as may be seen from the following two examples:

Leonora's aria in Paer's opera also has a dramatic coloratura going to up to *b* flat″ and concluding on a top *c‴* which may have served Beethoven as a model for the original version of his piece (Ex. 38).

As already remarked, Pizarro is from the point of the drama as important as Leonore but musically he is far poorer. More than his antagonist, he is an abstraction, the personification of evil *per se* and comparable to the blackest of stage-villains in Victorian melodrama. He even intends later to dispose of Rocco and Fidelio (Leonore) as the witnesses of his crime on Florestan! A paste-board figure then? Not really, for the Himmlers of Nazi Germany and the Berias of Stalin's Russia are the spitting image of Pizarro but on a monstrous (in both senses) scale. Beethoven was not the composer to be truly inspired by evil incarnate—it needed a Wagner (Hagen), a Verdi (Iago) and a Strauss (Klytemnestra) to make something credible of this one-dimensional figure. Moreover, if my theory is true that in his unconscious mind Beethoven equated Pizarro with the cause of his personal tragedy, his instinctive hatred of this character may have acted as an inhibiting force on his creative imagination. Admittedly, he achieved his best with him in the duet with Rocco (No. 8), but the

'Vengeance' Aria (No. 7) is scarcely more than a noisy piece of theatrical rage and fury. It is the only blot on an otherwise marvellous score.

'Vengeance' arias were a common coin in *opera seria*, and Beethoven did not have to go farther than Donna Anna's 'Or sai che l'onore' and the Queen of the Night's 'Der Hölle Rache' for a model of how to project one of the most genuine emotions of the human animal into musical terms. The permanent characteristics of this type of aria are wide leaps in the voice-part and a preference for high tessitura, and, in the orchestra, a ceaseless agitated movement. All this is to be found in Pizarro's 'Ha, welch ein Augenblick!' which happens to be in the same tonality as the two Mozart arias—D minor/major. The vocal line, with its ejaculatory high notes and skips, and its compass which extends over a twelfth (from low *A* flat to high *E* flat) demands not a baritone but a bass-baritone to ensure a fully sonorous delivery. (In Gaveaux, Pizarro is a speaking rôle; in Paer, he is a tenor.) The violence of the vocal part is matched by the violence of the orchestra, with its explosive syncopations, hammering *tutti* chords, and rapid arpeggios and scale runs. In short, voice and instruments are in a perpetual uproar. The aria is in the rare *bar* form—two *stollen* in D minor and an *abgesang* in D major in which the whisper of the frightened guards, 'Er spricht von Tod und Wunde', with its ascending chromatic harmonies, is the only subtle touch in this medicore piece.

Florestan is, dramatically speaking, an anti-hero. He takes no active part whatsoever in the action, he is a completely passive character who endures (in both senses) the things done to him. Florestan has a striking similarity to the principal figure in Beethoven's early oratorio, *Christus am Ölberg* whom Alan Tyson calls an '*Ur*-Florestan'.[30] Yet from the *moral* point of view, the point of view that mattered most to Beethoven, Florestan *is* a hero bearing, with despairing fortitude, his unmerited fate, in the knowledge of having done his duty in denouncing Pizarro. That Beethoven felt profound pity and compassion for this character who, following my hypothesis, may have symbolised to him his own tragedy of total deafness, is seen in Florestan's Recitative and Aria (No. 11). It is a most moving piece of music and shows Beethoven as a fine psychologist in that he tones down the heroic element to an imperceptible level of which we are only subliminally aware, except for the phrase in the *adagio*, 'und die Ketten sind mein Lohn' where Florestan breaks out into a more forceful lament over his fate. It is an aria related to the eighteenth-century type of *aria di mezzo carattere*.

[30] *See* Note 17.

As Beethoven had given sufficient space to the expression of Florestan's despair in the orchestral introduction, this mood is only briefly touched in the first eight bars of the recitative. He laboured a great deal at this recitative before he found its best shape in the 1814 version. Here are two of his sketches of 1804:

Ex. 16 a)

b)

But I suspect that before arriving at the 1805 version he must have seen a score of Paer's *Leonora* in which Florestan's recitative opened thus:

Ex. 17 a) Paer

b) Beethoven

c)

The similarity of shape between Paer's and Beethoven's phrases is so striking as to exclude the possibility of a mere coincidence. In the light of what I said about Beethoven's marked proneness in *Fidelio* to influences, it is for me a certainty that he modelled the beginning of the recitative closely on that of the Italian composer.

After an initial feeling of desolation and anguish Florestan's mood alters to one of resigned acceptance of his lot and trust in God's will. As in Leonore's recitative, Florestan's changes of emotion are caught in the music with graphic truth—note the plasticity and dramatic expression in the vocal line and the suggestive modulations from the opening F minor tonality via F sharp major and B major to E major from which a most exquisite cadence ('interrupted cadence' and chromaticism in which the rising bass in semitones is crucial to the harmonic logic of the whole) leads to the dominant seventh of A flat major, the key of the ensuing *adagio*:

Ex. 18

It is a very subtle point that Beethoven endows this recitative with richer, more sophisticated harmonies than we find in Leonore's recitative—suffering to be conveyed in music has always led composers to a more complex 'introspective' style of writing. On the other hand, the formal design of Florestan's monologue is the same as that of Leonore's great piece—a recitative followed by an *adagio* and *allegro* section which was of course the established form for the extended aria in the second half of the eighteenth century. But may this strict identity of the formal scheme not also be taken as a symbol for perfect conjugal union?

The opening of Florestan's 'In des Lebens Frühlingstagen' cost Beethoven an even greater amount of labour than the recitative—there are no fewer than eighteen different sketches for it. But the result is, as with Leonore's 'Komm, Hoffnung!', one of the composer's most inspired *adagios* flowing in a broad lyrical stream and with the vocal line shaped and balanced to perfection. Florestan's sad retrospect to a happy past is fully recaptured in this *adagio*, which, though harmonically in ternary form (with a middle section in C flat major), is virtually *durchkomponiert*.

In the 1805 version there stood in place of the present *poco allegro* in F major an *andante poco agitato* in F minor in which Florestan continues his retrospect, drawing a medallion of Leonore from his breast, as he does in Bouilly's original libretto. His mood is that of Dante's 'nessun maggior dolore che ricordarsi del tempo felice nella miseria' which seems to me to be far more in tune with Florestan's state of mind at that particular moment than the delirium of the third version. This F minor piece was a restrained and dignified expression of grief in a pure classical, almost Gluckian style:

Ex. 19

In 1814 Beethoven, apparently dissatisfied with it, first thought of replacing it with an *aria di bravura*, possibly to suit Radichi, the Italian singer of Florestan in the third production. But he was dissuaded by Treitschke who pointed out the physical impossibility of a man on the brink of death by starvation singing such an aria. Treitschke wrote a completely new text in which Florestan, seized by a hunger delirium, begins to have hallucinations and sees the vision of an angel in the image of Leonore who leads him to freedom.[31] This is of course a more interesting psychological situation than the one we find in the original version, yet in the context of the whole of Florestan's scene it seems to me rather contrived, as does also the fact that his vision of Leonore in the shape of an angel is immediately followed by her actual appearance in the dungeon. It is all too pat to carry conviction. Yet in itself the

[31] The last act of Goethe's *Egmont* has a very similar scene in which Egmont sees a vision of the goddess of liberty, looking like his sweetheart, Klärchen. It is probable that Treitschke adopted this idea for Florestan's scene.

new F major *poco allegro* is a superb piece of dramatic writing, conveying Florestan's fever phantasies and his overwrought, almost hysterical, state of mind by means of short, broken phrases and a high tessitura, with the vocal line circling around the theme on the solo oboe.

Florestan's monologue is prefaced by an orchestral introduction whose opening four bars are all but identical with the beginning of Beethoven's youthful *Cantata on the Death of Joseph II*, WoO 87, of 1790, (see Ex. 20 *a*, *b*), a work on which we shall have to say more later.

In expression, key and pace this introduction (already present in the 1805 version) foreshadows the corresponding section of the later *Egmont* Overture, and, as already said, its function is to paint the sombre atmosphere of the dungeon and prepare us for Florestan's state of mind at the opening of his recitative:

Ex. 20 a) *Cantata*

b) *Fidelio*

Sketches suggest, however, that Beethoven did not originally think of a proper orchestral prelude but wanted to begin, after a few introductory bars, with the recitative. This introduction is a magnificent piece of tone-painting and a study in the use of *appoggiature* for an expressive purpose, as witness the poignant 'sigh' figures (1st violins, oboe and bassoon) and the grinding *gruppetti* (2nd violins, violas and celli). In addition, there are sinister-sounding hollow drum taps on the tritone, A—E flat,[32] a suggestive use of rhythmic acceleration and, generally, a dramatic use of harmony.[33]

Of the four subsidiary characters in *Fidelio*—Rocco, Marzelline, Jacquino and Don Fernando—the Minister, a *deus ex machina*, is an episodic figure, while the chief rôle of the young pair is to provide light relief to the serious drama. Rocco, however, is dramatically a more important figure: he is deeply involved in the plot and, so to speak, the go-between between Pizarro and Leonore. The jailer is a *Biedermann*, largely concerned with the petty, small things of life; he wants peace for himself and his family and therefore obeys, fearfully yet faithfully, his superior authority (Pizarro). He has a kind, even compassionate heart allowing himself to be readily persuaded to take Fidelio (Leonore) down to the dungeon, and shows pity with Florestan. He can also be slightly cynical: when he tells Leonore, in the spoken dialogue before the Act I Trio (No. 5), that there is a prisoner in the dungeon who has been languishing there for more than two years, and when she puts the leading question to him: 'He must be a great criminal', Rocco replies: 'Or he must have great enemies, which comes to about the same thing.' One of his chief character traits is his greed for money—not quite honest, he tries to make something for himself from his official purchases for the prison (as he tells Leonore in the dialogue before the canon-Quartet [No. 3]); and as a realist he attaches great importance to this commodity as a prerequisite for a happy marriage.

Rocco's love of the shekel must have struck a sympathetic chord in Beethoven who himself was avid of money and not above slightly dishonest dealings with some publishers; and so he wrote for the jailer a delightful song dealing with just this trait—'Hat man auch nicht Gold beineben'. The little aria is in the style of a couplet, much favoured in *singspiel* and *opéra comique*, and has a simple strophic form—a repeated A–B–C. It is music in a tuneful, popular vein and intimately scored;[34] there is an amusing if perhaps naïve illustration in the mercurial violin figure when Rocco refers to the 'rolling gold coins in the pocket'.

[32] Minor details include the frequent employment of the chord of the diminished seventh—in classical music a particularly powerful means for suggesting pain and suffering; the avoidance, with the exception of a passage in B flat major, of major keys, and the (partly) chromatic descent of the opening bass line which is reminiscent of a passacaglia theme.

[33] Incidentally, the *marche funèbre* in Act III of Spontini's *La Vestale* (Paris, 16 December 1807), an opera the music and libretto of which Beethoven greatly admired, shows a notable family likeness with his introduction.

[34] The 1805 version contained a pair of trumpets and drums which Beethoven omitted from the 1814 version, probably on account of the martial colour these instruments introduced.

Berlioz praised this piece for its melody, its good diction and piquant orchestration in his *À travers chants* (Paris, 1862).

The Marcelline in Bouilly-Gaveaux is a *schwärmerisch* girl of sixteen who can only think of her Fidelio and marriage to him while she is capricious and opinionated with Jacquino. This is the girl we encounter also in Beethoven's opera, but there she is more charmingly vivacious than in the French work, and there is also a slightly pathetic side to her when at the end she realises her deception.[35] Marzelline is in herself not a truly comic character as she is in Paer where she is twenty years of age and treated as a figure from *opera buffa*. The comic aspect of her rôle lies in the sole fact that she loves a young man who ultimately proves to be a married woman in disguise, mistaken identities always being an effective stage effect. Her dominant emotion is persuasively portrayed in her Act I Aria (No. 2), the C minor *andante con moto* conveying her longing for Fidelio while anticipation of conjugal bliss is expressed in the *poco più allegro* section in C major—note here the increased fluidity of the voice-part and the gay flutter of violins. There were two earlier versions of her aria—the first all in C major which Beethoven discarded because he felt that it failed to project Marzelline's initial wistfulness, and the second in C minor/major which came very close to the present version.

Jacquino, who in Paer is a bass, is scarcely more than an appendix to Marzelline, jealously but faithfully trailing behind her. The fact that he has no aria to himself is evidence of the very subsidiary rôle he plays in the drama. He only takes part in two concerted numbers (Nos 1 and 3) and the two finales. As far as there is any attempt at a characterisation of this colourless figure, it is confined to his duet with Marzelline (No. 1) and the spoken dialogue.

And now for the concerted numbers of which we shall first consider those in which the action is halted and which serve to convey emotional states. The static number *par excellence* is the canon-Quartet (No. 3)—wholly superfluous to the action proper but a wonderful piece of inward, contemplative music which in mood, rhythmic shape and pace is prophetic of the 'Benedictus' in the *Missa solemnis* of nearly twenty years later. The text for this canon is not in Bouilly and was probably written by Sonnleithner at Beethoven's instigation who may have got the idea for it from a canon-Trio in Paer's opera, *Camilla o il sotterraneo* (Vienna, 23 February, 1799). The inspiration appears to be Rocco's preceding words to Leonore: 'Meinst du, ich kann dir nicht ins Herz sehen?' In this canon,

[35] In Gaveaux's last act finale she sustains her urge for matrimony when she exclaims: 'Mais où trouver un *vrai* Fidelio?'

Marzelline, Leonore, Rocco and Jacquino are caught in a moment of rapt ecstacy, opening the depth of their hearts and each expressing a different line of thought in character with their individual personalities. Like the famous quintet in *Die Meistersinger* and the great trio in the third act of *Der Rosenkavalier*, Beethoven's quartet is a lyrical ensemble of such magical quality that it reconciles us to the fact that, as in the Wagner and Strauss pieces, the different characters are not individually defined in the music, as Verdi did with such incomparable dramatic skill in the celebrated quartet of *Rigoletto*. The very choice of a canon made this impossible, which suggests that here the musician in Beethoven was stronger than the dramatist. It is a simple canon at the unison and octave with a free coda, based on a folksongish theme of eight bars, with each subsequent entry occurring at the same distance. The uninterrupted flow and polyphonic intertwining of the voices result in music of ineffable beauty, and thus shows that with the first moment of Leonore entering the musical scene Beethoven's imagination began to soar.

The opening duet, which establishes the relationship between Marzelline and Jacquino, is a vivacious *allegro* in typical *singspiel* style,

Ex. 21

in which the two characters share the same material, except for the girl's mercurial *fioriture* in the *stretta* coda. Here again Gaveaux has provided the model, for his duet shows the same florid writing for Marcelline in the fast coda, and there is also an affinity in motif between the two duets.

The first act Trio (No. 5) is a piece *di mezzo carattere* standing halfway between an 'action' ensemble—in it Rocco decides to ask Pizarro for permission to take Fidelio (Leonore) with him down to the dungeon—and a static number expressing Leonore's determination to fulfil her great task. Indeed, the energetic opening seems to have been inspired by her preceding spoken words: 'Ich habe Mut und Kraft.' In contrast to the canon-Quartet, Beethoven here attempts some delineation of the three characters in that Leonore and, sometimes, Marzelline sing (mostly) in sustained *cantabile* phrases while the jailer fills in the bass of the harmony (Ex. 21).

The clouding-in of the F major tonality by a turn to E flat minor, at Rocco's words, 'Ich bin ja bald des Grabes Beute', is as suggestive a touch of word-painting by harmonic means as are the forceful imitative entries of the voices by contrapuntal means. The trio consists of three sections, each with own material and thus approaches a 'composed-through' number, but Beethoven lends it unity by an all but pervasive rhythmic figure:

Ex. 22

In Act II there are two static numbers—the Trio (No. 13) and the second Duet (No. 15). The trio, in which Rocco and, particularly, Leonore, who has in the meantime recognised in the prisoner her husband, are deeply moved by the sight of the starving Florestan, is the most tender number of the whole opera. Its opening theme is remarkable for the gently undulating line, and the whole music flows in a broad lyrical stream reaching its first climax in Leonore's poignant phrase:

Ex. 23

In this trio as well as in the preceding Duet (No. 12), Leonore is shown in softer, more feminine colours than she appears in the first act.

The second Duet (No. 15) conveys the paroxysm of joy by which husband and wife, at last united after their trials and tribulations, are seized, and in order to achieve the maximum effect from the two voices, Beethoven keeps the vocal lines comparatively simple and straightforward and accompanies with an orchestra markedly less symphonic than in other numbers. The 1805 first version of this duet, which was longer than the present one by no fewer than 90 bars, was derived from the trio which the composer wrote for the abortive Schikaneder opera, *Vestas Feuer.*[36]

Ex. 24 a)

b)

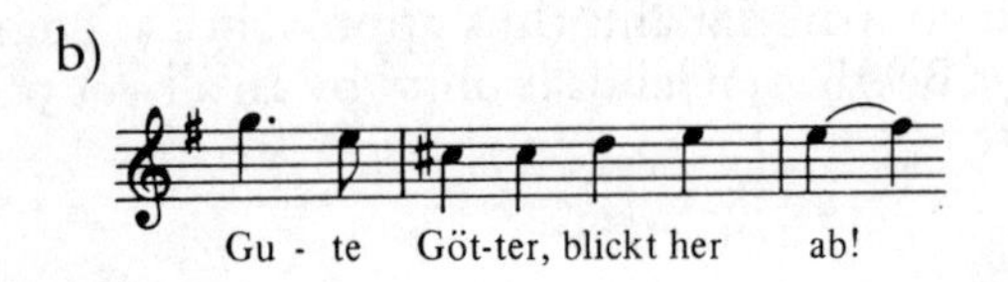

In the original 1805 version the tessitura of Leonore's part was vertiginously high; as Ex. 24 shows, her main phrase rose to the *b''* which (as we have noted already) recurs six more times in the course of the duet, and with a long sustained top *c'''* in two places, all of which was anticipated in the 'Joy' duet of Paer's opera. In 1814 Beethoven not only shortened this number very considerably but cut the *b''* in Leonore's motif (see Ex. 7) and inserted this note only once at the climax shortly before the end.

There are three 'action' ensembles in *Fidelio*—one in Act I and two in Act II. The first-act Duet between Pizarro and Rocco (No. 8) serves an imagined action, the Governor visualising his plan how to murder Florestan. His thoughts develop in two stages: he first tries, in bribing Rocco with a purse of money, to persuade him to commit the crime on the ground that the State demands the disposal of a subversive citizen;

[36] The trio was orchestrated by Willy Hess in 1953. Hess is also the author of a most comprehensive study, *Beethovens Oper Fidelio* (Zürich, 1953), as well as the editor of the new full score of the 1805 version (Wiesbaden, 1967).

when Rocco refuses, he tells him to dig only the grave in the cistern of the dungeon while he himself will do the killing, for only Florestan's death will restore his peace of mind. The duet is a completely *durchkomponiert* number, the music not only following the imagined action but also conveying Pizarro's various emotional attitudes—now cunningly persuasive, now imperious and overbearing—and Rocco's reactions to them. Beethoven draws on all his resources—thematic, harmonic, rhythmic and instrumental (the orchestra here includes three trombones, used sparingly in the opera)—to conjure up strikingly vivid images, as when Pizarro describes to the jailer how he will, hidden behind a mask, sneak into the dungeon and kill Florestan with a single stab of his dagger. Beethoven must have been so gripped by this verbal image that he set it twice, the first time in a sinister unison between voice and strings, the second time, with an eerie, creeping chromatic figure in the bass and halting syncopation on the first violins and violas:

Ex. 25 a)

b)

The duet belongs, dramatically and musically, to the finest numbers in the whole opera and succeeds in characterising Pizarro more succinctly and in greater depth than his aria.

On an equally high level yet totally different in mood and musical character is the Act II Melodrama and Duet (No. 12). The melodrama, marking the arrival of Rocco and Leonore in the dungeon, is a particularly apt preparation for their ghoulish task, and introduces two reminiscences—the oboe figure from the F major section of Florestan's monologue and the 'work' motif (Ex. 12) from the duet between Rocco and Leonore in the first-act finale. The exact date at which Beethoven composed the melodrama is not known. Although sketches for it dating from 1804 were found among those for the first version of the opera, the presence of that oboe figure, belonging to the part of Florestan's aria which Beethoven did not write until 1814, suggests that the original form of the melodrama must have been slightly different from the present one. This is the opinion of Thayer, Otto Jahn and Nottebohm, but Erich Prieger, in his edition of the vocal score of the first *Fidelio* (Leipzig, 1905) included the melodrama of 1814 (with the oboe figure). It is known that at the second production in 1806 the text of the melodrama was spoken without music.[37]

The ensuing duet is an outstandingly fine piece of musical realism illustrating the digging of the grave yet at the same time expressing Rocco's and Leonore's feelings as they proceed with their sinister work. Beethoven sharply sets off the jailer from the heroine: Rocco sings in an urgent *parlando* style, for he is most anxious to complete the digging before Pizarro arrives, and Leonore, here shown in her softer, more womanly aspect, is given expansive sinuous phrases:

Ex. 26 a)

b)

c) 1804

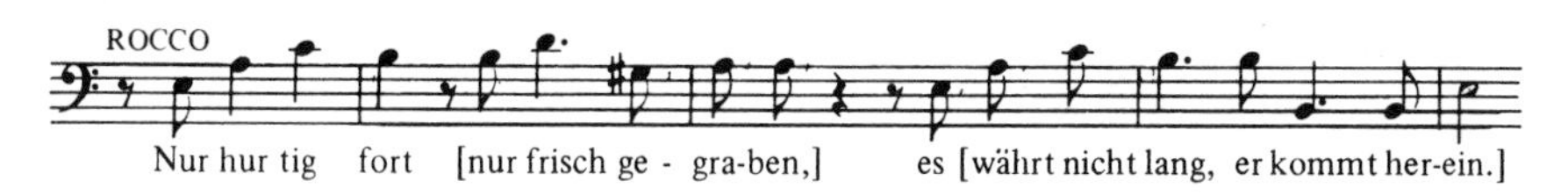

d)

The graphic realism is confined to the orchestra, with its circular 'digging' figure (Ex. 26*d*) scored for contra-bassoon[38] and double basses to suggest the fearful depth of the dungeon. In one of the

[37] *See* vocal score of the 1805 version ed. Erich Prieger (Leipzig, 1907), Introduct. p. VII, and Hess, op.cit (in n.36).

[38] This duet and the later Quartet (No. 14) are the only numbers in which Beethoven resorts to this instrument.

earliest sketches Rocco's *parlando* opened with a variant of Leonore's melody (Ex. 26*c*). On the other hand, Beethoven's original idea of suggesting the 'taking of breath' of the two characters by pauses in the voice-parts was later discarded. Incidentally, the rumbling phrase on the double basses and contra-bassoon imitating the rolling of the heavy stone to the edge of the pitch was found by Berlioz to be 'a piece of childishness'. The duet is, as was said, a rondo, with Ex. 26*a* fulfilling the function of a *ritornello* and with a symphonic development of the 'digging' figure (Ex. 26*d*).

The supreme example of an 'action' ensemble in *Fidelio* is the great Quartet of Act II (No. 14). Whatever the structural deficiencies and verbal infelicities of Sonnleithner's adaptation of Bouilly's original, he hit upon a single masterstroke which was to turn the *scène à faire*, which in Bouilly-Gaveaux unfolded in spoken dialogue, into a musical scene thus providing Beethoven with an opportunity to write the most dramatic ensemble in the entire opera. Paer also set this scene to music but since his *Leonora* was not produced until 3 October, 1804, Sonnleithner may claim priority, as his libretto was completed in late 1803 or early 1804. In the quartet Leonore and Pizarro meet each other face to face for the first time and Beethoven here is, rightly, more concerned with conveying the tremendous clash of the forces of good and evil than with a subtle and detailed psychological characterisation. This number represents at once the supreme climax of the opera (first part) and the peripeteia of the drama (second part). In the first part Pizarro makes three attempts to kill Florestan, each of which opens with this stabbing figure:

Ex. 27

This motif recurs, rondo-like, later and thus lends this *durchkomponiert* number a measure of thematic unity. Each of Pizarro's three attempts is, with increasing intensity, repulsed by Leonore—the first by her 'Zurück!', the second by her unaccompanied 'Tödt erst sein Weib!', and the third by her pointing a pistol at him. The spine-chilling moment is Leonore's outcry on which, as the sketches show (Ex. 28*a*–*c*), Beethoven laboured for some time. As can be seen from the following examples (*d* and *e*), the 1805 version of this phrase, accompanied and with a leap of a major third upwards, is unquestionably inferior to the unaccompanied 1814 version, which has its origins in the concept of Ex. *28b*:

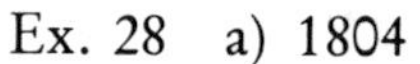
Ex. 28 a) 1804

b) 1804

c) 1804

d) 1805

e) 1814

The peripeteia of the drama begins with the first trumpet-signal announcing the arrival of the Minister in the prison after which follows an Intermezzo in B flat major, the home-key of the quartet being D major.[39] This *Un poco sostenuto* is a nine-bar hymn in which Leonore, Florestan and Rocco express their feeling of devoted gratitude for God's unexpected intervention, while Pizarro is in utter alarm and apprehension. This contrast comes out in the voice-parts: the first three characters sing in close harmony whereas the Governor has irate octave leaps downwards. The chorale-like melody shows a striking touch of orchestration in being scored for flutes and cellos which Beethoven repeated exactly in the *Leonore* Overture No. 3.

The rapt spell is broken by the sudden irruption of Jacquino and soldiers into the dungeon announcing to Rocco in spoken dialogue the arrival of the Minister. This has always seemed to me a clumsy piece of dramaturgy which unnecessarily destroys the dramatic tension and interrupts the musical continuity. From Pizarro's dialogue with the Captain of the Guard (before his duet with the jailer, Act I) we already know what the trumpet signals are meant to indicate, and therefore do not need further explanation. After the second signal the quartet could have easily continued and Jacquino and the soldiers could have appeared, when the music is over, to fetch Rocco and Pizarro. This innovation on the part of Treitschke compares unfavourably with both the Sonnleithner and Breuning versions where there is no such disturbing break.

In the second half of the quartet Leonore, Florestan and Rocco are seized by an overpowering mood of triumphant victory, while Pizarro curses the hour of his defeat. Throughout the quartet the latter is

[39] Beethoven was for some time undecided as to the choice of key for this number, considering in turn E flat major, G minor and A minor.

characterised by the same kind of vocal style as in his aria—ragged, wide-spanning intervals which also apply to Leonore's part in the first half where she displays the same extreme of agitation as the Governor. The maelstrom of warring emotions of this whole scene is mirrored in the orchestra in rapid arpeggios and runs, hammering note repetitions and tremolando-like figures on the strings. In passing it should be mentioned that in Pizarro's opening music there occurs in the bass a motif completely identical with a figure in the 'The Storm' of the *Pastoral* Symphony.

We now come to the two great finales (Nos 10 and 16) which partake both of the static or lyrical and the dynamic or dramatic. In the first-act finale the static element is represented by the Chorus of the Prisoners which from the point of view of the essential drama is, as in Bouilly-Gaveaux, an adventitious scene. Paer, in his opera, left it out substituting for it a quintet for Pizarro, Leonore, Rocco, Marcellina and Giacchino. But for Beethoven great choral masses as the symbol of united mankind played an important part in his creative imagination, as witness the Ninth Symphony and the *Missa solemnis*, and *Fidelio* was the first work in whose two finales he could give powerful expression to this symbolic idea. The finale of the first act is ternary, with the chorus flanking a central portion for the soloists, which may be said to stand for the development section in a symphonic movement. The opening and closing chorus of the prisoners in B flat, each with its own thematic material, are of about equal length and thus ideally balance each other. Joy at being allowed to see the light of day and breathe, if only temporarily, the air of freedom, is the mood of the first chorus—a sad farewell before their return to the cells, the sentiment of the second. This emotional contrast is reflected in Beethoven's different treatment of the two choruses. In the first the voices are divided into four parts (Tenor I and II, Basses I and II) whose successive entries at the opening and especially later at the words 'sprecht leise, haltet euch zurück!'—a fearful whisper which is like an anticipation of Verdi's choruses of conspirators—greatly enhances the liveliness of the texture (Ex. 29).

The closing chorus, on the other hand, is predominantly in two parts and combines with a concerted ensemble for the five soloists, which gives Beethoven the opportunity for some exquisite part-writing, in which the choral voices provide the harmonic basis.

While the action comes to a standstill in the two choral sections the central portion for the soloists serves to advance it culminating in Pizarro's fury at seeing the prisoners in the courtyard. Significantly, this section has development-like character which may be seen in the fact that it is 'through-composed', has several changes of key and, in

Ex. 29

the closing *allegro molto*, shows restless modulations. The only point of repose is the magnificent 'Work' Duet for Rocco and Leonore in E flat in which the jailer explains to her the task they have to accomplish in the dungeon. This *andante con moto* is the lyrical core of the whole first-act finale and is based on a one-bar motif from whose constant variation Beethoven builds up the structure for the greater part of this duet (see Ex. 12). The scoring, mostly for the warm-toned clarinet and bassoon, is noteworthy.

The second-act finale, taking place on the wide bastion of the prison, is essentially a scenic oratorio or cantata in which the action is confined to such minor happenings as the Minister's entry, the subsequent appearance of Rocco with Leonore and Florestan, the last still in chains, and Pizarro's arrest. In fact the real ending of the opera had, as far as the essential drama is concerned, been reached in the preceding 'Joy' Duet (No. 15), and that was probably the reason why Treitschke when revising the libretto first suggested to Beethoven to omit the original finale and close with this duet. The ideological significance of this finale is the glorification of conjugal love and the moral lesson to be drawn from it, the whole representing a magnificent, if static, stage-spectacle. But Beethoven's handling of the chorus and the soloists is such that it keeps the dramatic interest very much alive throughout. There are four principal sections which in their individual character are like the four movements of a symphony: an opening *allegro vivace* in C major (chorus); an *un poco maestoso* in C major leading to a *meno allegro* in A major (soloists); a *sostenuto assai* in F major (soloists and chorus); and an *allegro ma non troppo* in C major (soloists and chorus) which ends in a breathtaking *stretta, presto molto*, just as the finali of the Fifth and Ninth Symphonies. An early sketch (Ex. 30*a*) for the opening chorus of the final *allegro ma non troppo* section reads:

Ex. 30 a)

b) *Leonora*

c) *Fidelio*

Beethoven seems to have arrived at the final version (Ex. 30c) after seeing the score of Paer's opera where the last chorus opens with Ex. 30b. Beethoven interpolated the words for the opening choral section, which also recur later in the choral finale of the Ninth Symphony, from Schiller's *An die Freude*.

As in the first act finale, Beethoven treats the two choral sections in a markedly different manner. The first is for massed voices establishing the predominant mood of the finale with the greatest possible force. The second is ternary and has for its middle portions a five-part solo ensemble with choral interjections, while the repeat of the first section is characterised by a dramatic antiphony between the six soloists and the choral voices. As in the finale of the Ninth, in this last portion the tessitura for the choral sopranos and tenors is high and exacting, which is yet another instance of Beethoven being compelled by the poetic idea—here expression of extreme joy—to impose a considerable strain on the human voice.

The central portion, which stands for the inner movements of a symphony, is completely different in musical character and mood from the two flanking choruses. It begins with the Minister's noble *arioso* in which Don Fernando, in the king's name, grants the prisoners (were they all *political* prisoners?) their liberty, and contains the key-phrase 'Es sucht der Bruder seine Brüder, und kann er helfen, hilft er gern.' A brief agitated section marking the arrival of Rocco, Leonore and Florestan on the scene is followed by an *allegro* in A major in which the jailer exposes Pizarro for the criminal he is. This section is remarkable for its close-knit symphonic web in which an ostinato figure provides another good example of Beethoven's *accompanimento obbligato*. For me the chain-like succession of this ostinato always suggests the links of the chain borne by Florestan:

Ex. 31

Into the final part of this solo ensemble falls the arrest of Pizarro, preceded by a tremendous choral irruption, 'Bestrafet sei der Bösewicht!', which has the same impact as the explosive 'Barabbam' in the *St Matthew Passion*. An almost cosmic force lies in the unison phrase for the chorus and orchestra (Ex. 32):

Ex. 32

The following *sostenuto* in F major, in which, at the Minister's behest, Leonore unlocks Florestan's chains and the latter sinks into her arms, is the supreme moment in *Fidelio* of inwardness, and comparable in significance to the canon-Quartet (No. 3). All present—the solo characters, the prisoners and the people—stand transfigured in their contemplation of God's miraculous intervention and eternal justice. 'O Gott! welch' ein Augenblick!' is heavenly music, yet the extraordinary fact is that Beethoven took the melody, with only minor alterations, from a chorus in his youthful *Cantata on the Death of Joseph II* of 1790 when he was a boy of just nineteen:

Ex. 33 *Cantata*

This cantata was a glorification of one of the most humane and progressive emperors in more modern European history, and it was the parallel with the liberal king of whom Don Fernando is the ambassador, which may well have suggested to Beethoven the re-cycling of this theme in the finale of *Fidelio*. That no difference of style can be detected between it and the far more mature music of the rest of the original version of the opera written some fourteen years later, is testimony to the extraordinary precociousness of the youthful composer. Moreover, the inner identity of Beethoven's language when expressing religious exaltation is proved by the *Heiliger Dankgesang eines Genesenen an die Gottheit* from his Quartet, Op. 132, which again has a shape very similar to that theme from the early cantata.

III. A Companison between the Three Versions

In order to see the third *Fidelio* in its proper perspective and realise fully its improvements and few remaining defects, it will be necessary to attempt a comparison between the versions of 1805, 1806 and 1814. Beethoven's first poet, Sonnleithner, followed Bouilly's original more or less closely, even making in some instances a literal translation of the French text. But he expanded Bouilly's two acts into three by increasing the number of musical pieces from twelve in the French libretto to eighteen in his own and retarding the action by long stretches of uninteresting, tiresome dialogue. The result was a considerable diffusion of the original drama—nothing, for instance, happens in Sonnleithner's first act so that by the fall of the curtain the spectator is uncertain of the course the action will take. Moreover, Sonnleithner made the error of allowing the *petit bourgeois* element, so unsuited to Beethoven's intrinsic genius, too much room by the inclusion of verses for no fewer than five homely numbers—Marzelline's aria (No. 1), her duet with Jacquino (No. 2), a comic trio for the two and Rocco (No.3), the latter's couplet (No. 5), and a duet for Marzelline and Leonore (No. 10).[40] In addition, his second-act finale (now the first-act finale) ended most ineffectively with Pizarro's peremptory order to the guards to man the tower of the prison and watch out for the Minister's arrival to which the cowed fellows reply that he may rely on their loyalty and courage 'even if our blood flows'. The whole of the third act (the present second act) played, as in Gaveaux and Paer, in Florestan's dungeon. But recent concert and stage productions of the original *Fidelio*[41] have shown that from the dramatic point of view the appearance of the Minister and the people in the dungeon—Bouilly may well have had the storming of the Bastille in July 1793 in mind—is more telling than the present finale on the bastion of the prison, to say nothing of its advantage of uninterrupted

[40] See Appendix pp. 258–9.
[41] London Coliseum, Spring 1970.

continuity which in the 1814 version was destroyed by the interval of time it took for the change of scene. On the other hand, Sonnleithner's finale lacked the symbolism as well as the impressive stage-picture provided by Treitschke's finale. About the only point in Sonnleithner's favour is the fact that he gave Beethoven considerably more opportunities for truly dramatic music than did Bouilly for Gaveaux whose opera bears the significant inscription, 'Prose melée de chants', i.e. a play with music. Thus Sonnleithner turned his final act into a real music drama by transforming, as already remarked, the great *scène à faire*, which in Gaveaux progressed in spoken dialogue, into the occasion for the most dramatic music in the whole opera. Sonnleithner can also claim the merit to have realised that Pizarro, who in Bouilly is a speaking rôle, must be a singing part if he is to make his proper impact in operatic terms. To sum up, the original libretto of *Fidelio* was a most uneven mixture of some very good things with a lot of bad. But Beethoven who in the years 1804–5 was a novice in matters of the dramatic stage did not notice this, he did not see the libretto as a whole, and indeed, composed the musical numbers in exactly the order in which they followed in Sonnleithner.

Breuning's version of 1806 tightened the dramatic structure in that he went back to Bouilly's two acts, shortened much of Sonnleithner's spoken dialogue as well as the verses of some musical numbers, and threw out Rocco's couplet which Beethoven originally wanted to retain but with an entirely different text.[42] But Breuning preserved, possibly on Beethoven's insistence, the duet for Marzelline and Leonore and the comic trio (both omitted from the final version), yet, very strangely, made them succeed each other as Nos 9 and 10 immediately before the first-act finale,[43] while in Sonnleithner they stood widely separated from each other, the trio as No. 3 and the duet as No. 10 (see Appendix, pp. 258–9). But one of Breuning's scene transpositions was very apt. This was to let Leonore sing her recitative and aria (No. 8) immediately after the sinister duet of Pizarro with Rocco (No. 7) the last part of which she overhears. This provided a far stronger motivation for her following monologue than in Sonnleithner where it comes, without any compelling reason, after Leonore's innocuous duet with Marzelline. On the other hand, Breuning did

[42] Reproduced in W. Hess, *Beethovens Oper Fidelio*, p. 252.

[43] It is interesting that in the numbering adopted by Kinsky-Halm (based on earlier authorities such as Nottebohm), this trio and duet are still separated as Nos 3 and 10, following the 1805 version, but they qualify this by saying 'doubtful; see below' where they mention another place for them in the opera, and finally suggest the possibility of their having been cut before the 1806 production, a view to which I am much inclined. *See* Kinsky-Halm, p. 175.

nothing to improve the weak dramatic ending of Sonnleithner's second-act finale—Breuning's first-act finale. For posterity it was undoubtedly a blessing in disguise that Beethoven, after his *contretemps* with Baron von Braun, withdrew the score after the second performance in April 1806 and put it in his bottom drawer, for otherwise the opera might have never seen its third, and on the whole far superior version.

It was left to Treitschke to make the final improvements. He judiciously shortened as well as expanded the original text and thus gave it a more satisfying dramatic shape. He retained Breuning's two acts but cut out two of the five *singspiel* numbers (the comic trio and the duet between the two women) yet restored Rocco's couplet which was too good a piece to omit. The first two numbers changed places, the opera now beginning with the lively duet between Marzelline and Jacquino, instead of opening with the girl's C minor aria of the first version, in which it was, moreover, preceded by a lengthy spoken monologue— a most ineffective start for an opera. Again, Treitschke wrote a completely new text for Leonore's recitative in which she gives expression to her reaction to Pizarro's evil intention which was incomparably more dramatic than in Sonnleithner and Breuning. Here are the two texts:

Sonnleithner-Breuning

> Ach, brich noch nicht, du mattes Herz!
> Du hast in Schreckenstagen
> mit jedem Schlag ja neuen Schmerz
> und bange Angst ertragen.

Treitschke

> Abscheulicher, wo eilst du hin,
> was hast du vor, was hast du vor in wildem Grimme?
> Des Mitleids Ruf, der Menschheit Stimme,
> rührt nichts mehr deinen Tigersinn?

Incidentally, Treitschke's opening is an almost literal translation of Leonora's recitative in the Paer opera where she exclaims: 'Esecrabil Pizarro! Dove via? Che mediti? Che pensi?'

On Treitschke's invention of a new situation for the end of Florestan's aria we have already remarked (p. 220). Also the situation of the original second-act finale was radically altered in that it is now Leonore who in her compassion begs Rocco to allow the prisoners out of their cells into the courtyard which becomes the direct cause for

Pizarro's fury. In Sonnleithner, who followed Bouilly, this finale, which brings a change of scene, simply opened with the prisoners slowly emerging from their cells which, according to Rocco, is a regular daily practice. Admittedly, Breuning anticipated Treitschke in making Leonore express the wish to let the prisoners out into the open but she expresses this to herself in a brief solo scene. In both Sonnleithner and Breuning, Rocco sends the prisoners back to their cells with the consoling words that tomorrow will be another day. When Pizarro rushes on the scene in a fuming rage it is not because of the jailer's kindness to the prisoners, who by then have all disappeared from the scene, but because he has not yet obeyed his orders to go down to the dungeon and dig the grave. In Treitschke the various scenes of his first-act finale are far closer concatenated, resulting in a more concentrated dramatic development. Treitschke also added the text for the moving farewell chorus at the end, 'Leb' wohl, du warmes Sonnenlicht'.

He originally wanted Beethoven to finish the opera with the 'Joy' Duet No. 15 which, as already observed, constitutes the real end of the essential drama. But he then hit upon the excellent idea of a symbolic change of scene from the sombre dungeon to the bright, sunlit bastion of the prison as the place for the final apotheosis. As in Bouilly, the first two versions of the last finale (playing, as mentioned, in the dungeon) opened with a 'Vengeance' Chorus off-stage which Leonore and Florestan first interpret as being intended for them and they give up all hope for deliverance. When the Minister appears they beg him to show mercy to Pizarro, for the strange reason that the Governor found strength in his conscience ('Denn ihm gab sein Bewusstsein Kraft'), whatever this may mean. All this went by the board in Treitschke's version of the finale and it was also he who gave Don Fernando the moving words for his aria, 'Des besten Königs Wink und Wille'.[44]

Treitschke's inestimable merit was that by his improvements of the dramaturgy, his invention of one or two effective situations and some felicitous alterations of the text he enabled Beethoven 'to salvage a few bits from a stranded ship' and determined him 'to restore the desolate

[44] In Bouilly-Gaveaux, the Minister's address takes the form of an 'official' exhortation to the assembled women to emulate Léonore's example: 'Vous qui de Léonore applaudissez le zèle, la patience et l'intrépidité, femmes, prenez-la pour modèle, faites consister comme elle votre bonheur dans la fidélité'. To this the people reply:

Célébrons tour-a-tour
Le pouvoir et les charmes
De la constance et de l'amour!
Chantons, bénissons ce beau jour!

The Sonnleithner and Breuning versions contain nothing comparable to Treitschke's beautiful words.

ruins of an old castle' as the composer wrote to the poet in the spring of 1814. This was, however, an exaggeration, for the first *Fidelio* was, in spite of its dramatic defects, a strikingly impressive work musically.

The music

Before comparing the music of the three versions we must briefly consider the source-material for the *Fidelio* of 1805 and 1806. The position is as follows: no complete autograph score and no complete copies of it exist anymore—they were either lost or stolen; and there are no traces either of the orchestral parts used at the original production. However, there are copies extant of many numbers revised in Beethoven's own hand and even some manuscripts which he gave to Schindler, all of which was acquired in 1845 by the Königliche Staatsbibliothek, Berlin. It was from this material that an authentic reconstruction of the original score was made. The first scholar to take serious interest in these matters was Otto Jahn who in 1853 brought out a vocal score of the *second* version which he based on an incomplete vocal score made by Czerny in 1810,[45] Jahn also consulted orchestral parts in the possession of the Franz Seconda Theatre Company which were destroyed in World War II (Jahn's score, in addition, included numbers taken from the first version). More than fifty years elapsed before Erich Prieger published in 1905, the centenary of the original production, the vocal score of the *first* version and later (1908–10) issued a private edition of the original full score.[46] This has been reproduced under the editorship of Willy Hess by Breitkopf & Härtel (Wiesbaden, 1967) as the supplementary vols 11 and 12 to the *Gesamtausgabe* of Beethoven's works. The Appendix on pp. 258–9 shows that the original *Fidelio* was the longest of the three versions extending in round figures to 3,500 bars (without the overture) as against the 2,860 bars of the 1806 and the 2,830 bars of the 1814 versions. Each of its three acts brought a change of scene and each act was preceded by an orchestral introduction—Act I by an overture, Act II by the march (the original version of the march is lost; see Appendix, pp. 258–9), and Act III by a prelude. In 1805 Beethoven allowed his imagination to flow in a broad uninterrupted stream. But he got his priorities wrong in that in the first version the musician in him was often stronger than the dramatist. A glance at the Appendix proves that he was not concerned with or, possibly, not aware of the disproportionate length

[45] As was the practice, Czerny omitted all spoken dialogue and the overture, as well as the two finales.

[46] Prieger was also responsible for initiating a production of the first version of *Fidelio* in Berlin in November 1905, when it was conducted by Richard Strauss.

of such numbers as the first Trio of Act I (No. 3), Leonore's Recitative and Aria (No. 11), the original second-act finale (No. 12), the 'Joy' Duet (No. 17) and the third-act finale (No. 18). It would go far beyond the scope of this essay to examine in detail his revisions for the 1814 production. Suffice it to say that there is not a single number in the 1805 and 1806 versions which was taken over exactly as it stood there, into the 1814 version;[47] even the canon-Quartet was shortened by one bar! Beethoven's procedure was to cut some phrases altogether or cut some in one place and add others in another so as to achieve musical balance. There are numbers in the much cut 1806 version which appear even shorter in the 1814 version, such as the duet for Marzelline and Jacquino, the duet for Pizarro and Rocco, and Leonore's aria, while it is only the second-act finale which was extended from the 333 bars of the second version to the 421 bars of the third. In revising the opera Beethoven also loosened up close entries in concerted numbers and simplified vocal passages.

What reduced the length of the 1814 version very considerably was, in addition to a complete excision or shortening of parts of the spoken dialogue, the omission of the Trio No. 3 and the Duet No. 10 of the original 1805 version (see Table). The verbal essence of the trio in E flat major for Rocco, Marzelline and Jacquino may be summed up in 'Marry

[47] Kinsky-Halm, pp. 171ff, gives the following details regarding the 1805 and 1806 versions:

1805 version

Nos 1, 2, 3, 4, 5, 6 as in Carner
No. 7 (March) = that given in third version (38 bars)
Nos 8, 9, 10, 11, 12, 13 as in Carner
No. 14a (Melodrama); reference to Prieger's adoption of the 27-bar episode in the third version
Nos 14b, 15, 16 as in Carner
No. 17 = 289 (291?) bars
No. 18 as in Carner

1806 version

Nos 1, 2 as in Carner
(No. 3, Trio beginning with No. 3 of first version, 67 bars, 'doubtful')
No. 4 = Carner No. 3
(No. 5, Rocco's couplet, omitted)
No. 6=Carner No. 4, *but* 211 bars
No. 7 = Carner No. 5, *but* corresponding to that in third version (38 bars)
No. 8 = Carner No. 6, *but* 117 bars
No. 9 = Carner No. 7
(No. 10, Duet beginning with No. 10 of first version, 80 bars, 'doubtful')
No. 11 = Carner No. 8
No. 12 = Carner No. 11, *but* 544 bars
Nos 13, 14, 15, 16 = Carner Nos 12, 13, 14, 15
No. 17 = Carner No. 16, *but* 184 bars [?]
No. 18 = Carner No. 16, *but* 330 bars
Kinsky-Halm Nos 3 and 10 above correspond to Carner Nos 10 and 9 respectively, but Kinsky-Halm's number of bars is shorter in both cases. Czerny's 1810 vocal score gave the numbers according to Dr Carner's enumeration.

This comparison, which was made by Ates Orga, is reproduced with his kind permission.

in haste, repent at leisure'. It is pleasing, small-scale music in typical *singspiel* character belonging to the world of the jailer and his family:

Ex. 34

Essentially it anticipates the sentiments expressed by Rocco in his couplet and, moreover, held up the action of the original first act which was in any case slow-moving. The same may be said of the duet in C major between Marzelline and Leonore in which the girl builds castles in the air, telling Leonore (as Fidelio) how she imagines life as husband and wife, and not omitting a coy allusion to the future growth of her family.[48] Leonore feigns interest but in an aside begs Heaven to forgive her her deception of the love-lorn Marzelline. There is a comic irony in this situation which Mozart would not have missed, but Beethoven had no ear for this and composed a mildly inspired piece of music in the older style:

Ex. 35

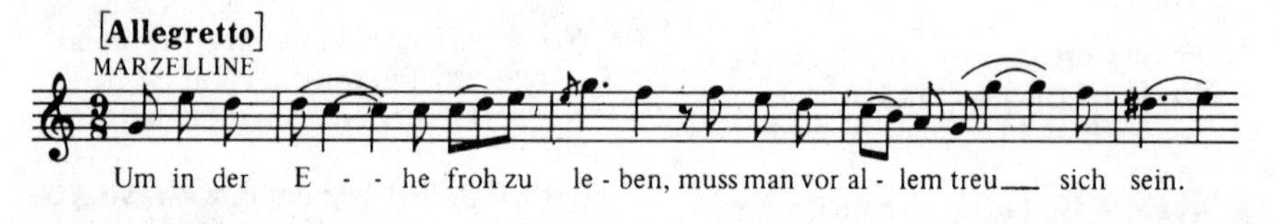

with an *obbligato* for violin and cello to indicate the temperamental difference between the two women. In this duet Leonore is seen to descend to the lower, confined sphere of Marzelline, which is alien to her true nature. As with the above trio, the omission of this duet from the 1814 version is no cause for regret.

Yet, what is to be regretted is Beethoven's excision of the recitative for the original 'Joy' Duet, No. 17 (No. 15 in the present version). In this recitative Leonore, overcome by emotion at the deliverance of Florestan, loses consciousness which makes her husband believe that she is dead. (This scene was in the original French libretto.) Her coming-to, his joy at finding her alive, her change from fear to

[48] *See* Note 23.

exultation—all this is movingly conveyed in this recitative, with its exquisite oboe solo:

Ex. 36

This was a situation full of warm poetry which Treitschke, unfortunately, replaced by a prosaic dialogue that merely serves the purpose of giving Leonore the opportunity to tell Florestan how she succeeded in entering the prison in a boy's disguise and becoming the jailer's assistant.

What is completely new in the third *Fidelio* are the recitative of Leonore's aria (No. 9) the F major section of Florestan's monologue (No. 11), the Prisoners' Farewell Chorus in the first-act finale, and the opening choral March and the Minister's *ariso* in the Act II finale. Compared with the music taken over from the 1805 version this amounts to very little—in round figures, altogether to 250 bars in an opera of 2,800 bars, in other words, less than a tenth of the total length. But in a statement published by Beethoven in the *Wiener Zeitung* of 1 July, 1814 he declared that 'the present version is in so far different from the previous one as almost any number has been changed [true] and more than half of the opera has been newly composed [untrue]'. This was, as the above calculation shows, a gross exaggeration possibly intended to induce the public to purchase the new vocal score (in an arrangement by Moscheles, supervised by Beethoven), whose forthcoming publication by Artaria the composer announced in this notice.

As already suggested, by 1814 Beethoven had made a considerable advance in the art of accompanied recitative, and how much inferior the original version of Leonore's recitative was to the present in dramatic expression, may be seen not only from its text (see p. 240) but also from the opening in E minor:

Ex. 37

To accommodate the various sentiments expressed by Leonore in Treitschke's new text, Beethoven lengthened the original recitative of 15 bars to 31 bars in the final version. On paper there is certainly a difference of style between the new recitative and the following *adagio* but, as in the case of Florestan's modified recitative of 1814, in performance this is scarcely to be detected. On the other hand, the first version of the aria was shortened by no fewer than 57 bars and, probably, pressed by Anna Milder (see p. 188), Beethoven simplified the vocal part (Ex. 14). In the 1805 version there was an accumulation of difficulties which made this piece into a true *aria di bravura* from which I quote two examples from, respectively, the *adagio* and the end of the *allegro*:

Ex. 38 a)

And here is, for a comparison, the cadenza of Leonora's aria in Paer's opera which was the model for Beethoven's vocal acrobatics:

Ex. 39

The new F major section of Florestan's aria we have already discussed (p. 220).

And now for a comparison of the two choral finales. In 1805 the first finale extended to 667 bars, in 1806 to 545 and in 1814 to 521 bars. The original 1805 finale was a curate's egg, with the bad part in the closing section beginning with Pizarro's second appearance. It opened with a *maestoso* followed by an *allegro* which shows the Governor as being more of a stage-villain than he is in the final 1814 version, while the music must be declared as not only conventional but even banal. All this was replaced in 1814 by the moving Farewell Chorus of the Prisoners which not only balanced the opening chorus but rounded off the first-act finale perfectly. As to the second finale, its first version consisted of 487 bars which Beethoven in the second version mutilated by reducing it to 333 bars, while in the third version he expanded it again to 421 bars.

The main improvement here is to be found in the opening section which originally began with a trite 'Vengeance' Chorus off-stage and was followed by a short duet for Leonore and Florestan giving expression to their fear that they were the object of this revenge. The 1814 version, playing on the bastion, begins with a rousing choral march in C major which, however, retains the dotted rhythm of the 'Vengeance' piece, succeeded by the Minister's noble address which is also completely new. In addition, Beethoven reduced the hymn-like F major section, 'O Gott! welch' ein Augenblick!', which in the first version extended through superfluous word repetitions to 96 bars, to 56 bars. The result of all these alterations was an appreciable gain in dramatic power and immediacy of effect of the two 1814 finales.

A little more, I feel, must be said about the second version. As we recall, in 1806 Beethoven, much against his own conviction, was persuaded to cut the music so drastically that it amounted to a brutal mutilation of the score, sacrificing to the time-factor the erstwhile logic and balance of several numbers. (Excessive length, we remember, was one of the chief points of criticism levelled against the first *Fidelio*.) Yet these ruthless cuttings had this advantage—they led to a considerable concentration of the sprawling dramatic structure and thus to an acceleration of the action. In 1814 Beethoven seems to have come to recognise this improvement of the dramaturgy—hence the singular fact that he based his revision very largely on the second version yet repairing as far as possible its distorted musical form which was a more difficult task to achieve than composing altogether new music. He also improved the harmonic and rhythmic texture of some numbers and made the orchestra a more integral and more eloquent part of the drama than it had been in the 1805 and 1806 versions.

Nevertheless, the original *Fidelio* was quite an extraordinary achievement for a composer making his first and, alas, only step into opera. After all, the 1805 version contained *all* the essential music we have in the 1814 version, such as the canon-Quartet (No. 3), the first-act Trio (No. 5), Pizarro's and Rocco's Duet (No. 8), Leonore's aria (No. 9), the orchestral introduction, recitative and *adagio* of Florestan's Monologue (No. 11), the 'Grave-digging' Duet (No. 12), the ensuing Trio (No. 13), the dramatic Quartet (No. 14), and the wonderful hymn of the second-act finale. Yet from a dramatic point of view, a point of view which must be among the prime criteria in the judgment of the opera, the 1814 *Fidelio* stands head and shoulders above its original version. Suggestions have been made[49] to construct the ideal opera by fusing the best of the 1805 and 1814 versions. This would not only go against Beethoven's own intention, it would greatly affect the unity of the two versions. They are each an artistic entity, they *must* be kept apart. But now that the full score of the original *Fidelio* is generally available it should be occasionally produced to ring the changes on the opera of 1814.

IV. The Overtures

Beethoven wrote four overtures for his opera—*Leonore* Nos 1, 2, and 3, all in C major, and the *Fidelio* Overture in E major. There are sketches even for a fifth overture as Joseph Braunstein informs us in his excellent study of the *Leonore* overtures.[50] Braunstein establishes once and for all the fact that Beethoven composed them in the order 1, 2 and

[49] By, for instance, H. D. Moser in the *Neues Beethoven Jahrbuch*, 2 (1925), p. 56.

[50] J. Braunstein, *Beethovens Leonore-Ouvertüren: eine historisch-stilkritische Untersuchung* (Leipzig, 1927).

3 and not, as Nottebohm[51] and others assumed, in the order 2, 3 and 1. The story that *Leonore* No. 1 was composed last, for a projected production of the opera in Prague in 1808, was put about by the unreliable Seyfried, the conductor of the first *Fidelio*, who based himself on a report in the *Journal des Luxus* of January 1808, according to which the opera was to be performed 'in Prague in the near future with a new overture'. Beethoven may have had the intention of writing a new overture but never carried it out since the Prague production did not materialise; or the 'new' in the above report was used in the sense of 'not heard yet in *public*'. We know that for the original *Fidelio* Beethoven wrote an overture which after a private rehearsal he discarded as too light and insignificant. This description can only fit *Leonore* No. 1 whose groping uncertainty and lack of inventive distinction are a sure pointer to its having been written first. We do best, I feel, to regard it as being in the nature of a fully completed sketch for the two later overtures which summarise the drama. What all three C major overtures have in common is a slow introduction opening on a unison (G), and the Florestan theme (Ex. 40), while the first subject of the *allegro con brio* of *Leonore* No. 1 anticipates the main theme of both *Leonore* Nos 2 and 3. In the case of *Leonore* No. 1, the Florestan theme is heard in E flat, while in the later overtures it is given in A flat, as in the opera.

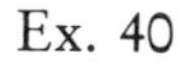

All three overtures show the influence of Cherubini's rhetorical style, using Cherubinesque figuration and displaying his predilection for strongly syncopated phrases:

Ex. 41 a)

[51] *Beethoveniana*, pp. 60–78. The late opus number of *Leonore* No. 1 (Op. 138) was due to the fact that the overture was not published until after Beethoven's death (by Haslinger of Vienna in the spring of 1838).

b)

c)

Leonore No. 1 has no trumpet-signals and no development section which is replaced by an *adagio* in E flat major quoting the 'Florestan' melody—rather incongruously, I maintain, since this melody belongs to the sombre, despairing music of the slow introduction. Beethoven must have felt this, for in *Leonore* Nos 2 and 3 he removed it to the slow opening. One other curious point in the first *Leonore* Overture deserves mention: the coda introduces a motif identical with the 'Ein Engel Leonore' figure in the F major section of Florestan's aria which was not composed until 1814.[52] Can it be assumed that in 1805 Beethoven had already ideas for that F major section of which he did not make use at the time? As far as I know, there are no sketches extant to prove this.

Leonore Nos 2 and 3 represent radical reworkings and a considerable extension of the first overture.[53] The step Beethoven made from *Leonore* No. 1 to the two subsequent overtures is comparable to his step from the Second Symphony to the *Eroica*. Their magnitude, *terribiltà*, and dramatic power makes these two overtures wholly unsuited as a preparation of the opening *singspiel* scenes of the opera. As Romain Rolland put it so forcibly: 'How can we descend from those epic heights to the babblings of the jailer's family?'[54]

Of the two overtures, *Leonore* No. 2 is a more faithful mirror of the

[52] *Leonore* No. 1. — *and* — *Fidelio* (1814 version)

FLORESTAN

ein En - gel, Le - o - no - re.

[53] The respective lengths of the three overtures are: 365 bars, 530 bars, and 638 bars. It should be added that *Leonore* Nos 2 and 3 were Beethoven's first symphonic works in which he employed trombones.

[54] 'Beethovens Leonore', *Europäische Revue* (Leipzig), June 1928, p. 177.

essential drama in that after the development section there is no formal recapitulation as there is in *Leonore* No. 3; instead, the music storms in a triumphant coda to its close and thus epitomises the apotheosis of the second-act finale of the opera. On the other hand, it contains something which has always appeared to me illogical from the point of view of the psychological drama. This is the fact that *after* the second trumpet signal, the symbol of Florestan's deliverance, Beethoven again quotes his theme which in the opera occurs in the situation in which this character is seen still suffering in chains in the dungeon. The composer must have become aware of this, for in *Leonore* No. 3 he cites the 'Florestan' theme only once in the slow introduction which portrays the dismal, despairing atmosphere of the dungeon.

Leonore No. 3 has a formal recapitulation after the development section which in terms of the essential drama brings us back almost to square one. It is not an overture in the established sense but a symphonic poem which sums up the inner, spiritual meaning of the opera, its only direct reference to it being the 'Florestan' theme, the two trumpet-signals and the hymn of the Act II Quartet (No. 14). An autonomous piece, this overture is completely rounded and aesthetically supremely satisfying music whose form is that of a Beethoven first-symphonic movement with a slow introduction.

The practice of performing *Leonore* No. 3 between the two scenes of the final act seems to have been initiated by Otto Nicolai at the Vienna Opera in the 1840s, and was followed by such conductors as Mahler, Toscanini, Furtwängler and Klemperer. Though personally I have no strong feelings about its inclusion in the opera, I am fully aware of the force of the argument that at the place where it is commonly played it recapitulates the dramatic essence of the opera just before the work ends and, moreover, anticipates the mood of the last scene in such a tremendous, overpowering way that we find it difficult to descend from it to earth again when the curtain rises. Hence the proper place for *Leonore* No. 3 is not the opera house but the concert hall.

It must have been some such consideration which in 1814 prompted Beethoven to compose the *Fidelio* Overture in E major though at first he thought of reworking *Leonore* No. 1 in that key and also introducing into it the trumpet-signals. But in the end he decided to keep the overture entirely free from any direct reference to or quotation from the music of the opera, except that the conspicuous use of the horns and the vigorous triad arpeggios upwards link it with the *allegro* section of the heroine's aria. As for its key of E major, suggestions have been made that Beethoven chose it with reference to the tonality of Leonore's aria or in analogy to the overture to Cherubini's *Les deux journées*, also in E major. This seems to me far-fetched. The simplest explanation is that he wished to write a prelude which led to A major, the key of the opening duet, and therefore selected its dominant key for it. The new features of the *Fidelio* Overture are that it avoids the huge symphonic structure of the two subsequent overtures and does not traverse the drama afresh. It stands halfway between the lighter and more earthbound sphere of *singspiel* and the world of heroic music-drama and thus serves as the ideal introduction to the opera.

TWENTY-ONE

PFITZNER VERSUS BERG

PFITZNER WAS A quirky, quarrelsome little man, always highly critical of the music of his fellow composers. In his public dicta about them he never pulled his punches. Moreover, he was an ardent German nationalist and reactionary—he liked to describe himself as the 'last German romantic'—who detested all modernism and internationalism in German art, a phenomenon which he attributed to the influence of the Jews, although he counted many friends among them. Endowed with an eloquent and most fluent pen, he left three hefty volumes of collected writings, some of them of a highly polemical character. Thus in 1917 he wrote a long essay, 'Futuristengefahr', a reply to Busoni's famous book *A New Aesthetic of Music*, in which he raised the alarm about the new tendencies that he considered detrimental to German music. His most important polemical essay was 'The New Aesthetics of the Musical Impotence', which was in the first place directed at the influential critic, Paul Bekker. As we shall see, it was this essay that induced Berg to challenge Pfitzner in a brilliant article of his own.

Bekker had written a book on Beethoven in which he spoke at length of the 'poetic idea' in which he saw the source of inspiration for virtually every one of the composer's works. What roused Pfitzner was Bekker's statement that Beethoven was in the first place a thinker and poet and only in the second place a musician. If Bekker, more correctly, had said that Beethoven was a thinker and poet in terms of music, I take it that all would have been well. As it stood, Pfitzner saw in Bekker's statement an imposition of extra-musical values on Beethoven's music which in his eyes was anathema. Bekker's second and perhaps cardinal sin was, according to Pfitzner, his failure to perceive the fundamental role played by inspiration in the composer's creative processes. Bekker, whose book contains not a single music example, hardly ever considers a theme or tune *per se* but is only interested in what happens to it by way of elaboration and development; that Pfitzner regarded as belonging to the intellectual sphere, so having little connection with inspiration. Bekker's third sin was to declare that the symphony from Beethoven to Mahler possessed, next to its purely musical values, a sociological one: it was *gesellschaftsbindend*, that is, it had the ability of bringing a large, heterogeneous crowd of people together and transforming it into a community assembled to share a great experience. All this represented for Pfitzner the intrusion into musical aesthetics of non-musical standpoints in which he saw the symptoms of decadence in German music. He sometimes uses a stronger word than decadence: he speaks of *Verwesung* (putrefaction). Incidentally, in this essay Pfitzner shows himself to be a veritable polymath drawing for his arguments on philosophy, politics, race theory (he extols Wagner's notorious pamphlet on Judaism in music), general aesthetics, morals, literature, drama and what have you. Pfitzner published his essay in 1920, and coming as it did from the composer of *Palestrina* it created a considerable sensation in German artistic and intellectual circles; he was widely accused of a deliberate distortion of the picture of contemporary German music and of airing hidebound reactionary views.

The tenor of his essay is the all-pervasive role played by inspiration in composition, without which, Pfitzner says, no great work can come into being, and the absence of which in modern German music he deeply deplores. The German word for inspiration is *Einfall*—literally, something falling into the mind from, as it were, outside: it implies that the artist is, at the moment of inspiration, completely passive, and feels to be merely the receptacle for something coming to him suddenly out of the blue. It is a phenomenon on which many artists have commented. In an earlier age inspiration was attributed to divine influence; that is why in mediæval paintings it was symbolised by angels. Pfitzner recalls this image in *Palestrina* when in Act 1 angels appear and sing the mass which the composer is just putting down on paper. Inspiration may often have slumbered or simmered in the artist's unconscious and perhaps needed a special stimulus to leap from the depths into the conscious part of the mind. There is evidence that, for example, Bach, Handel, Mozart, Schubert, Schumann and Strauss were subject to this kind of inspiration, which partly explains the speed with which they composed and the astonishingly large number of works they left. In Pfitzner's *Palestrina* there are at least two themes which bear the hallmark of spontaneous inspiration. One is the D minor theme associated with Palestrina as the humble and devout servant of God. Throughout the opera it recurs in the same shape and opens and concludes the work. The second *Einfall* is the theme symbolising the Council of Trent. It is a bigboned, tremendous idea of almost Brucknerian character and has great dignity when it is first heard in the prelude to Act 2.

In seeing in true inspiration the alpha and omega of composition, Pfitzner allots a cardinal role in artistic creation to the unconscious factor. Here is how he expresses this thought through the mouth of Palestrina, in that marvellous scene of Act 1 when the old masters of polyphony appear to him and spur him on to compose the mass. Palestrina says: 'You lived strongly in a strong age, an age which was deeply embedded in the unconscious—but the light of the conscious, a light fatal in its dazzle, is hostile to artistic creation.' In this connection Schönberg may be cited who said about himself that he was a 'Geschöpf der Eingebung' (creature of inspiration) and that he always composed instinctively. To which may be added a statement by the modern painter, Fernand Léger, who wrote: 'The creator . . . is caught between his consciousness and his unconsciousness . . . the subjective and objective interpenetrate in such a way that the creative event remains always a partial enigma for the artist.'

For Pfitzner the result of true inspiration is an organic musical whole which is not capable of being dissected and analysed. Its quality cannot be demonstrated but only felt. And as a supreme example of inspiration he adduces *Träumerei* from Schumann's *Kinderszenen*. Here, he says, inspiration and form coincide. What else, he asks, is to be said about it? All we can do is to shut out our conscious analytical mind and yield to an overwhelming feeling of rapture at its incomparable beauty. Every attempt at analysis is futile and to try to explain it in technical terms leads nowhere. It is interesting to note that for all the acuteness of his intellect and power of argument, in his approach to music Pfitzner shows himself non-intellectual, non-analytical and wholly emotive. Music for him is stuff not for the rational mind, but our feelings and sentiments, in other words, the instinctive and irrational in us. True, he does attempt an analysis of sorts in *Träumerei*, but he does it so superficially and so cavalierly as to indicate how insignificant technical description must be.

Now it was this section of Pfitzner's essay which Berg attacked in an elegantly written, satirical article which appeared in the June number (1920) of the *Musikblätter des Anbruch*, the house journal of the Vienna music publishing firm, Universal Edition. Pfitzner called his essay 'The New Aesthetics of the Musical Impotence': Berg reversed this and entitled his own essay 'The Musical Impotence of Hans Pfitzner's "New Aesthetics".' He begins by describing Pfitzner's wholly emotional reaction to Schumann's *Träumerei* as 'Schwärmerei' (gushing enthusiasm), and he rejects his view that the quality of its melody cannot be demonstrated but only felt. He then proceeds to a technical analysis; all who have read Berg's guides to Schönberg's *Gurrelieder* and the Chamber Symphony know how well he does this and what flashes of insight he shows. Berg first remarks on the central position *Träumerei* occupies in the set of 13 pieces: it is the seventh piece and thus divides the set into two groups of six pieces each. He then discusses Schumann's subtle variation technique in spinning out the melody and, by demonstrating that each of its cadences ends on a different chord, disproves Pfitzner's statement that *Träumerei* lacks harmonic variety and interest. He also draws attention to its strict four-part writing and says that the piece could just as well be played by a string or wind quartet or sung by a mixed choir.

Admittedly, Berg takes us a good way towards a demonstration of the inventive quality of *Träumerei*. But does he succeed in explaining why it is such a memorable piece? I do not think so. There are themes and melodies in classical music with a greater wealth of distinguishing features than Schumann's piece, and yet they do not strike us as memorable. On the other hand, there are tunes with a paucity of distinguishing features—think of folksongs and the operas of the middle Verdi—which, once heard, stick in the memory. Can we rationally ascertain wherein the difference between a memorable theme and an ordinary one lies? It is worth citing, in answer, what Alma Maria Mahler wrote to Frau Berg after she had read her husband's article: 'All the quotations from Pfitzner prove that he [Pfitzner] is right. Music is inexplicable, above all melody which is not A–B–C and X–Y–Z.' (That was how Berg marked the sections of *Träumerei* in his analysis.) Frau Mahler then asks—quoted in an unpublished letter from Berg to Schönberg, 21 July, 1920: 'Does Alban *really* believe that anything can be explained in this way—anything at all?'

Frau Mahler of course exaggerates when she negates the value of technical analysis. Analysis is needed, not only to rationalise aural impressions but also to discover relationships and correspondences in the structure and the formal design of a piece, to say nothing of its texture. Analysis is a *sine qua non* for a true knowledge of a complex piece of music, such as is necessary if one wishes to summon before the mind's eye its characteristic features or hear inwardly its directional progress from *A* to *B* to *C*, and so on. In short, without analysis—that is, without a deliberate intellectual effort—there can be no full and true appreciation of the music. Appreciation and aesthetic enjoyment are of course closely linked, but they are not interchangeable: the first belongs to the intellectual sphere while the second is the result of our emotional reaction. A listener must first respond instinctively and feel, as Pfitzner suggested, the beauty of a given piece. If this is his reaction then analysis will heighten his aesthetic enjoyment when he hears it again. If there is no positive response, then all analysis will be futile for him.

The seemingly insoluble difficulty in explaining in technical terms why one piece is memorable and another not lies to my mind partly in this: melody, harmony and rhythm, the prime parameters of Western music, interact in manifold ways which it is impossible to describe in verbal terms. Even if it were possible, any such description would fill pages and pages and yet would totally fail to conjure up the integrated impression which we receive through our ear. For the ear is capable of taking in instantly what in psychology is called a *Gestalt* or configuration, that is, to perceive a structured unity or whole which is more than the sum of its parts. This is a fundamental teaching of *Gestalt* psychology. I believe that it is in the difference by which the whole is bigger than the sum of its parts that our prime difficulty lies in explaining in technical terms why one theme is memorable and another not. To try to discover by analysis the beauty of an inspiration is like searching for the beauty of a rose by tearing off its petals. In the controversy about *Einfall* and technical analysis I thus take Pfitzner's side. There is no rational way to explain, as Berg seemed to think there was, one of the supreme aims of artistic creation: how to achieve significant beauty.

Appendix

Fidelio: Comparative Table

Version I, 1805			Version II, 1806
(Sonnleithner)			(Breuning)
Act I			*Act I*
Aria, No. 1 (Marz.):	97	bars, [C major] C minor/major	Aria, No. 1:
Duet, No. 2 (Marz. Jacq):	234	bars, A major	Duet, No. 2:
Trio, No. 3 (Roc. Marz. Jacq.):	106	bars, E flat major	(see Trio, No. 10)
Quartet, No. 4 (Leon. Marz, Roc, Jacq.):	52	bars, G major	Quartet, No. 3:
Aria, No. 5 (Roc.):	91	bars, B flat major	omitted
Trio, No. 6 (Leon. Marz. Roc.):	232	bars, F major	Trio, No. 4:
Act II			
March, No. 7:	?	bars, B flat major	March, No. 5:
Aria, No. 8 (Piz.):	122	bars, D minor/ major	Aria, No. 6:
Duet, No. 9 (Piz. Roc.):	181	bars, A major	Duet, No. 7:
Duet, No. 10 (Leon. Marz.):	98	bars, C major	(see Duet, No. 9)
Rec. & Aria, No. 11 (Leon.):	188	bars, E minor–[F major?] E major	Rec. & Aria, No. 8:
			Duet, No. 9:
			Trio, No. 10
Finale, No. 12:	667	bars, B flat major	Finale, No. 11:
Act III			*Act II*
Rec. & Aria, No. 13 Flor.):	129	bars, F minor	Rec. & Aria, No. 12 omitted
Melodrama, No. 14a:	?	bars	
Duet, No. 14b (Leon. Roc.):	122	bars, A minor	Duet, No. 13:
Trio, No. 15 (Leon. Flor. Roc.):	190	bars, A major	Trio, No. 14:
Quartet, No. 16 (Leon. Flor. Piz. Roc.):	207	bars, D major	Quartet, No. 15:
Rec. & Duet (Leon. Flor.), No. 17:	291	bars, C major G major	Rec. & Duet, No. 16:
			Finale, No. 17:
Finale, No. 18:	487	bars, C minor–C major	
Total:	3494	bars [+March, No. 7]	

Version III, 1814

(Treitschke)

	Act I	
97 bars, C minor/major	Duet No. 1:	210 bars, A major
220 bars, A major	Aria, No. 2: omitted	84 bars, C minor/major
52 bars, G major	Quartet, No. 3:	51 bars, G major
	Aria, No. 4:	87 bars, B flat major
210 bars, F major	Trio, No. 5:	202 bars, F major
30 bars, B flat major	March, No. 6:	38 bars, B flat major
115 bars, D minor/major	Aria, No. 7:	123 bars, D minor/major
181 bars, A major	Duet, No. 8: omitted	169 bars, A major
174 bars, E minor–E major	Rec. & Aria, No. 9: omitted	149 bars, G minor–E major
80 bars, A major		
68 bars, E flat major		
545 bars, B flat major	Finale, No. 10:	521 bars, B flat major
	Act II	
110 bars, F minor/major	Rec. & Aria, No. 11:	146 bars, F minor/major
	Melodrama, No. 12:	27 bars
104 bars, A minor	Duet, No. 12:	105 bars, A minor
148 bars, A major	Trio, No. 13:	158 bars, A major
207 bars, D major	Quartet, No. 14:	213 bars. D major
185 bars, C major–G major	Duet, No. 15:	124 bars, G major
333 bars, C minor/major	Finale, No. 16:	421 bars, C major
Total: 2859 bars		Total: 2828 bars

Index